SEARCHING FOR YOU

Books by Jody Hedlund

The Preacher's Bride
The Doctor's Lady
Unending Devotion
A Noble Groom
Rebellious Heart
Captured by Love

BEACONS OF HOPE

Out of the Storm: A BEACONS OF HOPE Novella
Love Unexpected
Hearts Made Whole
Undaunted Hope

ORPHAN TRAIN

An Awakened Heart: An ORPHAN TRAIN Novella
With You Always
Together Forever
Searching for You

ORPHAN TRAIN
BOOK THREE

SEARCHING FOR YOU

JODY HEDLUND

BETHANYHOUSE
a division of Baker Publishing Group
Minneapolis, Minnesota

© 2018 by Jody Hedlund

Published by Bethany House Publishers
11400 Hampshire Avenue South
Bloomington, Minnesota 55438
www.bethanyhouse.com

Bethany House Publishers is a division of
Baker Publishing Group, Grand Rapids, Michigan

Printed in the United States of America

Library of Congress Cataloging-in-Publication Data
Names: Hedlund, Jody, author.
Title: Searching for you / Jody Hedlund.
Description: Minneapolis, Minnesota : Bethany House, a division of Baker
    Publishing Group, [2018] | Series: Orphan train ; Book 3
Identifiers: LCCN 2018019436 | ISBN 9780764218064 (trade paper) | ISBN
    9780764232749 (cloth) | ISBN 9781493416103 (e-book)
Subjects: | GSAFD: Christian fiction. | Love stories.
Classification: LCC PS3608.E333 S43 2018 | DDC 813/.6—dc23
LC record available at https://lccn.loc.gov/2018019436

Scripture quotations are from the King James Version of the Bible.

This is a work of fiction. Names, characters, incidents, and dialogues are products of the author's imagination and are not to be construed as real. Any resemblance to actual events or persons, living or dead, is entirely coincidental.

Cover design by Jennifer Parker
Cover photography by Mike Habermann Photography, LLC

Author is represented by Natasha Kern Literary Agency, Inc.

18 19 20 21 22 23 24   7 6 5 4 3 2 1

And ye shall seek me, and find me, when ye shall search for me with all your heart.

Jeremiah 29:13

CHAPTER 1

NEW YORK CITY
SEPTEMBER 1859

Sophie Neumann nuzzled her nose against Danny's chest.

His arms tightened around her possessively. "You're my girl now. A Bowery Girl."

Bowery Girl. The coveted name should have sent shivers of delight through Sophie. Instead, the mention of it made her tremble with trepidation.

Danny lowered his head and pressed his mouth against her neck. His lips were slick and hot, especially in the September heat and humidity that lingered in the city air even though it was well past midnight. The dampness brought out the heavy scent of beer on his breath, as well as the acridness of bear grease in the pomade he used to slick back his hair.

She arched her neck to avoid the odor, telling herself she was only giving him more access. At the same time, she squeezed her eyes closed and tried to conjure pleasure at his touch. She'd enjoyed Danny's kisses and his caresses on previous nights. Tonight would be no different. She just needed to be patient and the affection would follow.

After all, he was Danny Sullivan, the head of the Dry Bones and one of the leaders of the Bowery Boys. He wore the usual gang attire—a long black frock, red shirt, dark trousers, polished boots, and a stovepipe hat. And he styled his hair similar to the other Bowery Boys, cut short in the back with ringlets of hair pasted down over his ears.

Although his clothing and hair blended in with the other gang members, he was easily the handsomest and strongest one in the Bowery neighborhood. She still marveled that of all the women who vied for Danny's attention, he'd decided he wanted her. He'd fought against two other Bowery Boys in bare-knuckle fistfights in order to claim her.

Of course, she hadn't really been interested in the other men. In fact, she hadn't been interested in getting involved with anyone—she never had. For the past two years, she'd always been on the move, running away from one asylum to the next, never having the time to invest in relationships other than taking care of Olivia and Nicholas.

But all that had changed a month ago when one of the mistresses at the Juvenile Asylum had informed Anna that she was too old to stay there any longer. Anna had been Sophie's only friend at the asylum. As Anna had packed her ragged bag of belongings, she'd pleaded with Sophie to leave too, assuring her that her sister Mollie would let them stay with her. After having a baby, Mollie had moved from the brothel where she'd been living and now had an apartment.

"We're old enough to get jobs," Anna had said. "We can be domestics in one of those fancy rich houses on Fifth Avenue."

"But we don't have any experience," Sophie argued.

"Then we can work in a factory or a sewing shop."

Sophie remembered all too vividly the sewing sweatshop her mother and sisters had worked in, one of many located in the crowded tenements on the East Side. Although Sophie hadn't been old enough to work alongside her family, she still recalled her mother and sisters coming home after twelve-hour workdays hot and exhausted, their fingers blue from the dye that colored the precut material they'd sewn to form men's vests.

In all those months, Sophie had never learned how to sew, not even a button. Besides, even if she and Anna found work as seamstresses, the pay was abysmally low. How would they be able to afford to live on it even if they stayed with Anna's sister? More specifically, how would she be able to clothe, feed, and take care of Olivia and Nicholas?

In spite of her reservations, Sophie had agreed to take up residence with Anna's sister in a tiny tenement on Mulberry Bend. The two rooms they shared with Mollie, three other women, and their children weren't nearly big enough for all of them. Still, the place was safe.

Now that she was Danny Sullivan's Bowery Girl, he would take care of her and wouldn't let any harm come to her.

"You're so beautiful," he whispered huskily.

With her long blond hair and bright blue eyes, she'd always drawn attention from boys. But in the past she'd been petite and thin, able to pass for a much younger child. Over the previous six months, she'd grown and filled out so that she'd had a much harder time deceiving the orphanage workers into believing she was ten or twelve years old.

At the Juvenile Asylum, she'd told the staff she was fifteen, even though she was drawing nigh to eighteen. They'd believed her, yet she knew her days of being able to stay with Olivia and Nicholas in the asylums was fast coming to an end, that soon enough the workers would get wise to her lies about her age and they'd force her out just as they had Anna. That knowledge was another reason she'd decided to live with Anna and her sister.

Danny's lips traced a path to her collarbone, and his hand on her back crept lower—too low.

"Danny, stop." She pushed at his chest, trying to keep her voice light and playful.

"You're mine now," he said breathlessly. "And I want you."

I want you. The words reverberated in her head and made a warm trail to her heart. When was the last time someone had wanted her?

Sure, Olivia and Nicholas wanted and needed her. But at five and three years old, that was to be expected.

But want—really want her? She couldn't remember a time in her life when anyone had valued her. She'd mostly just been a burden—to her overworked father after they'd emigrated from Germany, to her ailing mother before she'd died, and to her older sisters when they'd had no work and no place to live. Even during the past two years living in Boston and more recently in New York City, she'd always felt like a burden in the overcrowded and understaffed orphanages.

Having someone finally want her was a new experience.

She relaxed within Danny's hold. Surely there was nothing wrong with letting him touch her more intimately tonight? After all, he'd made a public declaration that she was his girl and forbidden to anyone else.

She shoved aside the guilt that slithered through the cracks of her closed conscience. She'd become an expert at locking guilt away into a closet at the back of her mind. Even so, Danny's too-personal touch embarrassed her. With the harsh yellow light spilling out of the Green Dragon, the other gang members who'd gathered in the narrow alleyway behind the dance hall would be able to see Danny's fondling.

Just a short distance away, Anna was locked into the embrace of Mugs, and they were kissing passionately. There were other couples hiding in the shadows taking pleasure in one another. It was normal and natural here among this crowd, even expected.

Better out in the dark than inside the saloon with its cigar-smoke-blackened walls, sticky floors, and broken chairs, with the scent of salted pigs' knuckles making her gag. Even worse were the girls dancing on the stage, twirling and flipping up their skirts to reveal their silk petticoats, and more. She hadn't wanted any of the other men to assume she was a dancing girl. Even though she'd sat on Danny's lap while he drank and played cards, she'd gotten too many bawdy comments and looks.

Danny's breathing and kisses turned heavy.

Sophie's mind flashed with the image of Mollie and her infant and the other two women who lived in the tenement with their children. None of them were married. None of them had set out to be single mothers. And none of them had dreamed they'd become prostitutes. But that was what they were.

"Danny, no." Sophie wiggled against him.

He didn't relinquish his grip, but instead tightened his hold. She squirmed harder. "I told you I want to wait until I'm married."

"You're just teasing me," he growled in her ear.

Irritation rose up to replace the tender feelings of belonging she'd had only moments ago. "I've always believed I'd save myself for marriage."

Even if her memories of her mother and father had begun to fade, their teachings were still deeply ingrained. And even if her faith had fled and gotten lost long ago, there was still a part of her that resisted giving up the search for it altogether.

As if finally sensing the seriousness of her resistance, Danny stopped groping and swore under his breath. He pulled back slightly, slackening his hold, but he didn't let go of her entirely.

For a second she waited for him to say more, to get angry or perhaps to belittle her for her stand. He was, after all, a Bowery Boy—tough and dangerous and determined. As a leader, he had a reputation to uphold, and he was accustomed to getting what he wanted. She hadn't known him long, and yet she'd already witnessed his violence when provoked.

Instead of lashing out, however, he pressed his forehead against hers and was silent.

The off-tune plunking of a piano came from inside the dance hall. The music blended with the distant wail of a baby from a nearby open tenement window, along with the shouts of an escalating argument. Such noises were so commonplace that she almost didn't hear them anymore. And she almost didn't notice the stench of the overflowing garbage bins at the end of the alley. After being homeless too many times to count, it was easy to become immune to the realities of street life.

Danny dropped a kiss onto the tip of her nose. "Fine, angel. We'll wait."

"You're not too disappointed in me?" she asked.

"I knew you were as innocent as a babe from the first second I laid eyes on you." He drew her closer again. "Beautiful and innocent."

"I'm not that innocent." She wasn't sure why his statement irked her, except that as the youngest of her sisters, she'd always been viewed as the baby of the family. Everyone had tried to shelter her from the problems, had thought she was too young to understand what was going on, had ceased their worried whispers whenever she came into the room.

But she wasn't a baby anymore. Not in the least. She'd had to grow up or give up. She'd had to do things to survive that would disappoint her sisters, things she didn't like to think about, things that threatened to loosen her carefully concealed guilt.

Danny brushed a kiss against her cheek. "You're an angel. My beautiful angel. And if you want, we can do things proper-like. We'll get married."

Married? She pulled back enough that she could see his face. Was he serious?

A sliver of light from the saloon crossed his face, illuminating his lopsided grin. "What? Don't you believe me?"

"Maybe. Maybe not." They'd only known each other for a couple of weeks, since the night Anna had dragged her out of the tenement to celebrate their freedom. At first, Sophie hadn't wanted to leave Olivia and Nicholas alone. But Anna had assured her the children would be safe, that they'd sleep and wouldn't even notice their absence. After all, Mollie and the other women left their children alone all night while they worked the corners and brothels all along the Bowery.

Was two weeks long enough to know if she wanted to marry Danny?

"My ma keeps telling me I need to find a nice girl and get married," he continued. "She said I ain't getting any younger."

Marriage to him would certainly take care of her housing problems. Thankfully, Mollie was kind enough and hadn't kicked her or Anna out for their inability to pay for their lodging. However, Sophie knew the kindness wouldn't last forever. Mollie needed to survive just like the rest of them. Sooner or later the young prostitute would need to find someone who could contribute to the tenement rent, and when she did, Sophie would find herself homeless once again.

Unless she married Danny. Then she'd finally have a home of her own.

How long had it been since she'd lived in a place she could truly call home? She supposed the tiny apartment above Father's bakery after they'd moved to Kleindeutschland from Germany had been a sort of home, although they hadn't lived there long before Father's heart attack and death.

"So, what do you say?" Danny asked. "Let's get married."

Sophie hesitated. What about Olivia and Nicholas? Would he be willing to take them in too? She doubted most men would. "It's a really nice offer," she started.

"Nice?" His voice rose with incredulity. The muscles in his jaw flexed, and his shoulders stiffened. He started to take a step away from her, clearly offended by what he assumed was her rejection, but she grabbed on to his arm.

"I have to take care of my little brother and sister," she said quickly, trying to soothe his wounded pride. "I can't abandon them."

"I heard those kids ain't even yours."

She shoved Danny's chest, willingly pushing him away, her temper flaring as it usually did whenever anyone insinuated that Olivia and Nicholas weren't hers. "They're mine. And if you want me, then you get them too." She jutted her chin and gave him her fiercest glower.

He glared back. Then his lips began to curl into a grin. "You're one sassy girl."

She shrugged. She supposed she was.

Before she knew what he was doing, he grabbed her arm and jerked her against him almost painfully. He locked one arm around her and at the same moment brought his mouth down upon hers. The kiss—if it could even be called that—was bruising, almost punitive. And when he released her mouth, his grip on her arm remained taut. "I like some sass in a woman," he whispered against her ear. "But don't ever forget who's in charge."

She didn't respond, didn't like his attitude, didn't like how he was hurting her. But she was smart enough to know when to keep her mouth shut.

He loosened his hold and then brushed a hand gently across her cheek. "Don't you worry now, angel. Two little kids don't matter to me so long as they stay out of my way."

His fingers on her cheek were clammy. She wanted to bat his hand away but sensed she'd pushed him far enough for one night. When he lowered his mouth to hers again, this time his kiss was gentle. She tried to make herself feel something for him, tried to ignore the warning clanging in her head, tried to tell herself she liked him and wanted to marry him. But the only emotion that seeped into her chest was hopelessness. It was a familiar visitor, yet unlike guilt, she couldn't lock it away. Whenever it came, it took up residence and was difficult to dislodge.

"What do you say we get married next week?" Danny whispered.

So soon? The words almost escaped, but she bit them back. The truth was, she needed him. Maybe he wasn't the perfect man. Maybe he wasn't the kind of man she'd dreamed of marrying, but he was good enough. After all, he cared about her, wanted her, and thought she was beautiful. He had a steady job as a butcher. He'd give her a home and had offered to shelter Olivia and Nicholas. What more did she need?

"All right," she said. "Let's do it. Let's get married next week."

He grinned and picked her up in a hug so that her feet no longer touched the ground. He'd started to swing her around when the ringing of a distant bell stopped him short.

It was a fire alarm, the call to all volunteer firefighters to hurry to action.

Danny's expression hardened. He set her down and jogged away, all thoughts of marriage clearly forgotten.

"Mugs and me'll guard the plug," he shouted to the Bowery Boys, who came out of the alley's shadows. "The rest of you get the fire engine and round up the gang."

The others rushed off to obey Danny's orders while Mugs helped him dump over a garbage barrel and empty the contents onto the street. Carrying the barrel between them, they raced out of the alley.

Sophie had observed Danny's brigade, the Dry Bones, put out a fire last weekend. The flames had engulfed an alley shack

15

containing the overflow of people too poor to afford a tenement home. The shack had been a flimsy structure patched together with loose boards and hunks of metal, and it hadn't been worth saving. But the volunteer firefighters had attempted to stop the spread to the tenements and businesses nearby.

"Let's go watch," Anna said excitedly, her dark hair and eyes gypsy-like compared to Sophie's fair coloring. She grabbed Sophie's hand and dragged her along after Danny and Mugs.

Sophie didn't resist. She'd been fascinated at the last fire, watching the group of men arrive carrying their fire engine. They'd quickly unraveled the leather hoses and hooked them up to a small device on the street called a hydrant that contained pressurized water. With crews of men manning the hoses, the fire was much easier to put out than with the buckets of water that were still used in some areas that didn't have the hydrants.

As Sophie and Anna ran down the Bowery trying to keep up with Danny and Mugs, the street grew noisier and more crowded the closer they drew to the fire. Sophie allowed Anna to guide her, weaving in and out of the onlookers, mostly hatless men and half-clad women who came out of the taverns and brothels to discover what was happening.

The bright light of the fire glowed above the rooftops, and when they turned a corner, Sophie recoiled at the sight of a two-story tavern with flames shooting out its lower level windows. Patrons stood outside a safe distance away, some gawking like spectators at a dogfight, others daring to go inside to rescue what they could.

Only a dozen paces from the corner was a hydrant, and Danny and Mugs were in the process of turning the empty garbage container upside down over the squat steel water source. When the barrel covered the hydrant, Danny hopped up onto the flat end and sat down.

Why was he blocking the hydrant instead of unplugging it

and getting it ready for the hoses that would soon arrive? If they didn't act soon, the fire would spread to the second floor of the building and perhaps to the other businesses connected to it. Every fire, no matter how big or small, had the potential to burn an entire city to the ground, especially since many old buildings were constructed of wood, not bricks.

From the opposite direction, a group of men wearing fire hats was fast approaching, hauling their engine.

"The Roach Guards!" Mugs shouted to Danny.

Danny nodded and squared his shoulders, his fingers closing around the bludgeon at his belt. Mugs had produced a lead pipe and held it poised to fight.

"I don't understand," Sophie said to Anna, who stood next to her. "What's going on?" Anyone who lived in the city for even a short time learned the names of the gangs. The Roach Guards was a powerful Irish gang and a huge rival of the Bowery Boys. That much Sophie understood.

In fact, she could still remember the riots of two years ago in 1857, now referred to as the Dead Rabbits Riot, when massive gang wars and wide-scale vandalizing and looting had taken place throughout Manhattan. She'd been staying at Miss Pendleton's Seventh Street Mission with her sisters the last summer they'd been together. While they'd remained safe inside the warehouse, the gangs had waged war until the National Guard and the Metropolitan Police started making arrests, finally bringing the rioting under control.

"The Dry Bones have staked their claim on the hydrant," Anna said, the flames casting a glow upon her features. Her lovely face was animated, and her luminous brown eyes were dancing. She was a few inches taller than Sophie and pretty in a wild, untamed sort of way. "They want the right to put out the fire and will fight off the other brigades until the rest of the Dry Bones show up."

"But the Roach Guards are already here. Does it really matter who puts out the fire as long as lives are saved?"

"It matters."

The men of the Roach Guards moved rapidly in spite of the heavy load of their hose engine. Long fingers of firelight gyrated across the raised bludgeons, brickbats, clubs, axes, and other makeshift weapons they carried in addition to the firefighting equipment. At the sight of Danny and Mugs guarding the hydrant, several of the Roach Guards broke away from the rest and sprinted forward.

Sophie clutched Anna's arm. "We need to get out of here."

Anna nodded toward the corner they'd just turned. "Don't worry. Our boys will be here soon enough to help with the fight."

As the first two Roach Guards reached the hydrant and swung their clubs, Danny and Mugs beat them back.

Sophie sucked in a breath, her body tense, her mind urging her to move farther away. But her feet failed to cooperate.

The shouts of men from around the corner told Sophie the Dry Bones gang was fast approaching. But would they arrive in time to save Danny and Mugs? The rest of the Irish gang was almost upon the two and would easily overtake them. As if realizing the same, Danny withdrew his revolver, pointed it at the closest attacker, and pulled the trigger.

A shot rang out. The Roach Guard crumpled to the ground like a puppet whose strings had been cut.

Only an instant later, Mugs aimed his revolver at the second attacker. Seeing what had happened to his companion, the other attacker started to retreat, lifted his arms to shield his head but was too late. Another shot exploded in the air. The Roach Guard's legs buckled, and he fell to the ground.

Screams erupted, and onlookers scrambled to take cover, now more afraid of the gunshots than the raging fire.

Amidst the melee, Sophie couldn't take her eyes off the gaping hole in the head of a young man no older than sixteen. Now lifeless, his blood stained the street. She was hardly aware that the Dry Bones brigade had surged from the corner until one of the men knocked into her, nearly sending her to the ground.

Within seconds, the warring gangs converged upon each other, their weapons and fists swinging.

Danny stood on top of the barrel, surveying the fight like a king. He held his smoking revolver in one hand and a bludgeon in the other. On the street beneath him lay the two Roach Guards, both unmoving and trampled in the fighting.

Nausea swirled in Sophie's stomach. She knew Danny was a fighter. She'd witnessed him battering several men who'd provoked him. But take a life? She hadn't wanted to believe he'd go that far, had clung to the possibility that maybe the Dry Bones weren't as violent and deadly as was rumored. Yet how could she deny it any longer?

"Mugs!" Anna shouted and started toward Mugs, who'd been knocked to the ground near the barrel.

At the sound of Anna's voice, Mugs lifted his head. "I'm fine, baby," he called to her even though his nose was spouting blood.

More shouting and the distinctive snapping of police rattles echoed above the fighting.

"Get out of here!" Danny motioned toward Sophie and Anna. He jumped from his perch and reached for Mugs, trying to help him to his feet.

Anna hesitated, watching the two men, the excitement from earlier replaced now with fear.

Danny glanced their way again, and seeing that they hadn't moved, he shouted again. "What are you waiting for? Run and don't let the leatherheads get you!"

The swell of people running from the scene pushed against Sophie. She stumbled but caught herself. The blaze from the leaping flames lit the street and the panic on the faces of those around her—men and women, like her, who had no desire to be anywhere near the crime when the police arrived.

With the momentum of the crowd carrying her along, she started to run at the mention of policemen. In the past, an encounter with one could have resulted in a charge of vagrancy and a trip over to Randall's Island, which was out in the East River.

From the outside, the tree-ringed island looked pretty, even pleasant. But everyone knew that the institutions on Randall's Island were nothing more than deathtraps. There were whispers that three out of four children who went to the unsanitary and overcrowded asylums there ended up dead. Some even said that common domestic animals were more humanely provided for than the almshouse inmates.

Sophie glanced over her shoulder only to see that several policemen had converged upon Danny and Mugs. Their leather helmets set them apart, as did their oak-handled rattles, which served as noisemakers as well as weapons.

"Don't look back," Anna said breathlessly, grabbing Sophie's arm and falling into place next to her.

"Shouldn't we do something to help them?" Sophie asked.

"The best thing we can do to help them is to disappear."

"Disappear? Why?" Someone jostled Sophie, and she tripped. Only Anna's hold kept her from going down.

"So that the Roach Guards don't find us."

"Why would the Roach Guards want us? We didn't do anything."

Anna released a humorless laugh. "If they catch us, they'll use us to get Danny and Mugs to admit to killing two of their men."

Fear crawled up Sophie's spine, and she picked up her feet and ran faster. She might not be good at much, but running away was something she'd learned to do well.

CHAPTER 2

"You have no choice," Mollie said in a whisper that was thin and taut with anxiety. "You have to leave the city."

Sophie peeked through the slit in the threadbare curtains to the street below. The light of dawn hadn't broken through the tall tenement buildings, and the shadows of the passing night lingered. Through strings of laundry that still hung in the narrow corridor between buildings, she couldn't see anyone on the street below, but that didn't mean Roach Guard gang members were planning to leave them alone.

"You don't think we're safe hiding here for a few days?" Anna's whisper was equally tight.

"Oh no, honey. You're not safe anywhere in the city." Mollie leaned against the door, not having moved since she'd arrived home thirty minutes ago. The fancy gown she'd donned at the beginning of the night was askew and wrinkled, the pretty coils in her hair were flat and lifeless, the rouge on her lips and cheeks faded.

If there had been even a hint of glamour when she'd left earlier, it was long gone. Instead, Mollie had dark circles under her eyes, made darker by the pallor of her skin. And her expression held an emptiness, as if every night she gave away more of herself. Perhaps eventually she'd have nothing left to give.

For prostitutes, the selling of their bodies night after night took its toll. Sophie had seen it often enough. Many of them turned to drinking to drown their guilt. Some were battered and bruised by their customers. Others succumbed to diseases. Whatever the case, very few of the women could stay fresh and pretty for long, and Mollie was no exception.

"The Roach Guards might not be on the lookout for you yet," Mollie continued in a low whisper, attempting to keep from waking the children who were all still sleeping in the next room. "But once they realize the two of you were there, they'll attempt to find you and make you testify against Danny and Mugs."

"We'd never do that!" Anna said vehemently from her spot in the apartment's only kitchen chair, positioned in front of a barrel they used as a table. The flicker coming from the stubby candle at the center highlighted the fear in Anna's eyes.

"They'd figure out a way to make you," Mollie replied. "Accuse you of being accomplices to the murder and try to get you arrested. Or maybe threaten to hurt someone you care about if you don't do what they say."

Sophie shivered and moved away from the window, hugging her arms across her chest. The air inside was laden with the stench of scorched fish and cabbage. The coming day promised to be as humid and stale as summer, but a chill wound its way to Sophie's heart and turned her blood cold.

What if the Roach Guards decided to hurt Olivia and Nicholas in order to make her testify against Danny and Mugs? Sophie had already checked on the two children when she'd arrived at the apartment. They'd been curled together and sleeping on the pallet on the floor right where she'd left them hours ago when she tucked them in and told them a story.

The realization that she'd put them in danger once again

spurred her into action. "I'm leaving," she said as she made her way across the front room, trying not to trip over the debris that littered the floor—discarded clothing, shoes, dishes, and toys. One of the other women who lived with Mollie was already asleep on the sagging sofa, having stumbled in drunk and fallen there fully dressed over an hour ago. She hadn't moved since.

"Where will you go?" Anna asked.

Sophie shrugged. "I'll find someplace. I always have."

"But where?"

Sophie spotted her bag underneath the sofa and dropped to her knees to retrieve it. "Maybe this time I'll head south to Philadelphia." She'd exhausted her welcome at the asylums in Boston and New York City. Maybe she could pick the pockets of the Philadelphia charities now.

"You know you won't be able to stay in the asylums with Olivia and Nicholas anymore," Anna whispered. "You're a woman now and it shows."

"I'll find work there."

"Then I'll go with you."

"That's fine with me." Sophie dragged the bag out, the contents inside bulging. She couldn't remember emptying her bag over the past two years. She'd never been anyplace long enough to truly unpack. And besides, she felt safer if she was ready to go at a moment's notice. Like now.

"Philadelphia's too close," Mollie said. "You need to go to a city where the Roach Guards wouldn't think to look for you, someplace where two pretty young women with two infants wouldn't stand out."

"I don't have the money to go farther away," Sophie replied. Actually she didn't have money to go anywhere. But she'd learned how to sneak onto steamers and stow away on the lower decks among the baggage and engines. She wasn't proud of the fact that she could get away with the crime, yet it was just one of the many sins she'd committed since running away from her family. What did it matter if she added one more offense to the long list?

"Take a train west," Mollie suggested. "I've heard there are plenty of jobs for women in places like Michigan, Illinois, or Indiana."

A lump of bitterness pushed into Sophie's throat. That was how she'd gotten into this mess in the first place, with her oldest sister, Elise, deciding to find one of those plentiful jobs for women in the West. They'd been happy at the Seventh Street Mission. They'd had a safe shelter, warm meals, and had been together.

Yes, Elise had lost her job as a seamstress when so many businesses had closed. Even so, Miss Pendleton, the owner of the mission, wouldn't have cast them out onto the street. Surely if Elise had asked, Miss Pendleton would have let them stay. After all, even when Elise left for the West, Miss Pendleton had allowed her and Marianne to remain at the mission, even when the mission was forced to close its doors to everyone else.

But Elise had been too proud. She'd cared more about making a new life than staying together. She'd abandoned them. Even though she'd promised she would save her earnings and send for them, she hadn't.

"What do you say, Sophie?" Anna asked. "Do you want to go west?"

"It's too hard to hide on a train." Sophie had only tried hiding in a baggage car once with Olivia and Nicholas and had almost been caught by a conductor before she'd slipped away and decided to stick with steamers. "And tickets for Olivia, Nicolas, and me would cost more than I could earn in a year."

The three women were silent for a moment. At the early hour of the morning, the tenement was eerily quiet. The noises of the nightlife had faded, and the normal busy chaos of the day hadn't yet started.

"Maybe you don't have to hide on the train or pay for the tickets," Mollie said, finally pushing away from the door. "Maybe there's another way."

"What way?" Anna and Sophie asked at the same time, although Sophie's question contained more derision than Anna's.

"The Children's Aid Society visitors were in the neighborhood yesterday looking for orphans. They said there's a group leaving for Illinois in two days."

Sophie shook her head adamantly. She and Marianne had run away from the Seventh Street Mission when Marianne had overheard Miss Pendleton talking about separating them and giving Olivia and Nicholas into the care of the Children's Aid Society. They'd fled to the Weisses' one-room basement tenement, mostly because Marianne had been in love with Reinhold Weiss and had pretended to be pregnant with his child, so that Mrs. Weiss and Tante Brunhilde would take them in. From the start, Tante Brunhilde had resented their presence and made their lives miserable, especially because Reinhold had gone west for work too and wasn't able to protect them.

Then that awful day had happened. Sophie had come home from school and discovered Tante Brunhilde had taken Olivia and Nicholas to the train depot to join a group of Children's Aid Society orphans bound for the West.

Sophie had panicked and decided that she'd go west with Olivia and Nicholas. After all, she'd been a burden to her sisters, first to Elise and then to Marianne. She figured they wouldn't mind if she left. Then they wouldn't have to worry about providing for her. They could go on with their lives, get jobs, and find husbands without her holding them back.

After making her decision, she hadn't told Marianne and certainly hadn't explained to Mrs. Weiss or Tante Brunhilde where she was going or why. She'd simply left.

When she'd arrived at the train depot and had asked about the train that left earlier in the day with the orphans, she was surprised to learn it had been delayed a day due to malfunctions with the train's engine and that the orphans had been taken back to the Children's Aid Society building for the night.

Sophie waited until darkness had settled and everyone was asleep before breaking into the headquarters and finding Olivia and Nicholas. She'd snuck them out and the next day hid on a steamer, which took them to Boston.

Now she couldn't imagine going back to the Children's Aid Society. Even if no one remembered Olivia and Nicholas from two years ago, she still harbored the desperation and fear from almost losing them.

"No. Absolutely not," Sophie said. "I don't want anything to do with the Children's Aid Society. And I won't send Olivia and Nicholas away—"

"You and Anna would go with," Mollie interrupted. "Join the group and get a free ride to the West. When you get to Chicago, you can get off and do whatever you want. You'll be able to disappear there, and no one will be able to track you down."

The rest of Sophie's words of protest stalled. Mollie's plan was so perfect and so simple it just might work.

Some of the exhaustion in Mollie's face dissipated with her growing excitement. "In fact, being a part of the large group of children would be the ideal place to hide from the Roach Guards. They wouldn't think to look for you among the orphans."

"But aren't Sophie and me too old to be a part of that group?" Anna asked. "Most of the kids are little, aren't they?"

"No, actually the visitor yesterday said they take children as old as sixteen, that the older ones are in high demand among families because of their ability to work."

"We can pass for sixteen, can't we?" Anna asked.

"Maybe," Mollie said, studying her sister through the growing light of dawn. "It's worth a try, and better than sticking around here and ending up like me."

Even if Mollie came home exhausted every morning, the young woman had been full of praise regarding her job as a prostitute, lauding her independence and her freedom from the restrictions of society. She left for work in cheerful spirits, making her job sound as glamorous as her fancy dresses. She'd even boasted about her wages exceeding those of seamstresses and factory workers.

Had that all simply been playacting, an attempt at justifying her choice? A thin veil of bravado over the difficult realities of prostitution?

"I thought you liked your job. But you don't really?" Anna finally voiced the question in Sophie's mind.

Mollie glanced at the door that led to the closet-like room where the children slept, including her one-year-old daughter, Jo. "It's all I have now, the only way I can take care of Jo. I have to make the best of the situation and can't let it get to me like some of my friends have."

"I'm sorry, Mol." Anna rose from her chair, crossed to her sister, and wrapped her in a hug. "I didn't know you felt this way. You're always so happy . . ."

Sophie couldn't tear her eyes from the sisters. Though they were only a couple of years apart in age, Mollie's exhaustion made her look at least ten years older than Anna. As with the other times Sophie had watched them interact, her chest expanded with an ache, an ache she'd tried to ignore and even dislodge altogether. But now the pain came rushing back, along with the need for her sisters. She missed them even though she didn't want to, and she longed to be wrapped into their embraces as she'd been many times in the past.

Her eyes misted. What were Elise and Marianne doing now? Where were they? Had Marianne finally joined Elise out west? Were they both safe? And happy?

Sophie blinked hard, forcing her tears away. Of course they were happy without her. She'd been difficult those last months together, stubborn and willful and angry. She hadn't been a supportive sister like Anna, but had instead made Elise's and Marianne's job of looking after her difficult.

She knew they'd been worried when she disappeared. They'd probably made a good effort at searching for her. But once they realized she was gone, surely they concluded they were better off without her.

There had been a few times during her worst moments of hunger and cold when she'd considered trying to track them down, had even thought about returning to the Seventh Street Mission and asking Miss Pendleton to help her. But Sophie had always held back.

At first her hesitation had been out of fear that someone would attempt to separate her from Olivia and Nicholas again. But now that she was stronger and wouldn't let that happen, she didn't want to see her sisters because she was embarrassed, and even a little afraid, of what they would think of her and the mess she'd made of her life.

No, she was better off on her own without them. She'd find a way to make things work. She'd become resourceful, and she could do whatever she set her mind to.

"Sophie?" came a soft sleepy voice from the bedroom doorway. Olivia stood in her nightgown, her long brown hair having come loose from her braid as it was prone to do since it was thin and silky. "What's wrong?"

"Nothing, Liebchen." Sophie didn't want to worry Olivia about the danger they were in.

Olivia's sights were fixed on the bag in front of Sophie. "Then why are we leaving?"

Sophie's mind raced to find a plausible excuse for having to move one more time, especially because lately Olivia had started crying whenever Sophie pulled out their bag. Sophie glanced at Anna for help. What should they tell the children?

Anna released Mollie and held out a hand toward Olivia. "We decided it's time for an adventure. Wouldn't you like that?"

"I don't want any more adventures." Olivia's voice wobbled. "I'm tired of adventures."

Sophie agreed with the girl. She was tired of moving and traveling too. She'd almost found a permanent solution by marrying Danny. He would have given her and the children a home so that they could finally stop running.

But by now the policemen had likely hauled Danny and Mugs to the Tombs, where they'd be put on trial and perhaps executed for the murders.

Her hope of a new life had gone up in flames just as swiftly as the wood-framed building had earlier that night.

"I don't want to go anywhere," Olivia said. "I want to stay here. Forever."

As if sensing the girl's escalating emotions, Mollie crossed to Olivia and brushed her hair back from her face, attempting to intervene before Olivia began to cry in earnest and wake the other children. "You'll get to ride on a train this time. Think of the fun that will be."

"I don't want to ride a train." Olivia's voice rose.

"Train?" another small voice asked behind Olivia. Nicholas moved past his sister and Mollie, looking for Sophie. At the sight of her kneeling on the floor in front of their bag, he raced to her, flinging himself into her arms.

Sophie easily caught and hugged him to her chest. At three, he was light and small for his age. As his thin arms wound around her neck, she bent her nose into his tousled brown hair and breathed in the soapy scent that lingered from the bath she'd given him last night in the metal sink on the second floor landing, the only spigot in the building that worked. Even with the handle turned all the way, it only gave a trickle, but it was better than nothing.

She'd been more of a mother to him than sister—the only mother figure he'd ever known since his real mother had abandoned him the first year of his life. Sophie had been taking care of him and Olivia ever since.

His warm body wiggled out of her embrace. He'd apparently reassured himself of her love and was finished with the hug. "I wanna ride a train," he said earnestly, his eyes wide and his expression serious. "I like trains."

"I know you do, Liebchen." Sophie tweaked his nose. "And because you like them so much, I decided we finally get to ride on one."

He gave her one of his beautiful baby smiles, one that never failed to melt her heart and remind her that everything she'd ever done, good or bad, was worth it.

"Why can't we stay here?" Olivia asked, her eyes brimming with tears. "Aunt Mollie is nice to us and so is Anna."

"Anna is coming with," Sophie said.

"That's right," Anna added. "I've always wanted to ride a train, haven't you?"

Olivia shook her head.

Nicholas bounced like the little ball on his bilbo catcher. The ball-and-cup game was his only toy, one Sophie had discovered discarded among the baggage during one of their steamer voyages. "Please, Olivia. I wanna ride the train. You'll like it too."

The little girl swiped at the tears that had begun to escape.

Sophie knew that for Nicholas's sake, Olivia would try to control herself. She'd mothered her brother too and would never do anything to disappoint or hurt Nicholas.

At a slamming reverberation of a door somewhere in the tenement, Mollie started and glanced to the entrance of their apartment, as if the Roach Guards might burst through at any moment. Sophie realized suddenly that they'd put Mollie in danger with their presence. The Roach Guards might harass her, perhaps even hurt and threaten her to divulge information about Sophie and Anna.

"You need to go," Mollie said, worry lines creasing her forehead. "Before daylight."

Sophie nodded and opened the bag. "Olivia and Nicholas, I want you to get dressed while I pack. We'll leave in five minutes."

Nicholas scampered to obey. Olivia hesitated. Her gaze met Sophie's and was filled with accusation.

Sophie focused on the bag. She would talk with Olivia later and try to explain why they had to move again. But for now they had no time to waste. They had to make use of the remaining darkness before dawn to reach the Children's Aid Society building.

She shoved aside the items within the bag, and her fingers made contact with heavy brass. It was her candle holder, the one Mutti had given her on her deathbed, the only possession she had to connect her to the life she'd once had. She traced the kneeling angel that was holding up a lampstand devoid of its candle. She didn't have to see it to know it was tarnished and had lost its polished shine.

"Remember not to lose your way in the darkness," Mutti had whispered through her last breaths. "No matter how lost you might feel at times, always keep His light burning inside you."

Sophie shoved aside the gift along with Mutti's words. Neither mattered anymore. She was as tarnished as the candle holder and definitely had no light left inside her.

She wasn't sure why she'd hung on to the heirloom. She'd kept it in her bag, refusing to bring it out in any of their temporary homes. Several times she'd considered selling it and using the money for shoes or coats for Olivia and Nicholas. But even in their most desperate predicaments, she'd kept the memento. Maybe because she knew it was her last link to her family. And perhaps her last link to God.

Whatever the case, it had come with her this far and would go with her as she ran away again.

CHAPTER 3

MAYFIELD, ILLINOIS
SEPTEMBER 1859

The blisters on Reinhold Weiss's fingers had burst and started to bleed, turning the palms of his leather work gloves damp and brown. The muscles in his shoulders and arms seared from the hours of swinging the scythe since sunup, six hours ago.

"Water break, Reinhold," Jakob called from near the edge of the alfalfa field. He held up a battered tin pail, no doubt full of cold, freshly drawn well water.

Reinhold nodded but didn't waver in the steady *swish swish swish* of the scythe. He would finish the section he was on before giving himself the luxury of quenching his thirst. He had to. There was too much to be done and not enough time to complete it all.

Once he finished the haying, the oats and wheat would be ready. The potatoes would soon need digging. And then the corn would finally be dry and ready for husking.

The alfalfa spread out before him, falling easily against the blade he'd sharpened with the grindstone last night. Tall and dotted with blue flowers, the alfalfa was alive with bumblebees and honeybees. While picturesque, the full bloom meant he was behind, that the hay was going more to fiber and losing its value for his livestock.

He shuffled and cut, shuffled and cut, leaving the clumps for Jakob to spread out with his pitchfork so that it could dry evenly in the sunshine. The hot spell would parch the alfalfa quickly, turning it from a vibrant green to a pale, dusty yellow. If the rain held off, he and Jakob might be able to finish by week's end, including raking the cut-and-dried hay into windrows, loading it onto the wagon, and hauling it to the barn.

The high afternoon sun coaxed a sweet scent from the freshly cut hay as it baked under the bright rays. A few butterflies and grasshoppers still rose into the air, protesting the loss of their shady sanctuary, while most of the other wildlife had decided to hibernate during the hottest part of the day. Even the red-tailed hawk that had been circling overhead earlier was gone, having given up on the easy prey of mice and rabbits that shot out of the alfalfa whenever his scythe drew too close.

As he neared the end of the wide path he'd cut, Jakob met him and held out the pail. Reinhold let the scythe's long handle slip from his aching fingers and fall to the ground. As he took the pail, his burning muscles caused his hands to tremble. He tipped the container and drank greedily, heedless of the water that sloshed over and dribbled down the front of his sweat-soaked shirt.

Jakob reached a hand out to steady the pail.

As small as the motion was, it unleashed a cyclone of helplessness inside Reinhold, helplessness at all he needed to get done during the harvest, helplessness at how much he still had to learn about farming, helplessness because he couldn't accomplish it all, even with Jakob's assistance. And now he was so tired he couldn't manage to guzzle water without making a mess.

He jerked the pail away from Jakob's touch. "I can drink by myself."

Jakob took a rapid step back and cowered, which only made the storm inside Reinhold swirl faster. At fourteen, Jakob was old enough to remember their father, his unbridled anger, and the destruction he'd rained upon them. Their father's outbursts had usually been unexpected and at the smallest provocation.

Had Reinhold become so much like their father that Jakob feared him?

Reinhold lowered the bucket and pressed his fingers against his trouser pocket, against the hard circular outline of his father's watch. The broken timepiece was supposed to remind him to be different, but more often than not it taunted him with the similarities. "I'm sorry, Jakob."

Jakob nodded but averted his gaze, peering behind him to the acres of hay that still needed to be mowed. Beneath the brim of the boy's wide straw hat, his green eyes held the sorrow of someone who'd seen and experienced too much in his short life.

Though he and Jakob shared the same green eyes, that was where the similarities in their appearances ended. Where Jakob had inherited their mother's brown hair and pale complexion, Reinhold took after their father with dark hair and swarthy skin. Jakob was as thin as a cornstalk and already promising to surpass Reinhold's stocky height of only five-foot-eight.

Jakob also took after their mother with his sensitive spirit. He'd been quiet and melancholy since he'd arrived in the spring. He'd shared briefly about what had happened to Peter during the previous winter, how their youngest brother, a newsboy, had been attacked, robbed, and left for dead on a New York City street corner.

It had taken only that short conversation for Reinhold to realize Jakob was plagued with guilt over Peter's death the same way he was. Reinhold had blamed himself since the moment he'd received the telegram about the boy's death. He should have brought both of his brothers to Illinois last fall after he'd purchased his farm. Even though it had taken him all winter to construct a house and barn, he could have built a temporary shelter. In truth, he knew that Euphemia Duff would have opened her home to the two boys the same way she had to him after he'd left the Turners.

If anyone was to blame for Peter's death, he was. Not Jakob. He'd told the boy as much, yet the shadows had remained in Jakob's green eyes all spring and summer.

"Thank you for refilling the water," Reinhold said before lifting the pail again and taking another long drink.

Jakob nodded and wiped his dirty shirtsleeve across his smudged face. The boy stank of sweat, having worn the same clothes all week. Reinhold had but one extra change of clothes too and knew he smelled as rotten as Jakob, if not worse. Both of them needed a good scrubbing, except that would mean having to take the time to haul and heat water, first for their baths, and second for laundry. And he simply didn't have the time. Already he was working well past dusk by lantern light. By the time he left the field, he had a dozen other chores waiting for him.

While Jakob did his best to lend a hand wherever he could, the boy was as ignorant in the ways of the land as Reinhold had been when he'd first signed on as Mr. Turner's farmhand. Thankfully, Mr. Turner had been a patient teacher, and Reinhold learned a great deal about running a farm during the year he'd worked there.

He'd believed he was ready for a place of his own. But he hadn't fully comprehended the magnitude of all he still had to learn. He certainly hadn't expected he'd struggle so much to get the work done. He realized now that was why Mr. Turner had hired two additional men to help him. The load was too much for one person.

The problem was, Reinhold couldn't afford to hire someone to help him. He'd paid every last dollar of his savings toward the down payment on the land, the farm tools, and the lumber necessary to build a house and barn. Now he had nothing left—not until after he made a profit from the harvest. Even then he'd have to pay down the credit he owed at all the stores in town before he'd truly see a profit.

"Are you hungry?" Jakob lowered a grain sack from his shoulder.

Reinhold was famished. He'd learned to make a few things on the old cookstove he'd purchased secondhand from another farmer in exchange for several days of labor. Eggs, beans, or fish. He was also getting fresh vegetables from the garden he'd planted behind the house. Thankfully, they weren't experiencing a shortage of food like they had in New York City during the depression and financial panic that had happened two years ago.

But when winter came, if he didn't earn a profit on his crops, and if he didn't learn how to preserve the garden produce, they'd go hungry.

Jakob opened the sack and began to pull out their lunch— hard-boiled eggs, slices of ham, radishes, carrots, and cucumbers.

"Thank you, Jakob," Reinhold said as he stuffed a piece of ham into his mouth.

For a moment, they ate in silence. The constant *zing-zing* of cicadas on fence posts and the distant trees was a sound he'd come to appreciate as much as the trilling of the crickets at dusk. The crackling rustle of the hay in the breeze and the distant warble of a songbird only made the silence more beautiful, and Reinhold allowed himself the rare pleasure of studying his land.

His land.

Every time he reminded himself that the land was his, he

was able to push aside his discouragement—even if just for a little while.

He was a poor German immigrant, a construction worker, a nobody. Yet here he was with a place of his own. He had more here in central Illinois than he'd ever dreamed possible.

The waves of green and gold of the ripening fields spread out on all sides, all one hundred twenty acres he'd purchased from the Illinois Central Railroad. Though he'd wanted to plow every inch possible and had grand plans for everything he'd grow, the plowing had taken longer and was harder than he'd anticipated. He managed to ready only one hundred acres, even with the neighbors helping him when they could.

Some of his property was no good for farming, particularly the rocky sections along the creek. Not only was his farm one of the farthest in Mayfield from the railroad, but he also didn't have a decent road that ran past his land. He'd have a harder time getting his harvest to market. But the drawbacks of the land had worked to his advantage, namely that the property had still been available when most of the farmland in the area had already been sold off.

He stared past the alfalfa to the cornfield. With their silky tassels, the stalks towered a foot or more above him. He'd already tested the ears and discovered they were ripe. However, he'd learned last year on the Turner farm that he had to wait to harvest and husk the corn until it was completely dry.

Beyond the cornfield on the west, the land sloped gently toward the creek where the only trees on his land stood—oaks, maples, and willows. Jakob had discovered wild blackberries growing in the brush in the valley earlier in the summer. And he'd provided a steady supply of bluegill and trout he fished out of the creek.

On the other side of the alfalfa field, on the eastern edge of his property, he'd built a simple two-story clapboard house with a living space and kitchen on the first floor and two bedrooms on the second. He and Jakob had painted the house white to weatherize the boards. But beyond the simple coating, the house was plain and mostly unfurnished, containing a few odds and ends of furniture given to him by neighbors.

He'd built the barn far enough away from the house that hopefully the livestock odors wouldn't waft into their living quarters. Of course, he didn't have to worry about too much stench yet since he only had one horse, one milking cow, a pig, and a few chickens, all of which he'd purchased from the Duffs on credit.

Eventually he planned to add another horse, as well as sheep. And he planned to bring his sisters west too. Thankfully, Marianne and Elise Neumann—or he should say, Marianne Brady and Elise Quincy—were caring for the girls in New York City and had been since his Tante Brunhilde had remarried last October.

After reading the telegrams and letters from Marianne and Elise, Reinhold knew they hadn't been able to locate their little sister Sophie, who'd run away two years ago. Because of the disappearance of their sister, they were all the more eager to help him with his. Both Marianne and Elise had married men from wealthy families and could provide his sisters with everything they needed and then some.

Although he was imposing on his two childhood friends by leaving Silke and Verina with them all these months, dread chopped like a hoe at his innards every time he considered bringing his sisters to the farm.

The truth was as stark as the horizon. He wasn't fit to raise them.

Besides, his home wasn't ready. He didn't have enough beds or blankets or other comforts. It didn't matter that the two had spent most of their lives sleeping on hard floors in crowded tenements without any hint of luxury, never knowing when they'd eat their next meal. They deserved more now, and he aimed to have more by the time he sent for them.

At nine and seven years of age, they weren't entirely helpless anymore and wouldn't need constant supervision. But they needed more—much more—than he could ever give.

Whatever the case, his first priority was harvesting his crops and taking them to market. Then he had to pay off his debts. If he had any money left, he could start adding more to his farm and then think about what to do regarding Silke and Verina.

Reinhold washed his meal down with the rest of the water from the tin pail. When he was done he was still hungry, but at least he would have more energy for the long afternoon ahead.

"I don't know what I'd do without you." He handed the pail back to Jakob.

Jakob nodded but stared at the ground and kicked at a clod of dirt. Though he never complained, Reinhold could tell his brother was discontent. After six months of living and working on the farm, he'd expected Jakob to adjust, to like the farm, to find a measure of fulfillment here. Sure, life wasn't easy. But living in the country with fresh air to breathe and space all around was still better than eking out an existence in the crowded city slums. Wasn't it?

Why, then, wasn't Jakob experiencing the same satisfaction when completing a job or the same appreciation for the beauty of the land?

Reinhold stifled a sigh and reached for the scythe. "Time to get back to work." As he straightened, a distant curl of smoke caught his attention. Against the clear blue of the cloudless sky, the dark gray line was distinct and made his pulse spurt with anxiety.

He couldn't be sure if the smoke was coming from his property or if the fire was on the Turners' land. But under the dry conditions of late summer, any fire in the area could quickly spread and take with it whole fields of crops. In fact, one gust of wind could fan a few sparks into an inferno, destroying everything he'd worked so hard to cultivate.

With a jolt, he started toward the smoke, heedless of trampling the alfalfa. "Looks like there's a fire!" he called over his shoulder to Jakob. "We need to put it out now before it spreads."

Reinhold ran hard, not bothering to stop and retrieve his hat when it fell off. Jakob's footsteps pounded behind him, urging him faster. When they rounded the field, Reinhold stumbled to a halt at the sight that met him.

His post-and-rail fence was on fire.

A new sense of desperation cinched his middle, drawing it tight. He'd bought the rail posts on credit, hauled them out to the farm, and spent hours constructing the fence to keep Mr. Turners' cows and sheep out of his alfalfa. He couldn't afford the loss.

"Take off your shirt!" he called to Jakob even as his fingers worked at his own buttons. Three posts and the connecting rails were in flames. Tongues of fire lapped at the boards on either side, and sparks had landed in the grass underneath.

How had the fire started? He scanned the area, searching for signs of what might have happened. Some farmers liked to set fires in the spring to burn off the previous year's growth. Mr. Turner had burned grass and leaves earlier in the year farther up on his land, and the pungent scent had spread everywhere.

Reinhold's sights snagged on the butt end of a cigar near the burning post. It was possible Higgins had been careless. That would have been just like the Turners' hired hand to smoke away from the house so he wouldn't get in trouble with Mrs. Turner. And it would be just like Higgins not to care how his actions affected anyone else.

Reinhold kicked at the nearest post and then cursed, giving

vent to his anger . . . and his remorse. Every time he thought of how he'd almost killed Higgins last year, the memory only fueled his self-loathing.

He stomped on the small flames in the grass and ground them out, all the while yanking at buttons. When he finally had his shirt off, he took the opposite end of the fence from where Jakob was and began beating at the fire with the garment, trying to put out the flames—or at the very least keep them from spreading.

Jakob swatted the flames too. But after several minutes of fighting the fire, Reinhold realized the boards were too dry and the flames as greedy as a hungry street urchin.

"Keep the grass from catching fire!" Reinhold shouted as he lowered his now-blackened shirt and began to tramp out the sparks in the grass again.

A faint call from the direction of the house drew Reinhold's attention. Barclay Duff and two of his boys were running their way.

Relief swept through Reinhold, and he lifted his hand to acknowledge them before he turned back to the fence with renewed zeal and hope. Maybe he could save the structure after all.

The two Duff boys arrived well ahead of Barclay, who was a hefty man, not just from the muscles he'd developed from all his farm work, but mostly because his wife kept him happy with a steady supply of pies, cakes, and cookies—a steady supply she'd made available to Reinhold when he'd lived there last winter. Euphemia's good cooking was just one thing among many Reinhold missed about his time with the Scottish family.

Fergus and Alastair, at twelve and fourteen, were the youngest of the five Duff boys. Stocky and muscular, they were hard workers just like their father. They took their shirts off and started pummeling the fire next to Reinhold. By the time Barclay joined them, his face was red and his breath wheezed from the exertion.

Even though the fire was mostly under control, Barclay stripped off his shirt anyway and helped until they'd extinguished every spark.

"Me and the boys were almost here when we saw the smoke," Barclay said as he swiped at the sweat coursing down his temple and cheeks. It ran through the smoke and ash and pooled at his thick mustache. "Pushed my team so fast the last half mile, I thought they might sprout wings and fly."

"I'm grateful you got here when you did." Reinhold wiped at his own perspiration and took stock of his rail fence. Three sections were blackened and crumbling, but the boards on either side of the burnt area were singed and nothing more. "Would have lost the entire fence if you hadn't shown up. Might have even spread to my alfalfa."

"I was more surprised than a catfish bitin' bait when I saw the smoke. Thought to myself what *Dunderheid* would think of burning grass on a dry day like today."

"Not me. I'm no Dunderheid." Reinhold toed the cigar stub in the charred grass. "If I had to take a guess, I'd say Higgins was out here smoking and avoiding Mrs. Turner's wrath."

Barclay made a disapproving sound at the back of his throat. "That skinny longlegs is a crabbit."

During Reinhold's months living with the Duffs, he'd grown accustomed to Barclay's strange Scottish sayings. And while he didn't understand everything that came out of Barclay's mouth, he'd learned well enough that the burly farmer was a fair man with a kind heart. Even though Reinhold hadn't deserved the ally, Barclay had become one anyway.

Barclay began to put his shirt back on even though parts of it were burned clear through. "Aye, sure do wish we had ourselves a way to teach that crabbit a lesson about behaving like a good neighbor."

"I guess not everyone can be the perfect neighbor like you, can they?" Reinhold tried to lighten his voice past the frustration cutting through him as sharp as a saw blade.

"That's for sure." Barclay gave him a beaming smile, one that lifted his mustache and lit his round face. "Ye won't find another neighbor like me even if ye searched the whole world over."

Somewhere over the past two years of hardships, Reinhold had lost his ability to jest and tease. But when he was with Barclay, that playful side sometimes emerged again. Barclay seemed to have a way of finding and bringing it out of him.

"And because I'm such a good neighbor, I was bringing ye news that ye'd be a pure idiot to miss."

"As much as I appreciate the invitation to one of Euphemia's dinners, I can't take the time this week." Reinhold was too embarrassed to admit that he'd worked last Sabbath and planned to do it again this week.

Barclay made another disapproving noise at the back of his throat. "Yer as stubborn as a raccoon holdin' a copper penny, don't ye know it? If ye'd take my offer of Alastair and Fergus's help, ye'd be done with the haying by now."

"You need them more than I do." The Duffs had moved to Mayfield Township four years ago from western New York after selling their dairy farm. Barclay had purchased three hundred sixty acres of prime land and was well on his way to having one of the largest dairy farms in central Illinois.

Barclay glanced at his two sons, who stood next to Jakob. Alastair and Fergus's legs stuck out of the bottom of their britches by several inches, their knobby ankles as scratched as their bare feet. They were growing fast, likely too fast for Euphemia to keep up with.

Their boisterous voices and laughter wafted as heavy and

thick as the smoke. Jakob was grinning, his face more animated than it had been all week—since the last time one of the boys had stopped by. Their easygoing manner always brought out the best in Jakob in a way Reinhold couldn't seem to do.

Barclay was fortunate his older sons still lived at home and hadn't branched out on their own. But they both knew it was only a matter of time before they married and headed off.

There was always too much work and never enough hands, even for the Duff family. And although Reinhold had taken Barclay's offer of help from time to time, he'd refused to make a regular practice of draining his friend's already limited resources.

Barclay wiped at his perspiration again. "We were just in town and heard the news that a train of them eastern city orphans is passing through soon. Ye need to go and get yerself a couple of boys."

Reinhold's mind flashed to the image of Liverpool, the hardened orphan boy Mr. Turner had brought back to the farm last summer. Reinhold had taken the time to talk with the boy, to encourage him and teach him a few things. He'd hoped to make a difference in the boy's life. But he'd only been fooling himself into thinking that was possible, especially when Liverpool had gotten into so much trouble.

Who was he to think he could take in any other orphans when he'd failed so miserably with Liverpool?

"They can help ye with the harvest," Barclay said.

The possibility of acquiring extra farmhands was tempting. If they were under eighteen years of age, like Liverpool, the families didn't have to pay the orphans wages. In exchange for work, the families were required to feed, house, and clothe the orphan children who came to live with them. More than that, they were asked to treat the orphans like members of their family, taking them to church and helping them to attend school.

Reinhold shook his head. If he couldn't take Jakob to church and didn't spare the boy the time off for school, he'd be hard pressed to do so for an orphan.

"Don't be a Dunderheid again," Barclay said, looking pointedly at his overripe hay. "Ye need the help. Get an orphan boy or two."

The scattered swaths drying on the ground reminded Reinhold of the many steps that went into haying, that he was only at the beginning of his harvest, and that he and Jakob had weeks of work left ahead of them.

"All right," Reinhold said, holding in a sigh. "I'll think about it."

CHAPTER 4

The squealing of steel against steel from an approaching train grated against Sophie's nerves, which were already frayed as thin as the bag she clutched.

"Stay right by my side," she hissed to Olivia and Nicholas, even as she drew them closer.

The people coming and going on the train platform swelled around the group of orphans, threatening to rip them apart. Sophie feared that a passerby would recognize her and Anna and point them out for the frauds they were. Worse, what if someone from the Roach Guards was in the crowd and recognized them?

Sophie darted a glance toward the depot. Several young men had been loitering on benches near the doorway before the group of orphans had arrived a short while ago. What if the Roach Guards had sent the men to prevent her and Anna from leaving town?

"Keep your head down," Anna murmured from behind, her voice laced with the same anxiety Sophie felt.

If only they could board their train car . . . then they could hide away again.

The day before, after they'd left Mollie's tenement on

Mulberry Bend, they'd skirted main streets and stayed to back alleys as they half walked, half ran to the Children's Aid Society, hoping all the while that no one would see them. They passed a drunk digging through a trash barrel. And they dodged an old woman setting up her corner vegetable stand with shriveled cabbages and potatoes.

When they'd finally reached their destination and pounded on the front door, one of the workers ushered them inside without any questions. The two grandmotherly women who seemed to be in charge of the gathering of orphans had been kind and didn't seem to recognize Olivia and Nicholas from their brief stay last time. Sophie supposed the Children's Aid Society workers saw so many children that they couldn't possibly remember all the faces and names.

Even so, she gave the Society workers a false last name as she'd done so often at the asylums. She would have attempted to disguise their first names too, yet she knew Olivia and Nicholas wouldn't have been capable of carrying out a name-change charade for long.

The women had provided them with the chance to bathe and had also given Nicholas a much-needed haircut. Then they'd offered each of them two new outfits, one to wear during their travels, and one to save for the day they were scheduled to meet their new families. Sophie had an easier time locating suitable garments for Olivia and Nicholas from among those available. But there were fewer choices for her and Anna, dresses that were plain and serviceable, nothing flattering or pretty or colorful.

Sophie gladly took what was offered, knowing if she didn't wear it for herself, she could sell it when she reached Chicago and fetch a fair price for other things they might need.

When the grandmotherly workers asked Sophie and Anna about their families, Sophie had explained that Olivia and Nicholas were her sister and brother and their parents were deceased. "No, no one wants us, and no one will care if we go west," she'd answered. That was the truth too, even if nothing else was.

They'd spent all of yesterday and last night with the other orphans inside the Children's Aid Society building. Sophie had recognized a few from the Juvenile Asylum, though most of them she'd never seen before. By the time they'd lined up to walk to the train station that morning, there were thirty-five children in their group.

Sophie slumped her shoulders, hoping to make herself invisible among the others. With her hair coiled beneath a new hat, at least she had a measure of disguise. Anna likewise wore a bonnet and had tilted it to hide her face.

"Here we are, children," said Mrs. Trott, the portlier of the two women who'd accompanied them. She stopped in front of a passenger car and motioned for them to stay near her.

Several compartments down, train workers were standing on top of a wagon-like car as a chute overhead dumped coal inside it. Although Sophie didn't know much about how trains worked, one of the other younger boys had patiently answered Nicholas's questions about the train ever since they'd arrived at the station.

"Thata one there," said the boy, pointing to the front train car. "That's the locomotive with the steam engine inside of it that makes this whole thing go."

"What's a steam engine?" Nicholas stood on his tiptoes and tried to see around the children in front of him to the locomotive. Nicholas had been thrilled to don his new clothes that morning—clean trousers and a matching coat, a crisp white shirt with a bow tie, and black shoes polished so shiny he could see his reflection in them. He even had a new hat and underclothes, more new items in one day than he'd had in a lifetime.

At the excitement and pride that filled his face when he'd finished dressing, Sophie should have been happy for him. Instead she felt strangely inadequate, as if somehow she'd failed the little boy by not being able to give him such nice things when he clearly craved them.

Olivia had been less excited by her new dress, although she hadn't been able to hide her pleasure over the new matching bow for her hair.

Thankfully, Olivia was less tearful today than she had been last night.

"Why?" she kept asking Sophie as they'd lain on blankets on the hard floor of the front room of the Children's Aid Society after Nicholas had fallen asleep. "Why do we have to leave again? Why can't we stay?"

Concerned that Olivia's whispers would turn into hysterics and wake everyone, Sophie had told Olivia some of the truth, that they were in danger if they stayed in the city.

"Promise that after this trip, we won't have to run away again," Olivia said, her sobs finally subsiding. "Promise we can find a home and never have to leave it."

Sophie had squeezed her eyes closed to fight back the sudden burn of tears. Find a home. It seemed like an impossible dream. But she had to do better for Olivia and Nicholas. She had to stop running away and needed to find a permanent place for them. "I promise," she'd whispered, kissing Olivia's forehead and drawing the girl into her arms. "I promise we'll find a good home this time."

Nicholas tugged at Sophie's arm, bringing her back to the busy train station. "Up, please. I wanna see."

Sophie hefted him to her hip as she'd done so many times in the past. His eyes widened as he took in the locomotive with its hissing engine and billowing smoke. "It's a dragon," he said in his most serious tone. "Like from the stories."

At his comparison, Sophie smiled.

"Will it eat me?"

"No, Liebchen." Sophie kissed his cheek. "It eats the black rocks. See, the men are feeding it right now."

Nicholas continued to watch in wide-eyed amazement.

"There you are, Mr. Brady," Mrs. Trott said with a thread of exasperation in her voice. She broke away from their group as a gentleman approached. He was dressed in a dark, crisp suit that spoke of wealth, but he had an easy air about him that lacked the formality of most in his social position.

"We've been waiting for you, as usual." Mrs. Trott leveled a matronly look upon the man.

Mr. Brady smiled, giving his face a handsome appeal and revealing a dimple in his chin. "I'm sorry for the delay, but we're not going with this time. My wife's sister, Mrs. Quincy, is overdue with her baby. And my wife doesn't want to leave her."

Mrs. Trott's eyes widened with dismay. "But, Mr. Brady, the children are ready and waiting."

Sophie stilled, as did the others around her, and their attention shifted to the conversation between Mrs. Trott and Mr. Brady. Did this mean they wouldn't be leaving today after all? Mollie had warned her and Anna that every day of delay in leaving the city would put them in more danger.

"Now, Mrs. Trott," Mr. Brady replied in an amiable tone that contained a Southern twang. "You have to know by now that I might be impulsive, but I care too much about the children to delay a placing-out trip."

Mrs. Trott gave him a grudging smile. "Yes, dear. You're a good boy."

"Thank you." As if sensing the children's attention upon him, Mr. Brady winked at them. "You'll be happy to know that Reverend and Mrs. Poole have agreed to take over for Mrs. Brady and me."

"Oh." The relief in Mrs. Trott's voice spread over Sophie and the other children, releasing the tension that had stiffened them only moments ago. Sophie supposed, like the rest of the children, that she was accustomed to disappointment, that it was as much a part of her life as breathing. Even so, she was counting on this train ride.

She darted a look toward the depot and the men still loitering there. One of them was studying her across the top of his newspaper with a hard, calculated gaze.

Sophie dropped her sights to the gleaming brass buttons on Nicholas's coat. Had she been discovered?

"Reverend and Mrs. Poole are on their way even as we speak," Mr. Brady continued. "I told the reverend I would assist with getting all the children on board and settled into their seats."

Sophie didn't wait for Mrs. Trott or Mr. Brady to give them permission to begin boarding. She pushed toward the metal stairs, holding Nicholas and herding Olivia in front of her.

As they climbed the steps and entered the train car, the fumes of the burning coal and the staleness of the compartment greeted them. Clusters of wooden benches facing each other spread out on either side of the aisle. The train car ended in a closet on one side, which Sophie guessed was the privy.

While the other little boys shot off down the aisle with shouts of glee, Sophie held tight to Nicholas until she reached a set of benches near the middle on the side opposite the train platform. She didn't want to chance anyone detecting them through the window while they waited to leave.

Anna sat down with Olivia on the bench directly across from her and Nicholas. Her friend visibly relaxed, extending her legs out in front of her and leaning back into the hard bench. "We made it," she said with a smile.

Sophie wasn't so sure. She wouldn't relax until the train was on its way. Nevertheless, the anxiety that had been plucking a dreadful rhythm finally ceased. Maybe everything would work out after all.

A short while later, Mr. Brady entered the train compartment, carrying boxes that he deposited at the front. He helped a few stragglers find empty seats, broke up a fight between two boys who both wanted to sit next to the window, and then showed another child to the privy. He seemed like just the kind of man these children needed—helpful and compassionate and yet confident and unafraid to apply discipline.

A feeling of anticipation permeated the commotion of the orphans, although Sophie could see the apprehension in some of the faces as well. She remembered all too well the first time she'd left New York City on the steamer headed to Boston, and the fears that had trailed along with her.

At least these children had homes waiting for them when they arrived. They wouldn't have to try to survive on the streets or find room in crowded asylums.

"When will we go?" Nicholas asked half a dozen times as he bounced with excitement on the bench, before a couple finally entered the train, red-cheeked and breathless, clearly having hurried to make the departure.

Mr. Brady greeted the couple as Reverend and Mrs. Poole. He talked with them at the front of the compartment for a few minutes before finally turning to wave good-bye.

As he bestowed a smile over the children, his gaze passed over Sophie, but then just as quickly snapped back to her. One of his brows quirked, revealing curiosity in the depth of his eyes, almost as if he thought he recognized her, even though Sophie was sure she'd never seen or met him before.

For a moment he stalled, and suddenly Sophie was afraid he'd seen past her deception, afraid he'd figured out she wasn't planning to stay with the group beyond Chicago, afraid he even knew about her witness to the recent gang murder.

She dropped her sights and focused on Nicholas, smiling at the boy and nodding even though she hadn't heard his most recent question.

Mr. Brady took a step toward her, and Sophie's heart jumped into her throat. What excuses could she give him? What story should she tell of the many she'd used to cover her trail these past months?

The lurch of the train beginning its journey stopped Mr. Brady. He hastily turned and made his way out the door, calling a farewell to Reverend and Mrs. Poole.

Sophie released a breath as Mr. Brady bounded down the metal stairs. Through the window she caught a glimpse of him leaping off the slowly moving train. He landed easily on the platform and then disappeared from sight as the train picked up speed and left the depot behind.

She sagged against the bench with a smile. "We did it," she said, finally agreeing with Anna.

"Yes, we did." Anna smiled back.

⁓⁓⁓

The clacking of the train against the tracks and the clattering of the compartment at the fast speed of twenty-five miles per hour had frightened Olivia for the first hour of the journey. She'd huddled against Sophie, her face pale and her eyes closed.

Nicholas, on the other hand, had pressed his face to the window, like many of the other children, exclaiming over each new thing he saw as the crowded city buildings had changed into the sprawling open countryside. Sophie wasn't sure he'd ever get his fill of viewing the passing farm fields, woodlands, and rolling hills that spread out on either side of the train for as far as the eye could see.

"Children, your attention please." Reverend Poole had risen from the bench at the front where he'd sat with his wife. It

54

was the first time he'd addressed their group since leaving, apparently having learned from previous journeys the futility of talking with the orphans until they had the opportunity to grow accustomed to the train and the scenery.

Both he and his wife were petite and certainly more reserved than Mr. Brady had been, having hardly spoken with anyone yet. Sophie liked Mr. Brady better, yet she hoped the Pooles' reticent nature would work to her benefit, that they'd take less interest in her and Anna, and ask fewer questions.

The children quieted, sat back in their seats, and focused on Reverend Poole. He wasn't young like Mr. Brady, but wasn't as old as Mrs. Trott. The hair that showed beneath his stovepipe hat was sprinkled with some silver, though his mustache and sideburns were still dark and untouched by age. He wore round spectacles that made his eyes appear wide in his thin face. They were keen eyes but not unkind.

"It is my greatest pleasure to welcome all you little ones of Christ on our journey together," he said. "How many would like to have nice homes in the West, where you can see chickens and pigs and cows every day and have your fill of apples and melons and wild blackberries?"

A chorus of chatter rose from the children, including Nicholas. "Chickens and pigs and cows?" he said, his eyes sparkling.

"And how would you like to have both a mother and a father, two parents who love you very much and will provide you with everything you need—warm meals, hot baths, clean clothes, and even toys?"

Again the children responded to Reverend Poole's question enthusiastically. Even those who had started to look frightened and sad as the reality of the trip set in regained some of their initial excitement. Sophie guessed that Reverend Poole was once again displaying his expertise, knowing how to cheer the children at just the right time.

Nicholas joined the clamor, clapping his hands and laughing. "Already your new mothers and fathers are preparing for you to arrive," Reverend Poole continued louder. "They're eagerly awaiting your coming so that they can give you homes."

Give you homes. Reverend Poole's words were mesmerizing, almost magical. For a moment they carried Sophie away to a fairy-tale world where real families with mothers and fathers still lived together and loved their children, where they gathered around the table for a meal, where they laughed and talked in front of the warm hearth fire in the evening.

The longing in Sophie for such a world rose sharply and swiftly, piercing her chest and reminding her of all she'd lost. If only her family had never left Germany. Maybe they'd still be happy together. She'd never understood why her father had lost customers to his bakery there and why he'd had to sell it. She knew it had something to do with a wealthy count who'd been angry with her father. But surely her father and mother could have worked things out if they'd tried harder.

"I want a home, a mommy and daddy. And a puppy," Nicholas said, his face now flushed with happiness. "The puppy can sleep with me. I'll let him."

Sophie started to smile at the sweet picture of Nicholas and a puppy, but then the smile froze at the realization that Nicholas believed he was just like the other children on the train, awaiting adoption into a new family. Sophie hadn't told him yet that they were getting off the train long before the others, that they would be living in the city like they always had, and that they wouldn't have a mother and father anytime soon.

Olivia had remained unsmiling through Reverend Poole's speech. And now she shifted to look at Sophie, her eyes pleading with Sophie to keep her promise to find them a permanent home this time.

Sophie feigned interest in the passing landscape. She'd have to tell Nicholas the truth at some point, but if she told him too soon, she risked him accidentally alerting another child or even the Pooles of their plans to abandon the group in Chicago. For now, she'd have to allow him to go on believing the fairy tale and then pray he'd forgive her once she told him it wasn't true.

CHAPTER 5

Nicholas and Olivia ran through the open field along the train tracks with the other children in a game of tag. Sophie sprawled out in the long grass next to Anna, letting the September sun warm her face.

The sunshine in the open countryside was so different from the sunshine in New York City. Brighter, gentler, and sweeter. At least that was what Sophie had decided during the past two days of traveling away from the city. They weren't allowed off the train at every small-town depot, but whenever the train stopped for refueling, the layovers were longer, with the Pooles herding them outside to stretch their legs.

As the two oldest among the orphans, Anna and Sophie helped supervise the children during their stops. Of course, Sophie hadn't revealed her and Anna's real ages and had allowed the Pooles to believe they were sixteen.

Both the Reverend and Mrs. Poole had been grateful for the assistance and assured the girls more than once that they would have no trouble finding domestic or farm work for them.

"Hardworking and morally upright girls like you are in very

high demand," Mrs. Poole had said. "Families will be fighting over which of them gets to take you home."

Sophie nodded and smiled the same as Anna, both of them pretending the prospect of placement pleased them. Perhaps the idea would have pleased Sophie if they'd planned to stay with the group. After all, every orphan fantasized about being wanted by a family, much less being wanted by more than one.

Yet they hadn't joined the group in order to be placed in homes. They'd joined for the ride west. That was it. Wasn't it?

"Do you miss Danny?" Anna asked, chewing on a spindly piece of grass. She'd discarded her bonnet as she usually did on their stops, letting the sun heat her face and toast her complexion a healthy brown, adding to her exotic look.

Sophie dug her hand into the thick grass, relishing its coolness against her fingers. "To be honest, I haven't thought of Danny much."

When they'd been together, she was enamored with his attention. But now that they were apart, she was more relieved than anything. Deep inside she knew she shouldn't associate with the gangs or with a man who cared more about establishing power than extinguishing a fire. Not to mention the fact that he was a cold-blooded murderer.

"I haven't thought much of Mugs either." Anna looked up at the fluffy clouds. "It's kinda hard to think about that life out here, isn't it?"

Sophie followed her gaze to the beauty of the sky—a sky she hadn't known existed from the narrow alleyways and dark tenements. There, it had been difficult to see beauty when desperation hung heavy, as gray and frayed as the dripping linens strung between buildings.

"I just wish Mollie and Jo could have come with," Anna said wistfully. "I'm worried about them."

"Do you think they're safe?" Sophie had worried about

Anna's sister and niece too. "What if the Roach Guards discover her connection to us?"

Anna's expression turned somber. "If they go after her, she won't tell them where we went."

"Unless they threaten to hurt Jo." Sophie wouldn't blame Mollie for doing whatever she had to in order to protect her daughter, even if that meant divulging their plans.

"We might not be safe in Chicago," Anna said, apparently coming to the same conclusion as Sophie.

"We'll just have to be careful and keep to ourselves."

"We reach Chicago tomorrow. And you know that both Nicholas and Olivia will have a conniption fit leaving the group, don't you?"

Sophie sat up on her elbows and watched Nicholas skip in the grass, completely oblivious to how the game of tag worked but happy to be running in the wide-open field—something he'd never been able to do in New York City. And never would do in Chicago.

His cheeks were flushed, his hair tousled, and his knees grass-stained. He was happier and freer than she'd ever seen him, playing the way every little boy should.

"We'll have to make up a story," Sophie said, thinking aloud, "make Nicholas and Olivia believe we're leaving the group only for a short time. Then we can go back to the train station later and show them that the group left without us."

Anna pushed herself up and watched the children as they played. "You might be able to fool Nicholas with that kind of plan, but not Olivia."

Sophie shifted her sights to Olivia, whose long brown braids bounced against her back as she screamed in joyful abandon and raced away from her pursuer. Olivia's anger at Sophie for making her move again had faded. Sophie had known it would. It always did.

"Olivia knows we're getting off in Chicago," Sophie said. "I told her."

"I think she wants to go live on a farm now too. Blast it all, the reverend and his wife have me half convinced to go work on a farm."

Sophie didn't respond, even though Anna had given voice to her thoughts.

"Would it be so bad to find homes?" Anna asked, longing turning her question to a plea.

Anna had lived on the streets longer than Sophie. She'd been thirteen when her mother was taken away to jail, and she hadn't heard from her since. For the first year, Anna had lived in the Ragpicker's Lot in the Bend, hiding among the stacks of filthy rags for warmth. Some rags were washed and resold, but most were simply collected and delivered to a middleman so the cloth could be shredded to remake into clothing or used to stuff quilts.

Some of the orphan children helped the ragpickers as they dug through trash, searching for anything that could be resold or reused—buttons, pieces of glass or metal, broken china, and even bones. Nothing was wasted.

Sophie always shuddered whenever Anna shared stories of her life, of how close she'd come to ending up a prostitute like Mollie. If not for being sent to an asylum after a police raid on the Ragpicker's Lot, Anna wasn't sure what direction her life would have taken.

"I want a home just like everyone else." Sophie chose her words carefully. "But I doubt we'll find anyone willing to take in the four of us."

"Won't we be okay so long as we're all close and can see each other?"

"No. Absolutely not. I've sacrificed everything to care for Nicholas and Olivia and keep them together. I won't let them be separated now."

"You've done a good job with them, and they love you," Anna said gently. "But what kind of life will you be able to give them in Chicago? Until we find jobs, we'll be homeless and hungry and have to go back to sleeping in doorways and stealing for food. To top it off, we'll have to keep hiding and moving around just in case the Roach Guards are searching for us there."

A sense of inadequacy crept back inside Sophie, the same feeling she'd had since the beginning of the trip, the one that told her she wasn't good enough for Olivia and Nicholas, that they needed more than she could give them.

"As long as we're together, that's what matters," Sophie said, voicing the same reasoning she'd used many times before to justify her choices.

"It might not be enough anymore." Anna was focused on Nicholas, who'd bent over to examine something in the grass— likely another insect.

"It's enough for Nicholas and Olivia and me," Sophie said, almost defiantly.

With cupped hands, Nicholas began to run to her, his eyes and smile alight with the thrill of all he was seeing and doing. He'd loved every moment of the trip so far.

"Look, Sophie! Look!" Nicholas bounded as fast as his legs could go. When he stopped in front of her, he held out his hand. He uncurled his fingers to reveal a long green bug with spindly back legs. The moment the bug was exposed, it jumped away with a whirring that had Nicholas giggling and darting after it.

Behind them, the blast of the train whistle signaled an end to their break. Sophie let Anna pull her to her feet, and together they rounded up the children, holding the hands of the youngest ones.

When they reached the depot, Reverend and Mrs. Poole counted all the children to make sure everyone had returned.

As Sophie helped Nicholas up onto the top step of the train car, she wondered what the couple would do in Chicago when they realized four children were gone. Surely they wouldn't delay the whole group to search for them. At least she prayed they wouldn't.

She glanced over her shoulder at Mrs. Poole, who was immaculately put together without a wrinkle in her skirt or blouse and not a hair out of place. How was that possible after two days of traveling in cramped conditions?

Mrs. Poole held a pencil and a notebook in which she kept roll. If Sophie made sure the notebook got lost in Chicago, then perhaps Mrs. Poole wouldn't notice the missing orphans until it was too late.

Guilt managed to open the closet door in her mind and stick out a foot. After how nice the couple had been, could she really repay them with such treachery?

As the children settled into their seats, Reverend Poole stood at the front of the compartment. "I hope you enjoyed the fresh air, children, for this will be our last reprieve until we reach Chicago."

Across from her, Anna raised her brow as if questioning again the wisdom of leaving the group.

Sophie pressed her lips together and gave a curt nod.

"But do not worry yourselves," the reverend continued. "All the fresh country air you could ever want awaits you in your new homes and will be much better for you than the foulness of city air. Moreover, we're rescuing you from the wretched influences, moral depravity, and evilness of your former lives. If left in such an environment, you would have grown crooked. But cut off from those influences and transplanted to a better place, you'll be able to thrive and grow straight and tall."

Sophie doubted any of the children understood the reverend's ramblings. She hardly did herself. Even so, she comprehended enough to second-guess her plans throughout the rest of the afternoon and evening.

Once darkness fell upon the train car and most of the children had quieted with sleep, she leaned against the window and stared unseeingly at the passing farmland. Nicholas had fallen asleep with his head in her lap, and his body curled onto the bench next to her. Olivia lay on the bench across from them, and Anna had taken the floor, her feet stretching into the aisle and tangling with others who'd bedded on the ground.

Was Reverend Poole right? Would country living not only take Olivia and Nicholas away from the crowds of the city but also the bad influences there? Sophie certainly didn't want them to grow up to become like Danny, Mugs, and Mollie—turning to gangs or prostitution. All this time, she'd thought the two would be better off with her, that she was all they needed, that as long as they stayed together it wouldn't matter where they were or how they got by.

Had she been wrong to steal them away from the Children's Aid Society two years ago? What if all this time they could have been living in a real home instead of orphanages? What if they'd had their own rooms instead of sharing a corridor with dozens of other kids? What if they'd had comfortable beds instead of thin, sagging, and often sour-smelling mattresses? What if they'd had thick, warm blankets in winter instead of thin and tattered covers?

By keeping them with her, maybe she'd deprived them of the love from both a mother and a father. And maybe she'd also kept them from the influence of a stable and godly family. She'd been far from godly, had in fact been a terrible example for Olivia and Nicholas. All she'd done was lead the two astray with her thieving and lying and waywardness.

The rhythmic clicking of the train seemed to whisper a truth she hadn't wanted to acknowledge before: *You're selfish. You're selfish. You're selfish.* Over and over, the words rolled through her mind as steadily as the wheels on the track.

She'd been selfish to keep Olivia and Nicholas instead of letting them find a family who would be able to take care of them the way they deserved. If she'd truly loved them, she should have considered their needs and what was best for them. Instead, she'd only thought about losing them and how empty that would make her feel.

She combed her fingers through Nicholas's downy hair. He was still young enough that he'd adjust to a new home and family without too much trouble. Sure, he might miss her at first, but with loving parents, lots of room to play, and plenty of fresh air, he'd thrive and soon forget how much he missed her.

The thought of him forgetting her sent a stab of despair through her chest so sharp that she sat up with the pain of it. Next to her, Nicholas shifted, turning over and burrowing his face against her lap. As if sensing her despair, he reached out until he found her hand. As his fingers curled into hers, the despair in her chest sank its talons deeper.

She couldn't let him go. She didn't care how selfish she was. She wasn't ready to lose the children. Not now. Maybe not ever.

⁓

"Hurry now," Sophie told Olivia and Nicholas as she forcibly propelled them away from the depot. She cast a glance toward the platform, where the other children waited for Reverend and Mrs. Poole to return from inside the central building.

She ignored the nagging voice in her head telling her the Pooles were counting on her and Anna to tend to the orphans while they were gone. She ignored Anna's silent questions, the ones asking if they were doing the right thing. And she ignored the silent whisper reminding her she was being selfish, the same whisper that hadn't allowed her to fall asleep until the early hours of the morning.

"I don't want to get penny candy." Olivia pushed back against Sophie's movement forward.

Sophie had found the penny on the ground at one of their earlier stops. Now it would come in handy as a way to lure the children away from the group and into busy downtown Chicago. At the early hour of the morning, the streets were bustling with people beginning their workdays. They'd have no trouble getting lost among the crowds.

But first she had to convince Olivia to leave the train depot.

"I wanna lemon drop," Nicholas said, more than making up for Olivia's lack of enthusiasm.

Olivia grabbed on to the edge of a passing bench. "I'm not leaving the depot."

"You've been talking about licorice and how you haven't had any for a long time." Sophie tried to keep her voice cheerful. "Now's our chance. Besides, we'll be back before anyone notices we're gone."

Olivia surprised Sophie by plopping down onto the bench and clutching the seat with both hands, almost as if she didn't intend to let go unless someone pried her loose. She glared up at Sophie with big brown eyes, which overflowed with resentment. "We're not staying in Chicago."

Sophie looked toward the remainder of the orphans who were only two dozen paces away. With all the sights and sounds of a new city, the children weren't paying them any attention. She had to sneak away now before anyone noticed them wandering off.

"Please, Olivia," she whispered, not caring that her voice was threaded with desperation. "You knew this was our plan all along. Don't give me trouble now."

Olivia lifted her pert nose in the air and jutted out her

chin with a defiance that had been showing itself more often. "They're your plans. Not mine or Nicholas's."

"I like candy. Don't you like it, Ollie?" Nicholas asked, coming to stand in front of his sister and peering at her with a serious expression that would have been comical had their situation not been so dire.

"We have to go now." Sophie reached for Olivia's hands and began to loosen her hold. "Stop being so stubborn."

"No!" Olivia cried out. Her outburst drew the attention of several orphans.

Frustration flooded Sophie. Why was Olivia making this so difficult? She tried to lift Olivia away from the bench, intending to fling her across her shoulder and carry her away if necessary. "Olivia, you need to come with me this instant."

Olivia refused to release her grasp on the bench. "You're not my mother. So stop acting like you are."

The words were a fist punch into Sophie's stomach. The air left her lungs, and she stared at Olivia, speechless and hurt. She'd been the only mother Olivia and Nicholas could remember. She'd loved them better than their real mother, who'd never cared about them even before she'd abandoned them.

The little girl clamped her lips shut and glared at her.

"What's wrong, Ollie?" Nicholas asked, putting a palm to his sister's cheek.

Sophie shook her head, warning Olivia not to say anything. But Olivia ignored her and focused instead on Nicholas.

"Sophie doesn't want us to find a home on a farm with a nice mommy and daddy. She wants us to stay here in Chicago and live on the streets."

At Olivia's declaration, Nicholas spun to face Sophie, his expression crushed, his joy ebbing away. "But I wanna live on a farm with a mommy and daddy. And a puppy and chickens."

Sophie released Olivia and let her hands fall to her sides in defeat. She met Anna's gaze over the children's heads. Anna only shrugged and silently seemed to say, *I warned you. What did you expect?*

"I wanna eat lots of apples and melons and blackberries," Nicholas said, his voice dropping with each word he spoke. When his bottom lip began to wobble and tears welled in his eyes, Sophie sighed.

"We want a real home," Olivia stated, plunging a blade into Sophie's heart.

Sophie clutched her chest and tried to breathe through the pain. What could she say now? It was clear neither of them wanted to be with her. Apparently she wasn't good enough, nor was her love sufficient.

Although she'd come to the same conclusion during the long hours of sleeplessness last night, it was one thing to admit her own inadequacies and another to have others point them out.

Didn't they understand she'd done the very best she could? Didn't they realize how much she loved them and all she'd sacrificed to keep them together?

Well, if this was how they felt about her, then she wouldn't force them to live with her, not when they didn't love and appreciate her in return.

She turned toward the street that ran in front of the depot. It was teeming with horses pulling carriages and wagons, as well as pedestrians hurrying among the businesses that lined the other side of the street.

The ache in her heart told her to lose herself in the crowd, to start a new life without the children. She'd be free to do anything she wanted. In fact, without the two holding her back, she'd have more opportunities at finding work, particularly as a domestic. Her life would be better and easier.

But even as she tried to convince herself to walk away from them and lose herself in the swarming metropolis of Chicago, she couldn't make her feet move. Maybe Nicholas and Olivia weren't her real children, born of her body, but she loved them as if they were. And the thought of leaving them at the mercy of strangers and an unknown fate was too difficult to imagine.

"Reverend and Mrs. Poole will be back any second," Anna said with a nervous glance at the depot door. "What do you want to do, Sophie?"

"You can go if you want." Olivia jumped up from the bench. "But I'm staying and so is Nicholas." She grabbed her brother's hand and began to march him back to the group.

Nicholas stumbled along without resisting. He looked at Sophie over his shoulder, his brown eyes wide with confusion and the beginnings of fear.

As much as Sophie's heart ached at their rejection, as much as she wanted to stomp off and let Olivia have exactly what she desired, she couldn't leave the children. Not yet, not without ensuring they were placed in a good and loving home.

If that was what they truly wanted more than being with her, then she could do nothing less than make it happen.

Nicholas struggled against Olivia, reaching a hand backward toward Sophie. "I don't wanna go without Sophie."

A lump rose in Sophie's throat.

"Sophie?" Nicholas asked, his voice ringing with anxiety. He twisted and freed himself. Before Olivia could stop him, he spun and ran back to Sophie.

She caught him in her arms, and for a minute she hugged him tightly, burying her nose into his silky hair and breathing him in. She let his sweet embrace soothe the sting of rejection.

He pulled back so he could look into her face. "Don't you wanna have a nice home and mommy and daddy too? With me and Ollie?"

Did Nicholas still want her? Maybe he assumed she would get to live with him at his new home. Maybe he believed they would stay together and be able to share the benefits of a new life. Sophie didn't know if such a placement was possible. Was there a family who might be willing to take in all three of them, possibly even Anna? Could she ask the Pooles to try to keep them together?

"What about chickens and apples?" he persisted. "I bet you'll like 'em real much."

Sophie nodded and attempted a smile. "I'm sure I will."

"Then let's go." He intertwined his hand with hers.

She let him lead her back to the group. For better or worse, she would stay with Olivia and Nicholas, and they would find a family together. She just hoped she hadn't made her worst mistake yet.

CHAPTER 6

Reinhold chanced another glance at the western horizon. The mounds of dark clouds were creeping nearer, like a coyote getting ready to pounce upon its prey. He guessed he had an hour before the storm caught them in its grip.

His attention shifted to the windrow that ran the length of the field in front of him. He and Jakob might have time to rake up and haul one final row to the barn before the rain came. Yet there were still three more to be brought in after that.

Maybe if they worked faster, and the storm held off a bit longer, they'd get to the others. He could only hope. For if they didn't get all the hay into the barn, then all the labor of the past week, particularly the spreading and drying of the hay, would come to nothing.

"We need to work faster," he called to Jakob with a nod toward the angry sky.

Jakob dug his pitchfork into the windrow and tossed more hay into the back of the wagon. Reinhold did likewise, driving himself harder, although he'd already been shoveling frantically and had been since before dawn.

"Jakob! Reinhold!"

The two paused to see Alastair and Fergus Duff running toward them, pitchforks in hand. At their approach, a flock of bobwhites flew up out of the long overgrown grass, their masked faces startled and their loud whistles perturbed.

"Da sent us," Fergus said breathlessly when he reached the windrow. Without waiting for Reinhold's permission, he stuck his fork into the pile and began pitching hay into the back of the wagon with a swift and easy motion that showed his expertise at haying. "When he saw the red in the sky this mornin' he knew we were in for a storm."

Alastair joined them, just as out of breath as his brother, likely having raced each other the mile or so from the Duff farm. Their sun-browned faces were flecked with sweat and bits of hay, their shirts stuck to their perspiring bodies, and their suspenders lifted the waists of their trousers high over their hips.

"Is your dad done with his own haying?" Reinhold asked, intending to send the boys right back home if Barclay was helping him at the expense of his own crop.

"We just got the last of it in the wagon," Fergus replied. At twelve, he was several inches shorter than Alastair. But what he lacked in height and muscle he made up for in determination. "Da, Lyle, and Gavin are putting it up in the loft right now. Said if you started to blether, to tell you to 'button up.'"

Reinhold could hear the words in Barclay's thick burr tinged with fatherly concern. His own father had never looked after him, had never cared about his needs. Rather, Reinhold had always been the one to take care of everyone else. Even if he didn't like to accept help because it reminded him of his shortcomings, Barclay's concern warmed him.

The boys threw their entire weight and all their energy into the task, even though they'd likely been haying since daybreak— after milking their large herd of dairy cows, which they had to do every morning and evening.

Like Barclay, his sons were talkative. And with their *blethering*, the time passed quickly, and as usual Jakob came out of his silent shell. They finished hauling a load of hay into the barn and were heading out for another when a raindrop splattered his hand.

"Get a move on, Daisy." Reinhold urged his chestnut Morgan faster. The crops could use a watering. But he needed the rain to hold off until he had the rest of the hay in the barn. Once the cut alfalfa in the fields got wet, he would have to leave it out until it dried again—that is, if it didn't get moldy first.

"Da told me to remind you that the orphans are coming through Mayfield today," Alastair said as they bumped along in the wagon.

As the rain became steadier, Reinhold suspected the rest of his hay was lost. They might be able to get more of it into the wagon bed, but even if they did, the hay would be soaked by the time they reached the barn.

Alastair shifted on the wagon bench next to him. "Said to tell you if you don't have the time to go to town, Mum is going to the meeting and can pick out a couple of boys for you."

Reinhold knew he should agree. Ever since Barclay had brought up the possibility of getting the orphans earlier in the week, Reinhold hadn't stopped mulling it over. If he'd had the extra hands this week, he would have gotten the hay in on time, and he wouldn't have found himself in this situation.

Still, he couldn't help but think that his taking in orphans would be akin to slavery. With the slavery debate growing more heated every time Reinhold went into town and heard the news, he was convinced that getting a couple of boys to do his work without paying them fair wages was hardly different from what was going on in the South with the Negroes being made to labor without compensation.

Reinhold hadn't ever experienced slavery, but the work he'd done in New York City had come close. With too many immigrants and not enough jobs, men and women alike fought over menial positions that paid pennies for labor that was worth so much more.

Even if the toil here in Illinois was unending and tiring, at least the farm was his. No one was taking advantage of him. How, then, could he turn around and take advantage of someone else, namely boys who were no older than Jakob and Fergus?

"Mum said she wants to get a young lady orphan," Fergus chimed in from where he rode in the back with Jakob. "Said she needs help harvesting and preserving her garden this fall. Told Da if she doesn't get the help, she won't be able to put away enough food to feed her army of men through the winter, since each and every one of us eats more than a horse."

Reinhold could hear Euphemia's voice speaking the words, just as boisterous and cheerful as Barclay's.

"'Course," Fergus continued, "Da claims Mum wants a young lady orphan so she can find a wife for Lyle."

At nineteen, Lyle was the closest of the Duff boys to Reinhold's twenty-one years. Lyle was a friendly young man and had done his best to welcome Reinhold during the months he'd lived with the Duffs. Gavin, at seventeen, had also become a good friend.

"Lyle said he doesn't need Mum meddling and finding him a wife." Fergus rattled on, raising his voice above the rumble of thunder and the growing patter of the rain. "Said he can have his pick of any of the young ladies in Mayfield he wants. So Mum told him to get a-picking."

Reinhold couldn't contain a grin as he imagined the conversation playing out between the mother and son at the dinner table—Lyle's loud, boastful comments, his chest puffing out, his eyes sparkling with excitement, and then Euphemia's no-nonsense, practical response that put Lyle right back in his place.

The laughter, the conversations, and the love around the Duff table was something Reinhold had never experienced before. While growing up, his home had always been full of tension and anger. And last year at the Turners', the dinner conversations had consisted mostly of Mrs. Turner complaining about one thing or another.

"So you want me to tell Mum to get you the orphan boys?" Fergus asked.

Thunder exploded overhead, and the sky opened up and released its torrent. Reinhold pulled on the reins and brought the wagon to a halt. The haying was done for the day, maybe even for the season. He didn't need the orphans now. Of course, there was still the rest of the harvest to bring in. But deep inside, he knew he had to do so honorably or not at all.

"Tell your mum and da I appreciate the offer," he said, "but Jakob and I are getting along just fine."

It was a lie. But it was the best excuse he could find.

❦

Sophie sat in the second pew with Nicholas on one side and Olivia on the other. As the church filled behind her with townspeople, Sophie had the overwhelming urge to drag the children out of the building and flee. The hard bench pressed against her as if to agree, prodding her to leave before it was too late.

Over the past couple of days since leaving Chicago, she'd come to the conclusion they'd made a huge mistake. She should have forced Olivia and Nicholas to sneak away from the group while they still had the chance, even if she'd earned their wrath. They would have eventually calmed down and realized the wisdom of her plan.

As it was, they were stuck. They had no place to run or hide, not out in the middle of nowhere. The farther south they'd ridden on the Illinois Central Railroad, the fewer farms and houses she'd seen. Sometimes miles passed with open plains the only scenery. The vastness of the prairie grass and fields spreading out endlessly was different from the woodlands, rolling hills, and even some rocky areas they'd seen while traveling through western New York and Ohio.

And the towns they'd passed through had gradually grown smaller and fewer in number. The Pooles had explained that, on this particular trip, they were revisiting two towns where the Children's Aid Society had already placed some orphans, but they were also venturing farther south to settlements more recently built so as to accommodate the newer farms along the railroad.

Mayfield. That was what the Pooles had called this particular town. Their train had arrived in the afternoon during a thunderstorm. They'd run through the rain and muddy Main Street to the Mayfield Inn. They'd been ushered to rooms where they'd been able to change into dry clothing, their second new outfit. Mrs. Poole had overseen the girls, helping them to wash up as well as fix their hair, while Reverend Poole supervised the boys.

Afterward they'd eaten a hot meal in the hotel's dining room. For most of them, Sophie included, the experience was the first time being in a hotel and the first time eating in a dining room. The pork loin with mashed potatoes and gravy, along with green beans and apple dumplings, was one of the best meals she'd had in a very long time.

She had vague recollections of enjoying delicious meals when her father was alive. He'd been an excellent baker and cook—at least that was what her sister Elise always claimed. Like their father, Elise had loved cooking.

With each bite of the fine meal, Sophie couldn't keep from conjuring Elise and Marianne's faces, even though she didn't want to. Most of the time she was adept at pushing aside memories and thoughts of her sisters. Thinking about them left her second-guessing everything she'd done and made her heart ache.

She'd learned it was easier to cope if she didn't allow herself to feel anything for her sisters, if she cut them out of her life completely.

After the meal, they'd walked over to the church. She and Anna had been tasked with the job of making sure the little boys, among them Nicholas, didn't jump in puddles during the short stroll. Thankfully, the rain had stopped, and they arrived dry, even if their new shoes were muddy.

A kindly older minister had greeted them and ushered them inside, instructing the children to sit in the front pews. Sophie shivered in the dark, damp interior, sitting between Olivia and Nicholas and praying no one would want them at this stop, that they'd be able to sleep together in the hotel. She needed to come up with a new escape plan.

Anna sat on the other side of Nicholas, her tanned face pale. She was fingering her rosary, a sure sign that she was nervous. Most of the time Anna kept the rosary hidden, along with the fact that she was Catholic. She'd even gone so far as poking fun at other Catholics when she'd been with Mugs and the other Bowery Boys, who were especially anti-Catholic.

Sophie didn't understand why it mattered whether a person was a Protestant or Catholic, any more than why it mattered whether a person was German or Irish. But she'd learned long ago on the streets that Catholics and Irish were despised by most Protestants, especially someone who was both Catholic and Irish.

"Please take your seats," the older reverend said from the pulpit. "We are starting later in the day than we did last year since so many of you are busy with harvesting. And we will try to finish up in a timely manner so that you can return to your homes and farms before darkness settles."

The thump of footsteps and the murmur of voices grew louder as more people entered the building. Olivia's hand slid into Sophie's. At the trembling of the little girl's fingers, Sophie squeezed tight. As belligerent as Olivia had been since the start of the trip, Sophie realized that she was frightened too. Olivia didn't have to speak for Sophie to see the questions running through her mind: Would anyone want them? And if so, what would their new home be like?

Nicholas, on the other hand, started to fidget with growing anticipation. He twisted around to watch the people coming into the church and then smiled up at Sophie. "Who's gonna be our new mommy and daddy?"

"We'll find out soon," Sophie whispered, hoping she was wrong.

After a few more minutes, the reverend called the meeting to order and began with a prayer. Then he introduced Reverend Poole, who took his place at the front of the church and explained the work of the Children's Aid Society, shared stories of children placed elsewhere, and then presented the terms for the families who desired to take a child home with them.

"You must feed, clothe, educate, and otherwise treat the child as if he or she were your own by birth. We also ask that you promise to bring the child to church."

Besides today, Sophie couldn't remember the last time she'd been inside a real church. She'd attended the chapel services at the Seventh Street Mission when she'd lived there, and she'd listened to Reverend Bedell speak about the saving love of Christ. But Christ certainly hadn't saved or loved her—not that she deserved saving or loving.

"We are confident each of you will do your best to care for these children and exert a godly influence over them," Reverend Poole continued. "However, we also recognize special circumstances arise when you may no longer be able to fulfill your obligation to the foundling. In that case, we will do our best to find a new placement for the child or bring him or her back to New York."

Back to New York? Sophie's mind sped with the realization that maybe there was a way to leave here after all. If things didn't work out, they could ask to return to New York. And on the train ride back, once they reached Chicago, they'd sneak away.

Sure, they might have to face the Roach Guards there if the gang had pressured Mollie to reveal their destination, but they'd just have to take their chances. For the first time in two days, Sophie let her shoulders relax. She finally had an escape plan. They weren't stuck in central Illinois.

With renewed confidence, Sophie stood with everyone else when Reverend Poole asked them to move to the front. Mrs. Poole arranged them in order from the oldest to the youngest. Since they were short on time, Reverend Poole said that he wouldn't present the children individually but instead invited people to come forward and make the acquaintances of the orphans.

"Introduce yourselves," the reverend said, "and then ask the children questions and get to know them to see if they are suited for you. It's better to ask too many questions than not enough."

Several farmers came forward right away to the oldest boys, who were a year or two younger than Sophie and Anna. One of the farmers felt the boys' arms, checking the size of their muscles. Another inspected the boys up and down, lifting pant legs and pushing up shirtsleeves.

Sophie decided that if anyone dared to lay a hand on her that way, she'd slap them rather than allow herself to be treated like a workhorse up for sale. When several couples finally made their way to the front, and one of them approached Nicholas, Sophie broke out of line and hurried toward the little boy.

A woman with dull brown hair knelt in front of Nicholas and spoke with him gently about whether he'd like to come live with them. From what Sophie gathered as she listened, Mr. Ramsey was a carpenter and not a farmer. He and his family lived outside Mayfield to the south on a small plot of land.

Nicholas beamed and nodded in response to Mrs. Ramsey.

Olivia squeezed next to Nicholas and grabbed his hand, apparently having left her place in the line when she'd noticed the attention the couple was giving to her brother.

"This is Ollie," Nicholas said, smiling at Olivia. "She's my sister."

The woman darted a sideways glance at Olivia, then returned her attention to Nicholas. Her features held the same weariness Sophie had seen all too often on the faces of the women in the tenements—a weariness that came not just from the drudgery of too much work, but also from the heavy burdens of a life that hadn't turned out the way they'd planned or dreamed.

Unease pricked Sophie. Wasn't life supposed to be easier and better here in the West? Weren't these people supposed to be happier? Godlier? Healthier?

"Mr. Ramsey and I already have a little girl," the woman said to Nicholas. "Our own Rachel is eight, and I think you'll like her very much."

Olivia's eyes widened and flashed with fear.

Sophie's unease turned into a gonging alarm like that of the city fire bells. "Nicholas and Olivia have to stay together," she blurted. "If you want a little boy without a sister, then maybe you should question someone else." Sophie motioned toward the other young boys in the group.

Mr. Ramsey, who'd been observing his wife's interaction with Nicholas with an air of detached coolness, turned brooding eyes upon Sophie. In his younger years, he might have been good-looking, but the passing of time had left him with yellowing teeth and several large moles, one on the tip of his nose. "Go on back to your place, girl. This isn't your concern."

"It's very much my concern," Sophie said.

"Sophie's my other sister." Nicholas reached for Sophie's hand.

Sophie refused to look away from Mr. Ramsey, giving back to him the same coolness he was giving to her.

Mrs. Ramsey stood and stepped between her husband and Sophie. "Please," she said in a soft-spoken voice that was filled with longing. "We've been wanting a little boy for a very long time. We weren't able to come to town last year and have been waiting for this group."

Sophie could sense the sincerity in the woman's tone and could see the emptiness in her heart. She'd apparently wanted to have more than one child, but for whatever reason hadn't been able to have additional sons or daughters. Now she saw Nicholas as her chance to make her family complete.

But what about Olivia? All of the girl's bravado in Chicago had disappeared. Only a scrawny, frightened girl remained.

Sophie tried to view Olivia through a stranger's eyes, the way the Ramseys might see her. She wasn't adorable in the same way Nicholas was. She was much more serious, with a plain face and nothing at all remarkable about her features. The other girls in their group who were Olivia's age were prettier and livelier and would attract new parents more readily than Olivia. In fact, Olivia's belligerence and anxiety might only scare families away.

Unless Sophie could work out a deal with the Ramseys . . .

"Nicholas expects both me *and* Olivia to live with him," Sophie said.

Mrs. Ramsey's face drooped, the dark circles under her eyes almost purple. She turned to her husband, but he shook his head curtly.

Before either could voice their objection, Sophie continued, lowering her voice so the children would have a difficult time hearing her. "I fully realize you can't keep all three of us, but if you take at least Olivia, you'll make Nicholas very happy. Without her, he'll be difficult to handle."

Mrs. Ramsey glanced again at Olivia, to her hand intertwined with Nicholas's.

"She'll make a good helper." Sophie had to convince this couple of Olivia's worth if she hoped to keep the two children together. "She's mature for her age and a quick learner. She'll be no trouble at all. In fact, you'll find her to be a blessing and not a burden."

"But we don't need another girl," Mrs. Ramsey whispered.

"Nicholas has never spent a day of his life apart from Olivia," Sophie replied louder this time, intentionally allowing Nicholas to hear her. "You'll devastate him if you won't let Olivia live with you."

"Ollie wants a mommy and daddy too," Nicholas said eagerly, looking up at the couple with so much hope that Sophie prayed they wouldn't be able to deny him.

Mrs. Ramsey looked over her shoulder at her husband. He was scrutinizing Nicholas. The cool detachment had lifted for an instant to reveal longing. For as much as Mr. Ramsey was clearly trying not to allow himself to want another child, particularly an orphan, Nicholas's sweet nature and charm was winning him over.

Mrs. Ramsey touched her husband's arm and leaned in to confer with him. With an exasperated sigh, Mr. Ramsey took hold of his wife and guided her several feet away. For a long moment they carried on a whispered exchange, until finally Mr. Ramsey threw up his hands and said, "You win. Do what you want, Caroline."

He spun and stalked away. Mrs. Ramsey watched him go, her

shoulders slumping. When he'd exited the building, she turned back to the children and forced a smile.

"We weren't anticipating taking more than one child, and we really had our hearts set on a little boy," she said as though that could explain away her husband's actions. "But I think we'll give both children a try. After all, Rachel has been complaining recently about not having enough friends."

Sophie wanted to sag with relief. She wasn't sure what she would have done if the Ramseys had decided they only wanted Nicholas and not Olivia. She certainly wouldn't have let them take him—she would have fought them if she had to. At the same time, she didn't want to disappoint Nicholas.

Though she didn't particularly like Mr. Ramsey, his wife seemed to make up for his deficiencies with her soft-spoken manner. Sophie just wished there was some way to find out more about the family. She wanted to ask Mrs. Ramsey some questions, yet she was at a loss to know where to begin. And everyone seemed to be in a hurry to make the placements and end the proceedings before darkness fell.

"Why don't you gather your belongings," Mrs. Ramsey said, "and we'll be on our way."

While Mrs. Ramsey talked with the children, Sophie dug through the bag they'd brought along from the hotel. She retrieved the bundles of extra clothing, several blankets, and the few toys she'd managed to provide for them. She wrapped everything into one of the blankets, tied the ends together, and handed it to Mrs. Ramsey.

"Is this all?" the woman asked in surprise.

It was Sophie's turn to be embarrassed. She'd provided for Olivia and Nicholas the best she knew how. Maybe they'd never had a lot, but at least she'd kept them from going hungry.

"Well," Mrs. Ramsey said in response to Sophie's silence, "we may not be wealthy, but we certainly can provide better than this."

Sophie was tempted to snap back at her, letting Mrs. Ramsey know that she'd given them her whole heart and all her love and that was better than material possessions. But the same guilt and frustration that had plagued her earlier rushed back with the force of a steam whistle. Olivia and Nicholas deserved so much more than she'd ever been able to provide. And now they would finally get it.

Nicholas happily placed his hand in Mrs. Ramsey's outstretched one. As the woman led him away from the orphans to the center aisle, Olivia stumbled along next to him, clinging to him and refusing to let go.

Sophie's own feet were rooted to the floor as they plodded along next to their new mother, someone who would take her place in holding them tight when they were sad, kissing their scratches and scraped knees, and telling them stories at bedtime.

Sophie's throat closed around the words of good-bye she wanted to shout. She didn't want to cause a scene, didn't want to make this harder than it already was. So she watched silently as the two precious infants who had belonged to her and were a part of the very fibers of her soul walked away from her for the first time.

Her eyes pricked with tears, but she forced them back. She wouldn't cry now. Maybe later when everyone else was asleep. But for now, she had to remain brave. Always brave.

She had to remember they would be better off in a real home. Much better than running around on the streets of Chicago, scrambling to survive. And they would still have each other. She'd find a home close by. Through all the adjustments in the days to come, they'd help each other through them.

Halfway down the aisle, Nicholas looked over his shoulder at Sophie. "Come on, Soph. Time to go to our new home."

Standing between Mrs. Ramsey and Olivia, he looked so little, so vulnerable. Sophie could picture him as a baby, when he'd been tiny, quiet, and afraid. It had taken some time, but he'd finally learned to trust her, to turn to her when in need and seek her when he wanted comfort.

Sophie forced a big smile, hopefully an encouraging one, even though her insides were shredding into pieces. She'd done her part with him. She'd gotten him this far in his life. Now it was time for someone else to help him grow into the young man he was meant to be. Hopefully Mrs. Ramsey was that person. Hopefully she would love Nicholas even more than Sophie had.

As though finally sensing Sophie's silent good-bye, Nicholas planted his feet and stopped, forcing Mrs. Ramsey and Olivia to a halt.

"Sophie?" He twisted around, his eyes filled with worry. Mrs. Ramsey clung to Nicholas's hand and so did Olivia, preventing him from retreating.

"I'm not coming with you, Liebchen," Sophie said, knowing she had to remain both calm and positive. "I have to go to a different home, one that needs an older girl like me."

She glanced to where Anna stood talking with a man whose wife and brood of children flocked around him. She surveyed the remaining orphans. As far as Sophie could tell, no other families were vying for another grown girl. What happened if she wasn't able to find a home here in Mayfield? What if she had to get back on the train and ride to the next town before someone took her in?

A quiet desperation stole through her. She had to find a place here so she could remain close to Olivia and Nicholas. Letting them leave with this stranger was hard enough, but she couldn't abide the thought of not being able to see them whenever she wanted.

"Maybe my new mommy needs an older girl," Nicholas said, looking up at Mrs. Ramsey.

Weariness seemed to fall over the woman's face, as if she'd

already waged enough battles for one day and couldn't bear the thought of fighting another. If Nicholas protested too much, would she change her mind and decide not to take the children after all? Then what would happen?

Sophie suspected this opportunity for the children to stay together was rare and likely wouldn't come to them again. She couldn't let it pass by. "Mrs. Ramsey already has an older daughter to help her and now she also has Olivia. So I need to stay in another home that needs me."

"But I want you to stay with me." Nicholas's eyes welled up with tears.

Sophie swallowed hard to keep the painful lump in her throat from rising and bringing tears to her eyes too. "I'll be close by. I promise."

"And we'll allow her to visit you," Mrs. Ramsey added in a soothing tone.

Sophie wanted to blurt out that she was planning to see Nicholas and Olivia as often as she wanted whether the Ramseys *allowed* it or not, that she didn't need anyone's permission to visit her children. But she couldn't do anything to jeopardize this placement. "I'll see you as much as you'd like."

"You will?" Some of the worry slipped from Nicholas's face.

"Of course I will. I'll learn how to ride a horse and come out to see you."

"And teach me to ride a horse too?"

"Your daddy will do that," Mrs. Ramsey said.

Nicholas beamed up at the woman. "And then I'll ride and see Sophie?"

Mrs. Ramsey hesitated. Sophie could sense the woman's inner struggle, that she wanted Nicholas to like her, but she also wanted to be truthful with him. And somehow Sophie liked her better for it. "Perhaps we'll ride over together to see her," she finally said.

The answer seemed to satisfy Nicholas. When Mrs. Ramsey started forward again, he didn't resist but walked beside her, chatting about horses. Mrs. Ramsey stopped to speak to Reverend and Mrs. Poole, along with several other distinguished-looking people.

Sophie guessed they were part of the committee Reverend Poole had talked about, the leaders of the town who had made the arrangements for the placing-out, who also helped to vouch for the families wanting to take in the children.

The committee members all greeted Mrs. Ramsey politely, which Sophie hoped spoke of their respect for her character. Mrs. Poole asked a few questions and took notes in a ledger, perhaps recording information about the placement for future reference. Within a few minutes, the arrangements were complete, and Mrs. Ramsey led the children to the door.

Sophie knew she should return to the front of the church and take her place next to Anna, but her feet propelled her to follow Olivia and Nicholas outside.

Mr. Ramsey was already sitting atop a wagon bench and holding the reins of a fine-looking team of horses. He held himself rigid as he surveyed the other departing families, some with an orphan and others without.

He didn't acknowledge his wife when she drew near with Olivia and Nicholas. He made no move to help her lift the children into the back of the wagon and didn't offer a hand of assistance when she climbed to the seat next to him. Sophie didn't know why his rudeness should bother her, but it did.

"It doesn't matter," she whispered as another family exited the church and pushed past her in the doorway. "So long as Mrs. Ramsey is kind, the children will be all right."

Mr. Ramsey gave a sharp command to the team, and the wagon lurched forward. Olivia and Nicholas nearly fell over with the motion, never having ridden in a wagon before. They righted themselves and grabbed on to the sides. Sophie expected the bumpiness to unnerve the children and was surprised when Nicholas laughed in delight.

With the growing dusk, sunlight touched on both of their heads, turning their hair a light brown that matched the color of the ripening wheat in the field next to the church. They were hers. They always had been and always would be, even if she could no longer hold them and take care of them the way she wanted.

As they rolled toward the road that led south of town, Sophie fought back a wave of panic at the thought of losing them, of perhaps never seeing them again. Then she reminded herself they were off on a new adventure, that they'd wanted a home like the one Mr. and Mrs. Ramsey would be giving them, that such a home with two parents was better than being raised by a single woman without any means to take care of them.

Even as the panic subsided, a feeling of emptiness was left in its wake, an emptiness so deep and wide that Sophie was liable to drown in it if she took one step forward. So she stayed in her spot by the door and stared after the wagon, watching the two little heads bouncing up and down.

Finally, Nicholas turned and looked back at the church. At the sight of her still there, he smiled broadly and waved. Olivia shifted and looked at her too.

Sophie managed to wave and smile at them, though she wanted to do nothing more than fall to her knees and weep. Instead, she continued watching the wagon with dry eyes until it was swallowed up by the tall wheat field and disappeared from sight.

CHAPTER 7

"Och, dinnae tell me I'm too late!" A short heavyset woman approached the church entrance. She regarded the departing families with dismay creasing her face.

Sophie could only shake her head, unable to squeeze a word past the tight ache in her throat.

"I knew I should have left those boys to feed themselves tonight," the woman said, wiping a splotchy red hand across her perspiring brow.

A bright yellow calico kerchief covered the woman's head and was tied under a fleshy and almost nonexistent chin. Wiry gray strands of hair escaped the kerchief and dangled across the woman's forehead and around her neck. She wore an equally bright yellow dress over a full bosom and rounded middle, reminding Sophie of one of the sunflowers she'd seen in passing from the train window.

"Och, this is all my fault, babying my boys too much."

Sophie was in no mood to talk to anyone, not after Olivia and Nicholas had just ridden away. Her heart was racing, urging her to run after the wagon and snatch the children from it.

"Can you tell me if there are any orphans left inside?" the

woman asked, standing at eye level with Sophie. At her slight frame and petite height, Sophie was rarely eye level with anyone, and yet she found herself staring into a pair of warm brown eyes.

Before Sophie could reply, the church door opened and several children darted past and scampered into the churchyard. A boy of about five years with a mischievous grin chased after two younger boys, who appeared to be twins. From their cries of protest, neither seemed especially thrilled at the game of chase.

A couple more children zipped past Sophie, quickly followed by a harried mother with a baby on her hip. Anna trailed after, and a tall man brought up the rear of the group.

Sophie awoke from her daze of pain and emptiness. "Anna," she said, reaching for her friend's hand. She couldn't lose Anna now too.

"I guess I'll stay with the Pierces," Anna replied, watching the children running and hollering. Her pretty face was filled with uncertainty, as if she too were wondering what they'd gotten themselves into. This wasn't what they'd agreed upon, was it?

Even with all of Reverend and Mrs. Poole's admonitions on what to expect, none of it had prepared them for the reality of the placing-out.

"You don't have to go," Sophie said.

"'Course she does." Mr. Pierce smiled at Anna congenially as he came alongside her. He stuck out his elbow, offering to escort her to the wagon. "We might look chaotic, but you'll find we're not all that bad."

Mrs. Pierce was yelling at the children to get into the back of the wagon. Her irritation was written in every taut feature of her tired face.

Seeing his wife's frustration, Mr. Pierce's smile diminished. He met Anna's gaze with clear, honest eyes that seemed to plead with her. While he wasn't a handsome man, he had an air of boyish charm that gave him an appeal difficult to resist. "She's going through a rough time of it. If you come, you'll be like an angel sent from heaven."

Anna hesitated.

The woman with the yellow kerchief frowned and looked as though she might speak.

"I promise to look out for you," Mr. Pierce continued hurriedly, "and make sure no one takes advantage of your help." His tone was so genuine and sincere that Sophie decided if Anna didn't accept his offer, she would.

As if sensing the opportunity slipping from her grasp, Anna nodded.

Mr. Pierce's smile returned, and he held out the crook of his arm again. This time Anna took the offer.

Sophie wrapped her friend in a one-armed hug before letting her walk away.

"How will I find Anna if I need to get in touch with her?" Sophie called after them.

"We're seven miles north of town on Huntington County Road," Mr. Pierce replied. "Come out and see us anytime."

Sophie nodded, the ache in her throat fading just a little. Maybe everything would work out after all. Olivia and Nicholas were together and had a nice new mother. And now Anna had a friendly place to go, even if the Pierce children were rambunctious and their mother harried. Perhaps Anna's presence would bring some peace to the home, and hopefully she would enjoy having a stable and pleasant place to live for the first time in years.

"Well now, looks like that's all settled," the heavyset woman said, staring alongside Sophie as Mr. Pierce lifted Anna onto the wagon bench instead of in the back with the children. He helped his wife up next. Sophie expected the woman to ask

Anna to climb into the back, but she settled the baby on her lap and didn't seem to mind Anna's presence in the least. Mr. Pierce jumped up and took his place next to Anna.

"She's your friend?" The woman beside Sophie shifted.

"Yes." Sophie waved at Anna as the wagon rolled out of the churchyard.

"Then you're an orphan." It was more of a statement than a question. Her voice contained an interesting lilt that wasn't Irish but sounded close to it.

Sophie couldn't tear her gaze away from Anna riding down the road. She felt the woman's scrutiny and wasn't sure how to reply. She'd never really considered herself an orphan, even when she'd lived in the asylums. Though both her parents were dead, she was old enough to take care of herself. She didn't need help or supervision the same way the younger children did.

Even so, she needed a place to live, preferably somewhere near Olivia and Nicholas so she could see them as frequently as she wanted.

Sophie spun and opened the church door. Was she too late to find a family here in Mayfield? Had everyone who wanted an orphan already picked one out?

She stepped back inside only to note that the sanctuary was now empty of families except for a few who were talking to the Pooles and the committee with their new children close by their sides. Sophie was surprised to see so many of the orphans still left at the front. Most of them had returned to the pews and were sitting or lying down. Several of the more energetic boys were wrestling each other near the pulpit.

"And who are you going home with, if you dinnae mind me asking?" The woman had come inside behind Sophie and was studying the children who remained as if looking for someone in particular.

The Pooles had been right—the oldest and the youngest had

been taken first. The teenage boys were gone, likely for their ability to help on the farms, as were the smallest, like Nicholas, who were still little enough that they weren't jaded or rough or rebellious, as was the case with some of the street urchins who'd lived on their own for so long.

"I don't have a home yet," Sophie answered. "Who are you looking for?"

"Well now." She turned her full attention to Sophie. "I think I might be looking for you."

"For me?"

"Aye. I came to find a young woman, and here you are. A wee one, that's for certain. But a bonnier lass I've never seen. You're standing at the door like you are waiting for me, though you should have been scooped up and whisked away already. It would be just like the good Lord to bless me with His favor even though I dinnae deserve it."

The woman's words didn't make much sense to Sophie, so she shrugged. "Why do you need a young woman?"

Although Sophie didn't have any other choices at the moment, something inside urged her to be cautious. She'd had to be careful and alert over the past two years. She wasn't naïve and knew that there were many people who took advantage of young women like her. Not that this plump, matronly woman looked like the type to sell her into a brothel. Nevertheless, her first instinct was always mistrust.

"I'll be honest with ye, lass," the woman said, looking her straight in the eyes. "I'm getting too old to handle all the work by myself. With a hardworking husband and five growing sons, I can't keep up with feeding and clothing them. I need an extra hand to help me with all the chores, especially with putting up the garden."

"So you live on a farm?" Sophie wasn't surprised. It seemed most of the people in Illinois did.

"Not just any farm, mind ye," the woman said with some spunk. "A dairy farm."

"What's a dairy farm?"

"We milk cows. Lots of cows."

Curiosity perked inside Sophie at the same time that anxiety prodded her. She'd never seen a real cow, much less milked one. Should she admit the truth? And what if she was honest and the woman decided she wasn't a blessing waiting at the church door after all and took another of the children instead?

"Oh, sure," Sophie said with feigned confidence. "I can milk a cow."

The woman's brows rose into the tight curls on her forehead. "You can now?"

Sophie kept her expression as wide-eyed as possible. She'd been told often enough that she had pretty eyes, that she could win over a person with one bat of her lashes.

"I wasn't expecting a young woman to help with the milking. My husband and boys take care of that. But I'm sure they won't mind a bonnie lass like yerself helping them in a pinch."

Sophie nodded. "How far away do you live from the Ramseys?"

"The carpenter?"

"They took my little brother and sister."

"Och, my dear." The woman lifted one of her splotchy hands and pressed Sophie's cheek. The touch was gentle, and her eyes filled with a compassion so warm and tender that the ache in Sophie's throat returned. "I dinnae know how you're standing there without falling apart. I know I'd be a blathering mess."

Sophie smiled even as the tears stung her eyes. She was going to like this woman.

"The Ramseys live a fair distance from our farm—five miles, maybe," the woman said, smiling in return, "but not far enough that one of my boys can't take you there whenever ye need to see your brother and sister."

Five miles. That was a long way to walk, but she could do it if she needed to.

"I'm Euphemia Duff. What do you say? Think you'd like to give me a try?"

Give her a try? Wasn't it the other way around? Wasn't Sophie the one who needed trying out? Euphemia probably wouldn't be quite so eager to have her if she knew all Sophie's many sins and faults. And she certainly wouldn't want her if Sophie admitted how little she knew about farm chores and *putting up* a garden, whatever that meant. But how hard could it be to learn?

"I'd be grateful for the opportunity, Mrs. Duff." Sophie searched her mind for proper manners. Along with the other things her parents had taught her, the manners were still there somewhere—perhaps a little dusty with disuse but not completely forgotten.

Euphemia took Sophie's hand and squeezed it. "Och, you must call me Euphemia. Or if you want to call me Mum, I won't mind that at all."

Mum. The word tumbled around Sophie's mind. She'd called her own mother Mutti, the German endearment. But it had been over two years now since Mutti had died, since life had unraveled one stitch at a time.

Maybe now she'd finally have the opportunity to knit her life back together again.

⁂

The wagon ride to the Duff dairy farm took the better part of an hour. Euphemia talked practically nonstop the entire way, which was fine with Sophie since her insides were tying themselves into a tangle of knotted questions the farther they rode from the church. Had she done the right thing for Olivia and Nicholas? Would they be happier and safer now? What would her own new life be like on a dairy farm?

Euphemia informed her that she had five boys ranging in age from twenty-five to twelve and that they all still lived on the farm. When she mentioned that she and her husband, Barclay, had been married for twenty years, Sophie guessed that Euphemia's first child was from a previous marriage, that perhaps she'd been a widow when she'd married Barclay. But Euphemia didn't offer an explanation, and Sophie didn't pry.

Euphemia told about how she'd come over from Scotland when she was about Sophie's age, how she'd been a milkmaid for a dairy farm in western New York and had learned everything there was to know about running a dairy farm.

Thankfully, Euphemia didn't ask Sophie any questions. She wasn't ready to share about her past or even much about her current situation, and she supposed Euphemia sensed that.

Darkness had fallen by the time Euphemia pulled the team in front of a barn with a peak roof projecting over a hayloft. It was one of the biggest barns Sophie had seen so far during the ride west. A lantern hanging from a rafter inside revealed horse stalls as well as pigpens.

"The cows are over in the other barn." Euphemia pointed in the direction of a long, low building that sat behind the barn and was connected with a fenced-in area.

"Does it always smell like this?" Sophie asked.

"Like what?" Euphemia asked as she clambered down from the wagon.

"Like . . ." Sophie tried to think of a delicate way to describe the waft of animal flesh and manure that was heavy in the air. Before she could say anything, the back door of the house opened, spilling light across the farmyard that spanned the barn and house, revealing a root cellar, a well, and clotheslines with linens still flapping in the breeze.

"Mum" came a boy's voice. "Did you get a girl?"

The boy was outlined in the doorway, stocky and broad-shouldered with a thatch of thick hair sticking on end.

"Fergus Duff, mind your manners!" Euphemia bellowed in a stern tone. Then she said to Sophie under her breath, "You'll have to forgive them, lass. They aren't used to having a girl around."

The boy hung his head and stepped outside, leaving the door wide open. Another boy appeared in the doorway, this one slightly taller.

Before Sophie could examine the boys more carefully, two other young men emerged from the shadows of the barn, framed by the lantern light.

"Mum," said the stockier of the two, coming forward and taking the reins. From his build and confident stance, Sophie could see he was older and more mature than his brothers. In the faint light of the barn, she couldn't distinguish his features but could see he was hefty, not as much as Euphemia, but still a large-sized man.

"Och, thank you, Lyle." Euphemia stood on her tiptoes and placed a kiss on the man's bearded face. "Why don't you help Sophie down from the wagon? I'm sure the lass is bone-weary after all her traveling."

Not wanting to be a bother, Sophie started to climb down on her own, but before she could find footing, wide hands were upon her waist and lifting her the rest of the way.

"There you are," the man said, setting her on the ground. The pressure of his hands was strong and yet gentle. Sophie expected him to linger, to take advantage of the close proximity. Any man she'd ever known would have. But he released her right away and took a step back.

"Welcome to the farm," he said with a warm smile, one that showed more of his familial resemblance to his mother.

"Thank you."

With the barn lantern casting a glow over her, he openly studied her, his eyes lighting with the appreciation she was accustomed to seeing in men.

"This wee bairn is my Lyle," Euphemia said, patting Lyle's arm. "Then there's my Gavin. And these two are my Fergus and my Alastair."

Sophie nodded first at Lyle, then Gavin, still by the barn door, and finally at the boys who'd walked over from the house and now stood nearby, staring at her with wide eyes.

The next hour was a blur as Euphemia gave her a tour of the farm buildings and house. She met everyone but Stuart, called Stu by his brothers. Euphemia had peeked into his room and came back out to say that he was already asleep.

Once the tour was complete, Euphemia propelled Sophie into a chair at the enormous dining room table and put a plate in front of her that was piled high with fried chicken, buttery homemade noodles, biscuits, and the sweetest jam Sophie had ever tasted.

Euphemia shooed the boys away with a broom and laughter, telling them they could ogle Sophie more in the morning. Sophie had assured the woman that she didn't mind, but Euphemia still swatted at the boys playfully each time they poked their heads into the room.

Once Sophie finished with dinner, Euphemia led her up the narrow stairs to the second floor, which consisted of two bedrooms—a large one for Euphemia and Barclay, and a smaller one next door with two twin beds.

"This room is for you, lass," Euphemia said. She lit a lantern on the pedestal table positioned between the beds that were neatly made with colorful quilts. A braided rug covered the floor and was bright with yellows, reds, and greens. A window had been opened, and a pair of cherry red calico curtains fluttered in a breeze that brought in the scent of the barnyard, a scent that seemed to be as much a part of the house as the bright colors.

"Make yerself at home." Euphemia opened a chest of drawers and pulled out several items that appeared to be boys' undergarments.

Had this room belonged to her sons? Of course it had. Who else would have used it?

"I can't take this room," Sophie said, retreating to the door. "I'll bed down on the kitchen floor."

Euphemia had opened the second drawer and was withdrawing more clothing. At Sophie's statement, she stopped rummaging, and her brows rose above confused eyes. "Kitchen floor? Now, why would you do a thing like that?"

"I don't want to take the room from your sons. They need it more than I do. Besides, I'm used to sleeping on the floor—can't remember the last time I slept in a bed. Even at the asylums, I bedded down on the floor so that I could be near Olivia and Nicholas."

Euphemia straightened and studied Sophie's face. Her eyes filled with something Sophie couldn't explain but that made Sophie suddenly self-conscious. Had she said too much? She wasn't a helpless orphan. And she certainly didn't need anyone's pity.

She strode to her bag in the corner where someone had placed it. She grabbed it and started back toward the door. She didn't need to stay with the Duffs. She'd find some other place, somewhere she could be on her own away from the pity and the raised brows.

"Now there, lass," Euphemia said. "Dinnae mind me. I'm as much an oaf as my boys at times."

Sophie's steps slowed, and she halted in the doorway. Helpless frustration coursed through her. More than anything she wanted to stomp out of the house and walk away and show Euphemia she was capable and strong and didn't need her pity.

At the same time, Sophie felt trapped. She had no place to go, and there was no one else who wanted her. And if she left now in the dark, she wouldn't know how to get back to town. Even if she somehow managed to make it there, what would she do then? How would she be able to hide in such a small town?

"I sometimes forget that I was a stranger once," Euphemia said softly. "I was on my own too and had to make a new life in a new place where everything was different."

At the woman's confession, Sophie pivoted.

"I dinnae do so well for myself those first few years," she continued, meeting Sophie's gaze, "and I made a great many mistakes I still regret. But I thank the good Lord He never treats us as our sins deserve."

Euphemia had made mistakes? This kind woman had sinned? It was Sophie's turn to study Euphemia's face to see the honesty in her eyes along with what appeared to be sorrow. What had Euphemia done that had caused such sadness? She seemed to have such a good life now, a prosperous dairy farm, and a large and loving family.

If this woman had made mistakes, she'd learned to move past them. Sophie wasn't sure she would be able to do the same. Nevertheless, maybe Euphemia would understand her. Maybe she wouldn't be as quick to judge as Sophie had first thought.

Sophie set her bag down on the floor.

Euphemia released a breath and then smiled. "That's a good lass. Now, as long as you live under my roof, you'll stay in the bedroom. I want to teach my boys to be good men, to respect women and sacrifice for them. You'll let me do that for my boys, won't you?"

"I'll try." Sophie looked around the room again. It was more spacious than any other place she'd ever lived. "But it doesn't seem fair that I have all this for myself and they have nothing."

Euphemia laughed. "Och, lass, dinnae be thinking they have

nothing. Fergus and Alastair are pleased as plums to be staying in the dormer room with their brothers. They've been asking to change for years and now's their chance."

Dormer room?

As if sensing her unasked question, Euphemia pointed to the ceiling above them.

The picture of a dormer room flashed into Sophie's memory. A low slanted ceiling, unpainted walls, creaking floorboards. And a bed big enough for three little girls to snuggle under a thick, down coverlet.

Her home in Germany. The memories were fading. She couldn't recollect much about those days before moving to New York, but the dormer room was one she still remembered. The cuddling between her sisters, listening to their whispered conversations, giggling together whenever they touched each other with icy toes.

"You best be abed," Euphemia said as she resumed her task of emptying the drawers. "We have a busy day of work ahead of us tomorrow. And the morn will be upon us before we're ready for it, that's for sure."

An hour later, Sophie lay on the bed, the softness of the mattress and pillow unfamiliar to her after so many years of sleeping wherever she could find a spot. Although she knew she should be grateful for the bed, for the clean sheets that smelled of lilac, and the safety of the room, silent tears slid from her closed eyes anyway.

The slumbering house was too quiet, with only the buzz of insects and the occasional noise of one of the livestock to break the silence. The anxious thudding of her heartbeat and the frantic racing of her thoughts resounded in the emptiness.

Her arms ached for Olivia and Nicholas. In spite of the chaos of their lives and all the moving, she'd always made time every night to tell them a bedtime story. Then, once she finished with the story, she hugged and kissed them good-night. Without fail. She'd never missed a night for as long as she could remember. Except tonight . . .

She could just imagine them in their new strange bed, holding each other, missing her, and crying out in loneliness.

"Why does it have to be this way, God?" she whispered against her pillow, muffling her sobs so that no one else could hear them. "Why does everything always have to be so hard?"

She didn't know why she was calling out to God after all this time of running from Him. In fact, she guessed He wouldn't hear her anyway. She was too far away. And even if she wasn't, why would He listen? She'd sinned too many times for Him to care about her anymore.

Amidst the heartache, Euphemia's gentle Scottish brogue whispered through her: *The good Lord never treats us as our sins deserve. He never treats us as our sins deserve. He never treats us as our sins deserve.*

Like the cool breeze bustling past the curtains and soothing Sophie's heated skin and hot tears, the words brushed over her broken soul, strangely soothing her pain. Not completely. But it was something. And tonight she desperately needed to cling to something or she wasn't sure she'd have the strength to go on.

CHAPTER 8

Sophie stretched and yawned, relishing the scent of bacon and coffee and something sweet. For a moment she just breathed in the delicious aromas. In her sleepy haze, she thought she could hear her father in the kitchen below.

At the ricocheting thud of a distant door, Sophie bolted upright and blinked until she was awake. Through the darkness she could see the fluttering of curtains and the outline of the closed bedroom door, her dress hanging limply from a hook on the back. With a start, she realized she wasn't in her father's bakery in Germany. She was in Illinois on a farm, living with strangers.

And Olivia and Nicholas were gone.

The hopelessness that had somehow disappeared for a few hours while she slept came charging back. She untangled her legs from the sheet and jumped out of bed. She was getting her children first thing this morning, and they were running away to Chicago. She didn't know how she'd manage to find money for their train fare, but she didn't care. She had to retrieve them.

As she donned her dress and plaited her hair, she heard more voices, the heavy trod of footsteps, the clanking of pans. But

103

all she could think about was escaping and finding Olivia and Nicholas. Whatever made her believe she could live without them? And how would they be able to survive without her? Surely they were both as miserable as she was.

Her fingers stumbled over each other as she slid on her shoes—the new pair the Children's Aid Society had given her. They were too big for her feet and had given her blisters, and yet they were much better than the old ones she'd been wearing. The leather had worn thin and was so full of holes that she'd had to patch the spots with newspaper.

Nicholas's shoes had been even worse. They were so tight that she'd cut out the fronts to make room for his toes.

At the remembrance of the awful condition of the shoes and Nicholas's delight when he'd gotten his new pair, Sophie's frantic motions ceased. She lowered herself to the edge of her unmade bed and stared at the closed door.

He was in a new home where he'd have everything he needed. He'd no longer have to worry about his toes getting cold and wet whenever it rained, or his lips turning blue in a cold breeze. He'd have his sturdy shoes and heavy coat and likely plenty of other warm clothes to see him through the winter.

She brushed her hand across the smooth clean sheets and the firm mattress and realized they'd probably slept in beds last night too. If she took them away from their new home, they'd be back to sleeping on the streets, in alleyways, in empty coal boxes, anyplace where they wouldn't be bothered by drunks or rats or policemen.

With a sigh, Sophie put aside the notion of walking over to the Ramseys and sneaking the children out of the house. Just because she needed them didn't mean they needed her in the same way. "You were selfish," she reminded herself. She'd kept the children with her because she'd wanted them. Now it was time to stop thinking about her desires and do what was best for them. If their new home was half as nice as hers, then they would definitely have a better life than what they'd had in the asylums or streets or even in Anna's sister's crowded tenement apartment.

Slowly, Sophie finished getting ready. When she finally left her room and started down the dark stairway, the friendly banter of men's voices rose up to greet her. She halted at the bottom step, the cheerful glow of lantern light from the dining room beckoning her down the hallway.

Even though dawn hadn't yet broken, she was late. She should have been up long ago, helping Euphemia with whatever it was she was supposed to do. Euphemia had told her the morning started early and that they would have a busy day ahead.

What would Euphemia think of her now? The woman had been patient with her last evening, but surely her patience would run thin if Sophie didn't prove her worth.

Sophie hustled down the hallway and stepped into the dining room. At the sight of her, every voice silenced and every pair of eyes flew to her. Barclay Duff sat at the head of the table, a mug of coffee lifted halfway to his mouth. Two sons sat on one side of the table and two on the other, all built with similar round faces, stocky shoulders, and hefty girths. They stared at her as though she were a street performer putting on a show.

Sophie stood awkwardly and stared back at them, unsure what to do.

As the silence stretched on, Euphemia came out of the kitchen carrying a plate piled high with griddle cakes. "Good morning, lass," she said, plopping the platter onto the middle of the table. "I knew ye'd stepped into the room the second my wee bairns fell silent."

"Good morning," Sophie replied, relieved at the sight of the woman with her warm smile and her cheerful blue calico dress. "I'm sorry I'm late. What can I do to help?"

"You can flip the last of the bacon before the pieces burn," she said with a nod toward the kitchen.

Sophie hurried forward, anxious to be away from the stares.

"You'll find an apron in the pantry," Euphemia said as she retrieved several empty plates.

The instant Sophie stepped out of the dining room, the clatter and conversation resumed, including Euphemia's good-natured scolding.

"You'd think you boys have never seen a girl by the way you're tongue-tied and making eyes at the lass," she said. "Now, mind you to be kind and not scare her away the first day."

Sophie halted in the middle of the kitchen. An open cupboard stood against one wall, revealing extra plates, bowls, and cups. Shelves on the wall next to it held crocks and tins and an assortment of what appeared to be baking supplies and spices. A worktable at the center was piled with vegetables that were still covered in dirt, along with crates underneath also filled to the brim.

Sophie had never seen so many vegetables. She recognized carrots, tomatoes, beans, onions, and beets. But she'd never seen them with their leafy tops still attached. Had Euphemia grown all these in her garden? And who would eat all the food? There was enough to fill every plate in an asylum dining hall.

She whistled softly under her breath. What was Euphemia doing with so much produce when there were so many hungry children roaming the streets?

Sophie's mind spun with memories of the many times she and Nicholas and Olivia had gone without food, even at the asylums where there was never enough to go around and most certainly not fresh produce like this. Even now, Sophie's stomach gurgled with hunger, a sensation she'd learned to ignore but that now prodded her to reach for one of the tomatoes.

Without a second thought, she slipped a tomato into the side pocket of her skirt. Next she grabbed a handful of the beans and started to shove them into her other pocket. At the sound of Euphemia's laughter from the dining room, Sophie stopped abruptly with her hand halfway in. "What are you doing, Sophie Neumann?" she whispered harshly.

Euphemia had been nothing but kind to her since the moment they'd met. And here she was repaying the woman by stealing food. And for what reason? She'd never stolen food for herself. It was always for Olivia and Nicholas. Only them.

And they didn't need tomatoes or beans. Not today. If Mrs. Ramsey's kitchen was anything like Euphemia's, then Mrs. Ramsey had likely provided Olivia and Nicholas with all the fresh food they could want and then some.

Sophie emptied her pockets but couldn't empty the guilt that had slipped out and was now taunting her with all the times she'd stolen from street vendors, out of the backs of wagons, or even right off the shelf of a store. Had thieving become such a way of life that she would do it even when she no longer had a need?

Near the window sat a big black stove with an enormous pipe that ran the length of the wall and disappeared into the ceiling overhead. The stove was churning out heat that made the kitchen hot even in the coolness of the morning. Pots and pans covered every burner, smoke curling up from one of them.

Was the bacon already burning?

"Blasted," Sophie muttered as she crossed to the stove. Sure enough, in a large cast-iron skillet slices of bacon lay shriveled and blackened in a layer of spluttering grease. She grabbed the long handle and started to lift the pan off the stove. But as her fingers made contact with the iron, burning heat seared her flesh, and she released the pan with a cry.

The skillet dropped to the floor, and hot grease splattered

Sophie's skirt, shoes, and the floor. She jumped back and gave another cry, this one of dismay.

Euphemia burst into the kitchen, her face wreathed with worry. "What happened, lass?"

At the sight of the pan on the floor with the charred strips of bacon in grease next to it, Sophie wanted to lie, wanted to come up with some excuse for why she'd failed to do the one thing Euphemia had given her to do.

Instead, she stared wordlessly at the mess and waited for Euphemia to berate her for not attending to the bacon, at the very least snap at her for being clumsy.

"Och!" Euphemia bustled toward Sophie.

When the woman reached for her, Sophie flinched, knowing she deserved to have her ears boxed or her cheeks slapped. She was surprised instead when Euphemia grabbed her hand, flipped it over, and examined the red splotches that were forming across her palm. "Ye've burnt yerself, lass. We need to get a cool cloth on your skin before it blisters."

Euphemia pulled Sophie toward a basin of water on a stand near the back door, dipped in a towel, and pressed the cloth against Sophie's hand. At the stinging contact, Sophie sucked in a breath.

"It'll take a few minutes for the cool water to help, but you just keep dipping and holding."

"Thank you," Sophie managed, once again attempting to find the manners she hadn't used in a long time. "I'm sorry about the mess."

Euphemia shook her head and tsked. "Dinnae you worry a thing about it. This is my fault. I should have known better than to send you near a hot pan on your first day."

The woman exuded a patience that was simply too good to be true. Surely it would run out soon. She'd get tired of Sophie's mistakes and ineptness and would eventually dole out the punishment she deserved. That was the way it always happened.

Euphemia glanced at the doorway, and seeing her four sons crowded there and gawking at Sophie, she shooed them with a towel. "Go on now. Skedaddle, and finish your breakfast, or I might just have to put you to work snapping beans."

At the mention of beans, the boys disappeared faster than beggars caught stealing from a street vendor. Euphemia chuckled, reached for a rag, and then picked up the skillet from where it had fallen on the floor.

"Lesson number one, lass." She placed the pan back on the stove on a side burner. "Dinnae touch the hot pans unless you have a towel in hand."

"Lesson learned." Sophie dipped the cloth in the basin again and reapplied the cool water to her burning palm. "I have to admit I haven't been in a kitchen in a long time. Not since my father died."

Euphemia used a wooden spatula to scrape the congealing grease from the floor.

"He was a baker," Sophie said, hoping that fact might work in her favor even if she'd been too young to assist him or learn anything from him. "If you want, I'll do some of the baking."

Once the words were out, Sophie wanted to slap herself with Euphemia's spatula. What was she saying? Her experience cooking during her stay at Mollie's had amounted to burned mush for almost every meal.

Thankfully, Euphemia didn't take her up on the offer. Instead, she showed Sophie how to clean out the pans and scrape platters, saving every dollop of leftovers in a slop bucket by the back door for the pigs. By the time the men finished their breakfast, the sun had risen and they exited the house just as noisily as they'd entered.

Euphemia instructed Sophie on washing the dishes while she took a plate of breakfast to Stuart. When Sophie finished, she tried to tidy the rest of the kitchen and the dining room the best she could while she waited for Euphemia to return and tell her what to do next.

Sophie mostly just stared at the spaciousness of the room with its solid oak table and chairs and matching hutch and sideboard. Although the glass cabinet doors in the hutch were dusty, the display of crocks and pretty plates was unlike anything Sophie had seen before.

The two-room tenement apartments she'd lived in could easily fit into one room of the Duffs' house. The dining room alone contained more furniture and knickknacks than her family had ever owned—at least that she could remember.

Hearing a shout from the direction of Stuart's bedroom down the hall from the dining room, Sophie left the dishrag on the table and went to investigate.

The bedroom door was open a crack, and at another bellow, this one distinctly male, Sophie peeked inside. With the curtains still closed, the room was shrouded in darkness. She could only see Euphemia's broad outline as she stood at the side of the bed and lifted a mug to the lips of a man sitting up against several pillows.

"You need a wee bit more," Euphemia was saying in a firm tone. "And you know I won't take your sass for an answer."

"Just let me be."

"Open up."

"No. I told you I don't want your help."

"I'm not giving up on you, Stu," Euphemia said fiercely. "And I don't want you giving up on yourself."

The man on the bed turned his head away from Euphemia so that he was glaring at the wall.

Euphemia chased his lips with the mug.

With a curse as foul as any Sophie had heard on the streets, Stu reached up and slapped the cup. It flew out of Euphemia's hand and banged against the wall, the liquid splashing out in a wet, tangled spider web.

The crash startled Sophie, and she accidentally bumped the door so that it creaked open several more inches. Both Euphemia and Stu swiveled her way. Sophie knew she should jump out of sight, but her curiosity was too strong. What was wrong with Stuart? Why was he in bed? And why was he giving up on himself?

She pushed the door open wider, allowing daylight to pour into the room and fall upon Stu. A thick beard covered much of his face and his hair was overlong, his cheeks gaunt, and his eyes sunken. Underneath the sheet, his limbs were thin, his bones poking up sharply. He was clearly sick and suffering.

The sourness of the room assaulted Sophie, reminding her of the privies, hallways, and stairwells in the tenements that were usually filthy with all manner of waste.

"This is Sophie," Euphemia said cheerfully. "The young woman I told you about who's staying with us and helping me."

For a long moment, Stu seemed to take Sophie in like a hungry beggar who'd stumbled upon a crust of bread. But then a dark cloud descended. His eyebrows scrunched in fury, and anger flew from his eyes and swung at her as fast as fists in an alley brawl. "Get out!" His hand shook as he reached for the plate on his bedside table. "Get out now!"

He punctuated his last word by throwing the plate at the door. With his lack of strength and the unsteadiness of his grip, the plate landed in the middle of the room on the rug. Even so, Sophie quickly backed away and closed the door.

She returned to the dining room, picked up the dishcloth, and resumed washing the table. Chagrin circled around her. She shouldn't have poked her head into the bedroom. Euphemia obviously had a difficult enough time with her son without Sophie making things worse.

When Euphemia entered the dining room carrying the plate her son had just thrown, Sophie stiffened her spine and waited for the words of censure she deserved. Euphemia paused and pushed in one of the chairs but didn't say anything.

Sophie peeked at the woman and was surprised to see sadness etched at the corners of her eyes.

"Dinnae mind Stu," she said softly. "He's like that with everyone."

"Why? What's wrong with him?" Once Sophie's questions were out, she realized how rude she was to pry.

"Poor lad was born a cripple," Euphemia whispered, looking out the window as if she were staring into her past. "He's had a rough time of it, more so these past few years."

"He's not able to walk?"

"Not without help."

"So he stays in bed most of the time?"

Euphemia nodded without shifting her gaze from the window. "He's only making himself more miserable."

Sophie wondered how Euphemia was able to care for him day after day when he didn't appreciate her help and treated her with disdain. She waited for Euphemia to break into tears or to complain about the burden she'd been given to bear with a crippled son.

But Euphemia's lips lifted into a wistful smile. "Sometimes God allows us to sink down in our own misery until we reach a low place where we're finally ready to look up and reach out for Him."

Once again, Sophie was at a loss with knowing what to say. She wasn't sure if Euphemia was referring to herself or to Stuart. Whatever the case, the woman's comment sounded like something her mother would have said. Sophie had the feeling Mutti would have liked Euphemia and was perhaps even now smiling down from heaven at the woman's wise words.

"In the meantime," Euphemia continued, "I'll keep on loving that bairn of mine the same way the good Lord loves me. That's about all I can do."

Sophie wasn't sure she'd be able to love Stuart if she were in Euphemia's position. In fact, she decided she'd do her best to stay away from the young man's room. If she didn't have to see him again during her stay at the Duffs', she wouldn't mind in the least.

"Now then, lass," Euphemia said, heading for the kitchen. "Let's start with churning the butter and gathering eggs. Then we'll get some bread rising before we preserve the beans."

Though Sophie hadn't a clue how to do any of the tasks, for a reason she couldn't explain she longed to help this woman, who carried a heavy load with not only the responsibilities of the farm but also a bitter, crippled son. The weight would have made even the strongest of people bend, perhaps even fall to their knees. But Euphemia hadn't let it crush her, and Sophie was curious to know why.

CHAPTER 9

Jakob jumped from the bench before Reinhold could bring the wagon to a halt in front of the Duffs' barn. His brother bounded toward Fergus with an eagerness that as usual seemed to point out Reinhold's glaring inadequacies, namely that the boy needed more companionship than Reinhold could provide. Jakob needed a home like the Duffs had, with a good mother like Euphemia both encouraging and scolding him.

And so did his sisters . . .

The telegram Fergus had delivered yesterday smoldered like a hot coal in Reinhold's pocket, the telegram from Drew Brady informing him Elise had delivered a fine baby girl and that mother and baby were healthy and well. Drew had mentioned that Silke and Verina were delighted with the baby and doing well too.

Although Drew hadn't asked when Reinhold wanted the girls to come live with him, Reinhold suspected the question was soon coming. Elise and Thornton would be busy with their new baby. Drew and Marianne had their work with the Children's Aid Society and were often gone on trips, helping to place orphans in homes. Neither couple would want to take care of his sisters much longer.

Reinhold brought the wagon to a stop near the hitching post. Lyle was already striding toward him and greeting him with a wide grin. He'd recently trimmed his scraggly beard and hair. His shirt was tucked in, and his trousers were clean. Clearly he was trying to impress the orphan girl.

"Had to come see our new lass for yourself, did you?" Lyle asked. "I knew you wouldn't be able to stay away."

"I'm only here because I fear your mum's wrath more than God Almighty's." Reinhold returned the grin. "When Fergus told me she planned to march over and drag me back here for supper tonight, I decided I better come of my own will."

Lyle laughed. But in spite of the shared humor, they both knew not to cross Euphemia. She was a woman to be reckoned with. After skipping church, working on the Lord's Day, and turning down her dinner invitations the past two Sabbaths, Reinhold knew he had to make time for supper or else Euphemia would make it for him.

"So that means you're not in the least curious about the lass?" Lyle asked as he helped Reinhold unhitch Daisy.

"Not in the least." And he meant it. When Fergus had delivered the telegram from Drew, the boy had been bursting with news about the orphan Euphemia had brought home.

"She's a real pretty girl," Fergus had declared, his eyes already sparkling with infatuation. "Lyle said he's gonna marry her someday."

Reinhold clamped a hand on Lyle's bulky shoulder. His friend was one of the kindest, gentlest souls he'd ever met. "You're a good man, Lyle. I'm sure you'll have no trouble winning her heart."

Lyle cast a sideways glance toward the house, as if hoping to catch a glimpse of the girl. He wore a crooked grin and had a glimmer in his eyes like he did whenever he was vying for the attention of one of the local girls—which happened to be one of Lyle's favorite pastimes.

Unfortunately, while Lyle enjoyed fishing for attention, he wasn't accomplished at it, and most of the eligible women ended up getting away. Maybe this time Lyle would finally hook the big one.

"I don't know, Reinhold," Lyle said with more uncertainty than Reinhold had ever seen in his friend. "She's too pretty for a man like me. And I freeze whenever I'm in the room with her."

Reinhold finished unbuckling Daisy's traces and rubbed his hand down her withers and across her flank.

"You're always so calm around the ladies," Lyle said. "How do you do it? I need some tips."

Reinhold was tempted to blurt out that his method was to stay detached. While he'd danced with a few of the girls at local barn parties, he didn't have any aspirations to get married. For a while he'd harbored feelings for Elise. He thought he'd loved her. But when she'd fallen in love with Thornton, he knew his love hadn't been enough for either of them.

Then last summer he'd almost married Marianne when she came through on her first trip as a placing agent. He'd discovered that she'd always liked him and had wanted to marry him. But then, as it turned out, she'd fallen in love with Drew Brady, her fellow placing agent, and hadn't wanted to marry him any more than Elise had.

The failed attempts to win the women had worked out for the best. After the fight that had almost killed Higgins, Reinhold decided he never wanted to get married, never wanted to burden any woman with his anger the way his father had burdened his mother. In fact, he loathed the thought of tying any woman to himself, not when the monster inside him was so volatile, and he didn't know how to control it.

"Tell me," Lyle persisted as they led Reinhold's Morgan into the barn. "How do you stay calm around the pretty women?"

Jakob, Alastair, and Fergus were already in the loft and taking turns swinging from the rope attached to the roof. Gavin had joined them as well. They flew in wide circles before finally dropping to the haymow below.

"Maybe if you tell yourself she's your sister," Reinhold suggested, "then you won't be so nervous."

"My sister? I don't know if I can do that." Lyle opened an empty stall and guided the mare inside.

"Then look at her like she's a friend. If you see her as just a friend, then you'll be able to talk to her like you do to me and get to know her without the pressure of more."

"A friend . . ." Lyle rubbed at his beard and seemed to mull over Reinhold's advice.

"Then again," Reinhold added as he reached for a brush and ran it along Daisy's flank, "if she's as pretty as you say she is, maybe you should get down on your knees and propose to her right away."

Lyle chuckled. "If I could get my voice working around her, I just might."

Reinhold soaked in the peace of the barn, the laughter of the boys overhead, the camaraderie of his friend. Why had he stayed away from the Duffs for so long? Their home was a soothing ointment on his aching soul.

When the dinner bell rang a short while later, the other boys rushed ahead of Lyle and Reinhold, who stopped at the bucket next to the well to wash their hands. At the waft of roasted chicken and gravy and mashed potatoes coming from the open kitchen window, Reinhold's stomach ached for filling as much as his soul did.

"Dinnae step foot into my house without washing your hands" came Euphemia's stern command to the boys. Her hefty frame filled the doorway, blocking their entrance. She pointed them back to the bucket, and her expression softened at the sight of Reinhold in the process of drying himself.

A moment later, as Reinhold stepped inside, she wrapped her arms around him in a tight hug. Though he wasn't a tall man, Euphemia's head barely reached his chin. He hugged her in return and at the same time caught sight of the *new lass*.

The young woman was standing at the worktable, slicing a loaf of bread and placing the pieces on a platter. Her pale blond hair hung in a single braid down her back with loose wisps of hair curling about her neck. Something about the delicate angle of her neck and ear struck him as familiar.

"You know better than to stay away from me this long, Reinhold Weiss," Euphemia said, squeezing him tighter.

At the mention of his name, the new lass stiffened. Her knife froze halfway through the remainder of the loaf.

"I don't care how busy you are," Euphemia continued, "you cannot forget about the people who love you or about the good Lord who loves you more."

"I'll try to do better," he said, unable to take his eyes off the new lass as she slowly pivoted.

At the sight of wide eyes as blue as a cloudless autumn sky, Reinhold fell back a step. For a moment he saw Elise, who had the same stunning eyes. But as he studied the delicately curved chin, the high cheekbones, and the perfectly rounded lips, he realized this woman wasn't Elise. This woman was shorter, slightly younger, and somehow more beautiful and alluring.

Silence had descended over the room. Euphemia was looking between him and the young woman, her brow creasing. And Lyle was staring at the new lass with unabashed admiration.

The other boys entered the kitchen, shoving and pushing and teasing each other. At the sight of the Duffs' new orphan girl, Jakob halted and his face lit up. "Sophie?"

"You know our Sophie?" Euphemia asked Jakob.

Jakob nodded and smiled. "She's Sophie Neumann. We were neighbors in New York."

Reinhold studied Sophie again, this time seeing a resemblance to the little girl he'd once known. "Sophie?" The name tumbled from Reinhold with a mixture of disbelief and excitement. Was this really Sophie Neumann?

Elise and Marianne had been desperate to find her, had searched for their sister for months, had even paid investigators to hunt her down. And they'd gotten nowhere. Now here Sophie was—standing before him in the Duffs' kitchen.

"I can't believe it," he said, grinning and taking a step forward. "It is you."

Instead of sharing his thrill, Sophie remained unsmiling, her eyes unwelcoming, and her stance like a doe caught grazing in the garden. She scooted around the worktable, her fingers trembling, then darted out of the kitchen.

Reinhold stared after her in confusion the same way the others did. Why was she afraid? Had she mistaken them for someone else? She couldn't have. Euphemia had said his full name, and from the way she'd stiffened, she'd recognized it.

That could only mean one thing. She didn't want to see him or Jakob.

At the distinct echo of the front door slamming shut, Reinhold's heart plunged within him like an empty bucket down a well. She was leaving, running away. And he couldn't let her do that, not now that he'd just found her.

"What's wrong with Sophie?" Euphemia finally asked. She turned first to Jakob and then to Reinhold, her rounded fists braced on her hips. "What did you boys do to her?"

"Nothing," Jakob said hurriedly. "I thought she'd be happy to see us."

"Me too." Reinhold started across the kitchen. "I'll go after her and find out what's bothering her."

Jakob began to follow him.

Reinhold motioned him and the others back. "Let me go first."

Jakob hesitated, his expression saying he wanted to chase after the girl, but his fear of Reinhold held him back.

Somewhere in the back of Reinhold's mind, he resented his brother's reaction and hated himself for it. Right now, though, he needed to focus on catching up with Sophie. He couldn't let her get away.

He bolted through the dining room, down the hallway that led past the parlor on one side and Stuart's bedroom on the other. He shot out the front door and stopped short, frantically scanning the yard. Through the leaves of the enormous maple that shaded the area he caught sight of Sophie. She was racing down the wagon path toward the road, her feet slapping the gravel and her braid bumping furiously against her back.

Not bothering with the stairs, he hopped off the porch and sprinted after her. "Sophie, wait!"

At the sound of his voice, she ran faster.

"Sophie, please!" He wasn't a particularly fast runner, but the stamina and muscle he'd developed over the past summer held him in good stead, and he caught up to her in no time. He grabbed her arm, giving her no choice but to stop.

She was breathing hard from her exertion, and possibly from fear, because she held herself rigidly and regarded him with frightened eyes. "Let me go."

He was still amazed at how grown up she was, how much two years had changed her from a girl into a woman. Maybe he'd changed too. "It's me, Reinhold Weiss," he said gently. "Don't you recognize me?"

Her breath hitched. Was she thinking of lying to him? Pretending she didn't know him? Why?

She glanced at the road that ran past the Duff farm and

then at his hand gripping her upper arm. "Please let me go, Reinhold."

From the soft way she said his name, she knew him. And this time when she met his gaze, a quiet desperation emanated from her pretty features.

"What's wrong?" Protectiveness surged into his chest. He'd always viewed her as he did his own sisters, with affection and concern. "Are you in some kind of trouble? I can help you."

She shook her head. "I just need to go."

"But you can't go yet." He had to make her stay for Elise and Marianne's sake. They'd be overjoyed to discover Sophie was safe and alive. If she slipped away and disappeared, how would he find her again? And how would he be able to live with himself knowing he'd had her within his grasp but lost her? Such news would devastate Elise and Marianne.

"Your sisters have been so worried about you." At the mention of her sisters, the panic returned to Sophie's face, and she struggled against his hold.

He refused to let go.

"Reinhold, please," she said, her big blue eyes pleading with him. "You can't say anything to them. Don't tell them you saw me."

"I can't do that. They have a right to know—"

"I don't want to see them again." Her words were brittle and final.

"But Elise and Marianne have been looking for you and will be glad to know you're all right."

"You can't tell them."

"How can I withhold such good news from them?"

Her eyes narrowed, and her nostrils flared. "If you say one word, I'll leave and you'll never see me again."

He could sense she was serious, that she really would go, and that this time she'd make sure no one ever found her. "I don't understand. Why don't you want your sisters to know where you are and that you're safe?"

She jerked and freed herself from his hold. Without answering him, she started striding toward the road.

He exhaled a frustrated breath and bolted after her. He'd have to do things her way, at least until he could figure out how to prevent her from running away. "Sophie, wait."

She kept walking, lifting her chin and refusing to look at him.

"Fine," he said. "I won't say anything to Elise and Marianne." For now. But he wouldn't tell her that.

"Promise me," she demanded without breaking her stride.

He didn't want to promise her anything. He wasn't a man who made vows and broke them. And if he promised her this, he knew he'd have to eventually break the promise. He couldn't withhold Sophie's whereabouts from her sisters for long. It would be cruel.

However, maybe in the short term, if he promised Sophie what she wanted, he'd be able to convince her she had nothing to fear, that she should be reunited with her sisters. He could help her do that, couldn't he?

"All right, Sophie. I promise."

Her footsteps slowed. "Do you mean it?"

"I'm a man of my word. You know that."

She stopped and turned to face him. This time the fear was gone, replaced with uncertainty. "Promise me again. Promise you won't tell Elise and Marianne you saw me."

The tension in his shoulders eased. "As long as you promise you won't leave the Duffs."

Indecisiveness flittered in her eyes.

"They're good people, Sophie. You couldn't ask for a better place to live."

She nodded as though having already come to that conclusion for herself. "I promise I won't leave the Duffs."

Reinhold had the feeling Sophie's word didn't mean as much as his, that she'd learned to lie to protect herself and that's what she was doing now too. Even so, he'd bought himself some time to decide how to handle the situation. At least he hoped so. "Good. If you'll stay, then I promise I won't tell Elise and Marianne you're here."

"Or that you've seen me."

"Or that I've seen you."

She studied his face as if testing the sincerity of his words. Then she smiled. The sight of her smile lighting up her face nearly took his breath away. Gone was the little girl he'd once known, and in her place was this beautiful young woman with bright eyes, a vivacious smile, and features pretty enough to render a man speechless.

No wonder Lyle was tongue-tied around her. And no wonder his friend wanted to drop to his knees and propose marriage.

Reinhold started to smile at the image of his friend falling to his knees in front of Sophie, but then he had the picture of other men running after her, brutal men who lived on the streets, men who would use a woman like Sophie to sate their needs before discarding her like rubbish.

The realization that she'd already been out on the streets and exposed to such men sent a tremor of fear through him as well as a burst of determination. He had to keep her safe and stop her from returning to the streets. If that meant he had to hurt Elise and Marianne for the time being, then so be it. Hopefully they'd understand why he'd chosen to withhold Sophie's whereabouts for a little while.

"Thank you, Reinhold," she said, this time more shyly. In her expression he could see some of the Sophie he used to know, the sweet girl who looked up to him and admired him.

"I'll do anything to make sure you're safe and happy, Sophie," he said earnestly. "You have to know that."

"You're wonderful." Her smile widened, and then she threw her arms around him and hugged him.

The embrace took him off guard. He instinctively wrapped his arms around her in return. He pulled her close and kissed the top of her head. All the many months of worry over Sophie, of wondering what had become of her, of thinking the worst had happened, and now here she was in his arms, alive and well. The thought brought a lump into his throat.

He held her tighter, as if in doing so, he could keep her from leaving.

She made no move to break from his hold. Instead she flattened her hands against his back and settled her cheek against his chest, against his heart. Her head nestled against his chin, her arms circled him in just the right place, and her curves melded into his body. Her very womanly curves . . .

The second the thought entered his head, he became instantly mortified. He swiftly released her and took a step back, praying she wouldn't see into his mind and discover what he'd just been thinking.

"It's good to see you." She peered up at him again with admiration. "You look older than the last time I saw you."

"Maybe that's because I *am* older," he said, keeping his voice light.

She laughed. "You have more muscles too," she said and wrapped her fingers around his bicep, "and your face is more rugged." She lifted a hand to his whiskered jaw and made a trail to his chin. He sensed a change in her, that she was seeing him as a man and not the boy he was when he'd left New York City.

Her eyes were trained upon his jaw and were so blue and vast that a man could easily wander in them and never get tired of the view. Her lips were slightly parted, the curves full and much too pretty. Her touch and her nearness and her beauty were captivating.

Drawing in a breath of self-rebuke, he took another step away from her, breaking her contact, and hopefully breaking the strange enchantment she seemed capable of casting over him with just one touch of her fingers.

"I can't believe you're really here," she said, still scrutinizing him.

"I have my own farm down the road." A motion on the front porch caught his eye. Euphemia was standing there, her apron and skirt fluttering in the breeze. She was watching them, likely worrying herself to death.

As much as he wanted to have Sophie to himself and ask her all about where she'd been and how she'd survived over the past two years, he knew they needed to return to the dinner Euphemia had prepared.

Besides, he had the feeling if he pushed Sophie to share too much too quickly, he'd only scare her away. She'd run from the Duffs the minute he left, and then he'd lose her and any chance of helping her.

"Euphemia's worried," he said, cocking his head toward the house. "Let's go eat. She's probably prepared a feast fit for a king—"

"A feast I helped her prepare," Sophie said, clearly proud of her efforts.

He stopped and feigned distress. "If you helped her, then maybe I'll pass."

Sophie laughed again and elbowed him playfully. "For that, I'm making you eat a double portion of everything."

As they bantered on their way to the front porch, Reinhold felt as though he was luring Sophie back to the house, back to safety, and back into the waiting arms of Euphemia, who would surely be able to convince her to stay even if he couldn't. When they reached the porch, Euphemia studied them as if attempting to solve a riddle.

"Is everything all right now?" she asked.

"I think so." Sophie arched a brow at Reinhold.

"Everything is just fine," he replied, hoping Sophie would be assured that her secret was safe with him.

ᴄᴏᵧᴇᴏ

The evening passed much too quickly for Sophie. After eating supper and helping Euphemia clean up, she'd had no trouble finding Reinhold outside sitting on a fence rail near the barn with one of Euphemia's sons. Reinhold had hopped down the moment he saw her, almost as if he'd been waiting for her.

"Let's take a walk," he suggested. They'd meandered to the rear of the house past Euphemia's enormous garden and through a newly planted orchard, finally stopping along the edge of the pond.

They'd only just sat down when the sun began its descent, bringing with it a darkness Sophie had never encountered in the city. Away from the reflections of house lights and street lanterns, the blackness would have been frightening except that the stars here were more visible, plentiful, and brighter than she'd ever seen. The crescent moon cast a warm glow over everything too.

Reinhold identified the night's noises for her—the trill of the crickets and throaty call of the peeper frogs—so different from the dance hall music and drunken laughter that often permeated nightlife in the city.

As they talked, she plied him with questions about her sisters, eager to hear every bit of news he had about them. He'd told her about his time in Quincy with Elise, about how she'd operated her own eating house. While there, she'd met and fallen in love with another man, a railroad tycoon. With a bit of chagrin he also shared about his failed engagement to Marianne last summer but how she'd also fallen in love and gotten married.

126

"A man by the name of Drew Brady, from a wealthy family too," Reinhold said, skipping a rock across the glassy surface of the pond. "He works for the Children's Aid Society."

Drew Brady who works for the Children's Aid Society. The name had a familiar ring. She'd heard it before, hadn't she? Her mind spun as she tried to place the name. She pictured the handsome gentleman who'd been at the train station in New York City, the placing agent who'd planned to accompany their trip. He'd lined up the Pooles to take the place of him and his wife.

Was Marianne his wife?

Sophie started with the realization of how close she'd come to seeing Marianne that day, if indeed the Drew Brady that Reinhold spoke of was the same Mr. Brady she'd seen.

He had reacted rather oddly to her, as if he'd recognized her, which had been strange because she was sure they'd never met. What if Marianne had described her? Or what if he'd seen the family resemblance? Sophie looked more like Elise than Marianne, but perhaps Mr. Brady had seen something in her face that seemed familiar.

What had Mr. Brady said about his wife and the reason they weren't going on the trip with the orphans? Had he said something about his wife's sister having a baby?

"Is Elise pregnant?" she asked.

"She had a baby several days ago."

Elise had given birth? Was the baby a girl or boy? What had she named it?

A yearning whispered in Sophie, the yearning for her sisters that she'd been unable to escape no matter how hard she'd tried to ignore it.

She was an aunt. She had a tiny niece or nephew. As much as she ached to see the new baby and hold it, embarrassment drove the idea away. If what Reinhold said was true about Elise and Marianne both having married wealthy men, then she was an even greater failure than she'd thought. They'd both obviously done well for themselves and had made something meaningful of their lives.

All she'd made of her life were mistakes.

Apparently both women had been able to move on without her there to hold them back, just as she figured they would. And yet somehow knowing they'd moved on without her and were doing so well brought an ache to her chest, a familiar ache that felt too much like rejection all over again.

With her shifting mood, she switched the conversation away from her sisters and asked Reinhold to tell her about his move to Mayfield and his efforts to start his own farm.

While he'd answered her questions about what he'd done since moving to the West, she sensed he hadn't shared everything. She couldn't fault him for keeping some of his life and feelings closed off, not when she'd done the same thing. She'd only given him a bare sketch of where she'd lived and what her life had been like since running away.

She was too ashamed to admit to him that after running away with Olivia and Nicholas, she'd resorted to thieving to keep them from starving. She'd become quite accomplished at breaking into shops and bakeries and stealing what they needed to eat. She'd even picked the pockets of people on the streets for change that she could use to buy food.

As time had gone on, she'd gotten into her share of fights with other street children, pushing and hitting and clawing for the right to a warm doorway or a coal box out of the biting wind. Even in the orphan asylums, she'd lied and cheated and stolen to make life easier and better for Olivia and Nicholas. She'd always justified her actions, telling herself that as long as Olivia and Nicholas were safe and happy, nothing else mattered.

But with each crime, with each sin, she'd pushed herself further away from God and from her sisters. She'd done so many things that Elise and Marianne would never condone, things they would never have done to survive.

Even when all three of them had been homeless and hungry, Elise and Marianne had found jobs and earned their food and shelter. They'd maintained their integrity instead of compromising time after time like she had.

The fact was, she'd sunk lower than she'd ever imagined she would. And after all she'd done, she was too afraid to face her sisters. They'd want to know how she survived. They'd see past any excuses she offered. And they'd see her for the terrible person she'd become.

When Reinhold finally led her back to the barn, he slowed his steps to match hers.

"I saw Olivia and Nicholas at church this morning," she said as they reached his wagon. Someone had lit a lantern and hung it from a post just inside the barn's open door, which helped to push back the darkness to the edges of the yard. "I was only able to talk to them for a few minutes."

Nicholas chattered endlessly about all the new things he'd seen and done. Olivia had been quieter and less enthusiastic, but she hadn't complained.

Sophie hadn't been able to stop thinking of the two all day. And the ache in her chest had expanded until she'd felt as though she'd explode with the need to be with the children. She'd wanted to walk over to the Ramseys and visit with them, but the day had gone too quickly, and before she knew it, Reinhold and Jakob Weiss were standing in the kitchen.

"I don't know the Ramseys well," Reinhold admitted. "But they seem like decent people."

"I hope so."

Reinhold stopped next to the horse that someone—probably Jakob—had attached to the wagon while they'd been on their walk. He ran a hand along the horse's muzzle affectionately, and Sophie couldn't keep from noticing how strong his hand was. And his arm. And his shoulders.

The lantern illuminated his profile, still thick and brawny but more pronounced than she remembered. The layer of dark stubble coating his jaw and chin made him look so grown up. The brown hair at the back of his neck curled along the collar of his shirt.

As if sensing her perusal, he shifted and looked at her. His green eyes were fringed with thick dark lashes. She'd always loved his eyes. In fact, she'd always thought Reinhold was handsome. Of course, half the girls in their New York City neighborhood in Kleindeutschland had thought so too, including Marianne. But at the time, Reinhold only had eyes for one woman—Elise.

Sophie could never understand why Elise hadn't returned Reinhold's affection. What was there not to like about him? He was sweet, kindhearted, and incredibly good-looking. Sophie was secretly glad Elise hadn't married Reinhold. He deserved a woman who would appreciate and love him in return.

As though sensing the direction of her thoughts, Reinhold's fingers on the horse's muzzle came to a standstill. His gaze moved languidly over her face, studying her the same way she had him. How did he view her now? He hadn't recognized her immediately, so she must have changed enough that she'd surprised him.

Did he like what he saw? Did he think she was pretty?

Something seemed to spark in his eyes, something that charged the air between them and made a warm trail through her belly. He jerked his attention back to the horse and resumed stroking between her eyes and down her nose. He wasn't a blushing man, not with his sunbrowned skin, yet his discomfort was palpable.

Sophie was used to men thinking she was beautiful. Danny

had fought for the right to claim her as his Bowery Girl because he'd thought she was more beautiful than all the other women. Even so, she'd never primped over her appearance or cared whether she was attractive.

However, standing in the lantern light with this man she'd always admired, a strange desire swelled inside her, a desire for him to see her in her own right and not merely as the younger sister of the woman he'd once loved.

She wasn't sure how to go about changing his view of her. Reinhold wasn't like the street boys she'd associated with. He operated by a different code of conduct around women. He wouldn't kiss her too intimately or grope her or pressure her to sleep with him the way Danny had.

Reinhold was too honorable and decent and considerate. He'd likely never allow himself to think of her as anything other than Elise and Marianne's little sister. Even if he might have an initial spark of attraction, he wouldn't act on it.

Or maybe she'd just imagined the spark. Maybe the draw was only on her part.

He stood silently for a moment, stroking the horse. Although she'd been frightened to see him earlier and had wanted to flee, she realized now that she was grateful he was here. He was someone solid, a safe link to her past, especially with his promise not to contact Elise and Marianne.

She knew he wanted to ask her more questions, wanted to understand why she'd alienated herself from her sisters. But how could she tell him she couldn't bear the thought of seeing them again after all she'd done? Then she'd have to face her wrongdoings, admit her sins not only to herself but also to him and her sisters. No, someday, if she was able to finally make something of her life, she'd contact them and show them she didn't need them, that she'd done just fine for herself.

In the meantime, she was too embarrassed for them to see

how low she'd fallen, especially now that she'd learned they were both so wealthy and happily married.

"Reinhold," she started, unsure how to voice everything inside her.

His eyes flew to hers. There was something intense and deep in them, something that once again charged the air between them and made her insides quiver with strange anticipation.

Before she could speak, their privacy was broken by the approach of the two younger Duff boys and Jakob from inside the barn. Jakob was still as quiet and reserved as he'd been in New York. After living on the streets for so long, she guessed farm life was as much a change for Jakob as it was for her. But from what she'd been able to tell, he was adjusting to his new life.

Reinhold had only briefly mentioned Peter's death. From the terseness of his comments regarding Peter and his two younger sisters still in New York living with Elise and Marianne, Sophie could tell that he didn't care to talk about his family.

Reluctantly, she stepped away from the wagon. She wasn't ready for him to go.

After settling onto the wagon bench, Reinhold started to roll away, tipping the brim of his hat in good-bye. Though he hadn't spoken to her again, something in his expression pleaded with her to stay at the Duffs', not to run away, that he wanted to see her again.

He wanted to see her again.

She let that revelation settle in her heart. Maybe she was making more of his look than he'd meant, but she didn't care. Reinhold Weiss wanted her to stay. And so she would.

CHAPTER 10

Sophie sat back on her heels in the dirt and examined her hands. Her fingernails and the grooves of her flesh were crusted with soil. And her skin was red and chafed.

Now she understood why Euphemia's hands were always so chapped. Between doing dishes, scrubbing vegetables, and washing up after chores, their hands were in and out of the water so often that Sophie was beginning to think she might end up washing her skin away. Or at least the soft beauty she'd always had.

She sighed before plunging her fingers into the ground and clawing at the stubborn carrot that refused to come out. A white hen scratched at the ground an arm's length away, pecking at the worms and other insects Sophie had exposed with the digging.

Among other chores, Euphemia had put Sophie in charge of gathering eggs. Sophie had expected the task to be an easy one, something she could learn quickly and so finally show herself to be worthwhile. Instead, gathering the eggs turned out to be just as difficult as every other farm chore she'd attempted.

During the spring and summer, instead of staying in the

chicken house, Euphemia allowed the hens to roam the farm freely, which meant some of them hid their nests.

"When the hens are allowed to feed on the fresh grass, seeds, and insects, their eggs are better," Euphemia explained. "The yolks are a darker yellow, which makes my cakes tastier."

For someone like Sophie who couldn't remember the last time she'd even had a crumb of something sweet, Euphemia's cakes and pies and cookies would have been fine without any eggs. But Sophie had refrained from commenting and had searched for the hidden hen nests in fence corners, unused feedboxes, and dark corners of the haymow.

Euphemia had shown Sophie some of the usual egg-laying spots and instructed her on the types of hen cackles that indicated whether a hen might be laying on the ground versus in high places. Even so, finding the eggs was much harder than it looked, especially because some of the hens seemed to make a full-time job of outsmarting her.

"If you dinnae get the eggs in time, they'll either be rotten or have a baby chick growing inside of them," Euphemia warned. "And we dinnae want baby chicks this time of year with winter right around the corner."

Sophie wiped a sleeve across her perspiring forehead. Several other hens fought over insects, their cackling reminding Sophie of the times Olivia and Nicholas bickered with each other. The two hadn't fought often because Olivia almost always gave in to Nicholas's whims. But they'd had their share of sibling disagreements.

It had been three days since she'd seen the children at church, and she wasn't sure she could wait another day to visit them. She'd asked Euphemia every morning if one of the boys could drive her over to the Ramseys'. But Euphemia had just shaken her head and said the boys had begun harvesting oats and couldn't be spared.

Sophie hadn't complained. It hadn't taken long to learn just how hard the Duff boys worked. They were up every morning by five o'clock to milk the cows. After milking and eating breakfast, they loaded drums of milk into the back of a wagon, and then Lyle or Gavin would take some to town to be sold to the locals before hauling the rest to the cheese plant.

While Lyle or Gavin was gone, the other boys fed and watered the cows. Euphemia explained that one dairy cow alone could guzzle a bathtub full of water a day. With thirty cows, the work of caring for them was never-ending. From what Sophie could tell, when the cows weren't needing to be milked or watered, their stalls required mucking or they had to be brought in from one pasture or another.

In addition to the cows, the men had to tend the fields. Euphemia had attempted to explain the types of crops that were growing, but Sophie couldn't keep track of anything except hay and oats. Apparently, the boys had just finished cutting and storing up hay in the barn for the coming winter to be used to feed the cows and horses. And now they were working on harvesting the oats.

She didn't envy the long hours the men spent out in the fields under the burning sun. But it hadn't taken her long to realize that the farmwife had just as much work, if not more.

Each morning, Euphemia used the cream drained off the milk and made pounds of butter in her churn. When finished, she divided the creamy mixture into crocks and stored them in basins of cold well water in the cellar, ready for taking to town.

Besides making butter, Euphemia was always baking or cooking something for the boys, who had ravenous appetites. Then there was the canning of the garden produce, the process of packing glass jars with vegetables and heating the jars in boiling water so the lids would somehow magically seal. Euphemia claimed the food in the jars would stay fresh through the winter, but Sophie wasn't sure she believed her.

In addition to the canning, they also dried herbs by hanging them in bunches, and they pickled various vegetables by soaking them in vinegar in heavy crocks. Euphemia said that they'd store the majority of the root vegetables—carrots, potatoes, onions, turnips—in the cool cellar where they could survive for most of the winter before going bad.

Sophie tugged at the thin leafy carrot top. The stubborn vegetable still wouldn't budge from the ground. Euphemia only needed half a dozen today for stew and said they'd wait to harvest the rest until just before the first killing frost. Sophie glanced to the long row of carrots that stretched out ahead of her and dreaded the day when she'd have to come back out and remove them all.

With the sun beating down on Sophie's hat, and the heat radiating off the soil into the air around her, a killer frost seemed like a fictional character in a book. Next time she told Olivia and Nicholas a bedtime story, she'd have to include an enemy by the name of Killer Frost. For long moments, Sophie let herself plot a new story with the new antagonist.

"There you are, lass," Euphemia called from beyond the fence that surrounded the garden.

Sophie snapped back to reality and closed her fingers around the leafy carrot top. She jerked it upward as if she'd been doing it all along instead of daydreaming.

"I'll be needing to ride to town for more laudanum for Stu," Euphemia said.

Sophie dropped her pretense of working and scrambled to her feet. "Can I come with you?"

"I wouldn't have it any other way, lass." Euphemia was in the process of fitting her bright yellow kerchief over her hair. "And while we're there, we'll ride over to the Ramseys' and see your wee brother and sister."

Sophie wanted to race to Euphemia and throw her arms around the dear woman. Instead, she clapped her hands together. "Thank you."

"We can't stay long, mind you," Euphemia added with a smile. "But I know how much you've been missing the bairns, and I have no doubt they've been missing you just as much."

They were on their way to town in no time, with Stuart's angry shouts ringing in their ears. "He's in pain," Euphemia said, as though that excused his atrocious behavior.

After stumbling into Stu's room on her first morning, Sophie had gone out of her way to avoid the young man. But even then, his curses and temper tantrums were difficult to miss.

"I don't understand how you do it," Sophie said as they jolted along the rutted dirt road with tall yellow weeds and thistles growing in the center undisturbed by wagon wheels and horse hooves.

"Do what, lass?"

"How you can be so nice to Stuart even though he's so rude to you." The words were bold, yet the question had been growing inside her every day as she witnessed Euphemia bustle to and from Stuart's room, caring for her crippled son without a word of complaint or anger.

To be sure, Euphemia's eyes had reflected sadness. And a time or two, she'd even seen Euphemia wipe away tears. But no matter how often Stuart pushed her away, Euphemia always went back.

"I think I would have left him to rot in his own filth," Sophie admitted.

"Dinnae mistake me for a saint, lass," Euphemia said with a mirthless chuckle. "I've lost my temper with the boy too many times to count."

Sophie shifted and searched for a comfortable position on the hard wooden bench that was bruising her backside with each bumpy roll of the wheels. "I can't believe you ever lost your temper. You're the sweetest lady I've ever met."

Euphemia laughed again, this time with pleasure. "Och, you're a sweet one yourself for saying so. But I wasn't always so patient or loving. I'm a bit stubborn, like my skillet when something's burned to the bottom. I haven't always let the good Lord chip away at my faults and clean me up the way He wanted to. But I'm learning to let Him do His work in His way. His scraping and cleaning might hurt for a bit, but then His character and beauty can shine through all my messes and mistakes."

Sophie fell silent. She'd made plenty of messes and mistakes in her own life. In fact, she wouldn't be in Illinois separated from Nicholas and Olivia if she hadn't gotten involved with Danny and the Bowery Boys. She'd known the gangs were trouble and that she should stay away. But she'd ignored the inner warnings, had set aside her good judgment, and had done what she wanted regardless.

Were the Roach Guards still searching for her and Anna? Would the law be looking for them as well, to testify against Danny and Mugs? She could only hope that the Roach Guards would decide tracing her and Anna was too much time and trouble. And if they'd decided to pursue them to Chicago, Sophie prayed they wouldn't learn she and Anna had stayed with the Children's Aid Society group and gone south.

Whatever the case, Sophie knew her skillet was much more charred and burned than Euphemia's had ever been. God might be able to clean up Euphemia and make her into a beautiful person, but her mistakes were too messy.

⁕

Sophie fingered the bolts of calico print and then moved to the ribbon. A dozen paces away, at the front counter of the general store, Euphemia chattered away with Mr. Wilson. Sophie had recognized him as one of the community members who'd sat in the back of the church as part of Reverend Poole's placing committee. He'd been polite to her the evening of the meeting and nice enough to her now.

Nevertheless, Sophie couldn't shake the discomfort at being in town. She'd thought it was just her, that she would need time to adjust to a new place. Today, however, she was distinctly aware of the unfriendly stares from other patrons that silently rebuked her to go back to where she'd come from, that her type wasn't wanted in Mayfield.

"Afternoon, Sheriff," Mr. Wilson said as the door squeaked open.

Sheriff? Sophie ducked behind a shelf that was piled high with an assortment of farming tools she couldn't begin to name. She feigned interest in a long-handled item that had a sharp, pointed blade at the bottom.

Why was the sheriff in the store?

Sophie's pulse sped with the need to find a back door and escape. She told herself she had no reason to run this time. Even though she'd been tempted to pilfer two apples from a bushel near a basket of squash, she'd resisted. She'd once again reminded herself that Nicolas and Olivia didn't need her to steal anything anymore. They could probably pick all the apples they wanted and were likely getting cakes and pies and cookies with rich yellow yolks just like she was.

"Lyle was sure talkin' up a storm about that there orphan gal you took in," said the new voice that Sophie assumed belonged to the sheriff. It was a testy voice and lacked the warmth and humor that Mr. Wilson's contained.

Sophie hunched lower, wanting to make herself invisible.

"Now, Sheriff, you know my Lyle, that you do," Euphemia said good-naturedly. "He's a good bairn, that one, but he's mighty anxious to find himself a wife."

A wife? Sophie bumped the farm tool, and it clanked against the others. She caught them all in time to keep them from crashing to the floor.

"He'd do well to stay away from those orphan gals," the sheriff said. "They're nothin' but trouble."

Mr. Wilson's and Euphemia's voices rose in protest, but the sheriff was louder and more forceful, drowning them out. "Most of those kids are crooks and criminals, and we don't need their like in our community."

At the sheriff's accusation, shame burned a trail through Sophie. He was right. She was a crook.

"Now, don't you go forgetting what happened here last summer with that orphan boy murdering one of his kind and dumping the body in Percy Pond and letting someone else take the blame for it."

"Och, Sheriff," Euphemia said, her voice ringing with consternation. "Crooks, criminals, or not, those bairns are in need of the love of the good Lord just as much or more than anyone else."

"Just don't come running to me," the sheriff continued, "if'n you find yourself in trouble on account of your orphan."

For several more minutes, the sheriff carried on a largely one-sided conversation with Euphemia and the store clerk. When he finally left, Sophie sagged against the tools. She didn't like that man and hoped she didn't have to face him anytime soon.

A short while later, when she and Euphemia rode out of Mayfield on the main road south of town in the direction of the Ramseys' place, Sophie sat quietly, unable to shake the ragged coat of shame she'd donned since hearing the sheriff's opinion of her and the other orphans.

"Dinnae you pay any attention to Sheriff Paddy," Euphemia said. She then reached over and patted Sophie's arm. "He takes his job seriously, and for that we're grateful. But sometimes he sees trouble when there is none."

Sophie nodded and tried to stuff her guilt and shame away

to the far corners of her mind where they belonged. "Did an orphan really kill someone last summer?"

Euphemia hesitated. Finally she sighed and nodded. "Not only did your Reinhold find the body, but the boy living with him at the Turners' was the culprit."

Sophie tried to digest Euphemia's comment, but somehow the only part of it she heard was *your Reinhold*. The idea of Reinhold being hers stirred the same longing she felt when she'd been with him, a longing she hadn't been able to squelch, which had been hovering in both her dreams and waking moments since she'd last seen him.

"Reinhold isn't mine, Euphemia," she said. "He loved my sister, not me."

"That may be. But in all the time I've known that boy, he's never shown interest in any other lass until he set his eyes upon you. Then he couldn't tear his eyes away."

"He's like a brother and only wanted to make sure I was doing all right."

"He wasn't looking at you like a brother. And you weren't looking at him like a sister."

Sophie shook her head in denial, but as Euphemia's eyebrows shot up, Sophie shrugged and then smiled. "Fine. I admit it. I've been admiring him. It's hard not to."

Euphemia smiled in return. "He's a good boy, that one. And he deserves a good woman to take care of him."

The warmth in Sophie's middle swirled at the thought of taking care of Reinhold the way Euphemia took care of her men. But just as soon as she pictured herself in Reinhold's kitchen, her guilt chased the image away. She wasn't a good woman. She didn't know the first thing about taking care of a man. And Reinhold certainly deserved someone better than her.

Besides, her first priority, as always, was with Olivia and Nicholas. She had to be ready to do anything for them.

A moment later, Euphemia slowed the wagon in front of a two-story home and adjacent barn a short distance off the road. At the sign above the barn, *Ramsey's Carpenter Workshop*, Sophie sat forward.

This was it, Olivia and Nicholas's new home.

She scanned the tidy front yard with several oak trees providing shade and sheltering a simple but sturdy home. It wasn't big but was well-kept with a fresh coat of white paint. A picket fence enclosed a big garden behind the house. The hedges and flowers and trees were all trimmed to perfection without a weed in sight. The privy behind the garden looked like it too had been recently painted. Beyond the cleared land stretched a tangle of shrubs and evergreens, likely the reason a carpenter and not a farmer had claimed the lot.

The barn wasn't as big as the Duffs', but the double doors were open and revealed a workshop and several pieces of furniture—a bedpost, a dresser, and a nightstand. Although Sophie wasn't an expert, she could see that Mr. Ramsey's workmanship was top quality.

As Euphemia pulled their wagon to a stop, Mr. Ramsey stepped out of the barn. He was wearing a leather apron and wiping his hands with a towel. Without his hat, his receding hairline made his forehead bigger and his moles stand out.

"Afternoon," Euphemia said pleasantly.

Mr. Ramsey didn't return the greeting but instead assessed them with open mistrust.

Sophie peered into the barn, hoping for a glimpse of Nicholas. Surely he'd be completely fascinated watching his new father at work, playing in the piles of saw shavings or whittling at his own little creations.

But a strange quietness greeted them. Not only was the barn silent, but the house and yard were too. Perhaps Sophie was just accustomed to all the noises on the Duff farm—the cackles of the chickens, the grunts of pigs and cows, the clattering of Euphemia in the kitchen, the boisterous laughter and teasing of the boys, even the constant whir of grasshoppers.

Whatever the case, the silence was unnatural, and it unnerved her.

"Since we were close by in town, I told Sophie I'd bring her over to see her wee sister and brother. She's been missing them terribly and—"

"They're not her brother and sister," Mr. Ramsey interrupted. "They said they're no relation at all to the girl."

Euphemia's mouth hung open for several seconds before she closed it.

Anxiety shot through Sophie. Should she contradict Mr. Ramsey and perpetuate the lie? She didn't want to disappoint Euphemia, didn't want the woman to dislike her. Already she'd given Euphemia enough hassle with all her deficits.

"Of course the wee bairns aren't Sophie's real brother and sister," Euphemia said before Sophie could decide how to respond. "Anyone can see so by looking at them. But they're family anyway. It's love that bonds people, not blood."

It was Sophie's turn to be surprised. Euphemia surely hadn't known she was lying all along, had she? Maybe Euphemia had guessed on Sunday after Sophie's interaction with the children.

"Don't matter." Mr. Ramsey crossed his arms as if he dared them to defy him. "They don't want to see the girl."

"Of course they want to see me." Sophie's backbone stiffened at the challenge, and she began climbing down. "Go tell them I'm here or I'll go find them myself."

Euphemia caught hold of her arm before she could hoist herself off the bench. "Och now, dinnae be rushing to fight, either one of you."

Sophie held herself motionless on the edge of the bench, wanting to run to the house and barge inside before Mr. Ramsey could stop her. But a new sense of loyalty to Euphemia kept her from acting on her impulse.

"I'm sure Mr. Ramsey won't mind letting the children come outside briefly, now, will you, Mr. Ramsey?" Euphemia's tone hinted he'd better allow it or she'd force her way into the house for Sophie.

Mr. Ramsey clamped his mouth closed before regarding them both with disdain. "They're not home right now."

Sophie glanced at the house, noting again the unusual silence and stillness. "Where are they?"

"Gone visiting neighbors with their new mother and sister." The lift of Mr. Ramsey's chin taunted Sophie to defy him.

She was tempted to spit in his face but held herself back for Euphemia's sake.

After a long moment of tense silence, Euphemia finally nodded. "Very well then. I guess we'll have to call again another day."

Mr. Ramsey didn't answer, but his expression told them they weren't welcome, that he didn't want them coming back.

Euphemia gathered the reins and prodded the team forward. As they turned onto the road leading back into town, Sophie's throat tightened with a disappointment so keen that she wanted to weep. She stared at the house, her arms aching to hold the children, her heart demanding to know they were happy and secure.

With a father like Mr. Ramsey, how could they be happy? Had she made a terrible mistake by allowing them to live with such a coldhearted man?

At a slight movement in the corner room of the second story, Sophie thought she saw a hand let go of the curtains and a face move out of sight. Her heartbeat sped. Was someone home after all?

Even as the wagon rolled away, Sophie craned her neck toward the window, praying for another glimpse. But if there had been someone, they didn't move again.

While she had no proof Mr. Ramsey was lying about the children not being home, the strong survival instincts she'd honed over the past two years told her that something wasn't right.

"Dinnae worry, lass," Euphemia said as she adjusted her rounded frame on the bench and settled in for the ride back to the farm. "Mr. Ramsey might be a wee bit difficult, but I believe he wants to do well by the children."

"He's not doing them well by refusing to let them see me." Sophie was unable to keep the bitterness from her voice. "I'm the only mother they've ever known, the only family they've ever had . . ." Sophie's voice cracked on the harsh edge of a sob. Embarrassed at the slip of emotion, she cleared her throat.

"There now, lass."

The gentleness in the woman's tone brought unexpected tears to Sophie's eyes. She had to blink rapidly to keep them at bay.

"It could be Mr. Ramsey thinks by cutting the children off from you in one swoop that he's giving them a fresh start. Maybe he believes this way they'll be quicker to forget about their past and quicker to accept a new family."

"I don't want them to forget about me," Sophie managed past her tight throat.

Euphemia's warm, strong fingers enveloped Sophie's. "You've loved them hard and well, lass. They'll never forget that. Never."

CHAPTER 11

The toe-tapping rhythm of the fiddle should have drawn Reinhold into the barn. Instead, it pushed him outside—to safety, to seclusion. To the solitary life he'd carved out for himself.

Perched on the paddock fence, he gripped the rough grain under his hands. From here, with his feet hooked under the next post, he had the perfect position in the waning light of evening to see the spread of the farm, including the barn. Horses and wagons were hitched here and there throughout the yard. The neighbors from all around couldn't resist the opportunity to congregate after a long week of harvesting. But he should have resisted.

"We have too much work to do," Reinhold had told Jakob after Fergus came over to inform them of the gathering at the Levelle farm.

Jakob hadn't said anything, had only gone back to shoveling out the pigpen, looking so wounded and forlorn that Reinhold had relented an hour later when he could no longer stand the silence.

Reinhold had told himself his change of mind had nothing to do with Fergus's declaration that Sophie would be at the party. But the truth was, he hadn't been able to put her out of

146

his mind all week. He'd thought of her when he was cutting oats in the fields, when he was mucking the stalls in the barn, when he was scraping his meager attempts at dinner from his plate, and even when he was lying on his bed in the dead of the night.

He could admit he'd liked being with her during dinner last weekend and talking with her afterward. He'd relished the walk to the pond and watching the sunset together. In the past, as the youngest of the Neumann sisters, he hadn't talked with her much except to tease her. But during their time together on Sunday, he'd shared more with her in one evening than he had with anyone else in an entire year.

Somehow his view of her had shifted and she'd become a friend. Not only could they converse easily, but she was a connection to his past, to his family, and to his people. After all, they'd both come from the old country as young children. They'd both had to adjust to a new language, a different way of life in America, and to a city overflowing with too many desperate people. They could relate to each other in a way he couldn't with anyone else.

Being with her had made Reinhold realize just how much he missed having someone who understood him. He missed having someone to talk to. And he missed having someone to listen to and care about. Elise had once been that person for him. And now, strangely, Sophie had stepped into his life, and in a single day had easily slipped into the empty place, almost as if she'd been made for it.

His gaze drifted again to the open barn doors and to the swirl of dancers and onlookers clapping their hands and stomping their feet in rhythm to the fiddle. He spied Sophie dancing with Lyle, whose bearded face was flushed as red as the stripes in his flannel shirt. Reinhold had never seen Lyle smile so broadly or his eyes sparkle with as much pleasure as they had since he'd asked Sophie to dance and she'd said yes.

Reinhold knew he should be happy for his friend. If this had been any other barn party and if Lyle had been dancing with any other girl, Reinhold might have chuckled at his friend's exuberance. But tonight, the longer Lyle danced with Sophie, the less Reinhold felt like laughing. In fact, the longer Lyle danced with her, the stronger Reinhold's urge grew to go inside and cut into his dance.

Sophie wouldn't ever get serious about a man like Lyle. Sure, she was smiling and laughing and having a good time, but she wasn't attracted to him—at least Reinhold didn't think so. And he didn't want Lyle to get his heart broken with a rejection from Sophie.

Besides, Lyle wasn't the right man for Sophie. Lyle was kind-hearted and hardworking and would make some woman a good husband. Just not Sophie. She was too spirited and independent and strong-tempered.

She hooked arms with Lyle and spun. The lanterns hanging from the barn rafters seemed to shine directly on her, highlighting her beauty. She was easily the prettiest woman there.

Which was why he needed to go in and break up the dance. He couldn't allow Lyle or any other local farm boy to try to win Sophie. She wasn't meant to live on a farm and endure the kind of hard work required of a farmwife. With Elise and Marianne now married to wealthy men, they would want more for Sophie than this kind of life. They'd seek out opportunities for her to move up in status just as they had. They'd be able to introduce her to eligible young men in their social circles who would provide everything Sophie wanted and make sure she never lacked for anything ever again.

Maybe farm life was good enough for him, Lyle, and Euphemia. But Sophie deserved so much more than this.

Reinhold unhooked his boots, released his hold on the post, and jumped down into the dry grass. In the shadows outside the barn, a young couple stood locked in an embrace. At his approach, they pulled away from each other.

Reinhold pretended not to see them. With how busy they all were, there were few opportunities for courting. He couldn't begrudge the young people their time together. Not that he needed time alone with Sophie. Even if he had taken pleasure from the walk with her last Sunday, his intentions had been friendly. Just as they were now.

He stepped into the spacious barn and hovered at the fringe, feeling suddenly awkward and nervous. Euphemia, Mrs. Levelle, and several other matrons stood behind a food table off to one side. It was filled with an assortment of baked goods that was likely one of the reasons Jakob had been so eager to attend the party. Even now the boy sat with his friends on hay bales in the loft, eating an enormous piece of cake.

Gavin and other younger men stood in a group eyeing the girls who weren't partnered up yet. They teased and dared one another, not yet ready for serious relationships but certainly beginning to lay their claims.

Barclay's boisterous voice resounded from the open entrance at the back of the barn, where he drank cider with neighboring farmers. They were laughing and teasing, having shaken off their worries, especially the constant pressure of hoping the weather and the passing of time would cooperate to allow a bountiful harvest.

Reinhold only wished he could shake off his worries as easily as the other men, even if just for one night. But the urgency of all he had left to do was a constant companion, reminding him that he needed to leave the party soon so he could fix the handle on a shovel and patch a hole in his work boot.

Reinhold scanned the dancers and easily found Sophie. Her blond hair stood out like a halo, tendrils framing her face, now flushed from dancing. Although she wore a plain blue dress that had no ribbons or frills, the simplicity only made her natural beauty more pronounced.

As the notes of the fiddle faded with the end of the song, Reinhold wound through the dancers.

Sophie spotted his approach before Lyle did, and a welcoming smile lit her face. "Jakob said you were here, but I didn't see you anywhere."

The thought that she'd been looking for him made his insides do a strange flip. "I wasn't planning on dancing, but I could tell Lyle needed a break. He keeps eyeing the cake table every time he passes it."

Lyle grinned but shook his head. "I'll get some later."

The fiddler began a new song, a slower tune. Lyle reached for Sophie, but Reinhold took hold of her arm.

"Are you sure you shouldn't get some dessert now?" Reinhold asked lightly, even though something inside began to coil tightly. For all his excuses, the truth was he didn't want to share Sophie with anyone else. She was his friend, and he wanted her all to himself. He wanted to spend time with her again, wanted to talk to her, see her smile and hear her laughter.

"With Jakob here eating everything," Reinhold continued, "you might miss out if you don't get something now."

Sophie's fingers slid around Reinhold's arm, and she sidled closer. The motion, although small, was apparently enough to let Lyle know whom she preferred. His grin slipped away, and he moved back a step.

Reinhold shifted Sophie around so they were facing each other, and he rested his hands on her hips. She lifted her hands to his shoulders and smiled up at him. "Let's see what kind of dancer you are."

"Not as good as Lyle," Reinhold said so that his friend could hear him and hopefully forgive him for interrupting his good time. "I'll probably bruise your toes by the time we're done with the dance."

As he began to move away with Sophie, he met Lyle's gaze over her head. Lyle's eyes were full of questions, and his brow furrowed. Reinhold silently pleaded with his friend to understand.

Lyle spun and shouldered his way through the other dancers, making a line for the door. Reinhold was tempted to run after him. But what could he say? How could he explain his actions when he didn't quite understand them himself?

Out of the corner of his eye, he saw Euphemia watching Lyle's exit and knew she'd witnessed their exchange. When she glanced back at Reinhold, he expected censure or even condemnation to cross the woman's face. Instead, she didn't seem the least surprised to see him with Sophie.

Sophie drew his attention back to her with her lively chatter and the excitement shining in her eyes. They danced through several songs, and the friendship he'd experienced with her last Sunday fell into place as easily as before.

When they took a break to eat, she told him about her futile trip to the Ramseys', her worry over Olivia and Nicholas, and how she missed her friend Anna, who'd gone to live with another family whose name Reinhold didn't recognize.

She asked him about his week and all the work he'd done. Although Sophie reminded him in many ways of Elise, she was also quite different. She listened better and was present in the conversation in a way Elise had never been. Elise had always held herself back. She'd been independent and stubborn and determined. Maybe she simply hadn't needed him the same way he had her.

Whatever the case, Sophie made him feel as if what he had to say was important. And he liked the way her eyes sparked with life and admiration when she looked up at him.

They danced again. And whenever anyone else dared to approach Sophie, Reinhold scared them away with a glare.

"You're not bad," Sophie said as the fiddler began to play a slow ballad.

He peered down at her face. Her delicate nose and slender cheeks and perfect lips were only inches away. "I'm not bad?"

"You're not a bad dancer."

"Believe it or not, I've been to a few parties over the past year." When he'd lived with the Duffs, Lyle dragged him to husking bees and other barn dances every chance he could.

She tilted her head slightly. "I'm surprised you're not married yet, especially with the way all the young ladies here look at you like you're their next piece of cake."

Were they? He doubted it. But did he detect a note of jealousy in Sophie's voice?

"I suppose that means you're still in love with Elise." She searched his face intently.

"Elise will always have a special place in my heart," he admitted. "But no, I don't love her anymore, at least not in the same way."

"Then you love Marianne?"

"No, we were never anything more than friends."

"There must be someone else now."

For a second he was tempted to boast about some of the women in the community who had pined after him, like Lucinda Turner. But what purpose would that serve? Was he hoping to elicit more of Sophie's jealousy?

"I'm not interested in anyone," he finally said.

Sophie's eyes seemed to fill with relief. But before he could read her face further, she leaned in closer and ducked her head. "Now that you have your own place, don't you want a wife to help you?"

Wisps of her hair brushed his cheek, the tendrils as soft and smooth as the silk under cornhusks. Her breath was near his chin and so warm. They danced close enough that he was suddenly too aware again of how grown up she was, how womanly. All it would take was a tiny amount of pressure with his hands at her hips to draw her closer so that her body would touch his, so that he could feel the soft sweet pressure of her.

Her lashes lifted, revealing a blue that had the power to pull him under like a strong riptide. From the widening of her pupils, he suspected that she could read his thoughts or perhaps see his desire, which was surely written all over his face.

"So do you?" she whispered, skimming her fingers along his shoulders.

"Do I what?" he whispered back.

"Do you want a wife?"

"Maybe someday." Even though he told himself he'd never get married, at the moment he couldn't fathom why he'd ever been so opposed to it. How had he made it this long without a woman in his life, and why had he ever thought he could get by without one? He longed for companionship, someone with whom he could share his life.

"Why not now?" Her thumbs brushed his neck, against his pulse, which had begun to throb with the desires he'd pushed aside for too long. He was a man, not a saint. And with this beautiful creature in his arms, he could think of nothing he wanted more than a wife.

As if sensing his desire, she slid her hands to the curls that hung over his collar. The touch nearly brought him to his knees. He basked in the sensation of her closeness, of her fingers in his hair, of the slow intimacy of the dance.

He wished they could be alone, especially as he became conscious of Euphemia's eyes upon them, of the other dancers sending glances their way, and of Lyle glaring at him from a distant corner, hurt darkening his countenance. He stopped dancing with such suddenness that Sophie bumped against him, only making him aware again of her body.

"What's the matter?" she asked with all innocence, having no idea the effect her merest touch had upon him.

He grasped her hand, wound through the dancers, and tugged her along after him toward the door. He didn't know where he was going or why. All he knew was that he was burning up, that he had to get out of the barn, but that he didn't want to leave her behind.

She didn't resist as he stalked out into the darkness that had fallen. She raced along after him, trusting him, even though she probably shouldn't since he didn't trust himself. He wanted to pull her into the shadows of the barn, like the couple he'd seen earlier. He wanted to slide his hands down her back, draw her as close as he could, and then take possession of her lips.

The temptation was so strong that he moved to the paddock fence post where he'd perched earlier in the evening and grabbed onto it. He was afraid of what he'd do if he didn't find a place for his hands.

The cool night air hit his overheated face, slapping him, waking him up, and reminding him of who Sophie was—the lost sister of two of his dearest friends. Maybe he could flirt with other women at barn dances and steal a kiss or two in the shadows, but he wouldn't—couldn't—do that with Sophie. It just wouldn't be right.

He had to get ahold of himself.

"What's wrong?" Sophie asked, standing beside him.

How could he explain the battle waging inside him? He was too embarrassed to admit his reaction to her, a reaction that went beyond the bounds of friendship, one that was taut with more longing than he'd felt in a long time—if ever.

He shouldn't be feeling this way about Sophie. Sweet, little Sophie. He shook his head. The problem was that he'd gone too long without real companionship. And now he was like a famished man, ready to devour a woman at the first hint of attraction. But he couldn't say that to Sophie, couldn't chance scaring her away with his inappropriate desires.

"Reinhold?" Her voice wavered with a hint of anxiety.

"I'm all right." What would Elise think of him at this moment if she'd been here to read his thoughts about Sophie? She'd probably slap his cheek and tell him to go home.

That was where he needed to go. He'd stayed at the party too long. "I should get going, Sophie."

"Did I do something to offend you?"

He glanced at her sideways. She was close enough that he could feel the warmth radiating from her arm. In the darkness, her eyes were wide and luminous. And too appealing.

His grip on the wood rail tightened. "No, you haven't done anything to offend me. It's not you, it's me. I need to keep my thoughts from wandering where they shouldn't go."

"Thoughts about what?"

Her breathy question set his heart racing again.

She touched his arm, then skimmed her fingers down its length.

He pushed away from the fence, away from Sophie, away from the temptation to treat her as anything other than his friend.

"Good night, Sophie." He turned away from her and strode toward his wagon without a glance back.

CHAPTER 12

Sophie belly-crawled toward the back door, trying not to think about the hordes of beetles and spiders and other bugs she was encountering. In the darkness of night, she couldn't see the insects. But she could hear them clicking and gnawing, their noises filling the night air. And she could feel them on her face, in her hair, and under her skirt.

She swatted at a buzzing near her ear and brushed at a tickle on her cheek. She stifled a shudder and then breathed out in relief as she made contact with a dry leaf instead of a spider.

"Just think about seeing Olivia and Nicholas," she whispered to herself for the hundredth time since she'd started across the Ramseys' backyard.

She'd crouched in the shrubs for hours until every light in every window had finally been extinguished. Even then, she'd waited for another hour—at least what felt like an hour—before she'd started making her way to the house, to Nicholas and Olivia, and to being together again.

While waiting, she'd tried not to think of Reinhold and the barn dance from last night. But the memories taunted her. She was giddy when he'd approached her and swept her away from

Lyle. The determination on his face had made her pulse thrum with a new melody, a tune that sang out that Reinhold had wanted to be with her. He hadn't once looked at the other girls, had hardly taken his eyes off her, so that by the time the evening was almost over she'd been floating like puffs of smoke.

Her Reinhold—as Euphemia had called him—had spent all evening with her. If she'd once admired him for his charm and the tender way he'd always regarded Elise, it couldn't compare to how much more she liked his attention upon herself instead. If she'd once thought him handsome, it couldn't compare to how much more striking he was to her now. If she'd ever thought she felt anything with Danny or any other boy, it couldn't begin to compare with the depth of feelings Reinhold stirred in her.

The truth was, her past admiration for Reinhold hadn't needed much nurturing to spring to life. But the other truth had become all too clear. Reinhold wasn't planning to change his view of her. He wanted to keep her at arm's length as Elise's little sister—even though she'd clearly seen the appreciation, even the longing, for her as a woman.

Maybe she'd been too bold with touching him in those last moments together. Maybe he thought she was a hussy. And maybe she was. She'd allowed Danny to be overly familiar with her, just one of her many faults.

She couldn't say exactly what was going on in Reinhold's head. But she'd realized at the moment he'd walked away from her that he was sending her a message. He had no intention of letting anything happen between them other than friendship.

"I don't care," she told herself every time she replayed his departure. "He has his life, and I have mine."

Right now, her life consisted of getting Olivia and Nicholas away from the Ramseys and then hopping the next train out of Mayfield. She couldn't let her growing feelings for Reinhold stop her from her first priority and what she needed to do tonight.

The pressure to see the children had been building since the failed attempt with Euphemia earlier in the week. After missing out on seeing them, Sophie had anticipated talking to both of the children that morning at church as she had the previous Sunday. But only Nicholas had come to the service with the family.

His little face had been pale, without any of the color she would have expected from someone playing for hours out in the sunshine and fresh air. The dark circles under his eyes were the telltale signs that he wasn't sleeping well.

All throughout the church service, Sophie had worried over Olivia and what had become of the girl. And her heart ached at the thought that Nicholas was having a difficult time adjusting to his new home. Maybe he wasn't able to sleep without her stories to lull him or without her soothing hands to calm him when he awoke at night. If only she could talk to Mrs. Ramsey and give her a few tips.

As soon as the reverend had spoken the last word of his lengthy benediction, Sophie had jumped up from her pew. However, the Ramseys were already gone. By the time Sophie made it out of the church, the Ramsey wagon was bumping down the dirt path out of town.

She hadn't cared who was watching or how improper it was for a young woman to run on the Sabbath. She'd chased after the wagon and called a greeting to Nicholas. He'd strained to stand up and talk to her, but the Ramseys' daughter, Rachel, had pulled him back down.

"Where's Olivia?" she shouted.

"She's just fine," Rachel had called with a cold stare she'd apparently perfected from her father's example. "She's a little sick this morning, that's all."

Sophie had been nearly inconsolable. That afternoon when the dinner dishes had been washed and put away, Euphemia asked Gavin to drive Sophie over to the Ramseys' to pay the children a visit.

Mr. Ramsey had met her at the front door. Once again he'd insisted no one was home and then asked her to leave. The longer she'd stood and argued with him, the more adamant he'd become, until at last he'd stepped outside, closed the door, and pointed his rifle at her.

Gavin pleaded with her to leave until she'd finally climbed up onto the wagon bench and allowed him to drive her away. All the while back to the farm, she'd silently fumed, and her resolve to return had only strengthened.

After she'd finished helping Euphemia with the evening chores, she managed to sneak off without anyone noticing. The walk had taken almost two hours since she'd had to stop and hide several times while wagons had passed by. But she'd made it and had hidden in the overgrowth at the back of the house, waiting patiently for everyone to finally go to bed.

This time she wasn't just visiting. She was getting Olivia and Nicholas and running far away. And she wouldn't let anyone stop her, especially Mr. Ramsey.

As she reached the back door, she raised herself slowly to her knees and swung the door partway open. She'd listened at the back of the house long enough to know that the door squeaked just before it reached its full capacity.

She crawled inside and gently closed the door behind her. Without rising, she crept on her hands and knees through an immaculate kitchen. Smoldering, banked coals in the stove gave her some light, enough to see that the Ramseys kept their home as spotless on the inside as the outside.

As she passed into the hallway and made her way to the bottom of the stairs, she hoped no one would be able to hear the soft thump of her knees against the hardwood floor. With every creaky step she ascended, she held her breath, waiting for

Mr. Ramsey to storm out of his room but praying desperately he wouldn't. She knew she had no right to pray. Even so, the whispered petitions tumbled out.

When she reached the top, she paused and studied the doors and tried to recall who was in each of the rooms. From her hiding spot in the brush, she'd attempted to gauge where Olivia and Nicholas's room was located. She guessed it was the one on the west end in the rear of the house. The lights there had gone out first. But she couldn't be entirely certain and knew that one wrong move would put her whole plan in jeopardy.

Hardly daring to breathe, Sophie crawled down the hallway. From what she could tell, there were three rooms—two smaller ones that took up the back of the upstairs, and a larger room at the front.

Her knees ached and her chest constricted, yet she didn't stop until she reached the final door. Once there, she pressed her ear against it and listened for any sounds that would confirm that the room belonged to Olivia and Nicholas.

Without hearing anything, Sophie turned the handle slowly. It opened easily, and she peeked through a narrow slit to see who was inside. The room was too dark to see anything, but at a familiar sniffling sound, Sophie opened the door further.

A sudden sharp intake told Sophie that Nicholas had heard the door open and that she needed to reassure him before he cried out in fear.

"It's me," she whispered. "Sophie."

He gasped, and his bed creaked with sudden movements.

"We have to be quiet." She scrambled in and closed the door behind her. Before she could catch a breath, Nicholas was already out of bed and had launched himself at her. He snaked his arms around her neck and buried his face against her chest.

She wrapped him in her arms and for the first time in two weeks felt whole again. She pressed her face into his hair and breathed him in. This was her baby, her boy. And she loved him more than her own life. That's why she'd been willing to give him up to a family, a small voice inside reminded her. That's why she'd let him go, so that he could finally have a stable home, loving parents, and a better life than she could give him.

If Nicholas reassured her that he and Olivia were happy, she'd walk away. She'd hug and kiss them both and then she'd leave. She'd do what she had to for them, even if she had to have her heart ripped out all over again.

But if they were even the slightest bit unhappy, she wouldn't hesitate to take them and run.

For long moments, she rocked back and forth, hugging Nicholas and letting his sweet embrace soothe the ache in her chest.

"I miss you." He pulled back and sniffled. "Why haven't you visited me yet? I've been waiting and waiting."

"I tried," she whispered, "but both times I came, Mr. Ramsey told me you weren't here."

Her answer seemed to satisfy him, and he relaxed against her, tilting his head back and allowing her to brush his hair from his face. His cheeks were damp from tears.

The realization that he'd been crying tore at her. She hugged him tighter. "Do you like your new home and your new mommy and daddy?"

His thin shoulders shrugged with a nonchalance that reminded Sophie of the way she responded all too often. Had Nicholas learned that from her?

"Tell me the truth, Nicholas," she said, smoothing his forehead and trying to see his expression in the darkness.

"My mommy is nice," he whispered. "But I miss you and Ollie."

"What do you mean you miss Ollie?" Sophie's heart stopped beating. "Where is she?"

"In the attic."

c✐✐つ

A pounding on the door jolted Reinhold upright from his bed. The wool blanket he'd covered himself with fell away. For a moment he stared around the bedroom shrouded in darkness and blinked, trying to orient himself and figure out what was going on.

More rapid thudding against the door prodded him to his feet and had him reaching for his trousers from the footboard where he'd discarded them.

In the room adjacent to his, he heard Jakob's bare feet slapping in hurried steps across the floor.

With one leg half in his trousers, Reinhold threw open his bedroom door and started down the steep narrow steps. "Who's there?" he called as he hopped into his other pant leg and jerked the trousers up.

"It's me, Lyle."

Halfway across the front room, Reinhold froze. He hadn't spoken with Lyle since the barn dance. He didn't go to church earlier today. He'd made up an excuse and declined Euphemia's invitation to supper, even though a sharp longing to talk to Sophie had swelled inside his chest until it had nearly hurt.

Reinhold glanced out the window at the moon and took note of its position in the sky. He guessed he'd been asleep for an hour or two. It was still early.

Why was Lyle here now, at this hour? Maybe he'd drunk one too many mugs of cider and decided to confront Reinhold about stealing Sophie away from him at the dance last night. In that case, Reinhold was in trouble. Lyle was a big man and a strong fighter. They'd wrestled for fun in the past, and Lyle hadn't been easy to pin down.

"What do you want?" Reinhold slipped his suspenders over his bare shoulders. Jakob's footsteps pattered on the floor behind him, and Reinhold held out a cautionary hand to motion the boy back.

"Mum sent me to fetch you." Lyle's sentence was muffled against the door.

"Why?" Reinhold approached slowly.

For a long moment, Lyle didn't respond, and Reinhold held himself back warily, suspecting he'd get a fist in his gut the moment he opened the door.

"Mum thinks you'll be able to help."

"Help with what?" Reinhold stood on the opposite side of the door, close enough to hear Lyle release a weary sigh.

"It's Sophie. Mum thinks she ran away."

Reinhold's blood chilled. He fumbled with the handle, suddenly not able to get the door open quickly enough. He practically tore it from its hinges as he swung it wide.

The moment Reinhold stood in front of Lyle, the big man roped his arm around Reinhold's neck and put him in a headlock so tight it nearly strangled him. "Where is she?" Lyle yelled, yanking at Reinhold. "Hand her over now."

The frustration coursing through Lyle's arms radiated into Reinhold. "I don't have her," he managed to choke out.

"You're lying!" Lyle jerked upward, cutting off Reinhold's breath.

A low flame of anger flickered to life in Reinhold's gut. His hands fisted, and his muscles twitched with the need to wrap his arms around Lyle's belly and take him down and pummel him. But Reinhold closed his eyes and forced himself not to move. If he gave life to the fire, if he lashed out, he was afraid he wouldn't be able to stop, the same way he hadn't been able to stop when he'd nearly killed Higgins last summer.

"He's not lying." Jakob's wavering voice rang out. "Sophie isn't here. She's never been here. Now let him go."

Lyle's grip loosened, but he didn't release Reinhold. "Where is she?"

The accusation in Lyle's voice sparked inside Reinhold, setting fire to the tinder and rapidly fanning the anger into hot flames. "Let me go!"

"Not until you tell me where she is."

"We don't know," Jakob said, his eyes wide and wild upon Reinhold, as though he realized Reinhold was rapidly losing control and would combust if he didn't do something to stop it.

His brother's worry acted as a mirror, revealing how dark and ugly Reinhold was on the inside. Seeing himself as he really was only added loathing to the growing inferno, until Reinhold couldn't keep it inside.

With a roar, he plowed forward, pushing Lyle until he tripped and fell in the grassy yard. Lyle landed on his back with such force that he released Reinhold.

Reinhold jumped on top of Lyle, pinned him to the ground with his knees, and brought his fist down hard into Lyle's stomach.

Lyle grunted, then bucked, attempting to dislodge Reinhold.

But Reinhold dug his knees in harder. His anger consumed all his thoughts, driving him to lash out and hurt someone.

"No!" Jakob said from behind. Before Reinhold could bring his fist down again, Jakob grabbed hold of his arm.

Reinhold swiveled and brought his other fist up, making contact with Jakob's chin. Jakob staggered backward and lost his grip upon Reinhold. He released a startled cry of pain and cradled his chin. Even in the dark, Reinhold could see the blood oozing from the boy's bottom lip.

The sight of it doused Reinhold's anger as rapidly as a bucket of water dumped upon a hearth fire. He rolled off Lyle and stood. His chest was tight and heaved with every breath. He couldn't make himself look at either Lyle or Jakob. He didn't want to see the reflection of himself, a monster, in their fearful eyes.

"We need to find Sophie," Jakob said, his voice wavering again.

The mention of Sophie's name was another bucket of water, this one ice cold against his face. His worst fear had come true. Sophie had run away.

"When did you last see her?" he asked Lyle as his mind spun with a thousand thoughts of where she could have gone and why.

"She must have left after supper tonight." Lyle slowly picked himself up from the ground. "That's the last time any of us saw her."

Reinhold's anxiety mounted with each passing second until it felt like it would strangle him. Was he the cause? She'd reached out to him at the dance, and he'd turned his back on her and walked away. It didn't matter that he'd done it to protect her from himself, from the longing he had for her.

Lyle rubbed his hands across his belly in the spot where Reinhold had hit him.

Reinhold looked away, but guilt slugged him in the chest anyway. "Did anything happen that would have made her want to leave?"

"She went to see her little brother and sister earlier in the day," Lyle replied, "but they weren't home."

Reinhold replayed the conversation he'd had with her about the visit earlier in the week, when Mr. Ramsey had insisted Olivia and Nicholas weren't there. It was too coincidental for them to be gone both times Sophie called. Perhaps Sophie had recognized that as well.

What if she'd gone back to the Ramseys'? And what if this time she intended to find the children and wouldn't take no for an answer? Even worse, what if Sophie managed to get the children and run away? She'd done it once in New York City under dire circumstances. What was there to prevent her from doing it again? What if she'd already found them and left? How would he be able to find them then?

He started toward the barn at a jog. "I think I know where she may have gone."

"Where?" Lyle asked.

Reinhold didn't stop to answer. Instead, he called instructions over his shoulder to his friend. "Go into town and stand vigil at the train station."

A moment later, as Reinhold hitched Daisy to the wagon, the sound of fading horse hooves told him that Lyle had done as he'd asked.

"I want to ride with you," Jakob said from the barn door where he'd positioned himself a safe distance away after handing Reinhold the shirt he'd requested.

"No." Reinhold buckled the final piece of the harness. "Someone has to be home just in case she decides to come here."

Jakob didn't protest but watched silently as Reinhold seated himself. Reinhold wanted to apologize, wanted to tell the boy he was sorry not just for hitting him but also for being such a lousy brother. But the words stuck in his throat.

As he started forward, he was surprised when Jakob spoke again. "If anyone can find her, you can."

Reinhold met his brother's gaze. By the light of the lantern that Jakob held high to illuminate Reinhold's path, he could see confidence in the boy's eyes, a confidence that reached deep into Reinhold's soul. His brother was offering him grace and love in spite of everything. He didn't understand why Jakob still cared, why he didn't hate him.

He nodded at the boy and hoped his eyes conveyed his appreciation and his wish that he could be different, that he could be a better man, that he could be anyone but his father.

At the sight of the boy's puffy lip still oozing blood, Reinhold swallowed hard against the despair that threatened to undo him. He promised himself he would work harder at becoming the kind of man Jakob could truly admire.

CHAPTER 13

Sophie strained for the latch, stretching as far as she could on her tiptoes. But the loop was out of reach. The pile of pillows and blankets from Nicholas's bed wasn't tall enough to boost her.

"We need something more," she whispered, staring at the attic trapdoor in the ceiling of the dark hallway, lit only by the faint moonlight in Nicholas's room.

Nicholas followed her stare. "Daddy uses a ladder."

Daddy. Sophie bristled at Nicholas's endearment for Mr. Ramsey. The man was a jailer, not a daddy. How dare he lock Olivia in the attic? What kind of man would do that to a little girl?

She wanted to call up to Olivia, to reassure her that help was on the way, but she couldn't chance making any more noise.

She returned to Nicholas's room, searching for anything she could use to raise herself higher. She couldn't waste time looking for Mr. Ramsey's ladder. She had to find something else. Here. Now.

"If I'm a bad boy, Daddy said he'd put me in the attic too," Nicholas whispered next to her, slipping his little fingers into her hand. "I don't wanna be stuck there. It's too scary."

The fear in his voice slashed at Sophie's heart. "I won't let him put you in the attic. Just as soon as I get Olivia down, we're leaving."

Sophie could sense his hesitancy. He'd said he liked his new mommy, that she sang songs and gave him warm bread. The woman had seemed kind when Sophie was with her, so she could understand why Nicholas might not want to leave her.

But why had Mrs. Ramsey allowed her husband to lock a child of only five years old in the attic? Especially for days? Even if the woman was opposed to such treatment, surely she could have done more to stand up for Olivia.

Sophie had tried to piece together all that had happened. But Nicholas didn't understand what Olivia had done to deserve the punishment, other than that she'd been a bad girl.

Olivia could be strong-willed at times, even quarrelsome. But no matter how the little girl had transgressed, she surely didn't deserve to stay in a cramped, windowless attic.

Sophie scanned the bedroom again, and her sights landed upon the small pedestal table next to the bed. "We'll use this little table." She crossed the room to retrieve it. "You hold the table steady while I stand on top."

He followed her, but then stopped and shook his head. "Daddy doesn't let me touch anything. He doesn't want me to make a mess."

Was that why the house and yard were so neat and flawless? Because Mr. Ramsey demanded perfection? "You can touch this."

"But he'll take away my dinner—"

"I won't let him."

Nicholas hung back. His fear fed Sophie's dislike and mistrust of Mr. Ramsey. It also unleashed remorse. She shouldn't have allowed Nicholas and Olivia to come here, should have heeded her reservations instead of ignoring them.

This was all her fault. And now she needed to set things right.

Silently and without any further discussion, she lifted the end table away from Nicholas's bed. Round like a stool, it was heavier than she'd anticipated. She managed to carry it several feet before having to place it down again. At the soft thud against the floor, she cringed and then held her breath, praying the ensuing silence and stillness in the house meant everyone else remained asleep.

She picked it up again, but before she could move, a voice cut through the darkness. "What do you think you're doing in here?"

Sophie gasped and dropped the furniture with a resounding *bang*.

Mr. Ramsey stood in the bedroom doorway, holding a lantern in one hand and his rifle in the other. The low flicker of the flame cast a jaundiced glow over the man's stark features and unsmiling, tightly drawn mouth.

He took a step into the room, grabbed Nicholas by the arm, and hauled the boy behind him. Nicholas cried out. The half sob, half whimper contained more fear than pain. Sophie knew Nicholas's cries enough to distinguish what they meant and to realize he was terrified of Mr. Ramsey.

She lunged after her boy, fully intending to pick him up and run from the house if that was what it would take to get him away from Mr. Ramsey. But before she could reach Nicholas, the cold barrel of the gun blocked her.

"Get out of my house right now." The man's voice was as steely as the long length of the rifle.

Sophie wouldn't let the man intimidate her. After all, she'd faced worse on the streets of New York City. "I'm not going without Nicholas and Olivia. Hand them both over. Then I'll be on my way."

He shoved Nicholas into the hallway and then spoke in an even tone over his shoulder to Mrs. Ramsey, who was hovering nearby and visibly trembling. "Take the boy into the bedroom and lock the door behind you."

"No!" Sophie shouted and tried to slip underneath the gun. But Mr. Ramsey brought the butt end down against her shoulder with a force that tore a scream from her throat and drove her to her knees. Even as she fought against the burning pain, she scrambled back to her feet.

Nicholas was openly sobbing now, and Mrs. Ramsey was murmuring to him even as she hurried to obey her husband and drag the boy away. Above, Olivia in the attic had begun to pound against the trapdoor and call Sophie's name.

"Olivia!" Sophie yelled in response. "Olivia! I'm here to get you!"

"Get out of my house before I drag you out!" Mr. Ramsey barked. The butt of the gun knocked against her again, this time in the middle of her back. It wasn't as hard or painful as the first hit, but it sent Sophie down to her knees once more.

"I won't leave without the children!"

"Oh, yes you will." Mr. Ramsey grabbed hold of her arm and began to slide her toward the steps as if she weighed no more than one of the scarecrows in the garden behind the house.

With Olivia's cries from overhead and Nicholas's sobs from behind the closed bedroom door, Sophie's resolve hardened, and she tried to grab on to something. Even as she fought against Mr. Ramsey, he picked her up, flung her over his shoulder, and started down the stairs.

"You're unfit to have them!" She kicked and hit. In spite of her flailing and yelling, he didn't stop until he reached the front door, opened it, and stepped onto the front porch. He dumped her so that she fell on her backside in the grass.

The impact jarred her as pain shot up her back. She wheezed for a moment and tried to draw in air as well as come up with a new plan. All she could think to do was fight back. She scrambled to her knees and pushed herself to her feet. Then she charged toward Mr. Ramsey.

He raised the barrel of his gun and aimed it at her.

"Sophie!"

At the shout of her name, Sophie halted. She spun to see a horse and wagon careening down the road in front of the Ramseys'.

"Sophie, wait!" the voice called again, this time more frantic. Reinhold's voice. Moonlight outlined his sturdy shoulders hunched over the reins.

She wanted to weep with relief at the sight of him. "Reinhold!" she cried and ran toward him.

He leaped down before the wagon came to a complete stop and strode toward her. She flung herself at him, and he caught her easily up into his arms and against his chest, crushing her in a hug so fierce she almost couldn't breathe.

For just an instant, she wanted to bask in the embrace and try to understand the meaning of his strong emotions. But too much was at risk, and they couldn't spare a single second. Not when she needed his help to rescue Olivia and Nicholas.

She pulled back enough that she could see his face, then tried to explain what had happened and how Mr. Ramsey was forcing her to leave without Nicholas and Olivia. "I can't go without them," she said, squeezing Reinhold's arms for emphasis. "Help me get them, Reinhold. Please."

"She's not taking those children." Mr. Ramsey spoke quietly from where he still stood on the porch, his gun leveled on them. "The Children's Aid Society gave them into our care, and we take our commitment seriously."

"They don't want to live with you anymore," Sophie said.

"Of course they're going to have a difficult time adjusting if their former caregiver insists on stopping by every few days."

"They're having a difficult time because you're cruel!" Sophie broke away from Reinhold, intending to march up to Mr. Ramsey and spit in his face.

Before she could make it more than two steps, Reinhold stopped her with an iron grip on her arm. "Wait, Sophie."

She was about to jerk away from him, but at the *click* of the rifle, Reinhold spun so that he stood between her and Mr. Ramsey. "Everyone needs to calm down," he said, holding her firmly in place.

"If you don't take her and get off my property, I'll shoot," Mr. Ramsey said, his tone low and hard.

"Give me my children!" Sophie shouted.

"They're mine now, not yours."

"They'll never be yours! Once Reverend Poole hears how you've locked Olivia in the attic, he'll take them away."

"And once I ride into town tomorrow and tell the sheriff you broke into my house and tried to kidnap my children, he'll take you away and send you right back to New York City to prison."

Sophie hadn't considered the implications of her actions, and she scrambled to come up with a response, something that could save both her and the children. But a strange cold hand of panic clamped around her throat and began to squeeze.

"You don't need to go to the sheriff," Reinhold interjected. "There's been a misunderstanding here, that's all."

Sophie couldn't speak past the panic's tight hold. What if Mr. Ramsey followed through on his threat and went to the sheriff tomorrow? What if the lawman arrested her and decided to send her back to New York City and she ended up on Randall's Island? What would become of Olivia and Nicholas then?

"Sophie's been missing the children," Reinhold explained. "All she wanted to do was see them. No one will fault her for attempting to do that."

"She needs to sever her bond with the children. They're ours now."

"I'm sure everyone will agree that visits now and then will help the transition go more smoothly." Although Reinhold's words were calm, they also contained the hint of a threat.

Sophie sagged against his back and closed her eyes. On her own, she was nothing, an orphan girl without any rights or power. With just her word against Mr. Ramsey's, he would win. But with Reinhold stepping in and standing up for her, she might still have a chance.

As if coming to the same conclusion, Mr. Ramsey said, "Take that girl away and don't let me see her here again. Next time I won't hesitate to call on the sheriff."

Numbly, Sophie let Reinhold guide her to the wagon and assist her up onto the seat. She held herself straight with her chin high as they rode away. But with each grassy acre of distance that came between her and the children, her chest and throat tightened with agony.

She'd not only failed to rescue them, she'd failed to do anything to make their lives better. In fact, her visit would probably only multiply their suffering.

With the edge of town coming into view, Reinhold tugged the reins and brought the wagon to a stop. He shifted on the bench to look at her. "Did he hurt you?"

"No." Sophie rolled her shoulder where he'd hit her with the gun. It would be bruised and sore, but the pain there couldn't compare to what she felt inside.

The moon was high overhead, casting ample light upon her disheveled hair and clothing. And likely showing every trace of her despair. She stared straight ahead, not seeing anything but Nicholas's face when Mrs. Ramsey had hauled him into her bedroom.

"Sophie." Reinhold's voice was tender and filled with such compassion that she couldn't keep her tears at bay. Several slid out and trickled down her cheeks.

"Ah, Soph." He stretched out a hand and brushed at the tears on her cheek before circling her shoulders. "Come here."

She didn't resist as he tugged her against his chest. His arms curled around her and pulled her close. Tears welled up, needing release, but she fought them back. She'd had to bear the burden of caring for Nicholas and Olivia alone for so long that she didn't know how to let someone share the load with her. Even so, her tears wet Reinhold's shirt, and she let herself sink into him, into his comfort, into his kindness.

After a little while she found herself telling him everything that had happened, starting with her failed afternoon visit to the Ramseys', her decision to run away, and then all that had happened once she'd sneaked inside the house.

He held her as she talked, quietly stroking her hair.

"I need to get them out of there, Reinhold," she whispered against his chest, settling in deeper, noticing the comfortable way his chin rested on top of her head. She closed her eyes at the gentleness of his fingers brushing against her hair and ear.

"Running away again isn't the answer," he finally said.

"I need to get away from here, and I'm taking the children with me." Except that tonight she'd learned she wasn't capable of getting the children away from the Ramseys on her own. She'd need assistance.

She pushed back from his chest so that she was looking into his eyes. "Maybe you can help me—"

"No, Sophie. I'm not helping you run away." He studied her face in the moonlight. "The whole ride over to the Ramsey place, I kept praying I wasn't too late to stop you. I don't know what I would have done if you'd already left . . ."

His voice contained a note of desperation that reached out to touch her lonely heart, the part of her that had felt unwanted for so long.

"You've been gone for so long, and I can't stand the thought of you being out there again without a home, without food, without anyone to take care of you." He lifted his hand to move a strand of loose hair behind her ear.

She was tempted to lean into his hand. She didn't want to tell him that she would have missed him. That was too embarrassing to admit. Aside from not wanting to face the difficulties of living on the street again, she also wasn't sure she was ready to leave the comfort and security that she'd found with the Duffs. She liked having her own room, a real bed to sleep in, and all the food she could eat. She liked Euphemia's cheerful company. She even liked having honest work to earn her keep.

But she would give it all up to make sure Olivia and Nicholas were safe and happy.

"I can't leave them with the Ramseys. I just can't."

He sighed. "I know."

"Then what should I do?"

He was quiet, studying her face as though he might find the answer there somewhere. "Maybe we can send a telegram to the Pooles and inform them of how the Ramseys are treating the children."

Sophie nodded, feeling the first plume of hopefulness all day. "Do you think they'll make the Ramseys give the children back?"

"It's possible. Especially if we have another place where the children can go."

"Where?" she asked almost breathlessly. "Is there another place? Would Euphemia let the children live with me?"

Her room was certainly big enough. The children could sleep on the beds, and she'd take the floor. There was enough food. She'd oversee them. Euphemia wouldn't have to do anything.

Reinhold shook his head. "She'd do it temporarily. She's got a kind heart like that, but she couldn't do it long term. Not with Stuart."

The rising hope inside Sophie plummeted. Reinhold was right. Stuart was not only demanding of Euphemia's time and attention, but he was also sensitive and sickly. Even though Olivia and Nicholas were mostly well-behaved children, they would bring more noise and commotion to the home, which would make things worse with Stuart.

"Isn't there anyone else?" she asked, unable to keep frustration from coloring her voice. She sifted through all the people she'd met since coming to Mayfield. Certainly there was at least one family willing to take in two additional children. A neighbor. Someone who lived close by. Then she could offer to help care for the children.

"You," she said, sitting up straight. "They could live with you."

Reinhold shook his head again, and his expression remained grim. "No, Sophie. I can't take care of Jakob decently. There's no way I could ever handle two infants—"

"I'll come over every day to help." A burst of excitement rippled through her. "I'm sure Euphemia will let me once I'm done with chores."

Reinhold's handsome lips fell into a flat line. "It wouldn't work. I don't have much yet. I'm barely getting by as it is. That's why I haven't brought Silke and Verina out here yet."

"I'll help with them too. This is the perfect solution, Reinhold. Don't you see?"

"No. Believe me, I'm not the solution."

"But you are," she insisted. "Euphemia told me you'd thought about getting a couple of orphans—"

"I didn't consider it." His voice was laced with exasperation. "And even if I had, I would have picked out older boys, not two young children who need a lot more attention than I could ever give."

"You always were the one to take care of your brothers and

sisters, even when your mother was alive. And you helped take care of me and Marianne and Elise."

Reinhold's back was stiff, and he stared straight ahead.

"Please, Reinhold," she pleaded. She had to make him understand what a brilliant plan this was. She reached for his hands and grasped them between hers. "I'm sure Jakob would help too."

The set of his jaw was stubborn, unyielding. "As an unmarried man, Reverend Poole might have allowed me to take older boys. But he won't consider giving me two little children. If he takes them from the Ramseys, he'll search for a proper home with both a mother and a father."

Sophie released a sigh as she realized he was right. Reverend Poole and the Children's Aid Society didn't have too many stipulations on families who took in children, yet they certainly wouldn't look favorably on placing two children as young as Olivia and Nicholas with a single farmer. They'd want him to be married first.

Married.

What if Reinhold married her?

For a moment, the idea was so ludicrous, so impossible, so impulsive she almost laughed aloud. But the thought of being in a position where she could adopt Olivia and Nicholas and finally make them hers sent shivers over her skin.

If she was married, she'd never have to worry about losing them again. No one would be able to take them away from her. They would be her children and she'd be their mama. Forever.

"I'm sorry, Sophie," Reinhold said quietly. "I wish there was another way—"

"There is." Then she spoke the words before her mind could find all the excuses why she shouldn't. "Marry me."

CHAPTER 14

Reinhold examined Sophie, grateful for the bright moon that shone directly overhead, offering enough light to see every line in her pretty face and every flicker in her expressive eyes. Even with the earnestness mingled with desperation, he still wasn't sure he'd heard her right.

Had she just asked him to marry her?

Her grip on his hands tightened. "If we're married, then Reverend Poole won't be able to say no to letting Olivia and Nicholas come live with us."

Yes, she had suggested marriage.

He blew out a tight breath. This conversation with her was going from bad to worse. Her suggestion that he take care of the children had been bad enough. But now she wanted to add herself to the equation and live with him too?

"Now hold on, Sophie." He attempted to keep his mounting frustration out of his voice. "We can't get married. That's taking this too far."

"I know it's a lot to ask of you," she said hurriedly. "To take care of me and Olivia and Nicholas. But I promise I won't be a bother. And I promise I'll do all the work of taking care of them."

"I don't doubt your ability to care for them—"

"I'll help you with your farm. I've learned a lot from Euphemia already, and I can do more than you think."

"I'm sure you can, but that's—"

"If we're married, then we can send for Silke and Verina. I'll be there to take care of them too."

He released another exasperated breath. He needed to do something about Silke and Verina now that Elise had given birth to her baby. But marrying Sophie wasn't the answer.

In fact, Elise and Marianne would be mad enough with him when they discovered he'd found Sophie and hadn't informed them. But if he married their little sister without consulting them, they'd be furious.

"I won't use you, Sophie." He'd allowed himself to get caught up into an engagement with Marianne last summer because of wanting to provide for Silke and Verina. Thankfully he'd realized how selfish he was before it was too late. He wasn't planning to make the same mistake now with Sophie.

"Of course you won't use me." She looked at him much too earnestly. "Marriage will be a way we can help each other. You'll be a father to Olivia and Nicholas, and I'll be a mother to Silke and Verina."

"No. This is crazy. I can't do it." He extricated his hands from hers, took off his hat, and shoved his fingers through his hair. He wanted to tell her he had no intention of getting married, of subjecting a woman to his moods and anger. Yet the needs he'd experienced at the barn dance were still too keen, and she'd likely see right through his excuses.

"Then there's someone else after all, isn't there? Someone you're in love with, and you just don't want to tell me."

"I meant what I said. There isn't anyone. Still, that doesn't mean you should be with me. You'll find someone better and richer, like your sisters did." He hadn't been good enough for either Elise or Marianne. Maybe they hadn't said so in words, but their actions had shown him well enough.

"Don't talk to me about my sisters," she said, her voice growing hard. "I don't ever plan to be like them."

He doubted Elise and Marianne would agree with her. Once they discovered Sophie was in Mayfield, they'd whisk her home and give her a life of advantage and comfort with everything she could ever want.

They wouldn't want her stuck with a poor farmer like him. How could he explain all that to Sophie? "Listen, Sophie," he started. "We can't be more than friends—"

"Then we don't have to share a bedroom," she said. Even in the darkness, he could sense the flush that rose into her cheeks at her bold declaration.

He squirmed and tried to think of how to respond.

Before he could find the right words, she continued, "We'll have a business partnership. I'll be like hired help. You can pay me by letting Olivia and Nicholas live with us. And giving us your name so I don't have to leave them ever again."

A business partnership? Could it work? He clearly needed the help around the farm. Even if Sophie didn't toil in the fields with him and Jakob, she'd be able to tend the garden, the chickens and the pigs, and all the other chores such as laundering and patching clothes, cooking meals, and keeping the place tidy.

"No," he said more adamantly. Why was he even considering her proposal? He wouldn't do this to her. He wouldn't trap her into this kind of life, not when so much more was available to her. "I won't marry you, Sophie. We have to find a different option."

"There are no other options," she cried. "You'll leave me

no choice but to go back to the Ramseys and try to sneak the children out again."

"You can't." His heartbeat had barely begun to slow down from earlier when he'd glimpsed David Ramsey on his front porch, his rifle barrel glinting in the moonlight, pointed directly at Sophie.

"You can't stop me." With a defiant shake of her head, she slid to the edge of the bench. Before he could grab on to her, she jumped down.

The fear from earlier roared back into his blood. He'd almost lost her. He loathed to think what would have happened if she'd succeeded in getting the children away from the Ramseys, then snuck aboard the train and ridden away before he'd known she was gone.

The truth was, she'd keep running and hiding for as long as she had to in order to stay with Olivia and Nicholas. He wouldn't be able to do anything to stop her from leaving. He was helpless to prevent it. Helpless to keep her here. Helpless to keep her safe.

Unless . . .

He watched her walk away, her footsteps determined. There was only one way to ensure she didn't run away again. "Sophie, stop." He hopped off the wagon and chased after her. She hadn't gone far, and at the sound of his voice, thankfully she halted. From behind, he captured her hand and wound his fingers through hers. Then he slowly rotated her so that she was facing him. "All right," he said softly.

"All right what?" she responded just as softly, a cautious note of hope in her voice.

"Let's get married."

She tightened her fingers against his and then lifted his hand to her lips and pressed a kiss there. The warm contours of her full lips near his knuckles flooded his middle with heat.

"You won't regret this," she whispered, lowering their hands but still hanging on to him tightly.

It was too late. He already did.

⌾⌾⌾

The moment Reinhold pulled the wagon onto the path that led to the Duffs', Sophie panicked. "Why can't I go home with you? Why do I need to go back?"

The road wound past the smokehouse and a storage shed, both of which seemed to grow faces in the dark and glare at her with accusation.

She didn't want to face Euphemia. Sophie doubted Euphemia would be angry with her for running away. During her short stay, she'd learned the dear woman was too kind and patient to get angry. But she was bound to be frustrated with Sophie for all the trouble she'd caused everyone tonight. And Sophie didn't want to experience that. It was easier to avoid people than to bear the brunt of their disappointment and disapproval.

"No, Sophie," Reinhold said in an exasperated tone, one that made her feel as though he viewed her more as a child than a woman. "You can't come live with me until after we're married."

"Why does it matter?"

"Because people will talk and assume the worst. And I don't want to harm your reputation in this community."

His words halted her protest. She'd likely ruin his reputation too, and she didn't want to do that.

"I think we should be married as soon as possible," she said. "Then when you send the telegram to Reverend Poole about Olivia and Nicholas, you can request that they come to live with us."

"I'll ride into town tomorrow and make arrangements with the reverend."

"And send the telegram?"

"Yes, and send the telegram."

She released a breath, trying to let go the anxiety over the children that had wormed inside her chest and burrowed there. But even with the new plan taking shape, she couldn't expel her worry completely.

She chanced a peek at Reinhold next to her on the bench. He'd been silent most of the way home. They'd stopped to retrieve her bag where she stowed it just outside of town. And they'd also ridden to the train depot to where apparently Lyle had been searching for her. Through it all, Reinhold's mood had steadily darkened.

"I'm sorry, Reinhold. I know this isn't what you wanted."

When he didn't contradict her, his silence pricked her heart. Even if this was an impulsive plan, now that it was set in motion, she could admit she liked the idea of being married to Reinhold. She certainly wouldn't protest becoming Reinhold Weiss's wife, even if under dire circumstances.

She just wished he wanted it too, even if only a little. But apparently he was doing this only for her and the children. He was noble enough that he'd do anything for her, like a medieval knight riding in to save the damsel in distress.

However, she sensed the slightest angst would make him change his mind. That was another reason she didn't want to encounter Euphemia. She had the feeling Euphemia wouldn't approve of a marriage of convenience for the sake of getting the children. And Sophie didn't want to give Euphemia the chance to talk Reinhold out of the marriage.

"Thank you for being so sweet and willing to do this for me and the children. I promise I'll do everything I can to make you happy."

"You don't have to make me happy, Sophie," he replied. "This isn't about me."

"I know. But I still want to try." Maybe she could eventually be a good enough wife that he would forgive her for making him marry her.

As the wagon rumbled closer to the house, the front door opened and light cascaded out over the front lawn, revealing Euphemia and Barclay and the boys. They were awake. And waiting for her. Lyle perched on the porch rail, having ridden back from town well ahead of her and Reinhold with the news that she'd been found.

She reached for Reinhold's arm and didn't realize she was trembling until her fingers made contact with him. "I can't do this, Reinhold," she said. "They'll despise me now."

"They'll be relieved to see you're safe."

"But Euphemia. She's been counting on my help. Once we're married, she'll be alone again."

"You'll come back and help her whenever she needs it."

"Yes, you're right." She tried to take in a deep breath, but as the wagon came to a stop in front of the house, panic swelled again, especially as Euphemia hurried down the porch steps.

Reinhold jumped down and rounded the wagon.

"Thank the Lord, thank the Lord," Euphemia called out.

Sophie gripped the bench and let shame lash her. She'd run away from this woman without a good-bye or a thank-you. After all Euphemia had done for her, for all she'd given her, for the love she'd freely bestowed, Euphemia deserved so much more from her.

Reinhold reached to assist Sophie to the ground, but she couldn't let go of the wagon bench.

"Everything will be all right, Soph," he said gently. "I promise."

She met his gaze. Even in the darkness, his eyes reflected his steadfastness and beckoned her to trust him. She nodded.

His hands encircled her waist, and he lifted her off. As her feet touched the ground, he wrapped one arm around her waist and drew her into the shelter of his side.

"Sophie's just fine," he said to Euphemia and the others.

But in spite of the security of Reinhold's arm, Euphemia barreled forward, wrapped her arms around Sophie, and drew her into the soft cushion of her body.

"Och, lass. My sweet little Sophie, lass." She rocked back and forth, her warmth and love surrounding Sophie and bringing sharp tears to her eyes.

She waited for Euphemia to say something about how much worry and trouble she'd caused. But Euphemia hugged her a moment longer, before pressing a kiss to Sophie's forehead.

"I'm glad you're back," she said, finally releasing Sophie.

Uncertainty gripped Sophie again. As if sensing her insecurities, Reinhold slipped his arm around her, drawing her back to his side. She leaned into the strength and protection of his hold. She let Reinhold explain where he'd found her and what had happened, including Mr. Ramsey's treatment of the children.

"I always said that *dunderheid* is as sly as a weasel in the cornfield," Barclay boomed. He'd thrown his coat on over his nightclothes. His head was bare and his feet stocking-clad. Clearly he'd been in bed, attempting to sleep. A quick glance at the younger boys and their attire told her they'd been slumbering too.

The morning milking came early, and her antics were costing everyone precious hours of sleep.

Barclay rubbed his hands together for warmth, not seeming to mind the late hour. "He's the one the sheriff ought to lock behind bars until he rots like a stinking potato."

"We all know how Sheriff Paddy feels about the orphans," Reinhold said more solemnly than Sophie had yet heard him. "If David Ramsey decides to make a case against Sophie breaking into his house, the sheriff will take his side and do his best to prosecute her."

Sophie shuddered, not sure whether out of fear or from the night air that had steadily grown colder.

"I won't let him lay a hand on the wee lass," Barclay said.

"And I won't either," Reinhold said, pulling Sophie closer. "Which is why I'm planning to marry Sophie just as soon as the reverend can perform the ceremony."

At his announcement, everyone erupted, and for several seconds they all talked at once, making Sophie cringe at their slew of questions.

"Sophie and I have already made up our minds," Reinhold stated calmly but loudly enough to be heard above the commotion. "It's the best way for me to keep Sophie safe and for us to gain custody of Olivia and Nicholas."

The voices died away. Sophie could feel Euphemia's eyes upon her, searching for answers. But Sophie avoided looking at her, too afraid of what she'd see there. What must the dear woman think of her now? That she'd somehow seduced Reinhold?

"Och, now," Euphemia said. "We best be going to bed all of us. The morn will be here in the twitch of a cat's tail, and we'll be needing our sleep since we have a wedding to plan."

Sophie's gaze darted to Euphemia, who was smiling at her kindly. "Wedding to plan?"

"You're the only daughter I have. You can't deny me the chance to plan a wedding, now, can you?"

Daughter? Did Euphemia consider her a daughter? Tears stung Sophie's eyes once again.

When Reinhold took his leave a few minutes later, she allowed Euphemia to lead her upstairs to her bedroom and didn't refuse when the woman helped her into her nightdress, covered her bruised shoulder with ointment, and then brushed her hair.

All the while Euphemia made plans for the wedding ceremony and the food.

"You can wear my wedding dress," Euphemia said as she plaited Sophie's hair. "We'll have to take it in here and there, of course, but it'll do nicely."

"I couldn't," Sophie said, feeling guiltier with every new suggestion Euphemia so enthusiastically made.

"Dinnae say no, lass. I won't be swayed."

Sophie perched on the edge of her bed with a colorful knitted blanket wrapped around her for extra warmth against the nip of the room. Even with the warm blanket, chills slid up Sophie's spine. After all the trouble she'd caused, Euphemia deserved to know the truth about her arrangement with Reinhold.

"Reinhold doesn't love me and is only marrying me because I begged him to." The confession tumbled out, the words falling over one another in quick succession. "He's too kind to say no."

"Och, dinnae think that, lass. Reinhold is verra good at saying no to the things he dosen't want. Believe me, I've heard him say no often enough. If he dinnae want to have you, he wouldn't have agreed to marry you."

"We're only forming a partnership," Sophie persisted. "He's helping me and I'm helping him."

The lantern on the bedside table bathed the bedroom. When she'd packed her bag earlier, she never expected to come back. Even though she was grateful for the opportunity to spend another night at the Duffs' home in this cheerful room with its soft bed and warm blankets, her chest pinched with urgency every time she thought of Olivia huddled in the attic, cold and alone and frightened.

"My marriage with Barclay started as a partnership." Euphemia's hands in her hair stilled.

"It did?" The statement caught Sophie off guard. Euphemia doted on her husband, always making sure his plate was heaped with food and his coffee cup filled to the brim. As often as Barclay stole kisses from Euphemia, it was obvious he loved his wife.

"When Barclay's mother died, he needed a woman to take over the upkeep of his home while he managed the dairy farm. Told me he was too busy to worry about keeping a wife happy, that he dinnae want the extra complications that came with love."

"So if he married you to be his housekeeper, then why did you marry him?"

"I needed a father for my bairn."

"For Stuart?"

"Not many men would have done what Barclay did for me."

"Seems to me that lots of widows get remarried to have fathers for their children."

She was silent for a moment. "I wasn't a widow."

Sophie sat motionless and tried to digest Euphemia's confession.

"When I came to America, I was a young lass and naïve, believing the first man who told me he loved me. I thought I could secure a good life for myself in my own plans and doin' things my own way. I was a milkmaid, and he was the owner's oldest son. I assumed he'd marry me and then I'd never have another worry."

Euphemia resumed her gentle ministration in Sophie's hair. "But instead of marrying me, he got me fired and kicked off the farm. Thankfully, he took pity on me and supplied me with enough money so I could pay for a place to live until the wee babe was born."

Euphemia was such a strong woman of faith that Sophie couldn't imagine her being anything else. It was almost as if she were speaking of another person entirely.

"I eventually found work as a milkmaid again," Euphemia

said. "But I had to lie and tell people that my bairn's father had died and I was a widow. That's what I told Barclay too."

"Then he doesn't know the truth?"

"He learned soon enough." Euphemia chuckled, her whole body shaking with the movement. "We were getting along real well. I even thought he might like me. Until I ran into Stu's father in town one day. Barclay was with me, saw the way that I reacted, saw the resemblance of my bairn to his father, and knew the truth."

"Oh."

"Och is right. Barclay despised me after that."

"But he still asked you to marry him when his mother died?"

"He said it was because then he'd have no temptation to fall in love, that he'd be able to focus on his work better." Euphemia finished plaiting Sophie's hair, tied it off with a ribbon, and lowered herself to the bed beside Sophie. "I figured if Barclay could see the truth about Stu's father, that eventually other people would too. So when Barclay offered to marry me, we both had every intention of keeping it a partnership."

"What happened?" Sophie asked, fascinated by Euphemia's story.

Euphemia laughed again, this time more soundly. "Och, lass. Surely you know enough about the ways of a man and woman to see what happened. I have four more sons to prove that we had much more than a partnership."

Sophie's cheeks heated at Euphemia's implication. "I can see that you love each other now. But how did you get to that point? When did it all change?"

"The changes were slow and happened over time."

Was that what she was hoping for with Reinhold? That perhaps he'd eventually see their marriage as more than a mere partnership, that perhaps he'd even come to love her over time?

"So you see, my wee lass." Euphemia patted Sophie's hand

on her lap. "When we're finally willing to let go of the messes we've made, the good Lord can step in and salvage the scraps."

Sophie studied Euphemia's chafed hand, the strong fingers that worked so hard every day. Could she be like Euphemia? Was there a chance that God could make something of the messes she'd made?

"Mind you," Euphemia continued, "not everything in my life is put back together perfectly, and poor Stu is proof of that. But the good Lord has pieced my life back together much better than I could have."

She squeezed Sophie's hand and then hefted herself up from the bed. "Time for some shut-eye, lass." She kissed the top of Sophie's head again and started across the room. When she reached the door, she stopped. "And dinnae worry about your Reinhold. I saw the way he was looking at you at the barn dance, and he'll be wanting more than a partnership before long."

CHAPTER 15

A line of sweat trickled down Reinhold's back between his shoulder blades, but he resisted the urge to itch it through his best shirt and coat. Even with the parlor windows wide open, the air in the room pressed against him, heating and constricting him.

Next to him, Barclay and the reverend talked amiably, trading news about neighbors, discussing the cooler temperatures, and wagering when they'd experience the first killing frost. Around the room, other guests mingled, some standing and others already seated and awaiting the start of the wedding ceremony.

Reinhold shifted and stared out the side window that overlooked the pond. Now with the beginning of October upon them, the water reflected the oranges and reds of the changing leaves. In the distance, the cornstalks had also dried and turned a burnt gold color.

The sight of the corn only reminded Reinhold of all the work he'd neglected over the past week. First he'd ridden into town to make the marriage arrangements, as well as place the telegram to Reverend Poole. Of course, once Reinhold had sent the telegram, word had gotten around town regarding the nature of his business and his complaint to Reverend Poole regarding the Ramseys' treatment of the orphans in their care.

After David Ramsey learned of the telegram, he'd made a visit to the sheriff and filed a report against Sophie, accusing her of breaking into his house. When Fergus had come running out to the farm to tell Reinhold the sheriff was planning to arrest Sophie, Reinhold quickly saddled his horse and rode to town again, this time to stop the sheriff.

No amount of threatening had deterred Sheriff Paddy, not until Reinhold had divulged that Sophie was related to both Thornton Quincy and Andrew Brady through her sisters. That had finally silenced the sheriff. Everyone knew that the Quincys' power and money could buy them just about anything they wanted. And the sheriff had already been rebuked once by Andrew Brady's father, a wealthy lawyer with many connections.

Reinhold had explained his plan to marry Sophie by the week's end and promised to make an honest, law-abiding woman out of her. With Reinhold's threats and reassurances, the sheriff agreed to wait to bring any charges against Sophie.

Reinhold prayed that everything would be just fine—that Reverend Poole would get their telegram and respond, that Sophie could be reunited with Olivia and Nicholas, and that she wouldn't try anything else that might get herself into trouble.

All week, Reinhold had also scrambled to find another way to save Olivia and Nicholas without having to marry Sophie. He'd mentally visited every family who lived in Mayfield, and even some he knew lived beyond the town. Yet he hadn't been able to single out anyone else who might be willing and able to care for both together. Some families might be willing to take one or the other of the children, but since Sophie was determined to keep them together, he'd run out of options. He had no other choice but to marry her.

He turned to face the roomful of guests Euphemia had

invited to the wedding—neighbors and friends from church. They would all witness the vows that would seal his fate. From this day forward, he'd have a wife.

Panic pressed against his chest. What was he doing here?

His sights went to the door. He could leave now, escape before it was too late. He wasn't fit to be any woman's husband, especially not Sophie's.

Unless he later gave Sophie an annulment . . .

The idea sprang up, burrowing through his befuddled mind. Sophie had brought up the possibility of having a business partnership, of not sharing a bed. If they didn't consummate their marriage, then once things settled down, once Sophie had custody of the children and felt safe, then he'd be able to contact Elise and Marianne and let them know everything that had happened. They'd come and get Sophie, and take her and the children back to New York City with them, and Sophie would be free to start a new life without him. With an annulment they'd be able to part ways without any guilt or repercussions.

He drew a deep breath and pulled his attention away from the door. Yes, he could do this. He'd marry Sophie now because it was the only way he could keep her out of danger. But later, once the situation was under control and Sophie was willing to contact her sisters again, they'd dissolve the marriage.

"Ah, Reinhold, my lad," Barclay said, clamping down on his shoulder and grinning like an oaf. "Ye are the lucky one today."

Reinhold managed a smile in return, the pressure in his lungs loosening. With the plan to annul the marriage, he could rest easier. Everything would work out just fine.

"Could tell the first night ye laid eyes on that lass, ye were smitten."

Reinhold wanted to refute Barclay's boisterous declaration that carried throughout the room. But at the attention that shifted their way, he decided against the denial. It was better if everyone thought he and Sophie were marrying out of affection. Then Reverend Poole wouldn't have any cause to question the marriage and refuse to place Olivia and Nicholas with them.

"With the way Lyle was skedaddling after her, no wonder ye moved fast."

Reinhold avoided Lyle's gaze. The young man leaned against the far wall, arms crossed, his expression saying he'd rather be anywhere else but here. Several times over the past week, Reinhold had almost saddled Daisy and ridden over so he could talk to Lyle. He wouldn't apologize for taking Sophie away from his friend. Sophie had never been Lyle's to begin with. But he owed Lyle an apology for losing control and attacking him the night Sophie ran away.

A sudden hush fell over the room, and all heads turned in the direction of the door.

Reinhold shifted his attention, and his heartbeat stuttered at the sight of Sophie standing there. She wore a lovely blue gown that was full and round on the bottom but rose to sculpt her body and outline every womanly curve, exposing creamy flesh at the curved neckline. His gaze continued upward to her pretty face, made more beautiful by the cascading curls arranged on the top of her head, the rosy flush in her cheeks, and the endless blue of her big eyes.

When she offered him a tentative smile, his chest constricted. She was exquisite in every way.

"Breathe, lad." Barclay nudged Reinhold in his side. The whisper was loud enough that it elicited laughter from some of the guests.

Reinhold dragged in a breath and forced his mouth into a smile even as a surge of doubts crashed into him. What was he doing? He couldn't marry Sophie. It was a terrible idea, and he needed to put a stop to it now before they proceeded.

But as she started across the room toward him, her eyes held his, so full of innocence and trust and beauty. If he let her go, she'd probably end up back in the city where some other man would swoop in and claim her. In fact, he was surprised she'd made it this long without someone attempting to have her. She was so beautiful that surely she'd drawn attention.

When she was only a few paces away, her steps slowed and her eyes questioned him, as though she could sense the war raging inside him.

He held out a hand, beckoning her.

Her smile widened, and she placed her hand into his. As her fingers made contact with his, the merest touch was enough to set his stomach to flight like a flock of geese heading south for the winter.

It was a reaction he needed to ignore. But as he stood with Sophie in front of the reverend, he decided that just for their wedding, for this moment, he wouldn't fight himself. He'd keep her at arm's length in the days to come, but not today. Surely it wouldn't hurt to appreciate her and the beautiful woman she'd become for one day.

The words, the vows, the prayers were a blur. He spoke when he needed to and told himself that he didn't need to feel guilty about making wedding promises because they'd both agreed they wouldn't have a real marriage. Maybe he hadn't spoken with Sophie about giving her an annulment, but once she was secure and had Olivia and Nicholas, she'd find the wisdom in his plan.

When the reverend ended with a prayer and benediction, she smiled up at Reinhold with a radiance that made him believe for just an instant that she truly was happy to marry him.

Across the room, Euphemia's smile was equally bright. She dabbed at her eyes before starting to issue instructions about the wedding feast she'd prepared.

"Now hold on," Barclay cut in, grabbing Reinhold before he

could walk away. "This wedding ceremony would be as boring as a cow chewing cud if the groom didn't give his bride a kiss."

Sophie ducked her head, her lashes falling to her flushed cheeks.

Reinhold shook his head. He couldn't kiss Sophie. It was one thing to hold her hand and let himself enjoy her warm touch for the duration of the wedding ceremony. It was another thing entirely to kiss her.

"Go on now," Barclay insisted jovially, his round face full of mischief. "Don't be a dunderheid, lad."

Reinhold caught Sophie's gaze and raised his brows, seeking her permission. He wouldn't kiss her now unless she agreed to the display, for that was all it would be—a display for their guests.

She shrugged her shoulders almost imperceptibly, as if to give her consent. And then she turned and lifted her face, allowing him access.

His eyes focused on her lips, curved in a shy smile. He could do this. He could kiss her and remain objective. The kiss wouldn't mean anything. It would be simple and quick and that was all.

He bent in, once again looking her in the eye and questioning her. Should they really go through with a kiss?

She lifted to her toes, closing the distance between their mouths. As her lips came against his, she closed her eyes but not before he caught sight of her yearning. The knowledge of her desire at the moment their lips collided was enough to create an explosion in his gut. Fire, light, heat sparked in brilliant hues.

His hands rose and he cupped her cheeks so he could deepen the connection. His lips moved against hers, fusing them together at the same time she molded her lips to his. The passion in her response caused a groan to work its way up the back of his throat. He was saved from embarrassing himself as Barclay's laughter penetrated the haze of his desire.

Reinhold broke quickly from Sophie. But even as she backed away, a hot pressure inside urged him to go after her and take possession of those lips again.

"Now, that's how it's done, lasses and lads!" Barclay said, clamping a hand on Reinhold's shoulder. Reinhold tore his attention away from Sophie and tried to smile and pretend that he wasn't so weak and breathless.

As they followed the guests outside to the tables set up in the yard for the wedding banquet, Reinhold attempted to calm his wildly beating heart. But every time Sophie's hand brushed his, or her arm bumped him, his sights returned to her lips. And every time she spoke or smiled, his attention shifted to her mouth.

As they ate, he acted as though he wasn't aware of his desire, yet she was too pretty and vivacious to ignore. And his longing stretched taut until by the end of the afternoon he crackled against the pressure.

"Go over there and kiss her again, lad," Barclay said as they stood in the waning sunlight, watching Sophie receive gifts from some of the women. "It's clear as the dawn that ye want to."

The other men standing with them laughed and added their own teasing to Barclay's.

"Euphemia, lass," Barclay called, steering Reinhold toward the women, "let the newlyweds be on their way. Reinhold's anxious to get his bride home—"

Reinhold cut off his friend's ribald comment with a jab to his side. Barclay and the other men laughed again. Reinhold couldn't contain a grin as he started toward Sophie. Somehow in just one day, one ceremony, he'd graduated from the fringes of the community and moved into the welcoming center. His neighbors saw him as more than just a young man now; marriage somehow validated him, made him older and wiser, earned their respect.

At his approach, Sophie met his gaze with a happy one of her own. Even if they weren't planning to have a real marriage, he was glad they would be friends, have a comfortable companionship, and perhaps even find a little happiness while they were together.

He wouldn't ask for any more than that.

⁂

Sophie paced the bedroom, hugging her arms across her chest. The nightgown Euphemia had packed for her was thin and did little to ward off the chill of the room. But it was silky, with pretty lace along the neck and hem.

She stopped in front of the bare window and peered out over Reinhold's farm—her farm now too. It had been dark when they'd arrived so that she'd only been able to see outlines of the house and barn and privy. Everything was smaller and much simpler than at the Duffs' place.

But she was proud of Reinhold for all he'd accomplished in less than a year. Even after her short time among the farming community, she'd gained an appreciation for just how hard he'd had to work to get to where he was.

And yet there was still a long way to go . . .

She'd only had to step one foot inside his house to see that he had the bare essentials necessary for survival. In addition to an old table, two mismatched chairs, and a cookstove, the kitchen contained two blackened pans, a dented coffeepot with a broken spout, and a few forks and tin plates. It was as dirty and unkempt as the rest of the house, which was as sparse as the kitchen.

Sophie had lived in enough squalor over the past years that the condition of Reinhold's home didn't bother her. But even as she'd unpacked and found places for their few wedding gifts, she'd tidied and cleaned as best she could. She'd do better tomorrow by the light of day when she could boil water and find soap and rags.

Releasing a tired sigh, she turned away from the bedroom window, walked over to the bed, and crawled onto it. Lacking any sheets, the flimsy straw-stuffed mattress was covered with a couple of wool blankets in sore need of a washing. The bed wasn't nearly as fresh and comfortable as the one she'd had at the Duffs'. But it was still a bed and better than most places she'd laid her head in recent years.

Although she hadn't spoken with Reinhold since he'd brought in the last load of wedding presents and headed to the barn, she suspected he'd insist that she sleep on the bed. He was too thoughtful and kind to do otherwise. Even so, she'd been waiting to see him, to say good-night, and more importantly to thank him again for giving her a home so that she could have Olivia and Nicholas.

That was all she wanted to do, she told herself, letting her fingers graze the silky sleeves of the nightdress. Euphemia's words from earlier in the week sifted through her head as they had many times: *"Dinnae worry about your Reinhold. I saw the way he was looking at you at the barn dance, and he'll be wanting more than a partnership before long."*

Did his kiss at the wedding lend proof to Euphemia's declaration? The kiss hadn't been simple, hurried, or awkward. Instead, it had been deep and slow and passionate. She thought again of the tender way he'd cradled her face, the fervent molding of his lips to hers, and she couldn't deny her longing for another kiss. Was that the real reason she was waiting for him to come back to the house? Because she wanted to kiss him again?

It was their wedding night after all. As they'd been readying to leave the Duffs' place, everyone had been teasing them good-naturedly, assuming they would spend the night together. In fact, Barclay had insisted Jakob stay the night with

Fergus and Alastair so that she and Reinhold could have more privacy.

Of course, Euphemia was well aware of the nature of her relationship with Reinhold, that they had only a business partnership. But she apparently hadn't informed Barclay, and she hadn't done anything to discourage the insinuations about Sophie and Reinhold being together.

Sophie leaned back into the sagging mattress, catching a whiff of the sourness of body odor and stale hay. The bed frame creaked, but otherwise the house was silent. She closed her eyes and willed herself to forget about Reinhold, about their wedding, and about his kiss.

But she couldn't. In her mind she replayed the afternoon and evening. It had been beautiful in every way—her dress, the ceremony, the meal afterward. The guests had been kind and welcoming, making her forget that none of her family or friends were there. At the very least, she'd hoped Anna would come, especially since she sent her friend a message to let her know of the wedding details. But she hadn't heard anything in reply.

After only a few minutes, Sophie sighed and sat up again. If Reinhold was still in the barn working, then maybe he could use her help. After all, he'd had to cut short his workday for the wedding. Without Jakob to assist, he probably had even more chores than usual.

She donned the shawl Euphemia had given her and made her way out of the house and across the farmyard with only the scant moonlight to guide her. At the barn door, she hesitated.

Light shone from the cracks in the plank door, and the steady tapping of a hammer greeted her.

She didn't want to bother Reinhold if he preferred to work alone. At the same time, however, she'd promised him that he wouldn't regret marrying her. She had to show him he hadn't made a mistake, that she could help him, that she might even be an asset to the farm.

Determined, she set her shoulders and slid the door open. The odor of horseflesh and newly cut hay rushed at her.

Reinhold sat on a bench in the center of a wide aisle that ran between stalls on both sides of the barn. A lantern hung directly above him and cast a glow over a curved metal blade on the bench. As the door squealed open, he paused in his work, his hammer suspended above the blade as his sights landed upon her.

"Hello," she said, offering him a smile, not sure why she suddenly felt so shy.

He lowered his hammer and wiped a sleeve across his forehead, brushing aside damp strands of his dark brown hair that hung in his eyes. "I thought you'd be asleep by now."

She realized she couldn't tell him she'd been waiting for his return. She didn't want him to think she was desperate for his company. She glanced around the barn and noted his horse in one stall and a reddish-brown cow in the pen across from it. The cow lifted its head and regarded Sophie with large eyes as though wondering who she was and what she was doing here.

Feeling foolish for disturbing Reinhold, Sophie clutched her shawl around her nightgown. "With Jakob gone, I thought maybe you could use some help."

Reinhold flexed his shoulders, rolling them as though to rid them of the tension that had built there. "I'm just repairing one of my tools. I have to get it ready for cutting more oats tomorrow."

"The Duffs are cutting oats too."

He brought his hammer down on one of the long teeth of the tool where it was bent. "We're all racing to get in the harvest before the frost."

She stepped farther inside, gaining confidence from the fact that he hadn't asked her to leave. She slid the door closed. Already moths and other bugs fluttered around the lantern, attracted to the light.

When Reinhold continued to work and didn't seem to mind her presence, she decided to explore the barn. As she ambled around, she asked Reinhold questions about his farm, his crops and livestock.

After sitting in the loft for a while with a mother cat and her litter of kittens, Sophie climbed down and decided she would stay with Reinhold and keep him company while he finished his repairs, especially since he appeared to enjoy sharing about his farm. She perched on the milking stool and began twisting hay the way Euphemia had taught her into the tight bundles they used for fuel.

As with the other times with Reinhold, she found that their conversation came easily, that he not only talked about his farm and the hardships he'd encountered but he also asked her about her hardships.

She found herself opening up and telling him about her thieving in order to provide for Olivia and Nicholas. When he didn't react with shock or condemnation, she shared about the last harrowing week in New York City, the involvement with the Bowery Boys, and how she and Anna had witnessed the murder of two Roach Guards.

"We had to leave the city," Sophie admitted, her fingers twisting another fuel bundle. "And we can't go back, not without putting our lives in danger."

He paused, letting his hammer lie idle on his knee while he studied her.

She wondered if she'd said too much. What must he think of her now that he knew she'd been involved in a gang?

"I guess that means you belonged to one of the boys?" he

asked, his brows coming together in a dangerous storm cloud above murky green eyes.

She wasn't sure how much more she should tell him about Danny. She didn't want Reinhold to think any worse of her than he already did. "Are you jealous?" she asked, trying to keep her voice playful.

He grabbed his hammer and swung it against a metal tine with a force that was sharp and angry. "Who was he?"

Her fingers tangled in the straw and came to a halt. "He wasn't anyone special—"

"But you were with him?" Reinhold's expression was almost pained as he watched her and waited for her answer.

Did he think she'd become a loose woman? She gave a short laugh. "It wasn't like that. I told Danny that I was waiting for marriage."

"His name was Danny?" he growled.

She smiled. "You *are* jealous."

"Maybe."

Her smile widened, and her heart warmed with his admission. "You don't have to be jealous. He didn't mean anything to me." Not the way Reinhold did. But she kept that thought tucked away.

He was silent for a moment, twisting his hammer and staring at it. Finally the storm clouds in his countenance seemed to dissipate. "I'm glad you're here, Soph. Away from all that."

"I'm glad I'm here too." What would have happened if she hadn't witnessed the murder the night of the fire? Would she still be in New York City living with Mollie and still involved in the gangs? Not for the first time, she realized her life might have veered the same direction as Mollie's. Or maybe she would have been married to Danny by now or gotten together with another Bowery Boy, someone who might not have been as patient with her as Danny had been.

Sophie didn't want to think about what could have happened. She'd made so many mistakes, she wasn't sure God could put her life back together even if He decided to try.

And yet He'd given Euphemia a fresh start when she'd made mistakes. Was He willing to do that for her too? Could He piece together her life here on this farm in Mayfield, Illinois, with Reinhold Weiss?

Reinhold tapped at the steel tine of his tool again, this time more subdued. Even so, his muscles rippled underneath his shirtsleeve. He was a strong man both outwardly and inwardly. She had no doubt he would provide for her and make sure she was safe. He'd already proven he'd do anything for her—even marry her so she could have Nicholas and Olivia again.

He was a good and worthy man. And she'd trapped him into marriage, had taken advantage of that goodness so she could have her own way. As usual, she'd resorted to her own scheming to try to clean up the mess she'd made with Olivia and Nicholas.

With a sigh, she leaned her head back against the stall door. No, she wouldn't involve God in her problems any more than she'd involve her sisters. She'd gotten herself into the predicament and she'd have to be the one to get herself out of it. It was too humiliating to think of the alternative, especially facing her sisters and admitting to them how wrong she'd been to run away.

If only she could put her life back together and fix it up pretty, then maybe she'd finally be ready to see her sisters again. They'd never have to know how many mistakes she'd made and how low she'd sunk.

Starting tomorrow, she'd begin again to make a new life for herself. And maybe this time, with Reinhold, she'd finally be able to make things work out.

CHAPTER 16

Silence awoke Sophie. For several seconds she didn't move. She nuzzled into the mattress and tried to catch the scent of Euphemia's delicious breakfast, the mingling of bacon and freshly ground coffee.

Instead, a deep intake of air filled her nostrils with the scent of musty hay.

Her eyes popped open. Bright morning light slanted through the windows that were devoid of the cherry-red curtains and into a room that was drab and colorless and dirty.

She wasn't at the Duffs' anymore. She was in Reinhold's bedroom. And it was the day after her wedding.

They'd talked in the barn long into the night, and at some point she must have dozed off. She remembered waking when Reinhold lifted her from the stool. She vaguely recalled him carrying her back to the house and up to the bedroom where he'd deposited her gently on the bed.

When he'd bent and pressed a kiss against her forehead, she'd wanted to wrap her arms around him and pull him down beside her. Thankfully she'd been too tired to make a fool of herself.

But now she'd overslept and had made a fool of herself anyway.

She scrambled off the bed. "What a great start to your resolution to make a better life here. He's probably already cooked himself breakfast and headed out to the fields."

She quickly donned one of her plain work dresses before hurrying down to the kitchen. A peek out the window showed the sun high in the sky, and she was ashamed to realize she'd slept half the morning away.

With all the work needing to be done, she'd wasted hours of the day. Even so, she dropped into one of the mismatched kitchen chairs and buried her face into her hands with a groan. Who was she kidding? She wasn't a farmer's wife. Even if she had been able to drag herself out of bed before dawn, she was inadequate. She'd watched Euphemia at her work and had helped her with numerous tasks, but that was different from managing everything for herself.

Where should she start? What should she do?

The stillness of the morning was broken by the rattle of a wagon and the clatter of horse hooves outside the house. Sophie sat up and pushed away from the table as fresh dismay crowded out her previous misgivings. She wasn't prepared to have company. Not this morning. Not here.

She'd only embarrass Reinhold. But what else could she do but make the most of her situation and attempt to be a good wife?

With quick steps she crossed the kitchen, flung open the door, and stepped outside. The morning sun blinded her for a few seconds, but at the sight of a bright yellow kerchief and a matching calico dress, Sophie felt like dropping to the ground and crying in relief. Euphemia was here.

"Good morn, lass!" Euphemia beamed down at her as she brought the wagon to a halt. "I see you've just pulled yourself from bed. I take it the night went well?"

Euphemia's question made Sophie flush, and she shook her head in denial. "No, it's not what you think. We talked in the barn while he worked. That's all."

The older woman hefted herself from the wagon. "Och, that Reinhold. He's a mite stubborn. But dinnae worry, lass." She lumbered toward the wagon bed. "With the way he kissed you yesterday at the wedding, I doubt he'll be able to keep his hands off you for long."

The heated flush sank deeper into Sophie. "He still views me as his friend."

"I guess you'll need to show him you're not just his friend."

"How do I do that?"

Euphemia chuckled as she lifted a crate out of the wagon and set it on the ground. "Now, lass, the good Lord gave you the beauty of a dozen women. It shouldn't be too hard to woo that husband of yours."

Woo her husband? Sophie shook her head. She couldn't remember anything about the way her mother and father interacted with each other. And even though she'd lived with her uncle and aunt for a while, their relationship hadn't been anything to emulate.

Euphemia hefted out another crate. Seeing Sophie's confusion, she chuckled again. "Find out the things he likes. Learn what pleases him."

Sophie nodded. "I know he likes his coffee strong and black. And that he favors your butterhorn rolls."

"That's right. You'll do fine, lass." She pulled a third crate from the wagon. "And if he needs a little more encouragement, then you can always tempt him with what's already his."

Sophie ducked her head at the bold plan, feeling the blush move all the way from her cheeks into her scalp. Since she'd trapped Reinhold into marrying her, she didn't want to coerce him or trick him into having a real marriage if he didn't want that. But maybe she could earn his love. Maybe over time, if she learned the things that pleased him, he'd eventually grow to love her.

"Och, lass. He'll come around."

Sophie hoped so. She hoped it more than she should.

"Now help me carry these boxes inside." Euphemia held out one of the crates. "We've got work to do."

As Sophie brought the crates and barrels into the house, she almost wept with gratefulness. Euphemia waved aside her words of thanks and set to work unpacking cleaning supplies, crocks of foodstuffs, and even a butter churn. Euphemia also produced bolts of material and spools of thread for making sheets, curtains, and rugs.

"I can't accept all this," Sophie said as she stared at everything now spread around the kitchen in piles, already giving the place a homey feel.

"Most of it is extra stuff I had lying around and don't need anymore."

"But it's too much."

"You tell Reinhold you'll pay me back by coming over and lending a hand with the rest of the preserving."

Reinhold was a proud man and wouldn't take charity—he never had, even in New York City when they'd been on the brink of starvation. Apparently, Euphemia had already anticipated Reinhold's reaction to the gifts. "And when you come," Euphemia added, "you bring anything left in Reinhold's garden, and we'll get it preserved too."

Euphemia showed her how to light the stove and set water to boiling. Then they scrubbed the kitchen, started laundry, and prepared a simple meal in readiness for Reinhold and Jakob's return for the noon meal.

When the two didn't come in from the fields, Euphemia helped Sophie bundle up the meal into a basket. Then she set out for home.

Sophie watched the wagon rumble away with a growing sense of trepidation. She wasn't ready to be on her own yet. But she also realized how much Euphemia had sacrificed by coming over. With all that Euphemia had to do every day, she couldn't afford to miss a minute, much less half a morning.

Sophie headed in the direction Euphemia had pointed out for her. She passed a field that had already been harvested. Beyond that, the level plain stretched in a lovely patchwork of gold, brown, and bronze. A few trees stood a distance away, their leaves changing from green to gold. The low clouds that had rolled in brushed against the color so that the fields and trees seemed to touch the sky.

In one field she caught sight of the sheaves—the oat stalks that had been gathered and banded tightly around their middles the way that Euphemia had described. As she drew closer, she finally saw Reinhold at work cutting the oats. Jakob was nearby, kneeling on the ground and binding the stalks into sheaves.

At her approach, Jakob stood and said something to Reinhold. He nodded but kept cutting, swinging with smooth strokes that caught the stalks and felled them.

"I brought you dinner," she said to Jakob as her gaze followed Reinhold's movements. Even with the cooler temperatures, he'd discarded his coat. His shirt was plastered to his back by perspiration, revealing every rippling muscle.

She lifted out the crock containing the ham, boiled potatoes, and green beans. She filled a tin plate for Jakob, and he took it gratefully.

"Reinhold," she called, but he didn't break from his steady rhythm.

"He won't stop until he reaches the end of the field," Jakob said. He spooned food into his mouth and swallowed it all in one motion.

Jakob was almost done with his second helping of the meal by the time Reinhold put down the tool and walked over.

Feathery pieces of oats stuck to his forehead and nose, along with smudges of dust. His cheeks and jaw were covered in a dark shadow of stubble he'd neglected to shave. But she found that she liked the shadows, that it gave him a rugged appeal.

"I've brought you a meal," she said with a smile, realizing she was happy to see him.

His return smile was tired, and she wondered how much sleep he'd gotten last night. Probably not much if he'd awoken before dawn to do chores and head out to the field.

As she ladled food onto his plate, his eyes widened. "How did you manage this?"

She laughed. "Are you telling me you don't think I'm capable of cooking an edible meal?"

His grin widened. "No. Not at all."

She liked the crinkles at the corners of his eyes, lines that his toil in the sun and heat had etched there.

"It's good," he said after a bite.

The compliment filled her with a sense of pleasure that was unlike anything she'd experienced before. She liked knowing she could please him and make him happy. And her conversation earlier with Euphemia rushed back. What were some other things she could do to woo him?

"I'm guessing Euphemia paid you a visit?" he asked.

"Is it that obvious?"

"She brought the ham." When his eyes met hers, they were full of questions.

"I'll repay her for everything she gave me."

He chewed slowly and stared off at the rest of the oat field still waiting to be harvested. A variety of emotions flickered across his face.

As though sensing their need for a private conversation, Jakob handed his empty plate to Sophie, thanked her, and returned to the sheaf he'd been bundling before her arrival.

For several minutes, Reinhold ate quietly. The breeze gently rattled the oats. Sophie soaked in the peace of the place, so different from the city life she'd known. She didn't miss the noise and chaos, she realized as she breathed in the scent of grass and soil and wind.

When Reinhold finished eating, he returned his plate to her. "As soon as everything is harvested and my debts paid, I'll be able to do more for you. I promise."

His words surprised her. Did he think she was disappointed in his home and what he was offering her?

"Reinhold Weiss, don't you think for a second that I care one bit about the material things you can give me."

He shifted to stare off into the distance again, his eyes troubled, his shoulders slumped.

She wanted to say more, wanted to tell him that nothing else mattered, that he'd given her so much more than she'd had in a long time.

She dropped his plate into the basket and reached for him. With one hand she tugged him near, and with the other she cupped his cheek, brushing her hand across the coarse stubble. Before she could rationalize or come up with excuses why she shouldn't, she stood on her toes and lifted her lips to his. She let her fingers stroke his cheek at the same time that her lips stroked his in a kiss that left no room for hesitation.

His eyes widened, and for a moment he didn't move, as if too surprised to react. Then his hand slipped to the small of her back and he began to press her closer. But as the reality of what she'd done crashed into her, she broke her lips from his and stepped away.

She dug her toe into the ground, too embarrassed to look at him. Finally she chanced a glance and found that his expression was unguarded, that he was studying her mouth as though he might grab her and finish what she'd started.

She sucked in a breath, and his gaze lifted so that she found herself lost in the deep lush green of his eyes. For a moment she could only stare, the air between them strangely charged, just as it had been yesterday at the wedding after they'd shared the kiss. She'd never known kisses could be so powerful, so enticing, so bonding.

With each thought of kissing him again, her breathing turned more shallow, until she took another step back, needing to put a boundary between herself and her desires.

Even as she moved to leave, she knew she had to say something. "You've given me a home, Reinhold. I haven't had that in a long, long time. As soon as Nicholas and Olivia are here, we'll be a family. And that's all I could ask for or want."

With that, she reached for the now-empty food basket, picked it up, and began to walk away. She sensed his eyes following her every move. And when she glanced over her shoulder at where she'd left him, he hadn't budged. His eyes smoldered with something she couldn't name but that sent her pulse skipping.

The admiration she'd once felt for Reinhold as a girl couldn't begin to compare to the new and thrilling feelings she had for him now. What was swirling inside her was so much bigger and more intense and beautiful that it made her chest hurt.

She was falling in love with her husband.

⁂

Through the darkness of the evening, Reinhold trudged wearily toward the house, following the bright light emanating from the kitchen window. He was tired down to his bones, and after finishing the chores he'd considered simply falling into a bed of hay in the barn and giving way to his need for sleep.

But the growling of his empty stomach prodded him out of the barn. He wasn't going to the house because he wanted to see Sophie, he told himself. It was only because he was hungry.

His thoughts returned to the meal she'd brought out to the field earlier in the day. Although he'd eaten his fill, a different kind of hunger had gnawed his gut the rest of the day, a hunger he didn't want to acknowledge.

"Forget it, Reinhold," he whispered to himself. If only she hadn't kissed him. Yes, it had been brief. But it had knocked into him like a strong prairie wind, and it had stirred all the desires he'd worked hard to tamp down the previous sleepless night after he'd carried her back to the house. When he'd laid her on his bed in her silky nightgown, he'd never imagined the difficulty he'd face in walking away from her. He supposed the desires that had fanned to life during the wedding had only added to the temptation to lie down next to her and hold her in his arms.

Only by sheer willpower had he forced his feet to exit the room. Rather than stay in the house anywhere near her, he'd returned to the barn, where he'd spent the remaining hours until dawn, rebuking and reminding himself of his resolve to keep their relationship platonic so he could eventually give her an annulment.

As he opened the back door that led into the kitchen, he took a deep breath, willing himself to be strong and to follow through on his plan.

She was sitting at the kitchen table, intently stitching a piece of fabric spread out before her. She held a thread between her lips and concentrated with a furrowed brow at pushing the needle through the edge of the material. A piece of her long blond hair had loosened from its braid and dangled over her flushed cheek.

He didn't want her to move so that he could go on looking at her all night.

At the sight of him, she dropped her needle, pushed away from the table, and stood.

"There you are," she said with a smile that welcomed him, a smile he could get used to coming home to every evening. "Jakob has already eaten and gone to bed. I was just about to fill a plate with dinner and bring it out to you."

With one sweeping glance he took in the simmering pot on the stove, the new shelf on the wall that was organized with crocks, the crates stacked underneath like additional shelves, the neatly swept and washed floor, and even a jar of wildflowers decorating the middle of the table.

In just a day she'd transformed his home from the dismal, dirty hovel it had been into a cheerful, even pretty, place that beckoned him to stay and sit and relax.

She hurriedly started to fold up the material and clear the table.

"Leave it," he said. "Don't pick up on account of me."

She paused as if debating the proper protocol.

"You're busy." He moved to the stove. "And I don't want to disturb you."

"You're not disturbing me." She crossed the room, grabbed a plate from a shelf, and motioned him back to the table. "I'm attempting to sew curtains, but who knew curtains would give me such a hard time? You'd think the material would be happy at the prospect of getting a home in the window and would cooperate a little bit more with my efforts."

The tension in his shoulders eased as he lowered himself into a chair. When she placed a plate in front of him of beets and turnips with ham, he relaxed even more, allowing himself to enjoy the pleasure of a delicious hot meal in his own home, in a bright and warm kitchen, with a beautiful and vivacious woman.

For now, it wouldn't hurt to pretend that all was right with the world, would it? That all of it was real, that this was what he had to look forward to every day of his future.

So long as he kept his hands off Sophie and resisted the temptation to kiss her, everything would be fine. She was his friend. He simply had to keep that at the front of his mind at all times, and then he could make their living situation work.

CHAPTER 17

With feet freezing against the floorboards, Sophie forced herself to dress before dawn even though the chill in the unheated bedroom tempted her back to the bed and the warm covers she'd abandoned.

She wanted more than anything to prove herself valuable to Reinhold. And she'd decided one way to do that was by providing Reinhold and Jakob with a hearty breakfast the same way Euphemia did for her men before they went out to the fields.

Yesterday, Sophie fried eggs and bacon and slathered thick slices of Euphemia's bread with butter for the two, though they hadn't come up to the house after their chores but had gone directly to the fields.

This morning she'd decided to take breakfast down to the barn for them. She made quick work of cooking the meal since she'd readied everything the previous evening before going to bed. Then she covered the plates and tucked them into a basket, along with the coffeepot and two empty mugs.

The sky was devoid of stars as she crossed the damp grass on her way to the barn. And the farm was so quiet she feared she might have missed them, that they'd already left to begin their long day of work.

When she entered the barn, she was relieved to see Reinhold in the horse stall, his broad shoulders showing above the railing from where he stood grooming and haltering the horse.

At the sight of her, Reinhold started, clearly surprised to see her. And Jakob had popped his head out of the stall where he'd been milking the cow.

"I won't let you go out to the fields on an empty stomach." She handed Jakob a plate first, hoping they weren't avoiding the house because of her. Then she crossed to Reinhold.

"We're heading to the gristmill in Dresden today," Reinhold said, taking the plate she offered him. "The oats need grinding."

She leaned against the rail, hoping he was pleased with her cooking. "What's grinding?"

"The mill breaks the grain kernels down and then bags them so they can go to market."

Between bites of breakfast and sips of coffee, Reinhold explained how the windmills harnessed wind power to operate the large grinding stones that were used in crushing not only oats but wheat, corn, barley, and rye, turning the grains into meal and flour that could then be shipped on the railroad to eastern markets.

"It's a busy time of year at the mill," he said, handing back his now-empty plate. "We may have to wait a while before we get a turn and might be home late."

"Then I'll keep dinner warm for you."

He nodded as he grabbed his coat from the pile of hay outside the stall. She couldn't keep from noticing his blanket and the imprint from where he'd slept.

He stuffed his arms into his coat and stepped past her, leading the horse.

Seeing that Jakob had taken the milk pail to the house and

that she had a moment alone with Reinhold, she stopped him with a touch to his arm.

His muscles stiffened beneath her fingers.

"I'm sorry for taking your bed. I didn't mean to cause you trouble."

"You're not causing any trouble."

She knew she ought to let him pass, that he was in a hurry to begin his trip to the neighboring town with the gristmill. But she let her fingers circle his arm instead.

"I stuffed the mattress with fresh straw yesterday, so it's plump and full."

"Good." He looked down at her fingers curled around his bicep.

After her kiss in the field two days ago, she hoped he'd sense she wasn't opposed to more in their relationship. But he'd kept a polite and friendly boundary between them whenever they interacted.

"You don't have to sleep out here, you know," she said shyly. "The mattress is big enough for both of us, especially now that I've stuffed it."

He inhaled a sharp breath and held himself motionless for a long moment. Finally he mumbled something strangled and hurried out of the barn as if the walls were on fire and crumbling in on him.

As the door closed behind him, embarrassment filled her. She wished she hadn't said anything to him about the sleeping arrangements. She didn't want things to be awkward between them, not when they had a comfortable friendship. Even so, she had to give him some hints of her attraction, didn't she?

"Find out the things he likes. Learn what pleases him." Euphemia's advice whispered in her head. She couldn't rush him, even though she wanted to. Instead, she had to show him she cared in the small things.

By the time Jakob and Reinhold had the horse and wagon ready, she'd managed to put together another basket for them, this one filled with hard-boiled eggs, cheese, biscuits and jam, and a few apples. She stood in the farmyard, basket in hand, as the wagon lumbered forward, the back piled high with the oats.

Through the growing light of dawn, she waited for the wagon to draw near before approaching and lifting the basket. "I've prepared something to tide you over to supper."

She was surprised when Reinhold halted, climbed down, and met her.

"Thank you, Sophie." He took the basket from her, his eyes lighting with appreciation.

She shrugged. "I don't know if it's enough—"

"It'll be better than nothing, which is what we took last time we went to the mill." He then gave her one of his rare smiles, and her insides warmed in spite of the chilled air.

"It's the least I could do."

He studied her for a moment, his smile fading. "If anything happens, do you know how to find the Duffs' place from here?"

Did she detect a note of worry? "Yes, I think I can make my way there."

"Maybe I'll stop by and ask Euphemia to send Fergus over at noon to make sure you're okay."

"I'll be fine." He *was* worried about her. She smiled at the realization. "This farm is like heaven compared to some of the places I've lived."

His brows pinched together. "But you'll be alone all day."

"I'll keep busy. And I have the animals for company."

"Are you sure?"

She bridged the span between them and pressed her hand to his cheek. "I can take care of myself, Reinhold. I'm not a little girl anymore."

"I'm well aware of that, Soph." The low timbre of his voice

made her quiver. And when his eyes dropped to her lips and lingered there, the growing warmth within her spread into her limbs.

Before he could take a step back, she reached for him and wrapped her arms around him in a hug. A hug was platonic enough, wasn't it? Surely she couldn't embarrass either of them with a simple embrace.

His arms caught her and returned the hug. She relished every second of it, but then forced herself to loosen her hold. "I'll miss you today." The admission was out before she could stop it.

He didn't release her. His fingers dug into her shawl at her back, and he pressed his lips against her crown.

She closed her eyes, wanting to lean into him and lift her mouth so he would kiss her there too. But with Jakob waiting on the wagon bench and watching them, she simply let herself bask in his nearness.

When finally he released her, he spun and climbed back onto the bench. He settled the basket on the floor between himself and Jakob and started down a worn path.

With the imprint of his lips lingering on her forehead, she watched them ride away, hugging her arms across her chest and wishing she still held Reinhold.

ᥫᩣ

The bulge of money in Reinhold's pocket made him sit taller as he rode away from the gristmill. The day had been never-ending, filled with a long, silent drive to Dresden, and then filled with an even longer wait for a turn at the mill.

But in the end, all the waiting had been worth it. He'd turned a sizable profit from the oats and only hoped his wheat and corn would do the same.

Now he and Jakob were heading home. To Sophie.

Somehow the thought that Sophie was there waiting for him

in the house he'd built, that she'd greet him with her cheerful smile and dish him up a hot meal drew a breath of satisfaction from his lungs.

The wagon rattled loudly now that it was empty of its heavy load. Without the weight of the oats, Daisy would be able to go faster for the return ride—at least he hoped so.

In the gray of the evening, Dresden's main thoroughfare was quiet, many of the shops having already closed for the day. The waft of roast beef and gravy lingered in the chilled air, making Reinhold's stomach rumble, inadvertently pulling his attention to the brightly lit windows of the tavern.

He and Jakob had eaten every crumb of food Sophie packed for them hours ago. He could still envision her shy expression when she'd handed him the basket, as though she truly cared about him and wanted to make his life better.

He had to admit, he hadn't expected much from Sophie given how young and inexperienced she was. He'd assumed she'd be another person for him to take care of the way he'd taken care of everyone else in his life. He hadn't realized she'd pay attention to his needs.

Yet she'd been sweet and thoughtful since the first day he'd brought her home. She'd managed the upkeep of the house and had started doing some of Jakob's chores. She not only delivered meals to him and Jakob in the field, but she'd also cooked him breakfast and brought it to the barn.

She most certainly wasn't a burden. In fact, he was surprised again at how much he was looking forward to seeing her when they arrived home. He was eager to tell her about the day, share the news he'd picked up as he talked with other farmers, and to see the glimmer in her eyes when he showed her his profit. She'd be proud of him, and his heart swelled at the thought.

The wagon rumbled past the general store. Even though the sign on the door said *Closed*, the shop light illuminated merchandise in a window display. His sights snagged on a fashionable woman's hat decorated with silk ribbons and flowers. Such a fine hat would look mighty pretty on Sophie.

He patted the bulge in his pocket. Beyond the front display, the storekeeper stood behind his counter, his head bent over his ledgers.

Reinhold slowed the wagon. If he tapped on the door, the owner would surely open up and let him purchase the hat. After Sophie's kindness, he wanted to give her something in return. During her time living on the streets and in the asylums, he doubted she'd gotten many gifts, especially something as fine as a new hat.

His lungs constricted at the remembrance of her tousled hair that morning, the golden wisps that had framed her delicate face. Her comment about the bed being big enough for both of them clanged through his mind as it had a dozen other times that day, along with her statement, *"I'll miss you."*

When she hugged him good-bye, he'd had to pry himself loose. And as he'd ridden away, he hadn't dared look at her again for fear he'd jump down, gather her in his arms, and kiss her until they were both breathless.

"Are we stopping?" Jakob asked from the bench beside him. The boy sat with his elbows resting on his knees, attempting to read an old newspaper left behind at the gristmill by another farmer.

Reinhold tugged on the reins. Yes, he'd do it. He'd buy the hat and surprise Sophie with it when he got home. Before he could bring the wagon to a complete halt, his sights fell upon a woman and her husband strolling hand in hand a short distance away. Her hat was similar to the one in the store window, but even more extravagant with feather plumes and ribbons displaying her wealth as much as the elegant gown and a fur-trimmed cloak pulled over her shoulders.

The man next to her was attired in equally fashionable attire, reminding him of Thornton Quincy, Elise's husband, one of the wealthiest men in the country. Elise and Thornton would be able to buy Sophie a hundred new hats, likely from the finest French milliners, not a simple hat from a general store in a small town in Illinois.

Reinhold slapped at the reins, sending Daisy back into motion. He steeled his attention ahead and ignored the hat in the window display.

He could pretend all he wanted that Sophie would always be there to greet him every time he came home from town with her breathtaking smile and beautiful blue eyes, but he couldn't forget she was only in his life temporarily. And he couldn't put off forever the telegram he needed to send to Elise and Marianne.

As much as he wanted to delay and allow their situation to continue unchecked, he would only make things harder on all of them if he didn't act soon.

He patted his pocket again and this time was reminded of just how little the amount was, how big his debts were, and how he couldn't possibly afford a hat for Sophie, even one as simple as the one at the general store. He couldn't afford it now and probably wouldn't be able to for a long time to come—if ever.

He wanted to cling to the dream of a life with Sophie in it as his wife, yet he knew it was just that—a dream. At some point he had to let go. If only he wanted to.

CHAPTER 18

Sophie stood back from the shelves in the root cellar and observed them, letting satisfaction surge through her. Jars of beans, green tomato pickles, watermelon-rind pickles, beets, and more lined the shelves Reinhold had constructed. He'd labored late for several nights to craft the simple shelves so she had a place to store everything.

All week, she'd worked to preserve the produce she'd picked from the garden, spending long afternoons in Euphemia's kitchen, cooking and storing food in jars and crocks. Now the shelves overflowed with the colorful assortment of vegetables.

With a final sigh of satisfaction at all she'd accomplished, Sophie gathered her skirt in one hand and ascended the ladder. As she climbed out of the underground cavern into the gray light of late afternoon, a gust of wind slapped at her, bringing with it a new chill she hadn't felt before.

She gathered her shawl closer and peered to the northwest at the dark clouds gathering on the horizon. When Reinhold had come up to the house at dawn for breakfast, he'd told her not to expect them back for supper, that they'd likely work late into the evening so they could finish harvesting the wheat this week and hopefully make another trip to the gristmill soon.

She already had soup warming on the stove and some of Euphemia's butterhorns ready to take out to him and Jakob for supper. Was it too early to go now?

"Sophie!" a voice called from the direction of the house.

She spun to see Fergus exit the kitchen, letting the door slap shut behind him. The boy ran toward her holding out an envelope. Except for Sundays to church, Fergus never wore shoes. But today he had on a scuffed pair of boots that had been patched and repatched, likely passed on from Alastair and Gavin, maybe even having once been Lyle's. He was also wearing a coat buttoned up over his stout frame. His cap was pulled low, but his ears stuck out and were red from the cold.

"Mum came back from town this afternoon with a telegram for Reinhold. She sent me over right away to deliver it."

Telegram? "Who's it from?"

"The Reverend Poole."

Sophie's pulse bounded forward in great leaps. It had been almost two weeks since Reinhold had sent the telegram to Reverend Poole, informing him of the problem with Nicholas and Olivia living with the Ramseys.

Two weeks too long. Two weeks of waiting. Two weeks of agony.

Thankfully she'd seen the children at church on Sunday. Reinhold hadn't wanted to go into town to the service, had claimed he needed to work. But when she'd said she would go without him, he'd relented and taken her. She hadn't been able to speak with Nicholas and Olivia, but she smiled and waved at them as cheerfully as she could, even though she'd been crying inside at the sight of Olivia's wan face and sunken eyes.

She'd wept later that night when alone in her bed, and she'd begged Reinhold the next day to send another telegram. He told her he would if they still hadn't heard from the reverend by the end of the week.

That was five days ago.

Fergus handed her the telegram.

She tore at the seal.

"It's for Reinhold." His brows slanted in accusation.

She was too anxious to respond to the boy. Instead, she unfolded the paper and read the message: *"Returning to Mayfield for follow-up visits soon. Will investigate situation then."*

Sophie read the message several times, and each time her heart sank a little further. *Soon* was ambiguous. It could mean tomorrow or it could mean several weeks. And she couldn't wait several more weeks to get Olivia and Nicholas away from the Ramseys.

But what else could she do? If she tried to sneak into the Ramseys' home again, Reverend Poole would label her a thief and deem her unstable and unfit to raise children. The best thing she could do was wait patiently. Surely when the reverend came and saw all she'd accomplished as Reinhold's wife, he'd be impressed.

With fresh resolve, she tucked the telegram into her pocket. She'd continue to be a good wife and prove she was capable, so that the reverend would have no reason to withhold the children from her.

"Mum also told me to warn you that the killing frost is coming tonight. If you have anything left in the ground, you best get it dug up and stored away."

Another gust from the north blew against Sophie, cutting through her shawl and dress with a new urgency. When at the Duffs' yesterday, Euphemia had believed they had another week, maybe two, before the killing frost. But with the ominous clouds rolling in and the nip in the air, she'd be wise to heed Euphemia's warning.

"Mum told me to stay and help," Fergus said with a nod toward the vegetable garden.

"Thank you, Fergus." Reinhold was proud and didn't like to accept charity, but Sophie wouldn't turn down help, especially not now when she was still learning so much about being a farmer's wife.

For an hour or more, she worked with Fergus in the vegetable garden, digging up the rest of the root vegetables, putting them in crates, covering them with hay, and hauling them to the cellar.

After Fergus left and as darkness drew nigh, she packed supper into a basket and began the long walk to the wheat field, only to find Reinhold and Jakob digging potatoes. Jakob dropped his shovel and ran to meet her. He devoured his supper as if he hadn't eaten in several days. Reinhold, however, left off his work more reluctantly than usual, casting worried glances toward the sky.

All the while as he ate, he had one eye on the northwest horizon and the piles of clouds drawing ever nearer.

She rubbed her hands over her arms to ward off the cold. "Euphemia sent Fergus to warn me that the killing frost is coming."

"I could feel it in the air too," he replied as he scraped the last spoonful from his plate. "We have to get the potatoes out of the ground and into the barn tonight."

"I'll stay and help."

"No, Soph. You're already doing enough. I won't burden you with this kind of work too."

She set the basket down and began walking toward Jakob. "Teach me what to do, Jakob." The boy looked between her and Reinhold with uncertainty. She'd quickly come to realize how much he respected, almost feared, Reinhold, and how he tried to keep everything even and calm around his brother.

Although Jakob hadn't questioned their sleeping arrangements or the nature of their marriage, she'd sensed his quizzical glances from time to time and knew their relationship puzzled him.

"You can show me," she assured Jakob. "If Reinhold doesn't want me here, then he'll have to carry me back, and I don't think he'll want to waste time doing that."

She cast Reinhold what she hoped was her most stubborn glare. Reinhold pressed his lips together and returned to the digging. Reluctantly, Jakob showed her how to find the potatoes among the dirt and roots Reinhold had overturned. In the growing darkness they worked by lantern light, searching for the dirt-encrusted potatoes more by touch than sight.

Jakob worked almost as quickly as Reinhold dug. While she couldn't find the potatoes as fast as Jakob, she caught on well enough that Jakob started digging up the withered tops of the potato plants along with Reinhold, stopping every few plants to help her locate the lumps in the hard soil.

After only an hour of working, her arms ached, and her nose and cheeks stung from the cold. She was grateful she'd thought to pack her mittens, because even through the knitted material her fingers grew stiff.

"Rain or sleet is coming soon," Reinhold called.

Jakob must have felt a change in the air too. "Should I go for the wagon?"

"Yes, and take Sophie back with you."

"I'm staying until the work is done," she replied, shoveling her hands deeper into the mound of dirt in front of her.

She could feel Reinhold's eyes upon her and sensed his frustration. The next time she glanced up, Jakob was gone and Reinhold was digging again, his coat straining at the seams against his shoulders and arms as he worked. Sophie could do no less. If Reinhold was willing to work tirelessly, if this farm and these crops were so important to him, then she wanted to do everything she could to help him succeed.

She dug until she couldn't feel her fingers. With the wind blowing harder, the lantern flames spluttered and the light flickered. When Jakob returned a short while later, driving the horse and wagon, he hopped down with a pile of grain sacks and began shoving the potatoes into the bags until they nearly overflowed. Then he would heft the bag into the back of the wagon and start to fill another bag.

Sophie worked behind Reinhold for what seemed like hours, searching for the potatoes among the clods and piling them up for Jakob to gather.

"Time to go, Sophie." As if from a dream, she heard Reinhold's voice speaking to her. She looked up and was surprised to see him kneeling next to her.

"I'm not leaving until you do." She tried to focus on the mound in front of her, but her fingers fumbled.

His hands came around hers, halting her choppy motions. She struggled against his hold.

His grip fastened more firmly. "I'm going. We have to get the potatoes into the barn before they get wet."

Setting aside one last potato, she sat back on her heels and realized for the first time that large drops of freezing rain had begun to pelt her.

She didn't protest as he helped her to her feet and lifted her into the back of the wagon, settling her in the midst of the lumpy sacks of potatoes. By the time they reached the barn, she was shivering. She tried to climb down, but Reinhold was there before her feet could touch the ground. He scooped her up and carried her with long strides to the house.

He lowered her to her feet in the dark kitchen. "Take off your wet clothes and get warmed up," he said gently, already opening the door and halfway outside again.

"What about you?" she said through chattering teeth. "You're wet too."

"I need to help Jakob unload the potatoes into the barn."
The door closed behind him before she could say anything else.

She stoked the stove until it was blazing and pumping out
heat. Then she thawed her fingers before going upstairs and
peeling off her wet clothes. After donning her nightdress and a
dry shawl, she returned to the kitchen, where she set the coffee
to boil and started warming the leftovers from dinner.

A short while later, Jakob came in dripping wet and blue-lipped.
He changed, then gratefully accepted and devoured a plate of
hot food before staggering back upstairs and dropping into bed.

Sophie peeked out the kitchen window. Through the hard
pellets of rain hitting the glass, she couldn't see the usual soft
light emanating from the cracks in the barn door. She guessed
Reinhold was tending to the horse and other animals, which
had been neglected while they'd been in the fields.

After watching him work tonight, after seeing his determination, strength, and passion for the land, she was filled with a
new respect for him. He inspired her to want to be better, work
harder, and sacrifice more. And he inspired her to love this place,
to fight for it, to make it into a home they could be proud of.

She'd never felt that way about anything before. After having been on the move from one place to the next for so long,
she'd never understood all the hard work that went into making
something come alive and be successful.

She slid the coffee and food off the heat, hung a blanket near
the stove to keep it warm, and then lowered her aching body
into a chair at the kitchen table. She spread her sewing out in
front of her and smiled at the picture of her waiting up for
Reinhold in ten or twenty years. Would they have a passel of
boys like Barclay and Euphemia had? Boys who would lighten
the workload? Or maybe they would have girls who would help
preserve the garden and sew new clothes for winter.

A touch to her shoulder startled her. She lifted her head

only to realize she'd dozed. At some point in her waiting for Reinhold, her eyelids had grown heavy and she'd laid her head down, intending to rest for just a minute.

She sat up and blinked. The kitchen was dark with the gray of dawn starting to show past the curtains.

The brush came against her shoulder again. "You should be in bed."

"Reinhold." She stood so quickly that she wavered.

He caught and steadied her. Through the low light of the lantern, she could see that he was still wet. His coat and shirt were plastered to his chest, and water dripped from his hat.

His fingers trembled against her waist, whether from exhaustion or cold she couldn't tell. All she knew was that she wanted to take care of him the same way he'd done for her.

"You need to get out of your wet clothes," she said, reaching up and taking off his hat, "before you catch a chill and end up sick."

She tossed his hat aside, helped him out of his coat, and reached for the buttons of his shirt. Her fingers flew down the front, and she had it halfway peeled off before she realized he hadn't pushed her away and insisted he could do it for himself.

Was he discouraged or just tired?

"How did we do?" she asked softly. "Did we lose a lot?"

"We did all right," he replied. "We got more into the barn than I expected to."

She let his shirt drop to the floor and then started to roll his wet undershirt up his torso. "Enough to pay off the debts?" He'd told her once before that his potato crop could be lucrative since not many farmers in the area were planting them. He'd netted a hefty profit last year from the potato field Mr. Turner had allowed him to plant, and he was counting on the profits from this crop to help alleviate some of his debt.

"I hope so." He lifted his arms and helped her free the tangled wet shirt from his skin.

She tossed it with the other clothing and reached for the front of his trousers. He caught her hand and paused. Only then did she become conscious of his bare chest. The glow from the lantern turned his skin bronze and outlined every sculpted muscle. At the realization that he was half-clothed in front of her and that she was staring at him like a brazen woman, she quickly spun away. She fumbled to find the blanket she'd had warming. Her fingers closed around it, and she thrust it in his direction without looking at him.

"I have some coffee and food waiting for you," she said as flames licked at her cheeks. Had she almost helped him remove his pants?

"I don't need anything to eat," he replied. "But I'll take a cup of coffee."

She reached for the pot and began to pour. At the thud of his pants joining his other wet garments, the coffee sloshed over the rim. Did she dare face him? But just as quickly as her embarrassment came on, she shoved it aside. He was freezing, and this was no time to worry about proprieties.

When she turned, he had the blanket draped over his shoulders and wrapped around his body. She handed him the mug. As he took it, the blanket fell away slightly to reveal his chest again. She turned back to the stove and busied herself by adding more fuel and stoking it.

"There," she said and latched the oven door. "Are you getting warm yet?"

"Starting to," he said with a loud slurp of coffee.

"Here." She picked up the extra blanket she'd had for Jakob. Rather than wait for Reinhold to free his hands to take the blanket, she tucked it over his shoulders and brought it around the front of him. She leaned into him and groped for the opposite end of the blanket that had slipped away.

"Thank you for helping." His voice rumbled near her ear as he leaned into the table and set aside his coffee.

"I didn't do much," she replied, finally making contact with the other edge of the blanket. She drew it around him more completely.

Before she could back away, he opened the blanket and folded her into the cocoon with him. The motion startled her, and she wasn't sure what to do.

He drew her closer. "We wouldn't have been able to get as much done without your help."

She didn't resist his embrace and laid her head against him. "I want to help you, Reinhold."

He nodded. Was he finally accepting his need for her? She closed her eyes and hoped so.

After a few seconds, he pressed a kiss against her head and began to release her. At the same time, he shuddered.

Rather than letting go, she snaked her arms underneath the first blanket, prying it back, and wrapped her arms around his body. "I'll help you get warm." She laid her cheek against his bare chest and leaned into him, attempting to transfer her body heat to his.

He held himself stiffly, his arms loose, as though he wasn't sure what to think of her boldness. He was only clad in his underdrawers now, which was completely inappropriate. Or was it? She was his wife, after all. And she loved him.

"For just a minute," she whispered, splaying her fingers against the cold flesh of his back. "I'll warm you for just a minute." She rubbed up and down his back, hoping the friction would thaw his skin.

After a few seconds, she could feel him relax against her. His arms slid around her and enfolded them both in the blankets.

She began massaging his back, working her fingers all the way to his neck.

His breath near her forehead was warm, as was the stretch of him against her cheek. She closed her eyes and relished the mixture of heat and hardness that emanated from his chest. The steady rhythm of his heartbeat thudded in her ear. He was a wall of strength, his arms like solid beams holding her up. She loved the security she felt within his embrace. It was unlike anything she'd known before.

She shifted her head so that her mouth brushed his chest. The sensation of his skin against her lips was more delicious than the sweetest of Euphemia's cakes. She went back for more, needing another taste.

He sucked in a sharp breath. His body grew rigid and his hold taut.

What was she doing? She blinked away the haze that had apparently driven away her good senses. Why did she seem to lose herself whenever she was with Reinhold? Even if they were married, this wasn't how she wanted to win him over.

She began to pull away, but then his lips grazed her forehead. His breathing was ragged. He shifted, and she waited for him to release her. She sensed he was holding back, that he was waging an inner battle. But instead of retreating, his fingers spread against her nightgown, moving her closer.

He buried his nose into her hair as though that was a safe place. Again he sucked in a breath, then let out a soft groan. He dug his fingers into her as he leaned in closer, his mouth hungrily seeking hers.

She only had to turn slightly for her lips to collide against his with a force that made her body tremble with wanting him. She deepened their connection in a long, breathless kiss. He lifted his lips away for a moment only to bring them down more eagerly, tangling together in a kiss that left her too weak to stand. She moved her hands to his arms to brace herself. At the same moment he let the blankets drop.

Without breaking his lips from hers, he swept her off her feet and cradled her against his chest. She wound her arms around his neck, savoring his nearness, the scrape of his stubble against her cheek, the pressure of his hands on her body.

With a heaving chest, he broke the kiss only to move his mouth to her jaw, then neck, then collarbone. The trail he made with his kisses fanned the sparks inside her.

"Sophie," he whispered, his voice low. "Tell me to stop."

"No . . . I don't want you to stop."

At her admission, he found her lips again. He claimed them in another kiss that tugged at her very core, pulling an invisible string taut. At the same time, she could feel him moving, carrying her toward the stairs. She wanted him to hurry, feeling an urgency she didn't understand.

As he took them up one step, then two, a pounding against the front door drew him to a stop. He pulled back, cutting off their kiss abruptly. As they listened, their heavy breathing filled the stairwell.

After several seconds, another knock sounded, this one more insistent. Who would be at their door at this time of the morning? Had Euphemia sent one of the boys to find out if they needed more help?

Reinhold backed down the steps and set Sophie's feet on the floor. He steadied her before releasing her and striding out of the kitchen into the front room.

Without the warmth of his body surrounding her, she hugged her arms and rubbed away the raised hairs. Her mind whirred with the realization she'd been kissing Reinhold and that he'd been in the process of taking her upstairs to the bedroom. She shivered again, this time with nervousness and anticipation.

She hoped the visitor was Fergus or Alastair and that Reinhold would send the boy on his way with just a word or two. When Reinhold returned, would he pick her up again? Would he resume where they'd left off? Or would they be shy and awkward with each other once more?

Reinhold's firm steps came to a halt in the front room. A *click* sounded as he unlatched the lock. Then he opened the door, and a gust of wind whistled around the windowpanes.

"How can I help you?" Reinhold asked, his voice formal and containing a note of alarm.

Sophie knew she wasn't attired to receive company and neither was Reinhold. Nevertheless, she crossed the kitchen and stepped into the front room. Through the growing light of dawn, she made out the hunched form of a woman standing outside, her long dark hair tangled and wet, falling across the torn shoulder of her bodice and revealing bare skin underneath.

"I need Sophie," the woman said through chattering teeth.

At the voice, Sophie started. "Anna? Is that you?"

CHAPTER 19

Reinhold swallowed hard, trying to force down the self-loathing that was pushing up like bile. What had he been thinking?

Using a towel, he lifted the steaming pot from the stove and headed toward the steps. Sophie was waiting for the water, had asked him to set it to heating so she could wash the young woman.

The moment Sophie had ushered Anna inside, the woman had collapsed unconscious on the floor. Sophie had helped him carry her up to the bed. And then she'd proceeded to undress her friend, sending him to fetch warm water.

All he'd been able to think about since retreating to the kitchen was the fact that he'd almost taken Sophie to bed. "What in all that's holy were you thinking?" he whispered harshly as he passed by his pile of discarded clothing and blankets on the floor.

But even as he chided himself, he stumbled, his legs turning weak at the memory of the softness of her body pressing into him, the hot mingling of their mouths, the delectable taste of her skin, and his desire for more.

He halted and closed his eyes, willing himself to forget about her low, sultry voice saying, *"I don't want you to stop."*

He *had* to stop. There was no other choice. As beautiful and desirable as Sophie was, she wasn't his. At least not forever. He only had her for a short time. He was her guardian, the one who'd found her after all the time she'd been lost.

His goal was to return her to her family safe and unblemished, so she could have all the privileges and luxuries Elise and Marianne would provide. After working so diligently to prevent her from running away and to keep her safe from other men who'd lust after her, he very well could have ruined it all in one unguarded moment.

What had he almost done?

The self-loathing rose in his throat again.

He'd tried to maintain a distance from her since their wedding day. Although he relished when she sat at the kitchen table with him while he ate dinner or when she brought her sewing into the barn at night and they talked, he always stayed several feet away. He'd been tempted a time or two to bend in and steal a kiss. But he'd been strong and good and had held himself back. Until today . . .

With his heavy footfalls thudding against each step as though he carried an enormous burden, he trudged upstairs.

He shouldn't have let her help him out of his wet clothing. She'd merely been trying to aid him in getting warm, but his thoughts had strayed into dangerous territory when she'd unbuttoned his shirt and tugged it off. He should have gone upstairs and changed on his own. Or at the very least made sure she was completely covered at all times instead of admiring the way her silky nightgown had clung to her womanly form.

But instead of fleeing from temptation, he'd told himself one little look wouldn't hurt. One small touch wouldn't affect him. One innocent hug to warm him wouldn't be wrong.

"What were you thinking?" he quietly berated himself again. The problem was, he hadn't been thinking. He'd allowed himself to get carried away with his desires—desires he didn't want or need.

As he reached the top of the dark stairwell, Sophie met him in the hallway. He could sense her worry more than see it.

"There you are," she whispered, reaching for the handle.

"Tell me where you want it," he said tersely. "And I'll carry it."

She led the way into the bedroom and removed several items from the crate next to the bed, including the angel candle holder she'd placed there. He remembered that it had belonged to her mother. Mrs. Neumann had given each of the sisters items from among her meager possessions, and he was relieved to see Sophie had kept the candle holder. If she'd hung on to it all this time, surely that meant she still felt some kind of connection with her family—her sisters.

If Elise and Marianne discovered he'd been kissing Sophie like a possessed man, they'd be disappointed in him. It didn't matter that Sophie was a grown woman and had proven herself to be capable and mature. They'd still expect him to treat Sophie like a sister, not a lover.

He placed the steaming pot of water on the crate and then moved out of Sophie's way.

With every day that passed, Sophie had stepped into the role of a farmer's wife as if she truly enjoyed it. She'd been an eager learner, catching on quickly to everything Euphemia taught her. In the two weeks of living with him, she'd transformed the farmhouse into a pretty but practical environment with curtains and rugs and decorations.

He appreciated all her efforts, not only with the house but also her hard work with harvesting the garden and preserving food for the winter. After building shelves in the cellar, he was excited to see the stores of food she'd brought in and was proud of her.

Jakob was thriving with her there, appreciating the regular

meals and having someone to talk to besides him. She doted on the boy, teasing and caring for him as if he were her own brother.

She'd proven herself to be of value in the fields as well. Although he hadn't liked subjecting her to harvesting the potatoes, he'd again felt a measure of pride and gratefulness for her willingness to do whatever needed to be done. She'd recognized how vital it was to get the potatoes out of the ground, and she hadn't rested until the work was done, even though she'd clearly been cold and exhausted.

Even now, after a sleepless night, she busied herself taking care of Anna.

In the pale light from the lantern she'd hung from the ceiling beam, he could see that Anna's face was bruised, her bottom lip swollen, and her neck scratched. From the condition of her clothing, he suspected she'd been assaulted.

Sophie had already told him about Anna during one of their late-night barn conversations. He knew Anna had helped Sophie find shelter in New York City, that Anna's sister Mollie had taken them in, and that Anna had fled west with her to escape repercussions from the Roach Guard gang.

Sophie dipped a cloth in the warm water, and that was when he saw the tears coursing down her cheeks. At the sight of her distress, he caught her arm and pulled her toward him. She didn't resist, but fell into him. "What's wrong?" he whispered. "Why the tears?"

"It's my fault this happened, that Anna's like this."

"Did she wake up and tell you what happened?"

"For just a few minutes." Sophie shuddered against him, and Reinhold drew her closer. All his reservations from only moments ago vanished with the need to comfort her. "If only we'd gone our own way in Chicago like we planned."

His entire being rebelled against the notion of her being in Chicago. "No, Soph, you did the right thing—"

"But Mr. Pierce is an animal. He forced himself onto Anna, and when she didn't cooperate, he attacked her."

"So he violated her?"

"She said she fought him off and then ran away." Sophie shuddered again.

Reinhold kissed her loose, silky hair.

"I shouldn't have let her go with him," Sophie whispered through her tears. "I should have fought to keep us together."

What if Sophie had been the one to go with the Pierces instead of Anna? Anger ignited deep inside Reinhold at the thought of any other man touching Sophie, much less hurting her. He hugged her tighter, grateful he'd found her, that she was here and never again would have to be homeless and susceptible to men like Mr. Pierce.

He ran his hand down the length of her hair, letting his fingers get lost there. He was suddenly conscious once again of her body against his, the softness melding into him. That same sharp desire he'd experienced in the kitchen rolled through him like a sudden hot fever.

He almost trembled with the need to taste her kiss, to fuse his mouth and body with hers.

At a mumbling from the bed, Sophie pulled back and wiped at her cheeks.

He reluctantly released her and started toward the door. Once in the dark hallway, he stopped and leaned his forehead against the wall, soaking in the coolness and attempting to control his erratic pulse. What was he doing? He thumped his head against the wall to knock some sense into himself. He'd just given himself a lecture about the need to keep his hands off Sophie. How could he have so easily given in to his desire?

Silently he cursed his weakness. If he allowed himself to take his pleasure with Sophie, he'd be no better than Mr. Pierce. Surely Sophie was just as vulnerable as Anna. They were both penniless and dependent on others for survival, which made them easy prey.

Even if Sophie didn't consider herself vulnerable in the same way as Anna, she still was. She needed him right now. She was relying on him to help her gain custody of Olivia and Nicholas. If the circumstances were different, if she had the means to take care of herself and already had the children, then she wouldn't have married him and wouldn't have kissed him.

Sure, maybe she thought she liked him. After all, she'd kissed him back and seemed to find pleasure in his touch. But the truth was, she wouldn't be here if she had a way to survive on her own. And if he allowed their passion to go unchecked, he'd be taking what she couldn't freely offer. He'd be using her, and he couldn't allow himself to do that.

He bumped his head against the wall again. He had to stick with their original plan to keep their relationship a business partnership. The problem was, he was too weak and apparently too enamored with her to maintain his resolve. He couldn't keep his hands off her or his desires in check.

There was only one thing left to do. It was something he should have done already, and he wouldn't put it off another day. He'd ride into town as soon as he finished the morning chores and place the telegram to Elise and Marianne. Surely by week's end they'd come and collect their lost little sister and take her home with them where she belonged. After looking for her all this time, they'd be ecstatic the search was finally over.

Yes, he'd promised Sophie he wouldn't contact them. But this was for her own good, for her protection from him, and for her future freedom. Maybe someday she'd understand and forgive him.

☙❧

Sophie lifted Anna's head and helped her to take a sip of coffee. Anna winced as the mug made contact with her split lip.

"I'm sorry." Sophie eased the mug away.

"It looks worse than it feels," Anna replied, lying back again. The skin around one eye was swollen and discolored with a mixture of black and purple, her cheekbone contained a bright red welt, and fingerprints marred her neck where Mr. Pierce had attempted to choke her.

"We shouldn't have come west with the orphans." Sophie placed the mug onto the crate next to the bed. But even as she said the words, she realized she was lying to herself. If she hadn't come west, she wouldn't have seen Reinhold again. And now that she had, she couldn't imagine her life without him.

"I could have just as easily gotten beaten up in the city," Anna said.

"But isn't life supposed to be better here?" Sophie sat in the chair she'd brought up from the kitchen and positioned next to the bed. "Reverend and Mrs. Poole promised that these families would provide good homes."

"And yours has," Anna said, looking around the sparse bedroom. "You ended up in two places that are both wonderful."

Sophie had already informed Anna about all that had transpired over the past month, telling her friend first about her home with the Duffs and then about marrying Reinhold so that she could get Olivia and Nicholas back. She hadn't explained to Anna the true nature of her relationship with Reinhold. How could she when she didn't understand it yet herself?

She wanted to sneak a few minutes alone with Reinhold and steal a few more kisses, and maybe this time she'd gather the courage to tell him she loved him. Maybe their marriage had started out with her using him to get Nicholas and Olivia, but it was more than that now, and she wanted him to know.

"I was content at the Pierces'. Until yesterday." Anna shivered, and Sophie tugged the blanket up to her friend's shoulders. "I thought Ben—Mr. Pierce—was a sweet man. He was always considerate and kind and friendly. Yet I should have realized he was trying to make me like him so that I'd sleep with him."

"How could you realize that?" Sophie smoothed a hand over Anna's cheek.

"Now that I look back, I can see all the signs. He confided in me that his wife was cold to him, and he complained she didn't love him anymore. She never got upset when Ben talked to me or spent time with me. In fact, she seemed almost relieved I was taking his attention. There were even times when I blamed her for being calloused and thought about what it would be like to become his wife in her place."

Anna's eyes turned glassy with unshed tears. "What if this was my fault, Sophie? What if he sensed that I liked him? What if I was too forward and made him believe I'd welcome his affection?"

"What happened isn't your fault," Sophie replied. "No man should force himself onto a woman, even if the woman really cares about him."

"But maybe I gave him the impression that I wanted him too."

Sophie pictured the way Anna had been with Mugs—kissing and holding him freely, going much further than Sophie had with Danny. Had Anna done the same with Mr. Pierce? "It doesn't matter how affectionate you were," she said adamantly. "No one should ever make you do something that you're not agreeable to. If it's not mutual loving, then it's not love."

Anna nodded, but her expression remained skeptical.

Sophie tried to think of a way she could reassure her friend further that she wasn't to blame in any way for what had happened, but a sound outside the window drew her attention.

Was Reinhold finally returning? He'd left shortly after finishing his morning chores, telling her he had some business to attend to in town. She'd pleaded with him to sleep, but he'd insisted he needed to make good use of the frozen morning for running errands he'd been putting off.

She could hardly blame him for denying himself sleep when she'd done the same. Between caring for Anna and preparing meals, she'd only managed to rest for a couple of hours in the chair while Anna had slept.

Her heart gave an extra thud at the prospect of seeing Reinhold again. She was surprised at how much she missed him while he'd been gone. Thoughts of their passionate kisses from earlier stole into her mind, stirring longing for more.

She pushed out of her chair, eagerness bringing a smile to her lips.

"You love him," Anna said.

It was more of a statement than a question. But it stopped Sophie. She weighed her friend's words before answering. "I always admired him. I guess it was easy for my admiration to change to love."

Anna regarded her with a somber expression. "Does he love you in return?"

"I think so." He'd kissed her like he loved her. But she wasn't naïve enough to believe that passion was the same thing as love. She sighed. "I don't know."

"Then be careful," Anna said. "A wise person once told me that if it's not mutual loving, it's not love."

Sophie's stomach fluttered at her friend's implication. "We haven't loved each other that way yet."

Anna quirked a brow.

"It's complicated," Sophie said.

"Are you planning to go your separate ways eventually?" Anna was as direct as always.

"No." They hadn't spoken of separating. At least she had no intention of it. She picked up the angel candle holder from the floor and placed it back on the crate in its spot of prominence. In all the places she'd lived over the past couple of years, she'd never put it out as a decoration. She'd used it as a weapon to break windows or locks, but she'd always tucked it back in her bag when she was finished.

But when cleaning the bedroom, she'd decided to liven it up. She brought in the crate, along with a rug and a colorful quilt Euphemia had given her, and it seemed only natural to put out the candle holder. It was still tarnished; she hadn't polished it yet. Even so, with all its imperfections, the candle holder looked at home here.

This was home now, wasn't it? This was what she'd been searching for—a safe and secure place she'd never have to leave. Just as soon as she had Nicholas and Olivia, she'd be truly happy. She'd have everything she wanted.

But did Reinhold feel the same way? What if he didn't want to be burdened with her and Olivia and Nicholas forever? What if he wanted to have his old life back without the worry of a wife and children?

She shook her head. No, he wouldn't be thinking that. He couldn't be. Not after the way he'd held her.

Sophie crossed to the window, pulled aside the curtain, and peered past the rain-streaked glass. Earlier in the day, a thin layer of ice had coated the grass and fields and garden, turning the green landscape into a frosted wonderland. Then, as the day progressed, cold rain had washed away the brittle beauty of the morning, leaving in its place a soggy, muddy earth.

The horse and wagon slogging through the mud and water wasn't Reinhold's. Neither was the thin man hunched over to ward off the chill of the day. His oiled cloak was wrapped tight, his hat tipped low.

Sophie speculated over the man's identity and was terrified at the prospect of Mr. Pierce coming to claim Anna. What if he barged into the house, stomped up the steps, and dragged Anna out of bed? How would they be able to stop him?

Jakob had arisen at dinnertime, eaten, and then headed off to fish for the afternoon. And Reinhold was still gone into town. She and Anna were alone and defenseless.

Just as the panic mounted, the newcomer glanced upward, as though sensing her looking at him from the bedroom window. A middle-aged man with spectacles, long sideburns, and a mustache stared up at her.

It was Reverend Poole.

CHAPTER 20

"Reverend Poole!" Sophie called as she stepped outside into the gray autumn afternoon. A chill permeated the air, and she hugged her shawl closer to her body.

She was disappointed he was alone, that Olivia and Nicholas weren't scurrying from the wagon bed, eager to see her. Maybe the reverend hadn't gone to the Ramseys' place yet. Maybe he was coming to talk to her and Reinhold first, to assure himself of their marriage and of the living situation.

"Good afternoon, Sophie." Reverend Poole had halted in a grassy section of the farmyard that hadn't been pecked clean by the chickens. "Or should I say good afternoon, Mrs. Weiss?"

Mrs. Weiss. The sound of it sent a thrill through her. She was Mrs. Reinhold Weiss, and she was no longer under the jurisdiction of Reverend Poole or any other New York City worker. She was free, her own person, and no longer had to worry about being sent to jail or an orphan asylum.

"Good afternoon, Reverend," she replied, attempting to use her best manners. She didn't want Reinhold to be ashamed of her as his wife. She didn't really know what was expected of her in greeting and welcoming company, but she had to try to make a good impression so that Reverend Poole would see she could take good care of the children.

He climbed down from the wagon bench and rubbed his gloved hands together as if attempting to regain warmth in them.

"Would you like to come inside for coffee?" she asked, thankful she'd had the foresight to pick up Reinhold's wet clothes and hang them to dry. She wouldn't want the reverend thinking Reinhold had undressed in the middle of the kitchen—even though he had, with her help.

Her cheeks heated, and she prayed the reverend couldn't see her thoughts.

"I wouldn't mind the chance to warm myself up," he said as pleasantly as always.

She pivoted toward the house.

Reverend Poole didn't follow her but instead rounded the wagon. "This little child of Christ is in need of warming too."

Sophie froze. As the meaning of the reverend's words penetrated and thawed her mind, she ran to the wagon bed, heedless of the puddles and the mud.

As the reverend pulled aside a wet canvas to reveal a lump under a pile of blankets, Sophie's breath hitched. And as a little hand poked its way out of the tangle of blankets followed by a familiar face, Sophie cried out and scrambled up into the wagon. At the same time, the child was free of the blankets.

"Olivia!" Sophie dragged the girl into her arms.

Olivia came willingly, flinging herself at Sophie and hugging her with a fierceness that made Sophie's heart ache. She could only imagine all the hurt, loneliness, and despair Olivia had experienced over the past month at the Ramseys'. The tightness of Olivia's hold and the sobs shaking her frail body told Sophie more than words could.

"It's all right, Liebchen," Sophie crooned, even as tears

slipped out and flowed down her cheeks. "You'll be fine now. You're with me."

Over the top of the girl's head, Sophie met the reverend's gaze. He smiled gently. "I'm always grateful to the Lord when we get to experience a happy reunion like this."

Sophie started to agree with him, but then released Olivia and searched the pile of blankets for another lump, another little body. She willed Nicholas to pop out and give her one of his endearing smiles. But the blankets lay flat.

"Where's Nicholas?" She shoved at the canvas, hoping to unveil Nicholas in the other corner, but her efforts were to no avail.

The reverend's smile faded. "I know you wanted to keep the children together—"

"Where is he?" Sophie pulled Olivia into her arms and clung to her, suddenly afraid that the reverend would take her away.

"The boy is still with the Ramseys," Reverend Poole said, his expression one of pity. "They were ready to part with Olivia, had apparently only taken her on a trial basis, but they love Nicholas and want to keep him as their son."

"The children must stay together." Desperation dug deep into Sophie's stomach. "They're brother and sister and need to be with each other."

The reverend shook his head sadly. "We often must split siblings, Sophie. You know that. But in this case, we can count our blessings the children will be in such close proximity to each other."

"They'll be even closer." Sophie's tone turned hard. "Because they'll both be living together right here."

"The Ramseys are making plans to adopt Nicholas."

"No!" Sophie cried. "They can't. He belongs with me and Olivia. We're his family."

"I've been informed that you're not really his sister."

Of course, Mr. Ramsey would have to expose her lie, undermine her trustworthiness, and create another reason not to return Nicholas to her care.

"It doesn't matter whether I'm related to Nicholas and Olivia by blood. I've raised them both since they were babies. I'm the only mother they've known."

"But now Nicholas has the chance to have a real mother and father—"

"I'm real—my love is real too."

The reverend studied Sophie for a moment, as though weighing her words, but then he shook his head. "I'm sorry, Sophie. The Ramseys took Nicholas during his greatest hour of need. And I have no just cause to take him away—"

"If being with his family isn't reason enough to bring him here, then all you need to do is investigate how Mr. Ramsey treats the children. He's cruel. He locked Olivia in the attic!"

"Mr. Ramsey explained everything." Reverend Poole waved his hand, dismissing her concerns. "Apparently the girl needed to be disciplined, and rather than use the rod, he decided to give her time alone to think about her naughty behavior."

From the way the reverend described the situation, Mr. Ramsey appeared almost benevolent. But Sophie had been to the house and had witnessed the cruelty for herself. Nicholas's fear, Olivia's pitiful cries, Mr. Ramsey's rage. It wasn't normal. And Mr. Ramsey wasn't nice.

"Something is wrong with that man," Sophie insisted. "His house is too neat. He's too controlling . . . and he wouldn't let me visit the children."

Reverend Poole cocked his head, the pity in his eyes now irritating Sophie. "A neat house is hardly something to complain about. And as for controlling, Mr. Ramsey explained that he felt you were trying to visit the children too often and that such visits would only cause the children to cling to their past instead of let go and become a part of their new family. I have to say, I agree with him."

Sophie could only watch the reverend with growing helplessness. Mr. Ramsey had already convinced Reverend Poole to side with him, and it was becoming clear that nothing would sway him.

Sophie moved to get out of the wagon, but Olivia clung to her so tightly that Sophie could hardly budge. Finally when she was standing again, she held Olivia like she used to do when the girl was much younger, with Olivia's arms wrapped around her neck and legs locked at her waist. Sophie could feel Olivia's bones sharply, and she weighed next to nothing. Not only had the little girl lost weight, but she seemed to have wilted over the past month, going from a strong-willed and talkative girl into a frightened, ghostlike shell of one.

If this could happen to Olivia after living with the Ramseys, what would happen to Nicholas? Sophie guessed he would fare better since the family actually wanted him. Even so, she didn't like Mr. Ramsey and didn't want Nicholas with him any longer. But how could she get him away?

The sound of horse hooves pounding the earth brought Sophie's head back up. She peered down the muddy path to the sight of another horse and wagon driven by a lone rider with broad shoulders, a stocky build, and ruggedly handsome features.

Reinhold.

Reinhold would help her. He could convince the reverend to give them Nicholas.

The reverend might not respect her, might still view her as an orphan girl who didn't know what was best. But surely he would listen to Reinhold.

Reinhold strained to keep his eyes open. For part of the last mile home, he'd dozed. The lack of sleep the previous night and the weariness of the day had finally caught up with him. Now, as he rumbled down the path toward home, the weight of all he'd done was overpowering, making him want to drop into the nearest haymow and fall into oblivion for just a little while.

Even though he wished he didn't have to say anything, sooner or later he'd have to tell Sophie. And he wanted to be well rested when he explained his actions.

All the way home he'd justified the telegram, told himself he should have sent it the first day he'd seen Sophie. Then perhaps he wouldn't be in his current predicament, wanting Sophie in his arms every time she turned around. Or thinking about how much he liked having her on the farm, as if she were meant to be there with him. Because she wasn't.

He stuck his hand into his pocket and grazed his father's watch, running his thumb along the jagged line in the cracked glass. The old thing had never worked, not even when his mother had given it to him after his father's death. At the time, he'd kept it as a reminder that he didn't want to become a brute like his father, a man who took out his anger on those around him.

But he'd ended up a brute anyway.

His anger was like a living and breathing dragon inside him. Although he kept it caged in the dark dungeon of his soul most of the time, there were times that it roared to life, spewing fire and wreaking destruction in its wake. And those times when he lost control scared and frustrated him.

He didn't deserve someone as beautiful and vivacious as Sophie. He didn't think he would ever hit her, yet his anger was dangerous. What would happen if it got the best of him? What if he ended up in jail and died there like his own father, leaving her helpless and alone and having to raise a family on her own?

No, she'd be better off with a different man, someone more

righteous than he was. That was just one more reason why he'd done the right thing today in sending the telegram.

He expelled a long sigh, his breath coming out in a cloud of white against the frigid October day. The wagon rolled slowly, his grip on the reins having loosened the closer he drew to the house. He didn't want to face her. Not yet.

But at the urgent call of his name, he lifted his head and tipped up the brim of his hat. Another wagon was parked in front of his house. A man in a stovepipe hat and long, dark cloak stood next to the wagon. The man wore spectacles and had a serious but not unkind expression. With his long mustache and thick sideburns, he had a scholarly appearance, certainly not the weathered, sunbrowned face of a farmer.

"Reinhold!" Sophie called again. She stood near the visitor and held a petite girl in her arms. Rather, the girl seemed to be clinging to Sophie. "This is Reverend Poole."

Reinhold drove the wagon until he was next to his visitor. As he rolled to a halt, he glanced between the reverend and Sophie, noting the tension in the air. He didn't know what had transpired since the reverend's arrival, but Reinhold's muscles became taut with the need to defend Sophie.

"Reverend Poole," Sophie said to their visitor. "This is my husband, Reinhold Weiss."

Reinhold knew he shouldn't savor Sophie calling him her husband, but he liked feeling that he belonged with her, even if only temporarily. He nodded curtly at the reverend. "We just received your telegram yesterday." Had it only been last evening when Sophie had come out to the field with the telegram and then stayed to help with the potatoes? It seemed as though it had been so much longer than that.

"I sent it several days ago before leaving Quincy," the reverend said. "I arrived in Mayfield this morning and thought I'd attend to the matter right away."

Reinhold hoisted himself from the wagon, his joints aching like those of an old man. As his feet touched the ground, a draft of fresh weariness blew against him.

"The reverend has brought us Olivia," Sophie said, cradling the child and pressing a kiss to her head. "But he said we can't have Nicholas."

Reinhold couldn't see Olivia's features, but in the years since he'd last seen her, she'd doubled in size and her brown hair had grown darker and longer. She'd been just an infant and now was a mature-looking girl, albeit still small in stature.

From the way she'd burrowed her face into Sophie's neck, he sensed her timidity and fear. He approached cautiously, digging into his pocket beyond his watch. He found the sugarcoated lumps at the bottom and pulled them out.

He'd splurged on the gumdrops for Sophie, remembering back to the days in Kleindeutschland when he'd occasionally bought candy for the Neumann sisters and Olivia and Nicholas, wanting to give them small moments of pleasure amidst the sadness of all their losses.

He hadn't been able to afford the candy then any more than he had today. Yet the sacrifice had always been worth it. He'd loved the way Sophie had giggled at his teasing and looked up at him with adoring eyes when he'd finally put the gumdrop in her outstretched hand.

Today he'd hoped the gumdrops would ease the sting of the news he had to deliver and remind her of the long past connection he had with both her and her sisters.

But for now, maybe the piece of candy would soothe Olivia's fear and assure her that life would be sweeter from now on— especially once Elise and Marrianne arrived and took Olivia and Sophie into their care.

"Do you remember me, Olivia?" he asked softly. "I used to give you these."

Sophie's eyes lit appreciatively at the sight of the gumdrops, and she smiled at him with both encouragement and approval.

Olivia tightened her hold around Sophie's neck.

Reinhold moved his hand closer, revealing the gumdrops. "You used to love them."

Olivia didn't move for a few seconds, then finally she shifted and peeked at Reinhold's hand. At the sight of the colorful mix of candy, she lifted her head from Sophie's neck and looked at Reinhold.

The little girl's face was thin, delicate, and plain, certainly not a face that would stand out in a crowd the way that Sophie's would. But her eyes rounded with recognition and interest.

He smiled and held the candy out further. "Which one is your favorite color?"

After studying the assortment, she chose a red one. She popped it into her mouth and then buried her face into Sophie's neck again.

"What do you say to Reinhold?" Sophie gently admonished the girl.

"Thank you" came Olivia's muffled response.

Sophie's eyes met his, and once more they filled with approval, an approval that sank into him and settled deep in his bones.

"The rest are for you," he said and held out the candy to her.

"For me?" Her smile widened into one of genuine delight.

He nodded and placed them into her outstretched hand.

Her fingers closed around the gumdrops. "You shouldn't have . . ." Her lashes lowered against flushed cheeks.

"I wanted to." Suddenly he wished he could bring home candy to her every time he returned from town. He'd put a piece into her mouth himself, graze her full lips, maybe even kiss the sugar off them, and then stand back and watch the pleasure ripple across her face as she tasted the treat.

A loud clearing of the throat drew his attention away from Sophie, making him realize he'd been staring at her lips. He stepped back rapidly and tried to clear his head through the haze of desire and exhaustion.

"I can see that yours is a happy union," Reverend Poole said and then cleared his throat again. "It would appear that your love for each other bloomed rather quickly, unless the love is a remnant from your previous friendship?"

The flush in Sophie's cheeks deepened.

Reinhold knew he ought to contradict the reverend. He and Sophie had never professed to love each other. Theirs was a marriage of convenience, a marriage that would soon be ending. But somehow he sensed such a revelation wouldn't impress the reverend, would perhaps work against Sophie's efforts to gain and keep the children.

For now, he needed to maintain the appearance of a loving husband.

"Sophie is easy to love." He didn't mean to look at her as he said the words, especially to meet her gaze. But he did. And he was surprised to see love shining in her eyes.

Did she love him? The possibility heated him instantly. If they'd been alone, if she hadn't been holding Olivia, he would have spanned the distance separating them and brought his mouth down on hers.

As if realizing his intentions, her sights dropped to his mouth.

The reverend coughed this time. "It's lovely to see you're getting along so well. Naturally I assumed that such a quick wedding meant that Sophie . . . well, was in trouble."

"Of course not, Reverend," Sophie stammered in mortification.

It took another second for Reinhold to grasp the meaning of the reverend's insinuation. Did Reverend Poole assume they'd had to get married because Sophie was pregnant?

At the insult to Sophie, anger kicked against Reinhold's ribs like a mule against a fence post. He took a step toward the reverend, his fingers balling into fists. He'd never hit a man of God, but he was sure tempted.

Sophie's hand on his arm halted him. "Reinhold's the most honorable person I know, Reverend. The truth is, we got married so we could provide a good and loving home for Nicholas and Olivia."

For a few seconds, Reverend Poole didn't speak. Instead, he studied Sophie, then turned his attention first to the house and then to the barn. His eyes were bigger than copper pennies behind his spectacles, taking everything in. Reinhold was afraid the man would find fault with some detail, perhaps realize how little Reinhold had, discover how much debt he still owed, or learn about the monster that lived inside him.

He doubted the man realized Sophie's connection to Marianne and Drew Brady, his fellow placing agents. Otherwise he likely would have raised more questions regarding their marriage, perhaps would have snatched up Sophie and Olivia and driven them away.

The pressure in Reinhold's lungs built as the reverend finished his inspection. When the man turned his attention back to Reinhold and gave a friendly nod, Reinhold exhaled.

"You've got a nice place here, Mr. Weiss."

"It's small but coming along."

"From what I've seen so far, I'm convinced you'll provide well for Sophie and Olivia."

"And Nicholas," he added.

"Nicholas is staying with the Ramseys." Reverend Poole adjusted his tall black hat as though readying himself to leave.

"We'd like him to be here with us," Reinhold insisted.

Sophie's soft body pressed against his side, her icy fingers gripping him tightly.

He slipped an arm around her waist, bracing her in the crook of his body. Her presence seemed so fitting, and holding her was as natural to him as breathing.

"I already explained to Sophie the nature of the placement and that I'm not at liberty to take Nicholas away from the Ramseys."

"He belongs with his sister and Sophie."

The reverend looked Reinhold in the eye. "I understand that everyone would like to be together. But I talked at length with Mr. Ramsey this morning, and he's quite determined to keep the boy. No amount of discourse could persuade him otherwise."

Something in the reverend's expression told Reinhold that he'd done his best to honor their request to have both the children. But he'd failed just as they had.

"Is there anything more that can be done?" Reinhold asked. "Anyone else we can contact regarding the placement and gaining custody of the boy?"

"I'm afraid we may not be able to do much," Reverend Poole said. "As long as Nicholas doesn't have any family to come forward to claim him, and as long as the Ramseys are taking good care of him, then we have no cause to take him away."

"But I am his family," Sophie said.

"Primary relatives," the reverend clarified, "particularly a father or mother."

Sophie started to argue, but Reinhold stopped her with a gentle squeeze. When she looked up at him, her eyes filled with tears. "What are we going to do?"

"We'll figure out something, Soph." Reinhold spoke with more confidence than he felt. "There has to be something we can do." He just prayed he was telling her the truth, that they would find a way to get Nicholas, and that it would be soon.

CHAPTER 21

Reinhold sifted through the potatoes he'd laid out on the hay. Some had gotten wet in their frantic efforts to get them dug and into the barn. And now they needed drying before he could take them to the market.

The barn door opened, and a burst of cold night air entered. Reinhold didn't glance behind him, guessing Jakob had finally returned from the Duffs' after fishing and hunting with Fergus and Alastair on a rare day off from working the fields. He couldn't begrudge the boy a day to be with his friends—something Reinhold hadn't been able to do at that age. By the time he was fifteen, he'd already been working long hours in construction so he could support his mother and siblings. He'd taken over the job of providing for his family after his father had landed in jail, and he'd been doing it ever since.

Soon he'd have Silke and Verina in his care. He'd told Elise and Marianne they could bring his sisters when they came. In addition to asking them to bring the girls, he'd let them know he'd found Sophie and that she was in Mayfield with him. He hadn't mentioned they were married. He reassured himself that small detail wasn't important, that he'd figure out a way to break the news once they arrived. He'd inform them of his plans to move forward with the annulment as soon as possible.

"Reinhold?" Sophie's voice startled him and made his heart speed with the desire he'd been fighting all day. He couldn't deny he enjoyed being around her. It didn't matter what they were doing or where they were, he liked having her near.

He started to step out of the shadows of the stall but then stopped. As much as he wanted to be with her, to see her, to hear her voice, he hadn't yet told her about sending the telegram. He'd considered waiting until the end of the week and letting Elise and Marianne ride out to surprise Sophie. But with the way news traveled around the community, Sophie would likely hear about his telegram from someone before too long.

"Are you already asleep?" she asked, coming into the barn farther, so that the lantern he'd hung from the rafter shone down on her. Even with her splattered apron still tied over her skirt and the wisps of hair that had come loose from her long braid, her beauty was stunning and never failed to amaze him.

Maybe he could put off telling her about the telegram until tomorrow. Tonight they were both tired from the previous night's work as well as the long day.

He moved out of the stall. At the soft crackling of hay beneath his feet, she turned his direction and then smiled.

"How's Olivia?" he asked.

"She's finally asleep."

Olivia had been silent and teary-eyed the rest of the day after Reverend Poole left. She'd eaten very little and was listless, clinging to Sophie almost constantly.

Sophie began to move toward him. Thankfully the maze of drying potatoes slowed her down and gave him time to stuff both hands into his pockets so that he didn't reach for her the way he wanted to. "You don't think Jakob will mind giving up his room for Olivia?"

"He'll be fine out here with me."

Sophie nodded reluctantly. "Maybe eventually we can use the front room as a bedroom too."

"Maybe." He squirmed with the realization that she wouldn't need to worry about bedrooms by the week's end. Elise and Marianne would be able to provide everyone with their own rooms and their own beds.

"Once Anna no longer needs my bed, Olivia can sleep with me," Sophie said softly, almost shyly. "But I didn't know how you'd feel about it . . ."

How he'd feel about it? Was she asking if he planned to continue where they left off this morning when he'd almost carried her upstairs?

Of course he wouldn't want Olivia there. That was how he'd feel about it. He'd want Sophie all to himself all night long. But he wasn't taking Sophie to his bed. Not now, not ever.

He ducked his head to hide his desire. "How's Anna?"

"She's afraid that if Reverend Poole discovers she's here, he'll force her to go back to the Pierces'."

"Once the reverend sees her wounds, he wouldn't dare make her return."

"But what if Mr. Pierce lies about what really happened? If Mr. Ramsey can twist everything to keep Nicholas, then it could happen to Anna too."

Reinhold didn't think the reverend would be so cruel as to make Anna go back. But he hadn't expected the reverend to allow Mr. Ramsey to keep Nicholas. "We won't tell the reverend she's here."

A hopeful glimmer lit Sophie's eyes. "Really?"

Reinhold hesitated. He couldn't keep Anna with him indefinitely, especially after Sophie left. Such a living situation would be scandalous. But he certainly couldn't hand her over to Reverend Poole and chance her having to stay with the

Pierces. He scrambled to find a solution. "Maybe Anna could stay with the Duffs. Euphemia keeps teasing me about stealing you away."

"Perfect!" Sophie clapped her hands together. "Euphemia would love having Anna. And I know Anna would love Euphemia."

Reinhold allowed himself a smile, one that contained his relief. "You can ride over tomorrow and ask her."

Before he could stop Sophie, she closed the distance between them and flung her arms around him. She laid her head against his chest and hugged him tightly. "Thank you, Reinhold."

He held himself stiffly, his arms at his sides, and tried not to think about how heavenly she felt or how much he liked her silky hair against his chin.

"You're so good to me," she said.

He relented and allowed himself to hold her and return her embrace. He knew he'd made a mistake the moment his hands reached the small of her back. Every nerve in his body became keenly conscious of the contact.

He could sense she was just as aware of him, and that realization only stirred his desire. There was no denying the attraction between them. It was alive and intense.

Her fingers unfurled against his back and slid upward. He closed his eyes against the sensation that rippled across his skin. He couldn't let himself get carried away again like he had earlier. But when she rose on her toes so that her nose and mouth caressed his neck, his hands flattened against her spine, drawing her closer.

They were alone. All he had to do was fall backward and bring her down with him onto the bed of hay. He wanted to kiss her again. Surely a few kisses wouldn't hurt them, wouldn't cause any problems.

But as he rubbed his jaw along her cheek and brought his

lips to the delicate spot beneath her ear, his heart clanged a warning. If he started kissing her, he wouldn't be able to stop. And this time they might not have an interruption like they'd had this morning when Anna showed up.

She shifted, and he reluctantly loosened his hold on her back. Just as he thought she was disentangling herself and stepping away, she returned, wrapping both arms around his neck and dragging him down until their mouths met.

For several heartbeats, he lost himself in the kiss, in a world where no one else could dictate their lives, where he could be with her and love her and never stop.

Did a place like that exist?

"Reinhold," she murmured, breaking the kiss.

"Hmmm?" He brushed a kiss against her cheek, against her temple and hairline.

"Reinhold," she whispered again, her breath coming in short bursts, "I love you."

Her declaration sent a chill rippling through him, making him shudder.

She leaned back and studied his face as if searching for his love in response.

Maybe she thought she loved him. Maybe their shared passion and kisses caused her to feel something that resembled love. But who could really love him, with the monster that lived inside him?

He had to put a stop to this attraction. He had to do it now. And he knew of only one way.

~~~

Sophie watched the emotions play across Reinhold's face like changing shadows tossed by the wind.

"I sent a telegram this morning," he said, his voice shaky and hoarse.

"What kind of telegram?" She wanted to return her lips to his and forget about everything but the two of them. If she kissed him again, surely he'd admit that he loved her too.

She could feel it in the way he held her and kissed her and touched her, the gentle but possessive way he claimed her. She wasn't just imagining this, was she?

But he stepped away, breaking the connection with her. "I sent a telegram to your sisters."

Time seemed to stand still, devoid of everything except the gentle rustle of the horse's tail, the steady chewing of the cow, and the sleepy snorts of the pigs.

Surely Reinhold hadn't done it. Surely she'd heard him wrong.

She clutched her apron, tangling her chafed hands there to hide their trembling.

"I expect Elise and Marianne will be here by the end of the week," he continued, his voice stronger now.

She hadn't heard him wrong. He really had betrayed her. And he'd broken his promise to her, the promise that he wouldn't contact them or tell them where she was.

She'd wanted to put her life back together first. After her marriage to Reinhold, she'd been on her way to proving she wasn't such a failure. With a handsome husband, a good home, and the ability to provide for Olivia and Nicholas, maybe she would have been able to face her sisters again with her head held high.

But if they came now, they'd discover she hadn't been able to truly care for Olivia and Nicholas, and that because of her poor choices the two children had ended up in a terrible placement with the Ramseys. They'd discover her marriage to Reinhold was contrived, and maybe they'd even find out she'd coerced Reinhold into marrying her.

With their rich, loving husbands, if they didn't scorn her, they'd certainly pity her.

Panic bubbled up inside her at the realization they would see her broken life in all its crumbled shards. No, she didn't want to reunite with Elise and Marianne yet, not until she could bring some order to the mess she'd made.

What should she do?

She darted a glance behind her toward the wagon, then to the horse stall. She still had a few days, maybe a week, before they arrived. She could be long gone by then.

Reinhold seized her wrist. "Calm down, Sophie. Everything will be all right."

She jerked out of his grasp and took a rapid step away. She slipped, and her feet tangled in her skirt, causing her to fall and land on her backside.

Reinhold held out a hand to help her up, but she ignored it and scrambled to her feet, glaring at him. How could he have done this to her? And more important, *why* had he done it? Especially after this morning, so soon after they'd been intimate with each other? So soon after making her believe that what they had was real?

"Why?" she asked as a stinging heat strained her lungs.

He stuffed his hands into his pockets, his broad shoulders slumping. "I should have told them sooner, Soph. After all the heartache and worry they've been through over you, they deserve to know you're alive and well."

"But why today?" she persisted. "Why now?" She knew she'd probably regret asking the question, but she needed to know the truth.

He hesitated, but then resolve settled over his features. "We formed a partnership so that you could get Olivia and Nicholas. And now that you have Olivia, I'm planning to release you of the partnership with an annulment."

"An annulment? But why?" She wished her voice didn't sound so needy.

"Under normal circumstances you wouldn't have married me. You were desperate and needed a solution to a problem. I was that solution, but that doesn't mean it's permanent."

Anna's question from earlier echoed in her mind: *"Are you planning to go your separate ways eventually?"* Had her friend seen the signs that somehow she'd missed?

"Then you never planned to stay with me?" Sophie asked.

"You deserve to decide who you want to marry," he replied.

"I chose you."

His face was darkened by the stubble he hadn't shaven that morning, and his green eyes were equally dark. "You had no other options. If you had any other choice, you wouldn't have married me."

Was that true? She supposed in some ways he was right. She wouldn't have needed him if she'd been able to save Olivia and Nicholas by other means. Nevertheless, she had no regrets about marrying Reinhold. He was a good and kind man. She couldn't ask for a better husband.

But what about him? Maybe he wouldn't have chosen her. Maybe he wanted a better wife. Someone who was more experienced with farm life, who wasn't intent upon bringing two orphans with her into the marriage. Someone who wasn't as tainted by the city streets.

The ache gathering in her heart spread through her chest. She thought she'd found a place to belong, a place she could finally call home. More than that even, she thought she'd found someone who would finally love her.

Why were the people she loved always abandoning her? First her father and mother, then Elise and Marianne. Now she was a burden on Reinhold. He didn't want her either.

"So you thought that by calling on my sisters to come here, you could be rid of me?"

"No, it wasn't like that, Sophie. I sent the telegram because of me, because after this morning I realized how easy it would be to use you."

So he wasn't denying the attraction that easily flared between them. He'd felt it too. But that's all it was to him? Just physical attraction?

"With the way things have progressed, I'm bound to do something I'll regret." He stared down at the hay beneath their feet, his arms straight and stiff with his hands still deep in his pockets. "And if I do take advantage of you, then I won't be able to give you an annulment and set you free."

She wanted to tell him she didn't want an annulment, that she wanted to have a real marriage with him, that she didn't want to be set free. But she'd already told him she loved him. Hadn't that been enough? If she said any more, she'd only be humiliating herself. Besides, she sensed he was determined to sever the ties with her one way or another.

"If you wanted to be free of me, you should have just told me," she whispered. "You didn't have to send the telegram to Elise and Marianne."

"They need to know you're all right."

"I'll contact them when I'm ready to do so."

"Because they've both married wealthy men, they can take care of you now." His words rushed out as if he needed to convince himself as much as her. "They'll provide the best of everything—food, shelter, clothes, and anything else you could ever want."

"Those aren't the things I want." Did Reinhold really think she'd take physical comfort in place of love? Surely he had to know that wasn't important to her, especially after all the sacrifices she'd made for Nicholas and Olivia. All along she'd chosen being with them and loving them over her own well-being. And she'd do the same for him.

"I know how important Nicholas and Olivia are to you,"

he went on, as though sensing the direction of her thoughts. "Maybe Marianne and her husband, Drew, can help us with Nicholas when they get here. Drew has connections with the founder of the organization and might know what to do to help."

She shook her head. "I don't want to involve them in my problems." After all, if Reverend Poole said that the Children's Aid Society's policy was to leave orphans where they were placed, why would Drew go against that and risk his job for her?

Sophie tucked a loose strand of hair behind her ear. After the long day of tending Anna and Olivia, her appearance was frightful. Worse, she'd just discovered that her husband didn't want her and that she no longer had a home.

What would Elise and Marianne think once they saw her and realized how pitiful her life was compared to theirs? After running away so she could keep Nicholas and Olivia together, she'd even failed to do the one thing she'd set out to accomplish. She was a failure all around.

"I don't want to see them." Tears stung her eyes.

"You have to," Reinhold said adamantly. "They're coming here for you."

"No. I refuse to see them." She tripped over the drying potatoes, suddenly desperate to get to the barn door. She wasn't sure where she'd go or what she'd do. All she could think about was leaving, getting far away before her sisters saw the brokenness of her life.

"Sophie, wait." Reinhold scrambled after her.

She fought back blinding tears and rushed to escape from the barn and from Reinhold. If he didn't want her in his life, then he had no business interfering with what she did or where she went.

Jerking the barn door open, she stepped into the cold night, letting the blackness envelop her. She'd taken only two steps when Reinhold's hand closed around her arm, bringing her to a stop. She twisted and tried to break free, but he held her tight.

"Please, Sophie. Don't do this."

"This is your fault!" A sob escaped before she could catch it.

"I just want what's best for you." His voice was raw with anguish. "You have to believe me."

"You don't know what's best for me!" she yelled, but the wind whipped away her words.

Ahead of them, a light glowed from her upstairs bedroom window, the room she was sharing with Anna. But all the other windows of the house were dark, seeming to taunt her that she was no longer welcome there.

Another gust of cold wind slashed at her, slicing through her clothes and sending the message that autumn could be as brutal as winter. She didn't look forward to the prospect of being homeless again with the constant pressure to find a warm place to spend the night. But she'd survived in the past, and she could do so once more if need be.

She struggled to free herself, but Reinhold gripped both of her arms, holding her in place.

"I hope you're not thinking of running away again," he said.

She debated lying to him so she could sneak away without his attempting to stop her. But the truth was, there was nothing he could do to prevent her from going, short of tying and locking her up. And she didn't think Reinhold would resort to Mr. Ramsey's harsh tactics.

"You've left me no choice but to leave," she answered.

"Please, Sophie." He started to wrap his arms around her, but she fought against him.

Frustration and helplessness welled up within her, and she pushed and pounded against his chest. But he stood immovable, keeping her in place. When she finally gave in to the futility of fighting him, she sagged and began sobbing.

This time, as he gathered her into an embrace, she didn't resist. She pressed into him and cried for all she'd lost—the time away from her sisters, the love of family, the safety of belonging, and of not having a home. She'd missed them and wanted to see them. Deep down she did.

But she was afraid.

Reinhold didn't say anything. He held her in his thick arms against his solid body, shielding her from the wind and the cold, until finally her tears stopped.

She sniffled against him, clutching his shirt and clinging to him, too weary to feel any shame for needing him. She didn't protest when he swept her off her feet and into his arms and carried her to the house. After entering the kitchen, he kicked the door closed and moved to the stairs. At the second stair, he paused. Or maybe she only imagined he did.

Was he remembering being in the stairwell last night? He'd held her then too. She'd thought he wanted her, even loved her. And because of that, she'd been ready to give herself to him. But all along he'd been biding his time, planning to end their relationship, keeping her at a distance so he could have their marriage annulled.

She sighed against his neck. Why was her life always breaking apart?

As they entered the bedroom, Anna's eyes widened at the sight of Sophie in Reinhold's arms. She quickly scooted over, and Reinhold gently laid Sophie on the bed next to Anna.

He surprised Sophie by taking off first one shoe and then the other before pulling the covers up over her. "Promise me you won't do anything rash tonight," he said, his forehead lined with anxiety. "Promise me you'll sleep the night right here. We will talk more about this in the morning."

She was too tired to run away tonight. Besides, Olivia was in no condition to go anywhere. And she still didn't have Nicholas.

"Promise?" he whispered, his eyes pleading with her.

She'd have to come up with a viable plan before leaving. She couldn't just pick up and go as she'd done so many times in the past. Although she didn't owe Reinhold any promises after his betrayal, she knew she couldn't leave him without saying good-bye first.

"Please, Soph." His voice was desperate, and she could feel Anna's questioning eyes upon her.

"I promise."

CHAPTER 22

From the bed, Sophie stared unseeingly at the gray sky outside the window. She'd awoken at dawn as she'd grown accustomed to doing. She'd checked on Olivia, who was still asleep, then returned to bed, unable to go down and make breakfast for Reinhold and Jakob.

A while ago she'd heard the kitchen door open and someone rummaging around the kitchen—probably Jakob looking for something to eat before heading out to the fields.

She'd felt a slight pang of guilt at her irresponsibility, at leaving Jakob to fend for himself, at not providing a hot meal to sustain him or Reinhold through the morning. She understood how hard they worked and how much energy they expended with the harvest. She'd witnessed and experienced it firsthand.

She should have gotten up and cooked them something. Except that Reinhold didn't want her. He'd made plans for her to leave.

A tear slipped down, and she swiped it off her cheek angrily.

Jakob would just have to get used to cooking his own meals again. That's all there was to it.

"You're awake?" Anna said behind her.

Sophie nodded.

Anna stretched, her cold feet brushing against Sophie's leg. "So are you going to tell me what happened, or will I have to guess?"

Sophie's throat ached from the need to cry, but she willed herself to be strong. She'd already shed too many tears last night in Reinhold's arms. She couldn't give way to her emotions again. "Turns out you were right. Reinhold wants us to go our separate ways."

The covers tugged away from Sophie as Anna rose to her elbows. "I wasn't right. In fact, I was completely wrong about Reinhold. I wasn't around him often yesterday, but even in the few times I saw him with you, I could tell he adores you, would do anything for you."

Sophie couldn't tear her gaze from the window, from the low, dark clouds rolling past. It was a mirror of her heart and soul. "It doesn't matter how much attraction he might feel for me. He made it clear last night that he never planned to stay married to me, that he intends to give me an annulment."

"You know as well as I do how to remedy that problem." Anna's voice was knowing. "Find a cozy part of the barn and pull him down into the hay with you. And don't let him up until—"

"Anna!" Sophie chided, heat flooding her face. "I don't want to coerce him into having a real marriage if he doesn't want one. If I do that, maybe he'll resent me."

"Or maybe he'll accept that the two of you belong together. Anyone with eyes in their head can see that."

Sophie swallowed past the pain. She'd wanted to belong to Reinhold. But she should have known that dreams like that don't come true. In fact, most dreams were just wishful imaginations of an impossibility.

"So what are you going to do now?" Anna asked, flopping back onto the bed.

Sophie remained motionless. Still facing the window, she replied, "I'm leaving."

"You mean, *we're* leaving."

For a minute, Sophie debated how to respond to her friend. She loved Anna and didn't want to lose her, yet why would Anna want to stay with her? "Do you really want to stick with me, Anna? I never do anything other than make mistakes."

"That's not true—"

"You wouldn't be battered up by Mr. Pierce if not for me."

Anna scoffed. "You had nothing to do with it."

"I brought us here."

"I have a mind of my own too, you know. I could have gone my own way long ago if I'd wanted to."

For a moment, they lay silently. The only sound was the wind rattling the shingles and whistling in through the cracks in the window.

"Listen, Sophie," Anna finally said, this time in a whisper. "I got a letter from my sister."

Sophie rolled over so that she was facing her friend.

In the gray light of the day, Anna's bruised face seemed even more discolored. Her wavy black hair was tangled and wild, but her dark eyes were solid and steady—something Sophie needed right now.

"When we first arrived, I sent Mollie a letter letting her know where I was," Anna continued. "I got a letter from her this week, and she told me Mugs and Danny were set free, that the police didn't have enough evidence to pin the murders on them. Apparently no one outside the Roach Guards would step forward to stand as a witness. Probably too afraid of the Bowery Boys and their retaliation to come forward."

"I don't blame them."

Anna nodded. "I guess Mugs wants me to come home."

"Back to New York?"

"Yes, and Danny asked about you."

Sophie glanced over Anna's head to the candle holder on the bedside crate. The brass angel finally held a candle. *"No matter how lost you might feel at times, always keep His light burning inside you."* Her mother's deathbed admonition whispered through Sophie.

She hadn't followed her mother's instructions. She supposed in some ways she'd already let the light of her faith grow dim even before her mother had died. Over the ensuing months, God's light inside her had been all too easy to extinguish.

Was it too late to rekindle the flame? What if she allowed God to light her path instead of continuing to try to find her way in the dark?

Sophie pictured the candle's flame driving away the darkness. Just one little flicker on one little candle could illuminate a whole room. She wanted that. No, she needed that.

"We could go back to the city," Anna whispered. "I'll marry Mugs, and you can marry Danny the way you'd planned."

In comparison with the depths of what she felt for Reinhold, any feelings she'd once harbored for Danny were shallow, not even real. At the time, she'd been caught up in Danny's importance as one of the leaders of the gang. And she'd needed him to fulfill her, to give her meaning, to provide for her.

Her inner ramblings ceased with a sudden realization. She'd been looking to Reinhold the same way—needing him to fulfill her, give her meaning, and provide for her. Her love for him had been selfish and about her needs. Maybe she'd tried to justify what she was doing by finding ways to help him. But ultimately she'd been selfish. Just as her love for Olivia and Nicholas had so often been selfish too.

"I could wire Mugs for the money for train fare," Anna said. "I'm sure he and Danny would find a way to get us home."

Home. Where was that? She certainly didn't think of New

York as home. She never had. But now this wasn't home either. Reinhold had made that evident.

"What do you say? Should we go back?"

She couldn't stay here, not with Reinhold giving her an annulment and her sisters coming for her. But she wasn't sure she could go through with marrying Danny, not after everything she'd felt for Reinhold.

"Are you sure we'll be safe there? Won't the Roach Guards still be after us to testify against Danny and Mugs?"

Anna hesitated. "I don't think so."

"Maybe we should try out Chicago first like we originally planned."

"I'm not going anywhere without Nicholas." A little girl's voice came from the doorway.

Sophie's heart sank. How long had Olivia been standing there listening to their conversation? She sat up to the sight of Olivia barefoot and in her nightgown, trembling from cold.

Sophie shoved aside her covers and hurried around the bed to the girl. She started to gather Olivia into her arms, but Olivia pushed her away, her eyes wide and filled with accusation. Sophie was relieved to see some of Olivia's spirit returning. Even if she was stubborn at times, that was better than the lethargic and weepy girl of yesterday.

"I won't leave Nicholas behind," Olivia said more forcefully.

"Of course we won't," Sophie replied. "We'll take him with us." Although she had no idea how. She'd already done everything within her means to get him away from the Ramseys.

But her answer seemed to be enough for Olivia. When Sophie reached for Olivia again, the girl fell against her, allowing her to draw her into an embrace.

"Yoo-hoo" came a woman's voice from downstairs. "Is anyone home?"

Sophie straightened. "Euphemia?"

"Yes, lass. I've come to lend you a hand."

Euphemia was here. Even if Euphemia wouldn't be able to solve all her problems, there was something calming and reassuring about the dear woman's presence.

Sophie clutched Olivia's hand, and together they descended the stairs. For several minutes, Euphemia made a fuss over Olivia, setting her up at the table and giving her oatmeal cookies from the tin she'd brought along. While Olivia ate the cookies, Euphemia busied herself putting the coffee to boil and cleaning out the greasy remains from the bottom of a pan.

Soon she had leftover chicken soup bubbling and biscuits baking and was bustling about the kitchen as if it were hers. "When Reinhold rode over this morning himself instead of sending Jakob, I knew you needed me."

"Reinhold rode over?"

"That man loves you, lass," Euphemia said with a smile.

Sophie shook her head in denial, the wounds of the previous evening still stinging.

"He never leaves his work for anything," Euphemia continued. "And he left it this morning for you."

Sophie mulled over Euphemia's words while she and Olivia ate soup and biscuits. Both Anna and Euphemia believed Reinhold loved her. She supposed there was no denying the attraction they felt for each other. But love?

Sophie suspected Reinhold had ridden over to the Duffs' place because he was worried about leaving her alone during the day while he was out in the fields. He'd probably wanted Euphemia to check on her and convince her to stay and see her sisters when they arrived.

Whatever the case, she was grateful Reinhold had gone after Euphemia. No matter his motive, the woman was a godsend.

Euphemia took food upstairs to Anna. And for a while their

voices drifted down the stairs, Euphemia's Scottish lilt and loving-kindness warming Sophie every bit as much as the soup.

"Och, what a sweet one that Anna is," Euphemia said as she hefted her portly frame down the stairs into the kitchen. "After missing you, Sophie, I sure will enjoy having another woman in the house again."

"Another woman?"

"Reinhold said Anna needed a place to live, said she couldn't return to the Pierces." Euphemia cast a sideways glance at Olivia as if to warn Sophie to refrain from saying anything more detailed around the little girl.

Should Sophie tell Euphemia about their plans to leave? To go to Chicago, or maybe even New York City?

"Anna says she's well enough to brave a wagon ride," Euphemia said. "Since you have your hands full enough now, I'll take her back to my house and nurse her from there."

Sophie supposed Reinhold was anxious to make other arrangements for Anna before the week's end, so he could avoid any more gossip than possible. He would suffer enough once people in the community learned she'd left.

"Only if you dinnae mind." Euphemia squeezed Sophie's shoulder. "Reinhold thought Anna would be safer with us if Mr. Pierce came around looking for her."

"That's true." Anna would be hidden better with the Duffs. Even if Anna only stayed there for a few days, as long as it took for Sophie to come up with another scheme for getting back Nicholas.

"And you know you're always welcome to visit Anna whenever you're lonesome for her."

"Thank you, Euphemia."

Euphemia waved her hand in dismissal. "Och, think nothing of it, lass. I'm just grateful the good Lord has given me the chance to have two daughters now instead of one."

Sophie swallowed her guilt at the realization that Euphemia would lose both her and Anna at the same time. It wasn't fair to Euphemia, especially after how wide she'd opened her heart to love them.

They didn't deserve such kindness from Euphemia. From anyone.

"I thank the good Lord that He never treats us as our sins deserve."

Euphemia's words wafted through Sophie. She thought often of Euphemia's story, of her pregnancy out of wedlock, of her bitterness toward God. And each time she remembered how much Euphemia had changed, fresh hope and longing swelled within Sophie.

Sophie stifled a sigh. She didn't want to leave Euphemia. She wasn't ready to leave anything in Mayfield, especially the man she loved.

But she had no choice. She just prayed that once she was gone, Euphemia would find the grace to forgive her, even though she wouldn't deserve it.

ে৩৲৹

"Can I name them?" Olivia asked as she stroked the fluffy body of the nearest orange tabby kitten while the other three from the litter crawled over their black-tortoiseshell mother who'd finally lain down for them.

Sophie knelt next to Olivia in the barn loft, where the mother cat kept her kittens safe and away from the larger animals. Now that the kittens were walking and getting bigger, they were in more danger.

The sweet scent of the newly cut hay wrapped around them, overpowering the other more unpleasant barn odors. The loft was cold, with the chilled October air seeping in through the cracks in the barn walls, especially now that night had fallen. But she'd brought Olivia out to distract her from her anxiety over Nicholas. The little girl thought of little else but her brother. After Anna and Euphemia had left earlier in the afternoon, the anxiety had mounted so much that Sophie was afraid Olivia would make herself sick.

"Maybe we should let Reinhold and Jakob name the kittens," Sophie said. After all, she and Olivia would be gone by the end of the week and wouldn't see the kittens ever again. Sophie scratched the orange tabby on the top of its head between its ears. It tumbled in its climb, rolling in the hay toward its mother.

Olivia giggled at the kitten's clumsiness.

Sophie couldn't remember the last time she'd heard Olivia's laughter. How long had it been? Weeks? Months? Whatever the length, Olivia didn't laugh often enough.

Sophie let her shoulders sink under the familiar weight of failure. Now that she had Olivia back, what made her think she could do better than before? Why had she thought the children would be better off with her?

What if Nicholas really would be happier with the Ramseys? With Reverend Poole's assurances that the Ramseys loved and wanted the little boy, maybe she should stop plotting how to take him away.

"I think we should name this one Orangey," Olivia declared.

"But then what about the other orange kitten? What will you name him? Orangey number two?" The orange kittens vied to nurse alongside the two kittens who had their mother's tortoiseshell coloring.

Olivia giggled again. "No, silly. We'll call him Cheesy."

"Orangey and Cheesy." Completely unoriginal pet names that only a five-year-old could appreciate. But since she and Olivia were leaving just as soon as Anna could go to town and get Mugs to wire money for their train fare, what harm would come of letting Olivia name the kittens?

Below, the barn door slid open, squealing its protest. Jakob appeared first, weariness in every step.

She was surprised when Reinhold didn't follow closely on Jakob's heels into the barn. Was he off running another errand? This time sending a telegram, telling her sisters to arrive as rapidly as possible so she wouldn't have time to escape?

Just as quickly as the bitter thought came, she released it. She couldn't blame Reinhold for her current predicament. She should have known he was too honorable to withhold her where-abouts from her sisters forever. If Elise and Marianne were as wealthy as Reinhold claimed, then no wonder he believed he was doing the right thing for her.

Was it possible her sisters could help her get Nicholas back?

Sophie shook away the prospect. She'd gotten by this far without them. She and Anna would figure out a way to get Nicholas without their help. With Anna's conniving, surely this time they could come up with a better plan for taking Nicholas away from the Ramseys.

At Olivia's antics with the kittens, Jakob stopped and peered up at them, probably not expecting to see them in the barn at this hour.

Sophie rose. "Hi, Jakob. I was just showing Olivia the kittens."

He nodded and offered Olivia a smile.

The girl didn't smile in return, but instead cowered against Sophie's leg.

"Don't worry," Sophie continued. "Supper is simmering on the back burner. It's ready whenever you are."

Jakob glanced toward the door as though making sure they were still alone. "Reinhold told me you're leaving, going back to New York with your sisters."

Sophie was tempted to lie and pretend to go along with Reinhold's plans. But she'd already decided she would say good-bye to Reinhold whenever she and Anna were ready to leave. She might as well be honest with Jakob too. "I'm going back, but not with my sisters."

Jakob was silent, his face pale, his eyes sad.

She shuffled toward the ladder.

"I wish you didn't have to go," he blurted. The moment the words were out, he cast his eyes down to his worn boots.

"I wish so too, Jakob," she said softly.

At her admission, he lifted his eyes, his expression confused. "Then why are you going?"

Before Sophie could answer, Reinhold burst into the barn, his face a mask of wild fear. "She's gone! Help me saddle Daisy."

Was he referring to Anna? Or her?

Neither Jakob nor Sophie moved, even as Reinhold rushed to the stall, grabbed the saddle from its perch on the rail, and threw it over the mare.

Jakob looked from Sophie to Reinhold, then back, understanding dawning in his eyes.

"What are you waiting for?" Reinhold tossed the terse question at Jakob. When Jakob shifted to glance to the loft, where Sophie stood stooped over with Olivia burrowed into her skirt, Reinhold followed his gaze.

At the sight of Sophie, Reinhold let go of Daisy and sagged against the stall wall. "Sophie," he said, his voice echoing with relief. "When I saw that the house was dark, and then when you weren't inside, I thought you'd left . . ."

"I'm still here."

"Praise Gott," he muttered.

"You're the one who told her to leave, aren't you?" Jakob said, his voice tight with accusation.

Reinhold pressed a hand against his chest as if to still his heartbeat. "That's not your concern, Jakob."

"It wasn't Sophie's idea."

Ignoring Jakob, Reinhold straightened and slipped the saddle off the horse.

"She wouldn't be thinking about going if not for you," Jakob continued.

"I said this isn't your concern." Reinhold threw the saddle onto the railing with more force than necessary.

Jakob glared at Reinhold. And Sophie could only watch them both, unsure what to say or do to make the situation better.

Finally, Jakob took another step toward Reinhold, his fists balled at his sides. "She's the one good thing that's happened to us, and you had to ruin it."

Reinhold stiffened, and his hands stilled around the shovel he'd just picked up.

Sophie sensed a storm brewing the same way a farmer could tell bad weather was coming.

"It's because you're a coward." Jakob's accusation echoed through the barn. "You're afraid to let anything good happen to you. Because then you might actually have to prove you're different than *he* was."

"That's enough." Reinhold's voice was low and tight. His fingers on the shovel trembled. "Go to the house. Now."

Bright pink dotted Jakob's cheeks, and his eyes glowed with the embers of emotion he'd obviously held inside for too long.

Sophie stepped onto the top rung of the ladder. She had to intervene before something bad happened.

"You think that by cutting everyone off, you won't hurt anyone," Jakob said. "Sometimes I wish you'd just hit me if it meant you'd let yourself care."

"Stop!" Reinhold roared. He spun around, his face contorted with fury. He threw the shovel against the wall with a loud *clank*. Then he started toward Jakob, every stride declaring his intent to pummel the boy.

Jakob lifted his chin and braced his feet, waiting for Reinhold to slam into him. Fear flashed in the boy's eyes, but he held his ground.

"No!" Sophie called. She began scrambling down the ladder. Jakob wouldn't be a match against Reinhold. "Reinhold, don't!"

Reinhold hesitated.

"You don't need to do this!" In her haste she fought against the tangled folds of her skirt that threatened to trip her. "Your fight isn't with Jakob."

She didn't know who the fight was with, didn't understand everything Jakob had said. But she knew Jakob wasn't Reinhold's real enemy.

Reinhold halted in front of Jakob, their faces inches apart. Reinhold's eyes were brutally dark, his nostrils flared, and his chest rose and fell with barely restrained rage.

Sophie wanted to shout out again as she jumped the last distance into a mound of hay. When she straightened, the brothers hadn't moved. In fact, Jakob hadn't even flinched. He held Reinhold's gaze with a daring glimmer.

She started toward them, intending to push herself between them to keep them from fighting. But as she slipped and slid across the hay, Reinhold took a step away—first a little one. As if that motion had broken the bonds holding him captive, he stepped back again, this time putting a large gap between himself and Jakob.

His eyes still held Jakob's. An invisible communication seemed to pass between the two. Finally, Reinhold nodded at Jakob before spinning and striding across the barn and disappearing outside.

Only after he was gone did Jakob allow himself to sag.

Sophie rushed to him, afraid he would crumple to the ground. As she grabbed his arm, he wiped his eyes, but not before she saw the tears.

"Are you all right?" she asked.

He blew out a long breath. And then she was surprised when he gave her a wobbly smile, his eyes still glassy. "I think maybe everything will be okay now."

Sophie didn't answer except to squeeze his arm. Maybe Jakob would be better off for having told Reinhold the things he'd needed to say for some time. In fact, she was proud of him for his courage to stand up to Reinhold and speak the truth. Jakob would only be stronger and better in the end for doing it.

But everything wouldn't be okay for her. No matter what Jakob might have said to Reinhold, nothing would change the fact that she was leaving.

CHAPTER 23

Reinhold wrapped the reins around his gloved hand and glanced at Sophie, who sat on the wagon bench next to him. She stared straight ahead so intently, he could tell she wasn't noticing the countryside they'd passed on their ride into town for church. She wasn't aware of the fields already cut clean, the dark soil damp from the rain, or the livestock grazing on the dying grass.

Normally, Sophie noticed the details and talked about it all. But today she'd been preoccupied, which caused worry to burrow into his core. He worried about her running away every single second of every single day. No matter where he was or what he was doing, his thoughts stayed on her and the possibility that she might disappear again.

When he arrived home after work two days ago to a dark house, he'd panicked, had assumed she'd left, and was nearly delirious with the need to go after her. At the sight of her in the barn loft with Olivia, he'd been weak with relief.

But what about the next time he came home to a dark house? Where would she be then? Even though three days had passed since he'd wired the telegram, and even though Sophie hadn't yet left, he could almost see her mind churning as she planned her next move.

Reinhold looked over his shoulder to the wagon bed, where Jakob and Olivia sat. The little girl had slowly shed her fear and was more talkative than Reinhold had expected. She seemed to have made friends with Jakob, who patiently answered all her questions and allowed her to tag along with him as he did his chores.

"Sometimes I wish you'd just hit me if it meant you'd let yourself care." Jakob's heartbroken declaration still haunted Reinhold's thoughts. He'd almost hit Jakob. He'd come within inches and seconds of it. But Sophie's cry of distress, along with the plea in Jakob's eyes, had shackled his arms and stopped him.

He'd realized in that moment that he hadn't let himself care about Jakob because he had been a coward, because he'd been afraid he'd hurt his brother.

"You're afraid to let anything good happen to you. Because then you might actually have to prove that you're different than he was."

Reinhold had mulled over Jakob's other words too. He could agree he hadn't let himself care and that he was afraid to let anything good happen. But he wasn't sure he needed to prove he was different from his father. He'd already become like the man. Was there any way to change that now?

He dragged in a breath of the crisp air laden with the promise of winter, of shorter, darker days, and of a slower rhythm. It was a time of slumber for the weary soil, a time when frost and freezing temperatures blanketed the land.

To the average city person, the bleakness and barrenness might appear lonely, even ugly. But to the farmer, winter was a necessity. Without it, without the rest, the land wouldn't be ready for the rebirth and the toil required of it in the spring.

Was that his life? Maybe he was thawing after winter. Maybe it was time for his own rebirth and the hard toil of sowing new seeds into his life.

The fact was, he hadn't hit Jakob. As much as he'd wanted to, he'd made the choice not to. Could he do that the next time? And the time after that? Was it possible that God could change him into a better man? He'd once thought so. Yet after nearly killing Higgins last year, he'd lost faith in himself, thinking God had given up on him too.

However, if Jakob hadn't lost faith in him, maybe God hadn't either.

His gaze slid to Sophie again. Her shoulders were stiff, her hands clutched tightly in her lap, and her pretty lips pressed in a straight line.

The familiar storefronts and businesses that lined Main Street loomed ahead. They were almost to church. His time was running out.

"Sophie," he said, forcing out his question before fear caged him again, "I can tell you're planning something. What is it?"

Her attention snapped to him, her blue eyes wide and revealing, telling him what he needed to know even before she spoke. "Anna and I are leaving tomorrow."

His chest suddenly felt as if it were on fire. His throat burned. He shouldn't have sent the telegram to Elise and Marianne. He wasn't sure what drove him to do it, except that he'd been afraid—perhaps afraid to allow himself to love Sophie, just as he'd been afraid to love Jakob.

"Where are you going?" he asked, his throat scratchy as though he'd breathed in smoke.

"Mugs and Danny didn't go to prison. Anna's sister said they've asked after us. Want us to return."

"You're going back to Danny?" The question came out as a hoarse whisper and contained an embarrassing amount of anguish.

Thankfully, Sophie seemed preoccupied, her hands now twisting hard in her skirt. "Anna is wiring Mugs for train fare. Once it comes in, we'll leave."

The prospect of any other man having Sophie—of even touching her—left a hot trail of bitterness in his stomach. But Sophie returning to Danny? A Bowery Boy gang member? Such a thought was pure torture.

"Sophie," he said, not caring that his voice was loaded with desperation. "You can't go back to him."

"We might stay in Chicago. We haven't completely decided what we'll do."

Reinhold wanted to protest, to remind her that Nicholas was stuck here in Mayfield with the Ramseys and that if she waited for Marianne and Drew to arrive, they might be able to help her gain custody. But before he could find the words to persuade her, she sat forward, her eyes trained on the church ahead.

He followed her gaze to a wagon carrying a family that had just halted in the grassy area next to the church. The man driving it hopped down and rounded his team. A small boy hunched into one of the corners. The boy's cap hid his face, but Reinhold didn't have to guess who it was.

The moment Reinhold brought his wagon to a halt, Sophie jumped down and started across the churchyard. Mr. Ramsey was busy hitching his team to a post, and Mrs. Ramsey was helping Nicholas out of the wagon. Neither noticed Sophie's approach.

Something in the determination of Sophie's steps made Reinhold's muscles tense. Without breaking his attention from her, he hopped down and followed her. "Secure the horse," he called to Jakob, who was assisting Olivia over the side of the wagon.

Within seconds, Olivia darted past him, flying toward Nicholas now walking hand in hand with Mrs. Ramsey and a young girl.

"Nicholas!" Olivia shouted.

At the sound of Olivia's voice, Nicholas jolted forward, breaking free of the Ramseys. "Olivia! Sophie!" he cried, his little feet racing toward his sister and Sophie. A wide, joyful smile filled his countenance and lit his eyes.

Both Sophie and Olivia were now running too. Sophie reached the boy before Olivia. She bent down, swooped him up, and then began to stride back toward Reinhold. With the boy securely locked into her arms, her sights turned to Jakob where he was tying Daisy.

Reinhold halted. Sophie's intentions were clear. Maybe this was what she'd been plotting during the ride into town—how to grab Nicholas and run.

"Stop!" Mr. Ramsey called.

Above Nicholas's head, Sophie's eyes locked on Reinhold and pleaded for help.

Reinhold surveyed the yard and the white clapboard one-room church. The door was open, and others were already entering. What did Sophie expect him to do? What could he possibly do? Especially with so many people here to witness their actions?

He returned his attention to Jakob, who was securing the mare. Should he order his brother to untie Daisy and attempt to ride away with Nicholas? As soon as the idea came, he tossed it aside. He could no more kidnap Nicholas from the churchyard than Sophie could. Already Mr. Ramsey was closing in on her and would catch her.

Her eyes continued to beg him to do something— anything—to help her regain the little boy who was more precious to her than her own safety and comfort. He loved that about Sophie—her devotion to the children, her willingness to do anything for them—so much that she'd run away and face cold, danger, and hunger just so they could be together again. He loved her fierce determination and her perseverance. He even loved that she was slightly crazy enough to grab Nicholas from the churchyard.

Was it possible that he was falling in love with her?

The idea sliced into his mind. But before he could ponder it further, Mr. Ramsey caught up to Sophie, grabbed her arm, and dragged her to a stop. Sophie screamed—a scream that contained a mixture of anger and pain.

The echo of her pain rose above the rest. When Mr. Ramsey jerked her around and slapped her cheek, Reinhold's anger exploded so that all he heard now was a roaring, his own, as he plunged toward Mr. Ramsey like an angry bull.

The slap caught Sophie across her delicate cheekbone with enough force that she screamed again, dropped Nicholas, and fell to the ground. In that instant, Mr. Ramsey shoved Nicholas behind him, away from Sophie.

Olivia drew to an abrupt halt, put her arms over her head in a gesture of self-protection, and cowered. The move was so reflexive, Reinhold was sure she'd had to do it before around Mr. Ramsey.

Reinhold barreled forward, his shoulder down. His roar was loud enough to draw Mr. Ramsey's attention. At the sight of Reinhold, the man's eyes flickered with concern for just an instant before he steeled himself, almost as if he hoped Reinhold would attack him with both fists flying.

Out of the corner of his eye, Reinhold glimpsed the other churchgoers pausing in the doorway to watch the fight.

"Prove that you're different than he was . . ."

Jakob's words, although just a whisper in his conscience, brought him to a halt. Standing only a foot away from Mr.

Ramsey, Reinhold's pulse hammered in his chest, his hands twitching with the desire to pummel Mr. Ramsey—to lash out at him for hitting Sophie.

Instead he rammed his hands into his pockets. For several seconds he stared at Mr. Ramsey, not knowing what to do next. If he didn't beat the man up, then what? He certainly couldn't let him hit Sophie and get away with it.

With anger nearly blinding him, Reinhold almost missed the challenge in Mr. Ramsey's eyes, the kind of look that dared Reinhold to punch him. Mingled with the challenge was the glow of white-hot rage.

Reinhold realized then that anger could manifest itself in more ways than just brute force. Mr. Ramsey's anger was contained deep inside him but was no less powerful and damaging. Neither letting out unchecked anger nor keeping it locked inside would lead to the kind of freedom Reinhold longed for.

"You hit my wife," he finally said through a clenched jaw, deciding that he'd at least say his piece and give voice to his anger.

"She took my child," Mr. Ramsey replied too calmly.

"By hitting her, you've proven to everyone standing here just why she should have the child and why you don't deserve him." Reinhold's words rose in the cool morning air. Except for Nicholas's soft sobs a short distance away where he'd found comfort with Mrs. Ramsey, the churchyard was silent, the onlookers observing with wide eyes.

As though recognizing how damaging Reinhold's words were, Mr. Ramsey's hard, unyielding gaze finally flinched. The man shot a glance toward the church door to a well-dressed man in a stovepipe hat and spectacles. There Reverend Poole stood with an arm around his wife, his large eyes seeming not to miss a detail of the scene playing out before him.

Had Mr. Ramsey hoped Reinhold would beat him up so that Reverend Poole would witness his out-of-control anger? If Reinhold had carried through with hitting Mr. Ramsey, he would have lost all of Reverend Poole's respect and any chance of regaining Nicholas.

The realization at what he'd almost done turned his stomach. At the same time he whispered a silent prayer of gratefulness that God had given him the strength to stop in time.

"She tried to take my son," Mr. Ramsey said, this time louder. Even though his voice was hard and forceful, Reinhold sensed a small crack, a wavering.

"You've been the boy's father for a few weeks. But Sophie's been his mother for years. He's Sophie's son, not yours. Now that she's in a position to care for the boy, she wants him back." Reinhold spun away from the man and knelt next to Sophie, who cradled her cheek. Her beautiful eyes were stricken, even apologetic as they met his.

He gathered her into his arms, drawing her close, needing her and everyone else to know that he was her protector and defender. She shuddered against him, which only stirred his anger toward Mr. Ramsey. Although his muscles twitched with the need to rise up and strike the man, instead he spoke as calmly as he could. "You shouldn't have hit her, Mr. Ramsey. You went too far."

With that, he picked Sophie up and carried her to the wagon, thanking God again that he'd controlled his anger and praying he'd have the strength to do so the next time. It would be a lifelong struggle, but he was ready to plow and sow and weed . . . and maybe someday he'd reap a harvest.

⁊⁊⁊

Sophie scrubbed at a plate in a basin of water, now tepid and greasy and spotted with the floating remains of their supper.

Next to her, Anna was drying and putting away the dishes, already seeming at home in Euphemia's large kitchen.

Sophie cast a sidelong glance at her friend. The bruises on Anna's face and neck had begun to heal, adding a yellowish-green to the fringes of the purple and black. The young woman had been unusually quiet during the meal Euphemia had prepared and now hardly spoke.

Spending Sunday evenings sharing a meal with the Duffs was a tradition Sophie would miss after she and Anna left. She would miss the boisterous sharing around the table, the teasing and the laughter, and the delicious scents and tastes of Euphemia's food.

She'd even miss the time after the meal. Usually the men moved to the front porch, where Barclay smoked his pipe and challenged the boys to checkers. Now that the evenings had grown colder and darker, the men congregated in the front room.

Even now their laughter resounded down the hallway and into the kitchen.

Through the kitchen door at the dining room table, Sophie smiled at the sight of Euphemia sitting next to Olivia, patiently teaching her how to knit. Euphemia would make a wonderful grandmother someday.

Just as quickly as the smile came, it faded at the realization that she wouldn't be here to witness Euphemia as a grandmother. She'd no longer be a part of this family or these warm and loving mealtimes.

"Sophie," Anna said hesitantly, "I don't want to leave."

Sophie's hands in the water stilled. She wasn't surprised Anna was feeling the same way she was. After all the places they'd lived, Euphemia's home was like stepping into the folds of a warm feather comforter. The love and joy wrapped them up and kissed them, holding out a future unlike anything they'd ever known.

It was an appealing offer, one that apparently Anna wanted to accept. Sophie'd wanted it too. Now that it had been ripped away from her, she realized just how badly she longed to stay and be Reinhold's wife, to be a helpmate to him, to be a part of this community of farmers.

Not only had she fallen in love with Reinhold, but she'd fallen in love with the kind of life that belonged to a farmer's wife. As difficult and laborious as the work had been, she'd never felt more fulfilled than she had that day she'd stocked the cellar with all the food she'd harvested and prepared from the garden. She'd loved learning how to cook and sew. And she'd loved adding a woman's touch to the farmhouse. She'd even loved working in the field with Reinhold—the satisfaction she'd felt in knowing that, by working together, they'd saved the potato crop.

But her love hadn't mattered, and now he'd given her no choice but to leave.

The familiar ache in her chest swelled, yet she reminded herself none of this was Reinhold's fault. She was the one who'd coerced him into marriage, who'd told him it would be a business partnership, who'd used him in her efforts to get Olivia and Nicholas back. He'd been kind enough to go along with all of it. In fact, he'd already done more than he'd bargained for. Like this morning before church . . .

She lowered her head and closed her eyes. What had she been thinking? There was absolutely no part of her kidnapping plan that made any sense. She'd been naïve to believe she could simply snatch Nicholas and leave the churchyard. Naïve and desperate.

But with time slipping away, she hadn't known what else to do.

She was grateful Reinhold had spoken out against Mr. Ramsey for hitting her. And he'd justified her rash attempt to run away with Nicholas. Even more than that, she was grateful he'd taken her back home, so she didn't have to face anyone's disapproval—namely Reverend Poole's.

She hadn't wanted to face Reinhold's questions again either, so she'd allowed Olivia to drag her out of the house. They'd hiked to the creek with Jakob, watched him fish, and then later climbed to the barn loft and played with the kittens. All the while she'd attempted to resign herself to the possibility that they would have to leave Nicholas behind.

But could she really do it? Could she really get on the train tomorrow and ride away without him? And yet how could she remain and face her sisters?

"Sophie?" Anna said, drawing Sophie back to the present moment.

She opened her eyes and tried to focus on scrubbing the dish and on finalizing their plans. She lifted the dish from the water and let the water drip away. "How much longer do you want to stay?"

Anna shrugged. "I don't know—"

A manly cough came from the doorway. Sophie jumped, and the wet plate slipped from her fingers. It landed on the floor with a crash, porcelain shards flying in all directions.

"I'm sorry." Lyle stepped into the kitchen, his round face turning red. "I didn't mean to startle you."

"Don't worry," Anna said. "It's my fault for not taking the plate from Sophie."

"I was just coming to refill my coffee of mug," Lyle said.

Anna cocked her head.

Lyle's face turned a shade darker. "Mug of coffee."

"Och." Euphemia bustled in from the dining room. In one sweeping glance she took in the broken dish as well as Sophie's dripping hands. Then her gaze swung from Lyle to Anna and then back. "I see my wee bairn is inventing excuses to be near the pretty girls and then scaring them in the process."

"No, Mum, it's not like that at all." Lyle darted a sideways glance at Anna.

"Well, since you startled the girls, you can help Anna clean up." Euphemia stepped into the pantry and reappeared a moment later with a broom before handing it to Lyle.

He faced Anna with an expression like a little boy at the general store who'd been told he could choose a handful of candy. Anna was already kneeling and picking up the bigger pieces. He lowered himself next to her, reached for a piece at the same time as Anna. As their fingers brushed, Lyle murmured an apology, but Anna only smiled.

Sophie stifled a smile of her own as she turned back to the remaining dishes. She liked Lyle. Even if he was a little awkward at times, he was a good man, just like Barclay. And he'd make a fine husband to some lucky woman.

With a start, Sophie glanced back at Anna. Was her friend attracted to Lyle? Was that why she wanted to stay longer?

Euphemia hummed as she started another pot of coffee. No doubt, Anna wanted to stay to be near Euphemia too. Who wouldn't?

"I'll finish for you, Sophie." Euphemia bumped Sophie with her wide hip as though to move her aside. "You go sit with Olivia and rest your feet."

Sophie shook her head and scrubbed at a wooden spoon. "I'm fine. Really I am."

"Dinnae make me swat you, lass." Euphemia wedged her large frame in front of the basin.

"I'm sorry for breaking your plate," Sophie said.

"Och, think nothing of it. It's not the first dish that's been broken in this kitchen, and it won't be the last." Euphemia plunged her hands into the dishwater and began to scrub a dirty pan vigorously. "We're human. We break things. It's what we do with the brokenness that counts."

It's what we do with the brokenness that counts.

Sophie rolled the words around in her mind, testing and tasting them. When she lowered herself into a chair at the dining room table, Olivia showed her the stitches she'd knitted all by herself—some sagging and too loose, others tiny and tight. Olivia's face beamed with pride, and her eyes glowed at her simple accomplishment. One day Olivia would look back on that first attempt and see her mistakes and likely unravel it and start over. For now, the misshapen twisting line of yarn was her best effort, and no one would criticize her for it.

In fact, Sophie praised her efforts and kissed her forehead, encouraging her to keep going. And as she did so, she realized her sisters had always done the same for her. They'd always encouraged her and believed in her.

Would they do so again if they saw the tangled mess she'd made of her life? She wished she could hold out her misshapen life as easily as Olivia had held out her line of knitting. But she'd kept her mistakes hidden for so long, embarrassed, guilt-ridden, and too ashamed to let her sisters or anyone else see the mess.

It's what we do with the brokenness that counts.

Could she let go of attempting to make the repairs her own way and finally hand the mess over to the One waiting to forgive her and repair her life in His way?

Sophie shivered at the prospect, then rubbed her hands up and down her arms. Olivia squinted at the yarn, her bottom lip captured between her teeth in concentration. Olivia would never willingly leave Mayfield, not if Nicholas was still here. Anna didn't want to go—at least not now.

And deep down, Sophie knew it was time to stop running from her mistakes and the brokenness of her life. She had to face her sisters before she could move on. She had to do it for them, for her, for them all.

She had to place the broken pieces into God's hands and let

Him start putting her back together. She'd never be the same innocent, sweet girl she'd once been. She was too cracked and chipped to ever go back. But if God could show His grace to Euphemia and create something new out of her life, Sophie would let Him do the same with her.

CHAPTER 24

"Are you ready?" Reinhold's call from the farmyard wafted through the open kitchen door.

"Coming!" Sophie replied as she finished tying the ribbon of her bonnet underneath her chin. The ribbon was still crooked, but she'd procrastinated as long as she possibly could. She couldn't put off leaving any longer.

She pressed her hands to her quivering stomach and crossed to the door. She took a final glance around the small kitchen. Everything was tidy, the fuel box was full of twisted hay, a fresh basin of water stood on the stand, even a pot of stew simmered on the stove.

This was good-bye, likely the last time she'd stand in her—in Reinhold's—kitchen. She'd wanted to leave it fully stocked and ready for Reinhold and Jakob when they returned later. Without her.

The tight ache in her throat pinched her airways and a suffocating sensation came over her, the same she'd felt since the ride home from the Duffs' place on Sunday two nights ago when she'd told Reinhold she wasn't leaving anymore, that she would stay and meet her sisters.

His relief at her news had been so palpable that his voice trembled when he'd responded, "It's the right thing, Soph."

She supposed it was indeed the right thing. Yet all she'd been able to think about was the enormity of Reinhold's relief and how much it had hurt to know he wanted to be rid of her and end their marriage.

When Mr. Wilson, the storekeeper and telegraph operator, had sent a messenger out to the farm on Monday morning with a wire that her sisters would arrive on Tuesday on the ten o'clock southbound train, Reinhold's relief had once again been as evident in his features as the dust from the field.

They'd spoken very little to each other since then. She hadn't been able to find much to say past the hurt that radiated in her chest. And he'd been silent too.

Now it was time to ride into town and meet the train that was bringing her sisters, their husbands, and her new niece or nephew. Silke and Verina were coming too. Sophie wanted to feel excitement at seeing Elise and Marianne again, but all she felt was dread. Even if she was trying to trust God to make His repairs in His timing, she wished He'd worked a miracle overnight so that her sisters wouldn't see how broken she was.

But no matter how difficult, she would face them. Today.

As she stepped outside into the sunshine, she had to fight the urge to run inside up to her room and barricade the door. She took a deep breath of the cool morning air and told herself she couldn't run, couldn't do things her way anymore. Instead, she had to hand control over to the One who could fix her brokenness. She was learning that the handing over was something she had to do minute by minute. Maybe today she'd even have to do it second by second.

She slowly pivoted to find three pairs of eyes upon her. Olivia and Jakob sat in their usual spots in the back of the wagon, and Reinhold was perched upon the wagon bench, reins in hand.

With his hat pulled low, his eyes were shadowed so she couldn't read them. But the grim set of his lips spoke of his own turmoil.

Was today hard for him too? Was he afraid of what Elise and Marianne would say to him, especially once they learned she'd been living here for over a month? Maybe he expected them to be angry with him for not contacting them sooner.

Well, he needn't worry. She planned to take all the blame upon herself. She'd explain to her sisters that everything was her fault, that Reinhold had wanted to contact them right away but hadn't because of her threats.

In the back of the wagon, Olivia's expression was filled with hope. The girl didn't remember much about Elise or Marianne. She'd been so young when she'd last seen them. But she was hoping—the same as Sophie—that the two wealthy sisters would find a way to help them get Nicholas back.

Jakob held Olivia on his lap. He shot Reinhold a look, one laden with questions as well as admonition.

As Sophie walked the short distance to the wagon, Reinhold jumped down and rounded the wagon to help her up as he always did. When his hand braced her hip, she ignored the warmth and strength of his touch. Before lifting her, the brim of his hat tipped up and unveiled his eyes, giving her a glimpse down into his soul, to the stormy anguish there.

The ferocity of the storm took Sophie by surprise. Before she could formulate a question or before he could heft her up, the rattle of a wagon drew their attention away from each other and to the path that led to the farmhouse.

Had the train arrived early? Maybe instead of waiting in town, her family had decided to ride out to the farm.

Reinhold steadied her on the ground and released his hold before taking a step away, almost as though he didn't want Elise and Marianne to catch him touching her. Was he afraid of what they'd think when they learned he'd married her? Yes, they'd be surprised. But they wouldn't disapprove, would they? Not with Reinhold, the man they both admired and loved.

Maybe Reinhold believed he'd fall short of their expectations now that they were married to important and wealthy men. After all, he'd made a point of bringing up how her sisters would be able to provide the best of everything for her now—food, home, clothes, and anything she could ever want.

"You should know," she said quietly. "Just because I've agreed to see my sisters doesn't mean I'm planning to join them permanently."

His eyes sharpened. "You can't run away again, Soph."

"I won't. But I've been on my own too long to go back to living with them."

He was silent as if digesting her news. "If you don't go with them, then what will you do?"

"I don't know," Sophie answered honestly. "I've been thinking about finding a way to stay in the area. I like Mayfield, and I like farm life." She considered pleading with Euphemia to let her room with Anna until she could find work. But she also knew that wouldn't be a long-term solution.

As the oncoming wagon bumped along the last wilted stretch of grass, Sophie's pulse sped at the sight of the driver wearing a bonnet and skirt. Was it one of her sisters?

The woman shifted so that Sophie could make out her features, and her pulse lurched again before sputtering to a stop. It wasn't Elise or Marianne.

It was Mrs. Ramsey.

The moment she brought the wagon to a halt next to theirs, something wiggled underneath a blanket in the wagon bed. A second later, a head emerged from one end and a pale face peeked out. "Are we there yet?" came a familiar voice.

"Nicholas?" Olivia said, jumping up from Jakob's lap.

Sophie's heart jumped just as suddenly. This was one of those moments when she was tempted to rush forward and try to seize control like she had at church. She wanted to scoop Nicholas up again and run far away where no one could take the little boy from her.

After holding him on Sunday, after feeling his thin arms around her neck and his satin hair against her cheek, her heart ached to hug him. But she forced herself not to move and to hand control over to God.

Nicholas stood, letting the blanket fall away. He glanced at Olivia, his eyes registering surprise. Then he looked at Mrs. Ramsey as though he didn't know whether to greet his sister or climb under the blanket again.

Mrs. Ramsey twisted on the wagon bench. Only then did Sophie read the sadness in the woman's tired eyes. "Yes, we're here."

At Nicholas's hesitation, Olivia paused at the edge of the wagon. She turned her attention to Mrs. Ramsey, her expression suddenly wary.

It was clear neither of the children understood why Mrs. Ramsey had driven to their home, especially after all the efforts the Ramseys had made to shelter Nicholas.

Sophie didn't understand either. The need to run over to Nicholas swelled inside so that she reached for Reinhold. She needed him, needed his strength, needed his help to hold her back. Her hand found his. She didn't care that her fingers trembled.

His fingers quickly enfolded hers. In a slight squeeze he communicated to her that he was with her in this difficulty, that they were in it together.

She squeezed back her appreciation.

"Good morning, Mrs. Ramsey," Reinhold said. "What can we do for you?"

"My husband discovered that your wife's family is arriving

this morning," she said softly. "And he instructed me to take Nicholas visiting for the day."

"So that you'd be away from the house if anyone came to see Nicholas?" Sophie's bitter question popped out before she could stop it.

Mrs. Ramsey nodded, her stooped posture one of defeat, not defiance. "I usually visit my sister down near Dresden. And this time I told my husband we'd stay a couple of days, maybe even a week before returning. My daughter Rachel is old enough to help at home while I'm gone."

Mrs. Ramsey was certainly ensuring that Marianne and Drew wouldn't be able to take Nicholas away, at least not this week. Did Mrs. Ramsey expect gratitude for coming and informing them of her plans? Sophie bit back her caustic response.

The woman began to descend from the wagon bench. As her shawl fell away and her sleeve rose, Sophie saw the bruises. Unmistakable welts in the form of fingerprints. The sight didn't surprise Sophie, not after the way Mr. Ramsey had so easily slapped her. Olivia had reassured her that Mr. Ramsey hadn't ever laid a hand on her or Nicholas or even their daughter Rachel. But he had no qualms about hitting full-grown women.

Sophie felt pity for Mrs. Ramsey while also offering up a prayer of gratefulness that Reinhold was working on handling his anger. Although she'd never met Reinhold's father, she'd heard the stories about his rage, about the fits he'd fall into, breaking and smashing everything in his path, and getting into fights at work and the tavern. She was confident Reinhold was well on his way to being a different man from his father—if he'd ever been like him.

With her feet planted on the ground, Mrs. Ramsey adjusted her sleeve and shawl before rounding the wagon. She reached inside for a small grain sack, lifted it out, and placed it on the grass.

"Come now, Nicholas," she said and stretched out her arms.
Nicholas scrambled to her. "I can get out?"

"Yes." She hefted Nicholas from the wagon and set him near
his bag.

Olivia finished climbing down and cautiously approached
Nicholas.

"How long can I stay?" he asked.

Mrs. Ramsey clasped her hands in front of her before meeting Sophie's gaze. "Forever."

Sophie's heart ceased beating, and her lungs stopped working. Had she heard Mrs. Ramsey correctly?

No one moved. The woman's answer had apparently startled
everyone, including Nicholas.

"Your husband said something on Sunday that I haven't been
able to stop thinking about," Mrs. Ramsey said in her soft-
spoken tone. "I've only been his mother for a few weeks, but
you've raised him for most of his life. You're his real mother.
You're the one he talks about, the one he wants when he's hurt
and hungry and tired, the one he cries for at night. It's clear how
much you love him and how much he loves you." She paused, her
voice cracking. "With that kind of love, he doesn't need me."

Nicholas was staring up at Mrs. Ramsey. He reached for her
hand. She took it and braved a smile for him.

"My husband claimed that Nicholas would forget about you
and eventually come to see us as his real parents," she continued.
"But while we may need him, he doesn't need us. He needs you.
And he belongs with you."

Sophie's throat constricted, and she couldn't formulate a
response. Instead, she nodded at Mrs. Ramsey, hoping her
expression conveyed the depth of her gratitude. The woman
was defying her husband by bringing Nicholas to her. She was
putting herself at risk and would probably have to face her
husband's wrath upon her return home.

"Will you be safe?" Reinhold asked, apparently coming to the same conclusion.

"He'll hear of my deed soon enough. By the time I return, I hope he'll be resigned."

Sophie hoped so too. Mrs. Ramsey's sacrifice showed just how much she'd grown to love Nicholas. She was willing to put the boy's needs and happiness above her own. And for that, Sophie respected, even admired, the woman.

Nicholas continued to hold Mrs. Ramsey's hand, his eyes wide. He'd always been a sensitive boy and tried to please everyone. Even if he'd only been with the Ramseys for a month, Sophie could see he'd grown attached to Mrs. Ramsey in his own way and didn't want to hurt her.

As if sensing the boy's inner turmoil, Mrs. Ramsey stooped and drew him into a hug. "You're back where you belong."

She straightened and walked away from Nicholas. She climbed up onto the wagon bench, retrieved the reins, and clicked a gentle command to the horses. As the wagon started back down the rutted path away from the house, Mrs. Ramsey kept her focus straight ahead, her face stoic.

Sophie didn't have to guess the sorrow and heartache the woman was working hard to hide. She knew the pain intimately from having lived through it herself. Though she wanted to call out her thanks or even a simple good-bye, the best thing she could do for Mrs. Ramsey was to allow her to leave with her dignity intact.

Nobody moved except to watch the wagon. When it finally disappeared from sight, Olivia started to cross to Nicholas. She smiled hesitantly at her brother.

When he grinned at her in response, she sprinted forward as fast as her legs would carry her. She dragged him into an embrace. He wrapped his arms around her and clung to her as though afraid he might be forced to leave.

Sophie broke away from Reinhold and rushed to the children. She grabbed them both in a hug and squeezed them. They wiggled against her hold and laughed. The sweet sound was more glorious than anything she'd heard in a long time. Only then did she feel the tears streaking her cheeks.

With both children in her arms, she lifted her face heavenward and whispered a silent prayer of thanksgiving. All her striving had amounted to more messes and brokenness. When she'd finally stopped trying to fix everything, God had stepped in and started to piece things back together in His way—a way that was completely unexpected and better than anything she could have accomplished on her own.

CHAPTER 25

Reinhold lifted Nicholas's grain sack and set it in the wagon next to Sophie's. A peek inside had revealed carefully stitched little outfits, additional shoes and hats, as well as a comb, soap, and several other necessities.

Mrs. Ramsey had been kind to send the boy away with so much. She could have delivered him with nothing more than the few garments he'd brought from New York.

Sophie's bag was fuller than when she'd arrived too. Euphemia had given Sophie some of her garments and shown her how to take them in to make them fit better. Among the soft lumps of clothing, Reinhold caught sight of the outline of the brass candle holder. The lampstand jutted through the thin fabric.

He closed his eyes against the image, against the finality of her leaving. All morning he'd fought the pain away, but now it sliced into him like the blade of his scythe and threatened to topple him to the ground.

Bending his head and attempting to suck in a breath, he grabbed the side of the wagon.

"She doesn't want to leave here." Jakob spoke from the wagon bed where he'd been resting while Sophie and the children enjoyed their reunion.

Reinhold straightened and met Jakob's gaze. The boy's eyes flickered with trepidation, and he held himself motionless as though fearing Reinhold might lash out.

Jakob still feared him but was learning to have courage in the face of his fears. Was it time for Reinhold to do the same?

He glanced to where Sophie sat in the grass with Olivia on one knee and Nicholas on the other. Her cheeks were still damp from her tears of joy, and she smiled with adoration at the two children, her fingers gently combing Nicholas's hair as he chattered away. They'd been that way for the better part of an hour. He hadn't wanted to interrupt them, had instead worked in the barn for a little while. But he supposed he couldn't delay the trip to town any longer.

Wearing the bright blue dress Euphemia had given her, she was especially fetching, her skin having taken on a honey color from her days spent in the garden and the farmyard. Her bonnet had come loose and now hung down her back, revealing golden hair the sun had bleached a shade lighter.

Yet as beautiful as she was on the outside, he'd learned her inner spirit was more so. Even now, with the children on her lap, he could see that she was a loving, devoted, and sacrificial mother. He could picture her with half a dozen more children at least.

Suddenly, more than anything, he wanted those children to be his. In fact, the thought of any other man fathering her children repelled him so that he had the urge to bend over and be sick. He couldn't make sense of his reaction except to finally admit that he loved her. Desperately. He didn't want to lose her, didn't want to give her an annulment, and certainly didn't want to hand her over to some other man.

He wanted her all to himself. Forever.

Releasing a shaky breath, he spoke to Jakob even while his sights were fastened on Sophie. "Take Olivia and Nicholas into the barn and play with them for a while."

Jakob scrambled out of the wagon bed. His brows rose above his questioning eyes.

Reinhold wanted to tell his brother he needed time alone with his wife, but he suspected Jakob would understand without him having to spell everything out. "You can keep them occupied, can't you?"

A slow grin crept across Jakob's face. "How long do you need?"

"As long as possible."

Jakob bobbed his head, his grin turning somewhat silly.

Reinhold started toward the house. "Sophie, I need to speak with you. In the house." He didn't wait for her reaction, didn't want to give her the opportunity to turn him down and insist that they start to town. After the visit from Mrs. Ramsey, they were running late. And now taking the time to talk would make them even later.

Behind him, he heard her murmur to the children.

"Let's go show Nicholas the kittens," Jakob offered, which was followed by Olivia's enthusiastic response and then Nicholas's. Reinhold released a breath of tension and whispered a prayer of gratefulness for Jakob's help and encouragement.

Reinhold entered through the back door into the kitchen and moved directly to the stove where he busied himself by pouring a cup of coffee. He had to have something in his hands or he might go right over to her, sweep her into his arms, and kiss her until they were both dizzy.

The door closed gently behind her. "What's wrong?" she asked, her voice laced with worry.

He finished filling his mug, replaced the coffeepot, then took a sip. Finally he turned, trying to slow the rapid thud of his pulse.

He knew he should be worried about what Elise and Marianne would say to him, but right now he was more concerned about Sophie's reaction.

How should he tell her he didn't want her to go? That he wanted to stay married to her? Was it too late after all he'd done to discourage their relationship? He'd rejected her when she'd told him she loved him. Why would she want him now?

She regarded him expectantly, her pretty eyes wide and innocent.

He lifted his mug and took another long slurp.

"I can tell something's bothering you." She crossed the kitchen toward him, as forthright as always. When she stood before him, he held his mug in front of him, a low wall of defense until he could figure out how to formulate the right words.

"Is it Nicholas?" Anxiety slipped into her question. "Do you think Mr. Ramsey will come after me and try to get him away?"

"No. He won't take Nicholas. I won't let him."

She lifted her eyes to meet his, and the sadness there ripped at his heart. "Maybe I'll have to leave Mayfield after all, so that he won't try to take Nicholas away."

Reinhold swallowed another mouthful of coffee, trying to gather the courage to say what he should have already.

She watched his throat as he swallowed, which made him all the more self-conscious. "I know you think I should go back to New York with my sisters. And maybe I should. Maybe that would be the safest place."

Was that what she wanted now? If she thought New York City would be the best place, who was he to stop her?

She was quiet for a moment. Finally she spoke. "Tell me the truth."

He didn't know what to think, especially because his desire to have her stay was selfish. He started to raise the mug to his lips again, but she intercepted his hand. With her eyes fixed on his, she pried his fingers from the cup and set it on the stove.

"Reinhold." She grasped his upper arms. "I know you want to tell me something. Please just say it. I can handle whatever it is."

Her touch sent heat rippling down his arms to his hands. Before he could deny himself, he reached for her hips. As he encircled her waist, her eyes widened. "You're right. I do want to say something."

She tilted her head just slightly in that perceptive way she had.

He wasn't an eloquent man. He didn't always know how to put his feelings into words. And this time he didn't care, didn't hold back. "I don't want to lose you. I want you to stay here with me and be my wife." He slid one hand around to the small of her back and tugged her closer.

When she came against him willingly and ran her fingers up his arms to his shoulders, his hope found life. She skimmed her hands back down as though relishing the feel of his arms. "I am already your wife."

"Yes, but I want to make you mine. All the way mine."

"Are you sure?" Her eyes were full of questions.

"I thought if you went with your sisters, you'd be happier and have a better life. But then you told me you wouldn't stay with them, that you want to find a way to live here and that you like living on the farm."

"I've been searching for this kind of life. And now that I have it, I don't want to leave."

He studied the earnestness that lined her face. "If you're sure—"

"Only if you are."

"I feel sick at the thought of having to say good-bye to you."

"Then don't." She smiled a slow, almost sensual smile.

He caressed the length of her backbone up to the base of her neck. With her hair pulled into an elegant knot, her neck was bare and smooth and beautiful. He let his fingers drift to the long stretch that ran from her ear to her collarbone.

A soft pleasurable sound escaped from her lips. Her fingers glided up his arms again, this time winding around his neck and landing in his hair, where she dug them deep. She surprised him by lifting her mouth to where his jaw and throat intersected. It was his turn to release a moan.

With her fingers wound in his hair, she captured him with kisses along his jawline and neck.

He bent in to her ear and whispered, "I love you. I'm only sorry for not saying it sooner, and for getting scared and pushing you away."

He could feel her lips curve into a smile. She kissed his neck again and took away all coherent thought save one. He wanted—no, needed—to kiss her.

He shifted his mouth in search of hers. "Kiss me, Sophie," he said hoarsely.

Her laugh was sultry, and her kisses shifted to his collar, to where his top button had pulled free. Her lips grazed the open place on his chest. He growled and scooped her off her feet and into his arms.

He started across the kitchen toward the stairs. He'd stepped onto the second stair when she loosened her hold. "Reinhold, wait," she said breathlessly.

"I'm finishing what I should have the last time we were in this spot."

"The children—"

"I told Jakob to keep them occupied."

She laughed again, her delight only stirring his desire. "So this is why you *really* called me into the house?"

"I didn't know if you'd forgive me, but I was planning to do everything possible to get you to stay."

"I guess you didn't have to work too hard at it, did you?"

He smiled. "Thanks for going easy on me."

She wiggled against him as though wanting him to put her down. He'd done so once and almost lost her. He wasn't planning on doing it again.

He started up the steps, this time without breaking his stride.

"My sisters," she said, looking up at him. "And the train—we have to go."

Her mouth was finally available for the taking. He lowered his lips to hers and silenced her with a kiss. She responded eagerly, melding and moving with all the desire that had grown between them. When he reached the bedroom doorway, he broke away for a moment.

"I'm not taking you to your sisters or the train," he whispered. "We're staying here. Home. Together. Where we belong."

With that, he stepped into the bedroom and kicked the door closed behind them.

CHAPTER 26

Elise Quincy paused on the top step of the private train compartment and surveyed the platform. Marianne sidled next to her and scanned the station, her brown eyes wide and full of excitement.

"Do you see her?" Marianne asked.

Except for the stationmaster talking with a gentleman standing next to his luggage, the platform was nearly deserted.

Elise peered through the depot door and windows, holding her breath in anticipation that at any second Sophie would come running outside and rush to meet them. Maybe *rushing* was expecting too much. But surely Sophie would be a little happy to see them, wouldn't she?

Thornton's warning from earlier resounded in her head. *"Reinhold sent the telegram. Not Sophie. And although you've been searching for her, what if she's not yet ready to be found?"*

Elise hadn't wanted to believe her husband, hadn't wanted to consider the possibility that Sophie didn't want to see them yet. After two years, why wouldn't Sophie want to be found?

"Where is she?" Marianne stepped past Elise down the train steps, landing with a hop onto the platform with childlike enthusiasm. Her new traveling gown was wrinkled from the long hours of sitting. Its pink floral print highlighted the rosy hue in Marianne's cheeks as well as the glow of her skin.

Elise had never seen Marianne as happy as when she was with Drew. After a year of marriage, the two were still like newlyweds with a smoldering passion that always flared whenever they were together.

While Drew tended to be too impulsive for Elise's taste, Marianne thrived on his jesting and spontaneity. She liked to tease him in response, often challenging him with dares he couldn't refuse. Like yesterday during their stay in Chicago, Marianne had insisted that Drew couldn't carry her from their train car to the depot without kissing her.

Of course, Marianne had won. But only because she'd used every feminine wile she possessed to lure Drew into kissing her. They'd clearly had fun in the process, so much so that Drew had suggested they stay the night in the hotel Thornton had recently built in Chicago.

Elise had vetoed the plan before Thornton gave in to the couple. Her practical nature and her need to be with Sophie had driven them the entire trip. She'd been the one to keep them focused on their mission. And as tempting as it had been to stop and sleep in a real bed for the night, Elise had pushed them onward.

Marianne's footsteps fairly skipped as she crossed to the depot and entered. "The train is arriving late. Maybe she was here already and left."

Elise glanced over her shoulder toward their luxurious compartment, debating whether she ought to wait for the others. Thornton had already told her to go ahead, that he would follow shortly with the baby. And Drew had said he'd watch over Silke and Verina.

She suspected the men had conspired together, wanting to

give her and Marianne the chance to have a private reunion with Sophie before bombarding the girl with introductions. On the one hand, Elise was grateful for their sensitivity, but on the other, she wanted Thornton by her side. Although she'd always considered herself to be strong and independent, somehow her life had woven together with Thornton's so completely that more and more lately she felt like they were the same tapestry, that they were like dangling lonesome threads when they were apart.

Was this how Mutti had felt after Vater had died? How had she possibly gone on without him? Now that Elise had her own daughter, she guessed Mutti hadn't given up because she'd loved her daughters more than her own life. Before Elise had held her newborn babe, she'd never known it was possible to love a child as much as she did. She would do anything for her baby, even die to save her.

Elise cautiously climbed down the steps onto the platform. She followed after Marianne and entered the deserted depot. Mustiness and the waft of stale coffee greeted her. The Mayfield depot didn't boast of an eating house the same way the Quincy train depot did. *Her* eating house, the one she'd so lovingly nurtured and grown. Even so, the stationmaster kept a pot of coffee on the corner stove for the few passengers who disembarked.

The main room was small and would have fit into the dining room of her Quincy home. Wryly she realized it would have fit into the pantry of the New York City Quincy mansion. There were still times, like now, when she couldn't believe she was living such a fairy-tale life, one of boundless resources and wealth.

Nevertheless, she could never forget the deprivation, weariness, and hunger from her previous life, the times when she and her sisters had nothing but each other. She wished she could say that had been enough. But somehow she'd let her pride, along with her need to prove herself worthy, drive her to be someone better.

When she'd gone west with the other women during the fall of '57, she'd convinced herself that it was the only way left, that she was merely trying to fulfill her promise to Mutti to take care of Marianne and Sophie. But in hindsight she could see that she'd been searching for more. Essentially she'd abandoned her sisters to pursue a life of her own.

If she'd never left New York City, and if she'd put her sisters' needs over her own, then perhaps they'd still be together. Perhaps Sophie would have felt loved and secure and wanted. She wouldn't have felt the need to run away. And they would have been together during the past two years.

As it was, Elise had cost them all the one thing that mattered most—their family. She'd talked for endless hours with Thornton about her conclusions, and he'd always reassured her that God could take any situation, no matter how much they botched things up, and He could still work things out for good.

Elise couldn't deny that God had been good to her in spite of her mistakes. Thornton was a devoted and loving husband and now father. She loved helping him bring about changes in the working conditions for the poor people in the various towns and companies he owned. She loved spending time in their home in Quincy and with their friends there. And even though she'd finally hired a manager for her eating house at the train depot, she still enjoyed working in the kitchen whenever possible.

"She's not here," Marianne said, peeking out the front window toward the quiet town beyond.

Elise stifled her rising disappointment. She should have heeded Thornton's caution, shouldn't have allowed herself to become so excited. "We'll have our trunks and personal belongings taken to the house that Drew has secured for us. Then we'll rest for a bit."

"Rest?" Marianne spun away from the window. "I can't rest. Not until I see Sophie."

"We're all tired," Elise said matter-of-factly, reaching for the door that would take her back to the train and to Thornton. "Besides, we could use a meal and a change of clothing before seeing her."

"I'm not tired or hungry. And I certainly don't care if I have dust and wrinkles in my clothing."

"Let's go to the house first."

"You can go. But I'm not resting until I see her." Marianne's expression turned stubborn. Elise knew Marianne blamed herself for Sophie running away. And even though Elise had said all she could to reassure Marianne that Sophie's leaving hadn't been her fault, Marianne had never been able to entirely let go of feeling responsible.

Elise guessed she and Marianne were alike in that way.

"Aren't you excited to see her?" Marianne asked.

"Yes, of course I am. But it's clear she doesn't share the same feeling."

As the reality of Sophie's absence sank in, the light in Marianne's eyes dimmed, as though she too recognized what it meant. They'd sent enough telegrams regarding their arrival day and time. If Sophie had been ready and willing to see them, she would have met them at the train station.

The depot door opened, ushering in the cool autumn breeze, along with the stationmaster. He nodded at Marianne, then turned his full attention upon Elise and gave her an ingratiating smile. "I'm honored to have you at my station, Mrs. Quincy. If there's anything I can do for you, anything at all, please don't hesitate to ask—"

"We're waiting for the arrival of our sister, Sophie Neumann," Marianne cut in. "Have you seen her this morning?"

The stationmaster lifted his hat and scratched his balding

head. "Don't know of a Sophie Neumann. Do you mean Sophie Weiss?"

"Sophie Weiss?" Elise and Marianne said the name at the same time.

"Yep. Reinhold Weiss up and married himself a young gal—one of those orphans who came through here back in September. A right pretty little thing who didn't look old enough to be marrying. But then again, what does an old man like me know about those kinds of things anymore?"

With every word the stationmaster spoke, Elise's consternation swelled. Why would Reinhold marry Sophie? She was years younger than he was and like a sister to him.

Marianne's troubled expression was filled with the same questions. Why would Reinhold marry Sophie? He wasn't the type of man to put pressure on any woman. He most certainly hadn't put any pressure on Elise and had willingly released Marianne from her commitment to him last summer. Reinhold had too much integrity and kindness to take advantage of Sophie.

"You're positive Reinhold married Sophie?" Elise asked.

The stationmaster nodded vigorously. "Yep, had a wedding at the Duffs' a few weeks back, and now they're living out on his farm. Got himself a small place northwest of the Turners'. 'Course, there aren't any good roads out that way, but it isn't hard to find."

Marianne nodded, apparently remembering where the Turners lived from her time in Mayfield the previous year.

"Heard tell that Mrs. Weiss has been trying to get her hands on a little boy that the Ramseys took in," the stationmaster continued, clearly accustomed to doubling as the town newspaper, sharing all the local gossip whether or not anyone asked for it. "She grabbed him Sunday morning before church and tried to run off with him."

Marianne's brows rose.

As the stationmaster spoke, the unease Elise felt inside began to grow. What was going on here?

"Some are saying she's the boy's rightful ma since she raised him, and that she deserves to have him back. Rumor has it that's why she married Reinhold in the first place, so she could have that little boy and his sister." The stationmaster dropped his voice as though someone might overhear him.

"Nicholas and Olivia," Marianne said.

"She's the boy's rightful ma since she raised him . . ." Elise digested the stationmaster's words. Was it possible that Sophie felt for Nicholas and Olivia the same kind of intense love that she felt for her own daughter? After all, Sophie had mothered the children from the start. They'd been babes when their father had died and their mother had abandoned them.

Elise wasn't sure how or when Sophie had joined back up with Olivia and Nicholas after Tante Brunhilde had taken the two to the Children's Aid Society. But was it possible Sophie had been willing to do anything and sacrifice everything, even die, to save them? She supposed she'd never understood Sophie's passion for the children, never took the time to understand . . . until now. Now that she had her own babe and realized the sacrifices parents were willing to make.

For several minutes, her mind attempted to make sense of everything. She only heard snippets of the rest of what the stationmaster was telling them, something about Reverend Poole from the Children's Aid Society and how he'd been attempting to intervene.

"Where can we rent a horse and wagon?" Elise interrupted.

The stationmaster stood with his mouth open, his sentence half finished.

"I thought you wanted to wait," Marianne started.

Elise shook her head. "We're going now."

Elise gripped the bench, her fingers stiff from not having let go since they'd left the main road. Yes, the rutted path through the yellowing grass was bumpy. But she wasn't afraid of falling off. If she was completely honest, she was afraid of facing Sophie. The excitement of earlier had faded in light of the stark truth of Sophie's current predicament.

"Do you really think Reinhold and Sophie got married so they could have Nicholas and Olivia?" Marianne asked from the driver's spot.

The late-October day was cold and breezy, but the sunshine warmed them whenever it decided not to hide behind the clouds.

"That's completely something Reinhold would do," Elise said. "Offer to marry Sophie so that she'd be in a position where she could have the children."

Marianne nodded. "I have no doubt Reinhold would go to great lengths to ensure that he treats her like a sister."

"Of course." But what Elise couldn't yet figure out was why Reinhold had only just contacted them, especially if he'd been married to Sophie for several weeks and perhaps had known she was in the community even longer than that.

"That must be it." Marianne pointed ahead to the roof of a house now showing above the tall grass that bordered either side of the path.

Elise straightened so she could see farther ahead, perhaps get a glimpse of the petite, blond-haired girl who'd always been a miniature version of herself. As the wagon rolled nearer, she could see that Reinhold had built a simple two-story house and had painted it white. It had no porch, no ornamental details, no extras. The only spot of color came from the bright calico curtains in the windows.

Beyond the house was a decent-sized barn. It too was a simple design, likely all Reinhold could afford. The farmyard surrounding the house and barn was barren in places. A few chickens roamed inside the fenced garden behind the house, but otherwise the place appeared lifeless.

"It doesn't look like anyone's home," Marianne said, bringing the wagon to a halt near the well. "Maybe they're out working." She glanced to the fields beyond the barn, to a distant patch of cornstalks.

A slight sway of the curtain in the upstairs bedroom caught Elise's attention.

Elise started to climb down. Someone was home, and she had a feeling it was Sophie. She'd begun to make sense of why Sophie might not want to be with them. But she had to see her sister, even if it was the last time.

Her feet had hardly touched the hard-packed grass when the house door squeaked open.

Reinhold stepped out, stockier and more muscular than she remembered. He rapidly closed the door behind him and combed his fingers through his tousled hair.

"Elise. Marianne," he greeted, his expression as hard as the rippling muscles visible beneath his shirtsleeves. His eyes regarded them coolly as though they were trespassing.

"Hello, Reinhold," Elise replied. She hadn't expected any warmth from him, not after the pain she'd caused him when they parted ways. But she certainly also hadn't expected him to be so cold, almost unwelcoming. "I hope we aren't disturbing you."

He glanced at the upstairs window. "Maybe."

The one word sent a flutter of trepidation through Elise.

Marianne had suddenly found a loose thread in the reins and was doing her best to tuck it back into the leather braid. Clearly Marianne was embarrassed to see Reinhold again since she'd rejected him for Drew.

Elise was tempted to send a caustic remark to Marianne about how she ought to take up sewing again, but she inwardly sighed instead. Reinhold would have every right to toss them off his property. But not before she accomplished what she'd set out to do. "We came to see Sophie."

"You shouldn't have come. She's not ready to see you."

At a movement near the barn, Elise shifted to see a lanky boy poking his head out of the barn door. "Hello, Jakob," she said. Even though she hadn't seen the boy in over two years and he'd grown at least two feet, she still recognized his face.

He gave a somber nod before turning his attention to Reinhold.

She did likewise.

Reinhold braced his bare feet apart and crossed his thick arms.

Her heart tumbled in her chest. He was serious. Sophie didn't want to see them, and he wasn't planning to go against her wishes.

"I'm sorry for sending you the telegram and inconveniencing you," he said, his voice softening just a little.

She nodded. "I'm sorry too."

Behind her, Marianne shifted on the wagon bench, which gave a faint creak.

Had they come all this way for nothing?

"I'll take good care of her," Reinhold said, breaking the silence. "I promise."

Elise studied his weathered, rugged face, noting the new lines next to his eyes and in his forehead. He'd aged since she'd last seen him. Or maybe it was the maturity in his eyes that made him appear older and wiser, a maturity that spoke of hardship pressing in and resulting in growth.

His expression also spoke of something else, something soft and delicate and yet powerful. Was he in love with Sophie?

Elise probed his countenance again. Was their marriage more than one of convenience after all?

He didn't back down from her scrutiny. His eyes were wide, allowing her to see deep into his soul to the truth. "I love her," he said simply. "And I plan to do everything in my power to make her happy."

She couldn't fathom the possibility that Sophie was old enough to be married. But she knew as well as anyone that street living had a way of making children grow up much too soon. "I'm glad Sophie has you."

His brows rose, as if her statement was the last thing he'd expected her to say.

"You're a good man, Reinhold Weiss. If Sophie had to get married, I couldn't ask for anyone better than you."

His Adam's apple moved in a hard swallow before he nodded at her, his eyes radiating gratefulness.

She glanced around Reinhold's farm again, this time seeing beyond the simplicity to the hard labor that had gone into everything. Reinhold was organized and tidy and diligent, and although the farm was still in its infancy, she had no doubt that over time he'd build it up to its full potential. And Sophie would be here to help him.

Maybe Sophie wasn't ready to see them today. But she would be close by, and maybe someday they'd be able to meet again. Elise turned toward the wagon to leave, then stopped and faced Reinhold again. "Will you give Sophie a message from me?"

"I'll try."

He was offering the best he could, and Elise would take it. "Tell her that I'm sorry—"

"We're sorry," Marianne interjected.

"Tell her we're sorry we didn't love her the way she needed, that we weren't there for her, that we didn't understand how much Olivia and Nicholas meant to her. Tell her that if we could go back and do it again, we'd never leave her . . ."

The farmhouse door squeaked open. A young woman stepped through and out into the sunshine. She was attired in a simple blue dress that molded to her full womanly curves. Her golden hair spilled in luxurious waves down her shoulders and over her chest and back, reaching almost to her waist.

But it was her eyes, her wide-as-the-blue-summer-sky eyes that made Elise catch her breath.

Marianne sucked in a breath too.

The young woman sidled next to Reinhold. He gathered her into the crook of his body, sheltering and shielding her all at once. His touch was intimate and gentle, like that of a lover. His eyes caressed her too, his adoration mingling with desire.

This was Sophie, her little sister. But she wasn't little anymore. At some point during their time apart, Sophie had turned from a little girl into a full-grown woman, a woman more beautiful than most. No wonder Reinhold was smitten with her.

Her gorgeous blue eyes glistened as she looked between Elise and Marianne.

Elise stared back in wonder at the transformation. The ache in her heart rippled with the fresh awareness that Sophie was almost a stranger to them. They'd missed so much of her life, hadn't been there to help her through all the difficulties she'd surely faced, and hadn't been there to ease the pain or to share the joys.

"I'm sorry," Elise whispered again past the ache that now clutched her throat. She wasn't sure if Sophie had heard what she'd said before, so she spoke the words again—letting the dam loose against the pool that had been gathering and pressing for release. "I shouldn't have left you, Sophie. You were—and still are—more important than anything else."

Tears welled in Sophie's eyes, and several spilled over. She didn't move to wipe them away, nor did she move to bridge the chasm that separated them.

"I know I have no right to ask you for forgiveness," Elise continued, needing to say everything that burned in her soul. "But I pray that someday you'll find the ability to forgive me."

More tears cascaded down Sophie's cheeks.

Elise's eyes stung, and she blinked back the moisture. "I want you to know that I love you. I always have and I always will."

As she spoke the words, her anguished soul seemed to find release, finally. Maybe she'd never have the kind of relationship with Sophie that she longed for. But she could live at peace, knowing that she'd been able to see her sister again.

Sophie's chest rose, and she choked back a sob. "You wouldn't say that if you knew everything I've done."

"Oh, Liebchen." She could only imagine what Sophie had done to survive on her own on the streets. And although Sophie didn't have the defeated and used-up look of a prostitute, Elise wouldn't have been surprised if Sophie'd had to resort to selling her body to survive. "There's nothing—and I mean nothing— that you could have done or ever could do that would make me stop loving you."

"I've lied, cheated, stolen—"

"None of it matters," Elise said fiercely. "All that matters is you."

"We've been searching for you for so long," Marianne said from beside Elise, openly crying. Elise didn't know when her sister had climbed down from the wagon, but she was grateful for her steady presence and support. "And now that we've found you, we only want you to know how much we love you. That's all."

Another sob broke from Sophie's lips. Reinhold pressed a kiss against her head. She leaned into him as though gathering courage and strength from his love. Then she straightened and broke from his embrace. She took a small, shaky step toward them, her eyes shadowed with uncertainty.

Elise had no uncertainty, no doubts, no reason to hold back. This was the moment she'd prayed for, the one she'd begged God to give her. And she wasn't going to let it slip away. In three long strides she reached Sophie, wrapped her arms around her, and hugged her with every ounce of love and strength she possessed.

"Oh, Liebchen," she whispered into Sophie's ear. "Oh, how I've missed you."

Sophie held herself stiffly for only a moment before sagging against Elise, her chest rising and falling with the intensity of her sobs. In an instant, Marianne was there too, wrapping her arms around both of them, her tears a sprinkling of love, relief, and joy.

Elise held on to both her sisters, never wanting to let go and whispering silent prayers of gratitude for God's presence in their midst. They'd each had to take different journeys in their search for Him. Their paths had been marked with their own unique trials and difficulties.

But He'd led them gently and lovingly, never letting go, finally bringing them to this place. Elise suspected this reunion wasn't the final destination, that they'd have many hard steps ahead yet to travel. But for now, she'd cherish this haven, this rest, this togetherness.

CHAPTER 27

At the screech of train wheels, Sophie pressed a hand over her stomach to quell her nerves and to ease the churning that had grown more frequent in recent days. She stared out the train window to the fallow fields covered with a dusting of snow, the dark loam a stark contrast with the pure white. The first buildings and storage bins loomed closer as the train slowed.

"How are you doing?" Reinhold's low voice rumbled near her ear.

She shifted to face him, his dark eyes watching her with concern. His face was freshly shaven, his jaw smooth, his muscles rigid. In his best shirt, vest, and coat, he was entirely too handsome. The gold chain from his new watch hung out of his pocket. He'd thrown his father's old broken watch into the flames one evening. Not long after, she'd surprised him with a new one. Having wealthy sisters had its advantages, especially since they were more than willing to loan her money.

Although Reinhold was handsome in his patched and worn

garments, with the soil and dust of the fields grooved into his skin, she appreciated the way he cleaned up.

She glanced at the children on the bench across from them—to Nicholas and Olivia, who had their faces pressed against the glass in anticipation of their stop. She peeked across the aisle to where Silke and Verina sat quietly reading books, which Marianne and Elise constantly supplied them.

The children were occupied, which meant only one thing . . .

"Kiss me," she whispered, leaning in to Reinhold and hungrily capturing his mouth with hers.

He just as hungrily obliged, his mouth fusing with hers for just an instant before she broke away.

She slipped a hand underneath his coat to his heart. His responding rapid thud told her he felt the same way she did, that he'd be waiting for the chance to get her alone sometime today—as he usually did—and kiss her longer.

"There's the depot!" Olivia called out.

"Look, look!" Nicholas cried.

Reinhold bent in toward her ear. "I love you, Mrs. Weiss."

She smiled. She loved hearing him whisper her name. Before she could whisper the endearment back, he slid his hand underneath her coat and splayed his fingers on her waist.

"I want to tell them," he whispered.

"Don't you think it's too soon?" She placed her hand on top of his.

"Don't you think they'll be expecting it?" he said with a mischievous grin.

From the first moment she'd seen Elise and Marianne that day two months ago in the farmyard, she and Reinhold hadn't been able to hide their love for each other. At least Elise and Marianne had known from the start how things stood between her and Reinhold.

That day had been truly memorable in every way. Not only

had it been a beautiful start to her marriage with Reinhold, but she'd also regained her family—all of her family, including Nicholas and Elise and Marianne.

Of course, Mr. Ramsey had ridden out the next day after hearing rumors of what his wife had done. He'd attacked Reinhold and demanded that he return Nicholas.

Someone had apparently alerted Reverend Poole of Mr. Ramsey's mission to regain the child. Since the reverend had still been in the area doing follow-up visits, he'd arrived at their farm in time to see Mr. Ramsey beating Reinhold. Even though Reinhold had wanted to strike back, he'd refrained.

The sheriff arrested Mr. Ramsey and locked him in jail for a week. Not long after his release, he sold his house, packed up his family, and moved away.

Sophie had been relieved to know he'd given up his fight to keep Nicholas and that he'd no longer be a threat. Marianne and Drew had also used their connections with the Children's Aid Society to speed up the adoption process so that she and Reinhold could legally make Nicholas and Olivia theirs.

"What does the sign say, Mommy?" Nicholas asked.

Mommy. Sophie liked the sound of it and shared a secretive smile with Reinhold.

During the first few days after Mrs. Ramsey had delivered Nicholas, he'd grieved in his own childlike way for the woman he'd grown to care about, the one he'd called Mommy. Sophie had assured him that she would be his new mommy, that he could call her that now if he wanted to. And he had. Sometimes she even caught Olivia using the term.

Maybe one day in the future, they'd no longer notice the cracks in the pieces of their life that God had put back together. Maybe the hurts and bad memories of the past year would fade away so they would see the whole masterpiece of all God had accomplished.

Sophie glanced out the window toward the train depot. "It says *Quincy*."

"After Uncle Thornton Quincy?" Olivia asked.

"Yes, after your uncle." Sophie peered outside at the town Thornton and Elise had helped to build. Beyond the depot, Main Street was a busy thoroughfare with buildings up and down both sides, along with businesses spilling over into neighboring streets. It was hard to believe the town had been hardly more than the depot and a few meager structures just two years ago when Elise had first arrived.

Sophie had been eager to hear all about Elise and Marianne's adventures. They'd stayed in Mayfield, making introductions, catching up, and spending time together before Elise and Marianne had taken their leave—Elise and Thornton traveling to Quincy, and Marianne and Drew returning to New York City.

When Elise invited them all to travel to Quincy for Christmas, Sophie had shaken her head in trepidation. Even though her sisters had assured her of their love and forgiveness numerous times, she still feared their rejection. What if they'd changed their minds about her after they had time to think about all she'd revealed to them regarding her years of survival on the streets?

Finally, Reinhold had been the one to make the decision to go. With the corn harvested and husked, with the pig butchered, and the new smokehouse filled with dried venison and fish that Jakob had provided, Reinhold told her the farm could get along without them for a few days.

He'd insisted on making the trip even though he was in the midst of building an addition to their home with the lumber Thornton and Elise had given them as a wedding present. He'd made arrangements for Fergus and Alastair Duff to stay on and take care of the livestock. But then Jakob had declined going along and offered to look after the farm even though Sophie had wanted to include him, wanted him to feel a part of their new family. Jakob said he was content at home with his new schoolbooks, now going to school with the other children whenever he could be spared.

With the harvest in and the farm under Jakob's watchful care, they had nothing stopping them from going to Quincy, not even the train fare. Since Thornton was part owner of the Illinois Central, he'd told them they could ride on it for free whenever they wanted.

Only Sophie's insecurity was holding her back.

"Look, look!" Nicholas shouted, his finger pointed against the window, his eyes wide, his face beginning to lose some of its baby chubbiness.

Sophie turned her attention again to the depot, and realized people were congregating on the train platform. Bundled in heavy coats and scarves and hats, they were laughing and smiling and waving.

"What does it say, Mommy?" Nicholas asked again.

"It says *Quincy*, Liebchen."

"No, the other sign."

Sophie followed the direction of his gaze to a sign that a young couple was holding. It read, *Welcome to Quincy, Sophie and Reinhold!* A curly red-haired woman held one side of it, and Sophie recognized her pretty freckled face immediately. Fanny, the Irishwoman who'd bullied Elise and Marianne at the Seventh Street Mission, but who, according to Elise, was now Quincy's premier seamstress and engaged to the town doctor. Sophie guessed that the good-looking man holding the opposite side of the sign was the doctor.

Sophie's heart expanded at the sight of her family. Elise and Thornton stood together, their baby girl sheltered against Thornton's broad chest. Sophie's eyes teared at the sight of her niece, Sophie, her namesake. Elise had named her firstborn daughter after her. The thought never failed to amaze her, the realization that Elise had never stopped loving her, even though she hadn't deserved it.

Next to Elise and Thornton stood Marianne and Drew with several of the orphans they'd apparently brought with them on this trip. The orphans were giggling and jumping up and down and thriving in the excitement, and Sophie prayed they would find good homes like the Duffs offered, where they would be loved and accepted for who they were. The moment Drew had laid eyes on her in Mayfield, he'd recognized her from that time on the train. It was only after Marianne had given him a long kiss that he finally stopped berating himself for not pursuing Sophie further.

The stationmaster in his crisp uniform was holding the hand of a redheaded boy. A petite woman with graying hair stood on the opposite side of the boy, holding his other hand. She beamed down at her son, clearly delighted in him.

There were others standing on the platform too, likely friends of Elise and Thornton, along with co-workers of Reinhold when he'd worked in Quincy doing construction. The sight of so many cheerful, welcoming faces brought the sting of tears to Sophie's eyes.

"Are you ready?" Reinhold asked, his voice and eyes brimming with emotion.

She stood next to him and wiped her tears away. Then she intertwined her fingers with his and moved into the aisle. "I'm ready."

As she started toward the door with her husband at her side, her children trailing, and her family waiting outside, Sophie hoped her mother and father could see them from heaven and know that they were still together even though God had taken them each their separate ways.

She'd never expected to end up here at this moment. But God had worked out the details more perfectly than she ever could have imagined.

Now unto him that is able to do exceeding abundantly above all that we ask or think, according to the power that worketh in us, unto him be glory in the church by Christ Jesus throughout all ages, world without end. Amen.

Ephesians 3:20–21

AUTHOR'S NOTE

Thank you for finishing the ride with me in this last book of my ORPHAN TRAIN series. I hope you enjoyed getting to know Sophie, the third Neumann sister, a little better in this story. And I hope you were as happy as I was that Reinhold Weiss finally got his well-deserved happily-ever-after. They both carried lots of heavy baggage during their journeys—the guilt of past sins and mistakes. And they had to learn how to let go of the weight so that God could help them move forward into the newness of the life He had planned for them.

In casting Sophie Neumann as an orphan, it was my hope to give readers a glimpse into what the orphan train movement was like from the point of view of the children who participated in it, showing a variety of ages, situations, and experiences. As I mentioned in previous novels, the Children's Aid Society (CAS), started by Charles Loring Brace, was the major placing organization of orphans in New York City from its inception in 1853 well into the twentieth century.

In 1859, during the time of *Searching for You*, the agency was still very much in its infancy. Well-meaning people like Brace saw the deplorable conditions under which orphans in New York lived, and they longed to make a difference in the children's lives. While their practices and philosophies might not necessarily align with how we choose to do things today, for the most part their efforts stemmed from the desire to improve conditions for the thousands of orphans living in both orphanages and on the streets.

In his well-researched book *Orphan Trains*, author Stephen O'Connor paints a vivid picture of what life was like for orphans in the nineteenth century in the immigrant slums of New York. He says that between twenty to thirty percent of children became orphans before the age of fifteen. That's roughly one in four children. A large number of children were considered "half orphans" because they'd lost one parent, and the other wasn't capable of providing for them adequately. If extended relatives couldn't help, the orphans ended up in asylums or living out on the street, taking care of themselves. Asylums, like the Infants Hospital on Randall's Island, typically lost around seventy percent of the children who went to live there due to unsanitary and overcrowded conditions.

It was in this climate that the Children's Aid Society hoped to make a difference in the lives of children through what was called its Emigration Plan. Similar to the indenture system that had been used since the founding of the nation, the Emigration Plan sought to reform poor children by placing them in respectable homes, where they might be influenced by godly Christian parents. In exchange for a home and basic necessities, the children were expected to contribute to the families. Brace idealized country families, believing that the best homes were found in rural areas. He said, "The cultivators of the soil in America are our most solid and intelligent class." Thus the Emigration Plan worked relentlessly to take children away from the "evil vices" of the city and place them in the more wholesome influences of the country.

Of course, the placements weren't always as ideal as the

Children's Aid Society hoped. I attempted to portray a variety of types of placement, giving light to both the positive and negative situations the children faced. During my research, I found numerous stories of real children who rode the trains, were adopted into loving families, and grew up to appreciate their new homes and lives. I also read just as many tragic stories of children who didn't fare well, who were placed in multiple homes, were abused, and struggled to find fulfillment for the rest of their lives.

By giving Sophie, Olivia, Nicholas, and Anna happy endings, it's not my intention to trivialize the heartache that many orphans experienced. But I do hope that you have gained a greater awareness of just how difficult a time the nineteenth century was for so many of our nation's children. I also hope that you gained an appreciation for the many families who opened their homes and hearts to homeless children. May their example inspire us to do likewise.

It was also my prayer in writing this story to help you—wherever you are in your journey—learn to let go of your burdens and guilt, to hand them over to the One who is waiting to bear the weight for you. He can take your brokenness and your messes and shape them into something beautiful and unique and unexpected—if you just let Him.

Jody Hedlund is the award-winning author of multiple novels, including the BEACONS OF HOPE series as well as *Captured by Love*, *Rebellious Heart*, and *A Noble Groom*. She holds a bachelor's degree from Taylor University and a master's degree from the University of Wisconsin, both in social work. Jody lives in Michigan with her husband and five children. Learn more at JodyHedlund.com.

Sign Up for Jody's Newsletter!

Keep up to date with Jody's news on book releases and events by signing up for her email list at jodyhedlund.com.

More from the ORPHAN TRAIN Series

When an 1850s financial crisis leaves orphan Elise Neumann and her sisters destitute, Elise seizes their only hope: to find work out west through the Children's Aid Society and send money home. On the rails, she meets privileged Thornton Quincy, who suddenly must work for his inheritance. From different worlds, can these two help each other find their way?

With You Always, ORPHAN TRAIN #1

More from Jody Hedlund

Take a journey across America and through time in this collection from some of Christian fiction's top historical romance writers! Includes Karen Witemeyer's *Worth the Wait: A Ladies of Harper's Station Novella*, Jody Hedlund's *An Awakened Heart: An Orphan Train Novella*, and Elizabeth Camden's *Toward the Sunrise: An Until the Dawn Novella*.

All My Tomorrows

Caroline has tended the lighthouse since her father's death. But where will she go when a wounded Civil War veteran arrives to take her place?

Hearts Made Whole
BEACONS OF HOPE #2

More from Jody Hedlund

You May Also Like . . .

Socialite Anna Nicholson can't seem to focus on her upcoming marriage. The new information she's learned about her past continues to pull at her, so she hires Pinkerton detectives to help her find the truth. But when unflattering stories threaten her reputation and engagement, she discovers that God's purpose for her life isn't as simple as she had hoped.

Legacy of Mercy by Lynn Austin
lynnaustin.org

Dr. Rosalind Werner is at the forefront of a groundbreaking new water technology—if only she can get support for her work. Nicholas, Commissioner of Water for New York, is skeptical—and surprised by his reaction to Rosalind. While they fight against their own attraction, they stand on opposite sides of a battle that will impact thousands of lives.

A Daring Venture by Elizabeth Camden
elizabethcamden.com

Annalise knows painful memories hover beneath the pleasant façade of Gossamer Grove. But she is shocked when she inherits documents that reveal mysterious murders from a century ago. In this dual-time romantic suspense novel, two women, separated by a hundred years, must uncover the secrets within the borders of their town before it's too late.

The Reckoning at Gossamer Pond by Jaime Jo Wright
jaimewrightbooks.com

BETHANYHOUSE

Printed in the United States
By Bookmasters